BLIND RETRIBUTION

ALSO BY K. T. ROBERTS

Educating Daphne

Kensington-Gerard Detective Series

The Last Witness
Elusive Justice
Deadly Obsessions

As Carolyn Hughey

Insanity Claus
Cupid's Web
Shut Up and Kiss Me

Romancing the Chef's Toque Series

Dishing Up Romance
One Menu at a Time
Catering to Love

Kindle Worlds

Gossip Girl: Lovers, Liars and Thou
Gossip Girl: Murder & Mayhem
From Princess to Prairie

BLIND
RETRIBUTION

K. T. ROBERTS

Montlake
Romance

Published by Montlake Romance, Seattle

www.apub.com

Amazon, the Amazon logo, and Montlake Romance are trademarks of Amazon.com, Inc., or its affiliates.

ISBN-13: 9781503939981
ISBN-10: 1503939987

Cover design by Cyanotype Book Architects

Printed in the United States of America

This book is dedicated to all the men and women in our military as well as those in law enforcement for their tireless efforts while risking their lives every day to keep us safe. My heartfelt thanks and appreciation for your service.

CHAPTER ONE

Helen Barrett opened the heavy door of her husband's red Lamborghini, slid into the beige bucket seat, and wiggled in until she felt comfortable. She shut the car door with a thud, and it locked into place. The aroma of leather enveloped her, and she instinctively inhaled. She couldn't believe she was sitting behind the steering wheel of her husband's prized possession. He never let *anyone* drive it . . .

Sliding her hands over the leather dashboard made her giddy. Seeing so many dials made her feel like a pilot preparing for takeoff. She smiled in the surrounding silence. It was . . . deafening . . . peaceful . . . eerie.

Helen sighed deeply. Contented heat pooled in her heart, knowing that Jeffrey was as much in love with her as she was with him.

Helen shook her head and glanced at her watch. It was later than she'd thought. They'd made love all night, like newlyweds. Now it was mid-morning. She couldn't remember the last time they'd stayed in bed this late on a Sunday. Luckily, they weren't leaving for Venice for their second honeymoon until late tonight, but it had been too long since she and Jeffrey had shared this kind of romance, and all she wanted to do was hurry back into his waiting arms.

She shook her head as she thought back over the last several weeks. What a crazy ride it had been. At first, she hadn't trusted Jeffrey's sincerity about wanting to make their marriage work or his confession that he'd never stopped loving her. But his actions had changed all that, and the hurt she'd felt for so long slowly disappeared after he'd proposed all over again and even planned an elaborate reception to celebrate their renewed wedding vows with family and friends. She was happier than she'd been in a long time.

Euphoria coursed through her body. She could live like this for the rest of her life, knowing she had all she needed—Jeffrey's love and devotion. This was wedded bliss—the mature kind of love that only comes after years of being with someone. This was even better than the first time they'd married fifteen years ago.

Helen pulled the seat belt across her chest, snapped it into place, and took another deep breath.

She inserted the key into the ignition, anxious to hear the roar of the engine, then heaved out one last breath before turning the motor over. An odd popping sound came from beneath the dashboard and echoed in her ears. *Oh God, what did I do wrong?* She sat for a few seconds waiting to see if the noise continued, and then a loud blast erupted and the hood of the car shot into the air. She screamed as rich red flames mushroomed across the windshield. Panicked, she screamed again. Confusion set in like rigor mortis, rendering her helpless.

Get out of the car! she told herself.

She tried to release her seat belt, but her fingers fumbled as if frozen. She pulled on the seat belt with force, trying to release the latch. Nothing.

A sudden intense blast of heat made her look down at her feet. Her sandals were in flames and for a second she was mesmerized as she watched the fire spread across the straps. Then the pain set in. She stamped her feet as hard as she could.

She screamed at the top of her lungs. "Jeffrey, help me!" Surely, he must have heard the blast.

She pounded on the door but couldn't find the handle. Her mother's voice echoed through her mind. *Everyone has to die from something.* Was she going to die? *No, dammit.* Not today she wasn't. "Jeffrey!" she screamed again, her throat sore from straining.

Hysteria overwhelmed her, and she banged on the window with all her might. Nothing happened and no one came. No one to help, not even Jeffrey.

She slammed her fist on the horn just as a second blast popped the trunk and rocked the car. Her voice, no longer audible, released a silent scream. Helplessness took over as the tears gushed down her cheeks and that old familiar pain Jeffrey had managed to erase resurfaced. She should have known better. Everything he'd fed her over the last two weeks was a lie, and like a fool, she'd fallen for it. The bastard never intended to spend the rest of his life with her. All he'd wanted was to silence her voice.

Orange flames engulfed her entire body in a thick blanket and she finally gave in to it. The sickening smell of burning flesh—her flesh—repulsed her.

The last blast under her seat was so intense it lifted the car into the air and flipped it over. Helen Barrett's charred body bounced like a rag doll behind the tight constraints of the seat belt. Thick flames punched through the billowy black smoke. Carbon fiber, thousands of glass shards, and steel fragments showered down in a deadly rainfall . . . alarms . . . shrill and deafening. And then, Helen Barrett's voice was silenced forever.

There'd be no wedded bliss.

There'd be no honeymoon in Venice.

There'd be no more Helen Barrett.

CHAPTER TWO

Cory Rossini removed the contents from his mailbox and walked back inside his brownstone. He hadn't realized he had so much mail after not checking it for a few days. He leafed through the envelopes and decided the pile was just a bunch of bills that he didn't feel like opening. He'd look at them later. He carried the pile over to his mantel and laid it down next to the baseball he'd caught at a few weeks ago at Yankee Stadium, now perched on its stand. It was enclosed in a glass case and destined to be given to his niece, Brooke, for her birthday.

He smiled, pleased that he'd caught that foul ball, but it brought back the harsh words exchanged between him and a beautiful woman. Her hand had been right there at the same time he'd caught the ball. If it hadn't been for the baseball glove he'd been wearing, she would have walked away with it. He remembered the feisty blonde, blue-eyed woman, with the voluptuous figure who had him swooning even though she was mad. Maybe it was the appreciative expression he'd had on his face that made her think he was being smug, because the more he'd smiled at her, the madder she'd gotten.

Under normal circumstances, he probably would have given the ball to her, but the snippy tone of her voice had reminded him of his ex-girlfriend, Lyndsey, and he'd stuck firm to keeping it. Besides, it was for Brooke. The poor kid had been through so much after she'd lost her leg to cancer, he thought having the entire team autograph it for her before her birthday would bring a smile to her face.

Although he'd convinced himself he'd done the right thing by keeping the ball, he couldn't escape the guilt he felt, nor get the image of the woman's face out of his mind. He'd even dreamt about her last night—not that he remembered exactly what the dream was about, but he remembered it had something to do with love.

Sadly, this last year had been disastrous in his life, and love was the last thing on his mind. Being suspended from the New York City Bar Association and banned from practicing law for six months had changed everything.

How could he stand by and watch Brooke die from cancer? With his brother-in-law out of work, no health insurance, and the surgeon who'd refused to do the surgery until he was assured he'd get paid, Cory had had no choice and he borrowed the money from his client's retainer fund. And then Lyndsey, angry because he hadn't wanted to get married after they'd only been dating a few months, told his partners what he'd done. At that point, the money had already been returned, but he'd lost his job, and the bar had still suspended him. What was so ironic about what had happened was that Lyndsey had been the one to suggest it. As a result, he'd sworn off women—possibly for the rest of his life. Then there'd been his knee surgery. He was recovering, but it was slow going. Yeah, it had been one hell of a year.

So why was he still thinking about this beauty two weeks later? And why did he want to know more about her? Apparently, a journalist thought their fight would make a good story and he'd snapped a picture of the two of them arguing. It had shown up on the sports page in the local paper, and for some reason, he'd cut that picture out. He told himself it was the novelty of being on the sports page, but he knew he'd only been fooling himself. Cory smiled to himself because he knew precisely why he'd kept the picture. So he could look at it anytime he wanted.

He walked to his desk and pulled out a magnifying glass and aimed it down onto the picture. Although part of his shoulder had been in the way, he had a partial view of her, but he wasn't likely to forget her beautiful face. His heart turned over. This blue-eyed bombshell was compromising his vow to swear off women. He placed the magnifying glass down and forced himself to forget about her. He'd never see her again anyway, so why was he wasting time? He needed to think more about what he was going to be doing with the rest of his life, or at least during this six-month suspension. Still, the image of this woman kept nagging at his mind, and apparently his memory of her wasn't going anywhere soon.

Even though the scene at the ball field had been unpleasant, he couldn't help but laugh because she'd tried playing the guilt card. He'd learned that spoon-fed guilt stuff at an early age from the best—his Italian mother. He'd even offered to buy the woman a hot dog and drink, hoping to relieve her stress, but that didn't work. It only angered her more because, he was certain, she thought he was patronizing her. Cory grinned. That little spitfire didn't mince words either. She'd flat out told him to go straight to hell and walked away as quickly as her legs would carry her.

CHAPTER THREE

Detective Maxine Turner, known as Max, arrived at the site of the explosion in Riverdale with her partner, Howie Spencer. She exited her car and whistled when she saw the mansion. "Holy cow, will you look at this place?" she said in a low voice.

"I think we chose the wrong profession, Max." Her partner, Howie, put his hands to his lower back and stretched as he took in the grounds.

Max eyed the house in awe. She remembered seeing a few mansions like this on a show on the Travel Channel during one of those rare occasions when she'd turned on the television to break the silence in her apartment. Her apartment was nothing like this house.

She loved the pitched roof, the brick and stone sheathing that stretched the entire length of the home, and its entryway tucked inside a turret that led into the main residence. Yeah, she wouldn't mind living in a house like this, with its park-like setting and grass so green it resembled a velvet carpet. Ornate flower beds with a variety of plants in hues of pink and lavender lined the fieldstone walkway leading up to the entrance. The trees throughout the property were just starting to change color and were ceremoniously showing off their brilliant reds, oranges, and yellows.

At the curb near the entrance to the long driveway, a uniformed patrolman stood guard, trying to control the curious neighbors now gathered and bombarding him with questions about what had happened at the Barrett residence. The first responders had secured the property with yellow crime scene tape to preserve the integrity of the evidence that had been strewn about the drive and lawn. Several investigators combed the property, looking for anything that could help reconstruct the last minutes of Helen Barrett's life. Any evidence would be taken back to the crime lab.

"Were you the first on the scene, Officer Jenkins?" Max asked when she read his badge.

"Yes, ma'am."

"What can you tell me about what happened here?"

"The husband said his wife wanted to pick up her prescription before they left on a second honeymoon." Max listened intently. "He gave her the keys to his Lamborghini, and she left while he was in the shower. Upon hearing the loud explosion, he rushed down the stairs. He shouted to the maid to call 911, but she was already outside."

"Which of them called it in then?"

"Neither. It was a neighbor." He checked his notebook. "A Mark Ginsburg, who was out walking his dog when he saw the car explode and immediately called from his cell phone."

"And you have his address?"

"Yes, ma'am."

"Excellent. Thank you." Max nodded in the direction of the two people standing to the side with their backs to her. "I assume that's the husband and their maid?"

"Yes."

"All right. Who is he? I didn't catch his name on the squawk box."

"He's one of those bigwig heart surgeons over at Mount Sinai." Jenkins checked his notes again. "Dr. Jeffrey Barrett."

Max screwed up her face. "I'm pretty sure I saw his face splashed across the *New York Times* recently, but I don't know why."

"A delicate heart transplant on a senator's kid, using some new procedure, I think," the patrolman said. "I remember it because it was such a risky new technique, done on such a young kid, right here in our own backyard. A state senator, as I recall."

"That's it." She pointed a finger at him. "Thanks, Jenkins." Turning to her partner, who was still eyeing the mansion, she asked, "You ready, Howie?"

"About as ready as I'll ever be."

The two stopped and stared at the smoldering pile of debris for a moment. The firemen were busy putting their equipment away after curtailing the blaze. Max glanced over in the direction of the bomb squad, which had already begun its investigation, when she saw the fire battalion captain in the distance.

"Why don't you go over and start questioning the witnesses," Max said to Howie. "I'd like to get the scoop from Zeke." Howie nodded in agreement and walked off. Max felt a tug on her heartstrings as she watched Howie's slackened pace. It was hard seeing him decline over the years. He was no longer the aggressive mountain of a man she'd first partnered with six years ago. Although Howie had maintained his slim six-foot build, his face was now drawn and tired looking, and that sparkle she'd seen in his brown eyes every time they'd solved a case seemed to die a little every day. She'd always thought of him as a father figure because he'd taught her the ropes, things she might never have learned if not for him during her rookie year as a detective. But it was more than that. He'd counseled her when she'd needed it, and hugged her as if she were his own daughter.

Max was pulled from her thoughts when the battalion captain, now approaching, called out to her.

"What's the status, Zeke?" she asked, standing next to him.

"Max, you know the drill. We're going to be here for a while, and your investigation will have to wait until we've completed ours."

"I understand." She nodded. "Can you give me your cursory view of the situation, though?"

"Oh, there's no doubt this was intentional. Those explosives were planted in the undercarriage in three places on that Lamborghini. It was as though the killer was trying to torture the victim by timing each explosive to go off one right after the other."

"So this person is no amateur then?"

"I think not," Zeke said with conviction.

Max pointed to the two garages adjacent to the carriage house in the back of the property and noted both doors were open. "A Lamborghini, huh?"

"Yes, ma'am."

"Doesn't it seem odd to you that his car wasn't parked in one of those bays?" Max asked, pointing toward the open garage.

"Yes, it does; unless he used the car earlier," he said. "Although I can't imagine anyone leaving that expensive car parked in the driveway and not inside the garage."

"Okay. That's a good place to start. I'll begin questioning my witnesses while you guys do your thing. Let me know when you're done." She glanced at the victim's husband and the employee, now talking with Howie. She stopped in her tracks and turned back to Zeke again. "Did the victim know what was happening? Was she conscious when the car was on fire?" Max asked, not really wanting the answer.

"I hope not. After the coroner takes a look at her lungs—or what's left of them—we'll know for sure."

"Poor thing. She never had a chance." Max sighed. "Okay, thanks." She turned and headed toward the trio.

"This is my partner, Detective Max Turner," Howie said when she approached.

"I'm very sorry for your loss, Dr. Barrett."

"Thank you," Barrett said before blowing his nose on a handkerchief he'd removed from his robe pocket.

"This is Maddie Thomas." Howie gestured with his hand. "She works for the Barretts and lives in the carriage house behind the main residence with her two sons."

The doctor's gasp drew their attention to the attendants who were placing what was left of Helen Barrett's charred body into a black body bag.

Max latched on to the doctor's arm and guided him away from the scene and closer to her vehicle parked at the end of the circular driveway. Barrett and his maid were already upset, and watching the investigators search the scene for body parts and debris would only upset them more. Although this explosion was on a much smaller scale than what she'd witnessed at the scene on 9/11 and in Afghanistan, the destruction scattered all over the fieldstones and lawn, and that unforgettable smell of explosives and human skin, caused Max to shudder. She had no desire to relive those moments of her past—in fact, she wished she could forget them entirely.

Eyeing a group of nosy, gawking neighbors slowly congregating behind the tape, Max suggested to the doctor that they talk in her car. She called out to Howie to tell him where she'd be as he led the maid to the white wrought-iron lawn furniture under a tree a short distance from the unmarked car.

Maddie's thick Jamaican accent rang out. "Poor Miss Helen is gone and now," she said to Howie, "I may not have a job." She blew out a breath. "I know I should not think about this now, but I have a family that depends on my salary . . . I don't know what I'll do."

Hearing the conversation, Barrett responded. "You'll always have a job with me, Maddie."

"Thank you, Dr. Jeffrey." Relief spread across her face as she lowered herself onto one of the filigreed white chairs. "You know, Miss Helen . . . she was always so good to me. And now—" She burst into tears. "I never see her again." Howie tried to console her by patting her back from the neighboring chair, but that didn't seem to work. He gave her his unopened bottle of water.

"I know you're upset, Ms. Thomas. I would be too, but I need to ask you a few questions to help with our investigation." She took the water, unscrewed the cap, and drank.

Max opened the back door of their police vehicle for Dr. Barrett. "It's quieter in here," she said. Barrett tightened the tie on his robe and held the two front pieces together before sliding across the seat.

Max stopped to glance in the direction of the wreckage in the distance before entering the car. From her experience, there was no doubt this bomb scene screamed military, and she wouldn't be a bit surprised if the technicians found proof of that on the fragments they recovered. Military bombs had color coding, serial numbers, and other markings identifying where the bomb was built and the weight of the explosive or whether there was a blasting agent included. Once the squad reconstructed the bombs, she would know. Max opened her door, seating herself next to Dr. Barrett. With pen in hand she began her questioning.

"What is that God-awful smell?" Barrett asked, wrinkling his nose and rolling down the window.

"Yeah, I know. We share cars with the other detectives, so there isn't much I can do about it. Unfortunately, at times our vehicles are used for transporting some unsavory characters." She made a face. "I think you get the picture."

"I don't know if I can stay in here," he whined. "It stinks."

"Okay," she said opening the door. "We can go outside to talk about what happened, if you'd rather." She exited the car and he followed suit.

"Detective, I'd really rather not talk at all right now."

"I understand that, Dr. Barrett, and I'm sorry, but it's important that we do," she insisted and launched right into questioning before he could resist again. "You work at Mount Sinai, is that correct?" He nodded. "Did you go out earlier this morning with your car?"

"No, Helen and I slept in this morning. We had a very late night after the party."

"Oh, you had a party? What was the occasion?"

"Helen and I renewed our vows," he said proudly as though temporarily forgetting he'd just lost his wife.

"That's a beautiful thing, and then to have something like this happen . . . I'm truly sorry. So you had a lot of people in your house, then?"

"About a hundred fifty or so."

"That's a really big party. Do you know of anyone who would want to hurt you or your wife?"

"I doubt it was anyone who attended the party. At least, I don't think so." His hands washed over his face.

"What about those who you didn't invite to the party? Do you think there were some who were resentful?"

"You mean, resentful enough to want us dead?"

Max's shoulder rose. "Have you had any squabbles with anyone?"

"The usual, I suppose."

"Will you clarify *the usual*?" she asked.

"Creative differences between surgeons. Sometimes it's something as silly as golf scores, but certainly nothing that would warrant *this*," he said, nodding in the direction of the explosion.

"I'd like the names of those individuals, please."

"I think it's silly."

"It may seem that way to you, but it would be appreciated."

Barrett's hands rose in defeat.

"Trust me, Dr. Barrett, it's usually the one you least expect." She tucked a lock of hair back away from her face and behind her ear. "Do you think any of your friends are jealous of your lifestyle or the success you've achieved within the cardiology community?" Max looked pointedly at Barrett.

"I'm sure most of them are jealous, but that doesn't mean they'd kill either one of us because of it."

In light of his recent loss, Max tried not to show a reaction to his pompous comment. "Listen, I'm going to need a copy of that guest list too. Can you get that for me?"

"You'll have to get that from the party planner." He shook his head as if trying to clear his mind. "I'm sorry. I'll have Maddie take care of it for you." His shoulders slouched. "I can't think straight."

"I understand." Max could see his mouth was dry and handed him a bottle of water. "Here, this might help that cotton mouth."

He accepted the bottle, twisted the cap off, and tipped his head back, taking a long swig. "Thank you."

"Here's the thing that I'm having a hard time trying to figure out, Dr. Barrett." Max gestured in the direction of the crime scene. "Why was the Lamborghini in the driveway? Given that you had one hundred and fifty guests here last evening, you would have needed the driveway clear, or did you use a valet service for the convenience of your guests?"

"Yes, we hired a valet service. I have no idea where they parked the cars, but they weren't in my driveway."

"All right. So getting back to the Lamborghini, I'm assuming the sports car was yours and your wife drove the Mercedes in the garage. Is that correct?"

"Yes."

"Okay, so can you explain why your car wasn't in the garage?" She popped a piece of gum into her mouth after offering him one. He seemed distracted and never responded.

Max held her finger up to her puckered lips in thought. "Was it your wife who left your car in the driveway? Can you think of any reason why she would have used your car last night when hers was readily available?" She frowned.

"No, I kept Helen pretty busy," he said with a slight grin. "After all, it was the start of our honeymoon. But what difference does it make now? She's gone, my car's gone, and my future is looking pretty grim without her." Max thought it was odd he even mentioned the fact that his car was gone.

"Dr. Barrett, why did you mention that your car was gone in the same sentence as your wife? It seems like an odd thing to say after what just happened."

"Oh, I don't know. Sorry. I guess I'm still in a state of shock."

"So who left the car in the driveway overnight?"

He shifted from one foot to the other, obviously trying to control his emotions. "I left the car in the driveway, but honestly, I can't seem to remember why at the moment."

"Please try to focus, Dr. Barrett. These points are crucial. With a two-hundred-thousand-dollar price tag for a Lamborghini, I'm just having trouble trying to figure out why it would be left outside, unattended. It's like an invitation for trouble. Do you think leaving it outside was a conscious decision?"

"Right," he fired back, "like I left my car in the driveway all night just hoping someone would come along and plant a bomb." He lowered his head into his hands.

"Relax, Dr. Barrett, I wasn't pointing fingers. I'm just trying to find the truth so I can solve this case and find out who killed your wife. Can you help me understand what happened here from yesterday morning to where we are right now, because I'm confused."

"I went to work at the regular time," he said. "I performed a heart transplant mid-morning, then made rounds and waited to talk to the cardiologist who was going to cover for me while Helen and I were away. I needed to bring him up to date."

"Okay. And what is this cardiologist's name?"

"Warren Decker." Max jotted the name down in her notebook. "He was also running late. When I noticed the time, I knew Helen was going to be upset if I didn't make it back before the guests arrived, so I drove home like a maniac. I pulled in the driveway and I guess I left the car without even thinking about it. Unfortunately, some of the guests had already arrived."

"I'll bet your wife was really ticked off that you were late, huh?" Max said, nodding encouragement.

"No, not too much." He smiled. "She was so excited about having another magnificent wedding, it actually didn't seem to faze her."

"I don't suppose you remember who was here at that time, do you?"

"Let's see." He shut his eyes. "My parents, her hairstylist, her clothing designer . . . and I think the florist was just leaving."

Max noted the information on her pad. "Did your wife drive your car often?"

"No." He smiled slightly. "This was the very first time."

"Really? Didn't she want to drive it?"

"I'm sure she did, but . . . well, the truth is, I didn't like or want anyone messing with my toy."

Max tilted her head, her lips puckered again. "Hmm, how interesting. I'll bet that caused a lot of friction."

"It did."

"Yet today, you decided it was okay? What made today different?"

"Let's just say I was trying to remedy the error of my ways. And now, oh God." He lowered his head. "I don't know what I'm going to do without her." Dr. Barrett looked toward the house. "Please excuse me," he said, and walked in the direction of the mansion. "I need my cell phone to call family and let them know."

"Whoa!" Max said, pulling him back. "I'm afraid not. It's a crime scene."

"But the bomb blew up outside."

"I understand that, but we need to be sure there are no bombs inside the residence. And the squad won't know that until they do a thorough search of the entire property. Okay?"

Barrett sighed. "I didn't think about that," he said, and then jerked back when a sudden flash blinded him. Surprised, Max whipped around and came face-to-face with a cameraman and a reporter who'd managed to sneak into the taped-off area.

Before Max could move, the reporter shoved a microphone into the doctor's face. "Did you plant those bombs, Dr. Barrett? Did you kill your wife?"

"Get out of here," Max yelled. The reporter persisted while the cameraman began filming. "If you don't get the hell out of here," Max warned, "I'm going to arrest you for trespassing. You know better than that."

Noticing the conflict, Howie rushed over and ripped the camera from the cameraman's hands, opened the back, and pulled out the memory card.

"Hey, you can't do that," the angry cameraman shouted.

"Well, he just did," Max said. "Now, get your ass out of here."

"I'll have my boss call the mayor," he threatened.

"You do that," Max said and clicked onto a call when she heard her cell ring. "Turner." She nodded. "Perfect timing. The media is harassing the doctor out here on the driveway. Okay. Thanks." She turned to Barrett. "The house has been released. We can go inside."

The doctor blew air from his puffed-out cheeks. "Thank God."

"Howie," Max called out to him, "inside." She pointed toward the residence. "They're done."

Maddie headed toward the front door. "I have to make breakfast for Dr. Jeffrey," she said. "He hasn't had anything to eat since last night."

"That's okay, Maddie," Barrett said, putting his arm around her shoulders. "I don't think I can eat anything anyway." He looked back down the driveway at the reporters.

"Where shall we continue our questioning?" Max asked him.

"We have a den and a sitting room. Either one is fine," he said, distractedly.

"Hey, do you have surveillance cameras?" she inquired.

"Of course. I never even gave that a thought."

"I want to see the footage. Does it record on a disk that I can take with me?"

It was obvious Barrett was still rattled by the reporter's intrusion. He rubbed his forehead. "I can't seem to remember if it does." He held his eyes tightly shut as though trying to cut the world out. Releasing a deep sigh, he opened them. "It does, and yes, you can take whatever you need."

Max noticed Howie signaling her just before she reached the threshold of the front door. "I need to see you for a minute," he whispered. She excused herself and followed him off the front steps.

"What's up?"

"The maid just told me the victim and the doctor had a rocky marriage, and that his wife threatened to leave him several weeks ago."

Max released a quick disgusted snort. "How interesting." She kept nodding her head. "This crap makes me crazy." Sucking in her bottom lip, Max wondered if that was the reason the doctor didn't seem as heavy-hearted as she'd expected. Or maybe it had more to do with how surgeons were trained to keep emotion out of their work. Together, she and Howie walked inside the home and back to their respective witnesses.

Maddie automatically walked through the kitchen toward what appeared to be the den, Howie following her.

"I guess we'll be sitting in the sunroom, unless you're allergic to plants," the doctor said to Max.

"No, I'm not." Max followed close behind, through the kitchen and out into a glass-enclosed room lined with planters holding beautiful flowers in varying shades of red, orange, and white. Large indoor potted trees reflected the serenity of the wooded area visible through the windows.

"Helen and I always loved this room," he said. "It afforded us the privacy we sought after a busy day."

The earthy smell of freshly watered plants spiraled up Max's nose and reminded her of a pleasant time during her teenage years when she'd spent time working in a florist's greenhouse.

A cluster of four plush lemon-yellow swivel chairs surrounded a large glass coffee table that used a planter as its base. Max admired the unique design and then noticed that Barrett had automatically sat in one of the chairs without inviting her to do the same.

"May I sit?" she asked.

"Yes, of course. I'm sorry."

"How long were you and Mrs. Barrett married?"

"Fifteen years."

"And how was the marriage?"

"Ah," he said, shaking his head. "I guess Maddie mentioned our marital issues." He stopped and stared at Max.

"Does that mean you wouldn't have mentioned them?" Max asked.

"No, of course not. I was getting to it." He shrugged. "We had difficult times. I'm not going to deny it. That's why it was my idea to renew our vows and rekindle the love we had when we were first married."

"I'm sorry, sir, but given that your wife was planning to leave you a few weeks ago . . ." Max paused. "You see where I'm going with this, Dr. Barrett? The renewal of vows with a hundred fifty friends witnessing the event"—Max screwed her face up—"you suddenly allowing her to drive your car—"

"Wait a minute." He cut her off, his voice growing louder. "What exactly are you saying?"

"Mr. Barrett, I'm just doing my job."

"It's Dr. Barrett," he said sharply.

"Forgive me, Dr. Barrett. Now that I know about the marriage troubles, I have to say you did have motive and opportunity."

"But you're taking my recent overtures toward my wife out of context." He paused for a few minutes, appearing to collect himself before continuing. "I know you detectives believe the spouse is the obvious suspect, so let me just squelch that idea right now. Let's start with the bombs. I have no doubt those bombs were meant for me, and I also have no doubt who could have planted them."

"I'm listening."

"Jack Hughes."

Max jotted down the name on her pad. "Ah, so you do have an enemy." He shot her a look. "Tell me about him and why you think he did it."

"I hope this doesn't wind up in the newspapers, but Helen was planning to leave me for Jack, and I talked her out of it. All she ever wanted was for me to show her that I loved her."

"Are you saying she was having an affair with this Mr. Hughes?" Max questioned.

"Yes, she was. For about a year."

"How do you know it was anything more than just a friendship?"

"Because I had her followed by a private investigator when I began to suspect something was going on. When the PI confirmed my suspicions, it was a wake-up call, and I realized what I would be losing if she left me. Before our troubles, we had something very special."

"What is the name of that private investigator?" she asked.

"Rodney Gilchrest."

"And he has photographs."

"Yes, he does."

"I assume you confronted her?"

"I did, and that's when she told me she was leaving me for Jack. At first, I was angry, but after I thought about it, I realized all Helen ever really wanted from me was love and devotion. We had that once, and I knew if I showed her how much she meant to me, we could rekindle what we'd lost. I had to put my ego aside, and that's when I begged her to stay and I made those promises that I fully intended to keep. That bastard Hughes took that away from me."

"I'd caution you about being so adamant about him killing her." Her brows rose. "We'll question him and see where it goes from there." She jotted down more notes. "It sounds like you know this man well. Can you tell me where you met?"

"He and I have been arch-rivals since high school, if you can believe that, always trying to outdo one another, whether it was driving the best car, dating the most popular girls in school—anything that was competitive, we challenged the other."

"I'm concerned about some of the things you've said here today, Dr. Barrett. I know you're upset about your wife, but I can't help but wonder if convincing Helen to remain with you was more about proving something to this Hughes guy."

"Absolutely not," he shot back. "I don't need to prove anything to anyone."

"Except this Mr. Hughes?"

"Well, okay." Barrett bristled, his chest rising from a deep intake of air. "At this point in my life, I've made my mark on society while Hughes is still trying. He's a shoddy artist who lost his fortune on bad investments and I'm a successful surgeon. Seriously, Detective, which man would you have chosen?"

"What I'd like to know, now that you've brought it up, is are you saying the only reason you believe your wife stayed with you was your money?"

"No." His eyes closed in frustration. "I'm just saying I had more to offer her than he did."

Max had her doubts about his devotion to his wife. His vacillating tones when he spoke of her were curious. "Do you know where he lives?" she asked.

"Hilary Gardens."

"Is that the building over on Mercer Street?"

"Yes. I don't know where in that building, but I guess you can get that information."

"Thank you." She noted the information. "Okay, Dr. Barrett . . . how about we move on to something else?" Max could see he wasn't happy about her shutting down his ego trip. "Please continue about Helen giving up Jack to stay with you."

He huffed out a frustrated breath. "At first, Helen was skeptical, but when I suggested I wanted to renew our vows . . . you know, to wash the slate clean—have a new beginning of sorts so we could leave all the other crap behind and start fresh—she agreed to stay."

"And that's all it took?" Max asked.

"No. I had to promise to work fewer hours at the hospital and find more time to play and travel. Once I agreed to those stipulations, she decided this was where she belonged—right here with me."

Max kept a watchful eye on his reactions. "So how did this Mr. Hughes take it when she broke off the relationship?"

"Just as you'd expect. He was furious. He even came to the hospital and stared me down in the cafeteria. I suspect it was right after Helen told him it was over and I was the winner. I don't know, maybe he thought he was going to scare me."

"And did he?"

"Hell no." Barrett's brows pulled together.

"Did he threaten you?"

"Not really, but he didn't like that I'd told him to stay the hell away from my wife." Barrett rubbed a hand over his mouth. "I have no doubt if I'd hung around a little longer, he would have seen fit to threaten me."

"But he didn't."

"The guy has one helluva temper. I'm also sure he knew she wasn't allowed to drive my car, so why wouldn't he try to extinguish me so he could have Helen all to himself?"

"Unless I can prove your claim, Doctor, it's merely speculation. But it's a good place for us to start our investigations." Max noticed the way he was glaring at her and wondered if he'd expected her to stop questioning him and leave immediately to arrest Jack just on his authoritative claim. "We have a lot more than that to investigate before we can draw any conclusions."

"You know," he said, looking past her shoulder, "I knew the minute I laid eyes on Helen that she was going to be my soulmate. She was such a caring person. And"—his voice softened—"did you know that Helen opened a preschool for children from the ages of two to five years old because we couldn't have children? It's called The Little Tykes Academy. Isn't that precious?" he asked.

"No, I didn't know that. I hadn't heard of it before today, but that is a wonderful way to fill a void."

"I really loved that about her." His eyes became glassy. "Honestly, there's not another person on this planet who could ever take her place." His fingertips reached up and massaged his temples.

"Want to take something for that headache?" Max asked.

"No, it can wait." He paused then continued. "As for the troubles in our marriage, we just got a little sidetracked, that's all. When she finally agreed to stay," he said, "I wanted her to know there'd be no more holding back, that she was more important to me than my toy, so I gave her the keys to my car to prove it. Now, I'm sorry I did. But if I hadn't, you'd be questioning her right now instead of me."

His odd comment gave Max pause and had her feeling unsure of how to take it. Was he saying he wished it was him, or that he was glad it was her? She stood upright, deciding she'd had enough information for one day and could come back another time to question him. "All right, Dr. Barrett, we're going to end this session for today. I'm sure we'll be talking again as evidence develops."

"And you're going to question Hughes, right?"

"Yes, that's the plan." She buttoned her jacket. "Can you get that surveillance footage for me?"

"Of course." She followed him down the hall to a closet filled with monitors. He placed the disk in a slim jewel case and handed it to her.

When Max heard the maid call out to the doctor, she realized Howie must have wrapped up his conversation too. She closed her notebook and nodded to Howie, who was now standing in the hallway. On the walk back to the vehicle with her partner, Max had an unsettled feeling in her gut about Barrett.

CHAPTER FOUR

"Hey," Max said, turning to Howie as she slid behind the steering wheel. "Did the maid ever mention the name Jack Hughes?"

"No." Howie frowned, his eyes hooded in question. "Who's Jack Hughes?" he asked.

"Our victim's boy toy."

"Ah, now we're getting somewhere." Howie gave a shake of his head and snickered. "I think it's interesting how most people envy these wealthy jet-setters. If they only knew how screwed up most of them are, they wouldn't waste another minute on wishing they were them." Howie blinked. "So tell me more about Barrett."

Max began filling Howie in on the details of her conversation with Jeffrey Barrett as she pulled out of the driveway and onto the main street.

"No doubt we'll be paying a visit to the boyfriend."

"No doubt," Max said with a nod. "But Barrett's emotions ran hot and cold; I'm just not sure about him. This is what has me confused. How does a husband forgive his partner who cheated on him?" Her lips tightened. "I think something's fishy, but I don't have a clue about what to even suggest it might be." Max's chin jutted out. "So, tell me what the maid gave you about their marital issues."

"She said they fought constantly and went for long periods of time without speaking. From what she told me, it sounds like they lived as married singles and even slept in separate bedrooms. That's why she was so happy to see them get back together."

"Married singles? Separate bedrooms? A cheating wife? Wow. Now I understand why Barrett didn't tell me about any of those things." Max cussed out a driver who cut her off. "Did you see what that jerk just did?" she shouted.

"It's nothing new in this city. Ignore it."

Max forced a breath out to relieve the tension. "Did this Maddie say anything about seeing either of them with a lover?"

"No." Howie tapped his hand on his thigh. "But we need to keep in mind that now that he's her only source of income, Barrett just became Maddie's highest priority."

"Exactly, and you can't blame her for wanting to protect him. Did she mention seeing anything strange happen after the party?" Max passed a slow-moving car, honking her horn with impatience.

"No," Howie said, shaking his head. "She claims that after cleaning up, she left the residence and walked back to her place so exhausted, she plopped down on the bed, fell asleep, and didn't wake up until this morning. She even fell asleep with her clothes on."

"Is she married? Did her husband see anything?"

"She's married and, like I said before, she lives with her two sons. Hubby's still in Jamaica taking care of her other kids."

"Tell me about the sons," Max asked, subconsciously sliding her hands back and forth over the steering wheel.

"Both in their twenties, clean records, each has a job. One works at the local pizzeria doing dishes; the other works at a securities firm sorting mail."

"Did you talk to them?"

"I would have if they had been home."

Max looked at him quizzically.

"They're in Jamaica visiting their father."

"How convenient. When did they leave?"

"She didn't say, but I'll check with the airlines for the time frame."

"Did she say when they were due to return?" she asked.

"I neglected to ask."

Max huffed out a frustrated breath, making her irritation known without saying anything. Howie defended himself.

"I know, Max, I know." Howie's hand lifted in surrender. "I'm sorry. I had intended to ask, but listening to her tell me about the Barretts' relationship issues, and then my realizing that just a few weeks later they were renewing vows, I was thinking about other questions, and the conversation just never got back to her sons."

"But you did get their names so you can do a check on them?"

"Yes, boss lady, I did," Howie said with a salute. It was his way of letting Max know she was treating him like a rookie.

Max cleared her throat. She knew she had a tendency to be a little too aggressive. "Thank you," she said. "Before you verify the sons' records in the database, though, double-check Jack Hughes's address. Let's go to see him right now." She gave him the street name, then listened to the clicking sound of Howie's nimble fingers gliding over the keyboard. "He's right. It's on Mercer Street, right in the heart of the Village." Howie stopped talking and stared at her profile.

"What?" she asked. Max knew what was coming next. Whenever Max showed irritation toward him, Howie would try to make nice. She pushed her annoyance aside and reminded herself of all their years together. She owed him some slack.

"What's new with you?"

"Other than going to a Yankees game a few weeks ago, I haven't been out much."

"What Yankees game?" Howie shot back with surprise.

"Didn't I tell you?" She knew she hadn't, nor had she intended to today, but the words just seemed to slip out. Howie was shaking his head.

"Well, my brother-in-law had a ticket he couldn't use, and Julie made me take it because I don't get out enough. She thought I might meet someone who was interesting and I'd start dating."

"And did you?"

Max smirked. "Oh yeah, I met someone all right."

"Great," Howie said with enthusiasm.

"No. It wasn't so great."

"I'm sorry to hear that," Howie said. "What happened?"

"A foul ball came into the stands. I reached for it at the same time the guy in front of me did, only he had on a baseball glove and he got it." She huffed. "I let him know that I thought it was unfair, and I wanted it for my nieces, but he told me the same thing." She humphed. "Yeah, like I really believed his story." Her knuckles on the wheel were white with strain. "And then the bozo offered to buy me a hot dog and a soda, like that was some kind of peace offering for being an asshole."

"Did he give you the ball then?"

"No." She reached for another piece of gum and popped it into her mouth.

"Did you take the hot dog?"

"Hell no. He was a jerk . . . except I have to admit he was hot."

"Ah, so he piqued some interest."

"No, he didn't."

"You're lying."

She glanced over at him with disbelief in her pose.

"Every time you lie, your chin juts out." He laughed. "You liked him." Max shot him a dirty look. "Go ahead, admit it."

"Well, maybe a little, but I'm still mad about that ball."

"Uh-huh," Howie said.

"Stop patronizing me."

"I'm not, Max. But sometimes I know you better than you know yourself."

Her hand flew in the air. "Okay. You got me. But I'll never see him again anyway—even if I go to another Yankees game. We weren't in box seats. They were just regular seats." Max rubbed her earlobe. "And you know, the other damn thing that annoyed me about Mr. I-know-you're-dying-to-date-me was his confidence."

"Sounds like your kind of guy," Howie said with a silly smile on his face. "Describe him in five words."

"He was average."

"That wasn't five words," he teased. "Go ahead, tell me just how average this guy was," he egged her on.

"Tall, trim, dark curly hair with deep green eyes and the deepest cleft in his chin that made him . . . well, very appealing." She sighed. "Too bad he was such an asshole."

"Ah, now see, that was more than five. You liked this guy."

"I did not," Max said, giving Howie a light punch in the arm.

"And what did your sister say when you told her?"

"Who? The matchmaker?"

"Do you have another sister?"

"No." Max released a low laugh. "Uh, I only told her a little bit about him. Mostly that he was a jerk." Distracted by the traffic, Max groaned and flipped on her siren to move drivers out of the way. The loud *whoop, whoop* had some cars moving over slightly, but without anywhere to go, the few inches made little difference. When the light changed, the traffic moved up enough for Max to take a side street. "Awesome," she said, turning off the siren and easing down the quiet street, where residents sat on the steps in front of their apartment buildings taking in the fall weather. A group of young boys played on the sidewalk, and one of the kids grabbed the cap off his friend's head and flung it into the street. He darted out in front of the car. Max stopped short, stretched her arms out, and then gripped the steering wheel to release the tension. She closed her eyes and took a deep breath.

Howie rolled down the window and chided the group. "That was clever, punks." The only response he received was a cluster of fingers all giving him the bird.

"Nice." He rolled the window back up. "These kids today have no respect. If they were my kids, I'd kick their asses all the way around the block."

"Yeah, well, everything seems to be acceptable these days. Chances of them changing are next to none." Making a right-hand turn, Max was curious about Howie's opinion. "So what did you think of Barrett?"

"I'm having a hard time believing he didn't do it." Howie's eyebrow quirked questionably. Stretching his fingers out, he counted out the reasons. "First, the wife cheated on him for who knows how long; second, she was planning to leave him not long ago—and then all is forgiven a few weeks later and they renew their vows? Seriously? With statistics showing eighty-three percent of spousal murders being committed by the partner, I think we need to take a long hard look at him," Howie said.

"And we will."

"And another thing," Howie said, "don't tell me you were falling for his crying jag. I think that was his guilty conscience working overtime for killing her."

"We've seen it enough times," she said, making her last turn onto Mercer. Noticing there was no on-street parking, Max found a public parking garage across from the swanky apartment building Hughes lived in. She drove down the steep slope to the attendant, holding out her badge, and he flagged her on. After thanking him, she pulled the car into a parking space close to the elevator.

"Okay, let's do it." Howie nodded, maneuvering out of the car. Stepping into the elevator, they rode up to the street level, crossed over Mercer to the entrance of Hilary Gardens, and walked up to the clerk at the reception desk. They identified themselves. "We're here to see Jack Hughes. Can you tell us where his apartment is located?"

He entered the information into his computer. "Would you like our security officers to assist you?"

"No, but thanks for the offer. We're here on a private matter."

"Let's see." His eyes focused on the screen. "It looks like he's on the thirty-second floor, unit 3212. I'll call Mr. Hughes and let him know you're on the way up."

Max tapped her foot impatiently while waiting for the elevator to stop. Outside the apartment door, Max gave a hard knock. After a few seconds, Jack Hughes answered. He was a handsome man in his late thirties to early forties with sandy-blond hair, a full mustache, and rimless glasses that showcased deep blue eyes. "Can I help you?" They held out their badges and introduced themselves. "What can I do for you?" he said, his eyes narrowed suspiciously.

"Do you know Helen Barrett?"

His lips thinned. "What about her?"

"May we come inside, Mr. Hughes?" He begrudgingly pulled the door open the rest of the way to a magnificent view of the Empire State Building out his windows. Max took a look around his apartment. She was more interested in answers than his décor, but it was so beautiful, she couldn't help herself. The accent wall was painted a dark brown and set the theme for the color palette. On that same wall was a stucco fireplace with a crackling fire that cast a golden glow across the floor. Art deco pieces were scattered throughout the living room, with overhead spotlights highlighting the most appealing parts of the room and intentionally drawing the eye to remain and linger, but his question drew her attention.

"What about Helen Barrett?" he asked impatiently.

"She's dead."

The expression on his face sagged into disbelief. Muscles in his jaw flickered, making it obvious he was struggling to hold back tears. He swallowed hard, his hands fisting at his sides, and then he opened his mouth to speak. "That son of a bitch . . . he finally did it?"

"Who is *he*?"

"Jeffrey Barrett. That's who."

"You say that like you know he threatened to kill her."

"He's told her on numerous occasions that he wished she were dead," he said with authority.

"Did she tell you that, Mr. Hughes, or did you actually hear him say it?" Howie asked.

"No, I'm afraid I can't make that claim. But he's been mistreating her for a long time. I just had this feeling something was going to happen." He paused to collect his thoughts. "How did she die?" he asked in a low somber voice.

"A car bomb."

Caught by surprise, the man gasped. "He actually put a bomb in her car?"

"It wasn't her car; it was his car." Max noticed Hughes's eyes begin to smolder with anger. Max continued. "He's really suffering over the loss."

"Yeah, I'll just bet he is. That's bullshit. He's acting. He should be your lead suspect." Hughes hesitated, and the sudden reality of Helen's death seemed to remove the wind from his sails. He crossed his arms and pressed them against his stomach then ambled toward the sofa and slowly sat down in a trance-like state without inviting either of them to sit. "Helen wasn't allowed to drive his fancy car, let alone ride in it," he blurted out. "Was she standing next to the explosion?" Max could see he was distraught over the news.

"No, she was about to drive it," Howie said.

He seemed momentarily confused. "Really? Since when?" He made a disgusted noise. "Oh, I get it." His mouth moved to the side. "Barrett promised her the moon to convince her to stay with him." Hughes became silent again, a tear rolling down his cheek. He swiped at it with the back of his hand. "But that's not why you're here, is it?"

"How well did you know Mrs. Barrett?" Howie asked.

"Well."

"How well is *well?*" Max's head automatically tipped to the side.

"Intimately."

"As a couple?"

"Yes, as a couple."

"Mr. Barrett told me that after your breakup with Helen, you visited him at the hospital. Would you care to tell me what that was all about?"

"I wanted him to know that I was going to watch him."

"Did you threaten him?"

"No. I thought he'd get the message by the way I stared at him."

"To freak him out, so to speak?" Howie asked.

"Exactly."

"Can you tell us where you were last night between the hours of nine o'clock and ten this morning?" Max asked.

"Right here," he answered quickly, then clamped his mouth shut while his expression grew sterner. "For God's sake, you can't actually believe I had something to do with her death?"

"Please answer the question, Mr. Hughes," Max said.

"Sure, I can answer your question, but hell, it isn't going to make me any less of a suspect. Like I said, I was here. All night. By myself."

"Is there anyone who can verify that?" Howie asked.

"Like I said, *by myself,* until the early morning hours, licking my wounds after Helen dumped me for Jeffrey. I guess she didn't love me as much as I thought she did. And now, I've lost the greatest love of my life and can never get her back." He leaned forward and rested his elbows on his legs, cradling his head as though blocking out the news. "Oh my God, I can't believe she's gone."

"You had no visitors, saw no one in the hallways?" Max asked.

"How many ways do I have to say it? Alone is alone. Check with security if you don't believe me."

"When was the last time you saw Helen?"

Jack swallowed hard, causing his Adam's apple to flex. He opened his mouth to speak, then clamped it shut and paused, obviously struggling to get the words out. Tears formed in his eyes. "I . . . I guess it was yesterday." Using his thumb and forefinger, he swiped the tears from the corners of his eyes inward toward the bridge of his nose.

"Is that when Helen told you it was over between the two of you?" Max asked.

"No. She told me on Friday."

"But you didn't want to take no for an answer?"

"Something like that. I was madly in love with this woman. I knew Jeffrey was giving her a line of bullshit, and I just couldn't give up what we'd spent time cultivating."

"Is that the same day you visited Jeffrey at the hospital?"

"Yes."

"Did you see Helen anymore after that?"

"I did. I called and invited her to lunch on Saturday."

"Can you tell me where you had lunch?"

"It was La Fontaine on Twelfth. A favorite place of ours and one we frequented quite a bit." He pursed his lips together tightly. "That was my last-ditch effort to convince her she was making a mistake. I thought . . . well, never mind what I thought." He stared wordlessly. "Do I need a lawyer?"

Max jotted down the name of the restaurant. "Do you think you need a lawyer?" She asked with raised brows.

"No. Dammit, I have nothing to hide."

"That's good, Mr. Hughes, because if you do, we will find out, so you might as well tell us now."

"I have nothing to tell you. I swear, we broke up and that was it."

"How long had you two been involved?"

"A year, two months, three days, and"—he checked his watch—"nine hours."

His specifics about how much time they'd had together caught Max off guard, and Jack didn't miss her expression. "That was to show you how much I loved Helen."

"I'm sure you loved her, Mr. Hughes, but after being involved all that time, you expect me to believe you broke up just like that?" Max's voice was curt. "No fallout? Just cut and dried?"

"No," He shrugged. "I took it harder than she did. I couldn't convince her Jeffrey was pulling the wool over her eyes, but she bought it." He sucked in a breath. "And now she's dead." His head shook in disbelief. "I guess it's true that you can't make someone love you," he said, his voice cracking.

Max didn't know why she thought Jack's sad act was for her benefit. "We checked your record, Mr. Hughes," she said, "and it appears you have a few priors. Care to tell us about those?"

"Just barroom brawls over some broad." He gave a dismissive raise of his shoulder. "I was much younger then. That's all. No biggie."

"Hmm, not quite, Mr. Hughes. Our records indicate one of the victims filed a complaint against you, so it wasn't, as you say, 'no biggie.'"

"So I have a temper! So what?"

"A temper that has gotten you into quite a bit of trouble. Did you ever hit Mrs. Barrett?"

His eyes widened in complete surprise. "Of course not," he exclaimed vehemently. "I get into trouble trying to protect women, not abuse them. Those priors were over men treating women badly in my presence." He stopped talking and stared out the window, tears spilling from his eyes. "I can't believe she's gone." He wiped his tears with a tissue he'd pulled from the box on the end table.

"So you're a regular Prince Charming, huh?" Max mocked.

"I'd like to think I am. But as you can see, it hasn't made a bit of difference. I still don't have Helen, nor will I ever."

Out of the corner of her eye, Max noticed a photograph on his bookshelf. She picked it up and scanned it, glancing at Howie, who came over behind her and looked over her shoulder. It was a picture of Hughes in his military uniform standing in front of a warning sign that read *Explosive material, authorized personnel only.*

"Looks like you were in the military."

His brows furrowed together. "Yes. Why?"

"Because we believe our killer has military training in the use of explosives."

"Detective, you're trying your damnedest to make me the primary suspect here, aren't you?"

"So I guess this answers my next question about you having explosives training in the military?" The words spilled from her mouth.

He blew air from his puffed-out cheeks. "Yes, I did. Are you happy now?"

"I'm trying to solve a murder here, Mr. Hughes." Max tapped her pencil on her pad and looked at Howie. "Okay, I think we're done for today." Tired from standing, Max shifted her weight onto her other leg. "We'll be in touch, Mr. Hughes. Don't leave town." Hughes didn't reply, but he didn't have to. His peeved expression said it all.

Stepping into the elevator, Max blew out an annoyed breath. "Let's stop at the security office. I want to see the surveillance video myself to find out whether our suspect is telling the truth or not about being in his apartment all night."

"Those guys aren't going to let you see anything without a warrant."

"I know, but it's worth a try. You know, the old cliché, you wash my back, I wash your back?" Max gave him a questionable look. "It's worth a shot."

"I think this is going to be a high-profile case and we need documented proof we did this by the books," Howie said, giving her a side glance.

"What did you think of Jack?"

"I was having a hard time trying to read him. He seemed genuinely upset, but I'm just not sure. He could just be a good actor. What did *you* think?"

Max paused for a few seconds. "If his intent was to kill the doctor and he found out he'd killed her instead, I would think he'd have a hard time trying to control his emotions. What has me concerned are all those priors and his military background." The doors opened and they made their way over to the front desk.

"Where is your security office?" Howie asked.

"It's down on the basement level."

"Thank you." They headed back to the elevator and pushed the Down button. "When we get back to the station house," Max said, "I want to check his financials—Barrett's too, for that matter."

"Why are you checking those so soon?" he asked.

"Something Barrett said about Hughes losing his money from a bad investment that has me curious. Judging from that swanky apartment, he must have had plenty of money to afford it. Either one could have paid someone to plant those bombs. Maybe that's what we'll find in the financials. What really boggles my mind is a husband forgiving his wife after she'd been cheating on him for more than a year, especially with his archrival."

"Yeah, it does seem suspect. Do you think our victim was playing them both?" Howie asked.

"In what way?"

"Obviously, I'm speculating, but if the doc's rival is Jack, and the Barretts' marriage was on the skids . . ." Howie shook his head. "Was our victim using Jack to get what she wanted from her husband?"

"That's a damn good question," Max said, happy to see that Howie was taking the initiative—something he hadn't done since announcing his retirement. "I'm not sure we'll ever figure it out now that Helen Barrett is dead."

Howie knocked on the door of the security office. The smell of nicotine hit Max like a windstorm when a hefty guard opened the door. Stepping inside, Max crinkled her nose. A curling stream of smoke from his lit cigarette lingered overhead like fog. Noticing her expression, his yellow-stained fingers crushed his cigarette out in an ashtray overflowing with cigarette butts. "Sorry, ma'am."

Howie was the first to show his credentials. "We'd like to see your surveillance from last night. Specifically, the thirty-second floor."

"Do you have a warrant?" the guard asked.

"Okay, so you're going to play tough. All right," Howie said, "we'll be back tomorrow."

"Sorry, detectives, but we have to protect the privacy of our residents, you know that."

"Yeah, and what about protecting the health of your residents?" Howie asked sharply. "You realize you're breaking the smoke-free work environment law, don't you? If de Blasio finds out, you'll be fined up the wazoo." The guard remained silent.

Back at the precinct, Max called Brian, their A/V technician, and asked him to set up the machine for the Barrett surveillance. Summoning Howie, they anxiously marched into one of the rooms to watch. "It appears that most of the wedding day deliveries were from a variety of service providers," Howie said after watching it for a while.

Max squinted her eyes to focus on the screen when she saw Jeffrey pull into the driveway at four o'clock in the afternoon. She watched him get out of the car. As soon as he walked to the front of the house, an older woman met him, and it appeared as though he was being scolded.

"That's probably his mother," Howie said with a chuckle. "I can almost hear my mother doing the same damn thing."

"Yeah, but we don't know that for sure," Max pointed out. "Are you ready to do some flatfooting over the next week or so?"

"You mean like my last hurrah before I leave?"

"Yeah, something like that," she said.

"You know how much I've always hated canvassing?"

"I do, and that's why I'm suggesting we do that as your last assignment. It'll really make you happy about getting out of here. You'll have no second thoughts."

Howie laughed. "Not to worry. Having second thoughts has never been an issue. Not getting out of here fast enough has."

The pair continued to view the screen when the video turned to nightfall and the screen blackened. "It doesn't look like anything is happening here," Max said.

Brian shut the machine down to allow it to cool. "That's the end of the file," the technician said.

"Okay. Thanks, Brian."

"Phew." Howie sat back and scrubbed a hand over his face. "Boy, I'm bushed. The granddaughter is taking drama at Hunter College, and we sat through her first performance last night, and we were up way past my bedtime."

"I'll bet your family is happy about you retiring," she said.

"Yeah. You remember that little cabin we have in the mountains of North Carolina?" Max nodded. "Well, as soon as I get that golden handshake, we're out of here. I'm so ready to go where there's peace and quiet. No sirens, no break-ins, just good old country living. I think we'll even spend the holidays down there."

"The whole family?"

"Yep, the kids and grandkids. It should be fun. You'll have to come visit us sometime when you want to get away from this rat race."

"I'd love that. How many bedrooms do you have in the cabin?"

"Four. Plenty of room for you."

"Well, I might just take you up on that." Max yawned. "Oh, excuse me." She covered her mouth. "Your yawning is contagious."

"My sentiments exactly. Listen, I have a few more things to do and then I'm leaving," he said and waved to her. Max wasn't thrilled Howie had been leaving early over the last month, but she told herself that after thirty-six years in the NYPD, he deserved it.

Her first order of business would be to fill the boss in on what was happening. He liked to be apprised of every detail, and she didn't mind. It actually helped her organize her thoughts about what had been done and what needed to be done. Making her way to his office, Max passed several detectives talking on phones at their desks and others who roamed around the office chatting with coworkers or checking databases.

She remembered the first time she'd walked into the precinct. It was nothing like she'd imagined. No frills, just a huge room with steel desks lined up in rows, open seating with partners' desks facing one another, and file cabinets surrounding the perimeter of the office, ceasing only when there was a doorway to an interrogation room.

"Hey, Bower," she said to one of her coworkers. "How's your day going?"

"Probably not any better than yours," he said dryly.

She laughed and continued toward the boss's door. Lieutenant Wallace was a tall, dark-skinned man who dressed impeccably. Every day he wore a tailored suit with a different pocket square that matched his tie. He'd been with the department for a few years, and was very adept at leading his people. He took no bullshit from those who defied him, and he got the job done. Max had no problems with the man, though some of her peers did.

Lieutenant Wallace was filling out a form. Without looking up he called her inside.

"How'd you know it was me?"

"I always know when it's you standing at my office door."

"Why? Do I smell bad or something?"

He laughed and gestured for her to sit. "I didn't know you smoked," Wallace said.

"I don't. It's a story that you don't want to know about."

"All right," he said, "give me a brief overview of your case. I've already spoken to Zeke. Not a very pleasant scene, I understand."

"Not at all." She removed her jacket and sat on the chair by his desk. "We have two suspects. The husband and the boyfriend."

"Which one are you leaning toward?"

"You know, I'm still puzzled. We don't have enough evidence yet. Each has their own set of issues. Barrett had a cheating wife, Hughes got jilted, both men wronged by the same woman." She filled in the details of what they'd learned. "Got the surveillance from the Barrett household, but not from Hilary Gardens where the boyfriend lives. The security guys are playing hardball and want a warrant."

"That *is* the proper protocol, Turner," he said, smirking.

"Yeah, but I just thought we'd try. Being Sunday, I have to wait until tomorrow to call in the warrant, but Howie did try at my suggestion."

"Speaking of which, I'm going to partner you with Neal Riley starting tomorrow. He's getting a transfer from the NARC Unit and is ready to try something else."

"That's great, Lieutenant."

The lieutenant chuckled. "My first thought was to pair you with Rosie"—he smirked again—"but I figured that might be rough sledding for the department when you two get into a squabble over who's going to take the lead," he said in a playful voice.

"That was definitely smart thinking, Lieutenant."

He winked. "Just trying to get a rise out of you, Detective, but it doesn't look like I succeeded."

"No, you didn't. Of course, I'll do what you want, but I wouldn't like it one bit . . . and frankly, neither would Rosie." She blew out a breath. "Thank you for choosing Neal. I've seen him a few times on those rare occasions when I've gone to The Alibi, and from what I've seen he seems like a nice guy." She also liked that he reminded her of one of her favorite actors, David Caruso, who played a law enforcer on *CSI Miami*.

"With Howie leaving in two weeks, I think it's a good time to make the break, since you're not that far along in the investigation."

"Okay, but I don't want Howie feeling like I'm just dumping him. He's been very influential in making me the detective I am today."

"What do you mean? He knows you'll eventually be getting a new partner."

"I know," Max said. "But I actually suggested he do some flatfooting today to finish out his time. I don't want him thinking I requested the change."

"I'll take care of it with him. But honestly, he hasn't been looking so good lately. I don't want his last days on the force to be more stressful. Let him ease out of his job in preparation for his retirement."

"That's very nice of you." The lieutenant shrugged. "Have you told Riley yet?" she asked.

"Yeah. I talked to him this morning."

"And he was okay with it?"

"He was more than okay."

"Good." She stood. "Thanks, Lieutenant." Max sighed, concerned about her partner's feelings. "Howie's finishing up on some paperwork, so I think I'll stop and give him a heads-up, then I'm heading home for the night. See you tomorrow."

Max felt a twinge of guilt burning inside her over the change and what Howie would think. Returning to her desk, she was disappointed to find that Howie had already gone for the night and had left a note and his file folder in her center desk drawer. She took a fast look at the note, which stated Jack Hughes was on the brink of bankruptcy, and a notation in the file that he wanted to speak to her about something. She closed the file, deciding she'd had enough for one day. "Tomorrow's another day." Stretching her arms overhead, she yawned. It was definitely time to leave for the night. She reached for her jacket, zipping it up all the way, then shoved the files in her briefcase. The office was just beginning to fill up with the night detectives who shared their desks.

Outside, Max shivered when the wind picked up. Even though the days were warm, the evenings had begun to feel chilly, and she knew it was just a matter of time before the white stuff would begin to fall from the sky.

A few blocks away from the precinct, she walked into Berg's Deli. She'd been hankering for a Reuben sandwich for a week now, but hadn't quite made it to the deli because she'd always gotten sidetracked by her investigations. Tonight though, she'd satisfy that desire.

"I'll have one of those Reubens to go," she said to the owner's son, Sean, who appeared to be a little sweet on her. "And one of those barrel pickles to go with it." She'd been to other delis in the city, but not one was as authentic as Berg's. "Please pack it good, Sean."

"You headed out to arrest someone, pretty lady?"

"Not tonight." Sean was fascinated by the stories he'd heard about the NYPD and their old cases. He called them his collection of "takin' down the bad guys."

Sean handed her the bag with a wink. "Good to see you, Max. Don't make it so long next time."

"It has been a long time. I'll try to remedy that."

She knew her sandwich would be packed in a Styrofoam container with an overabundance of fries, and the pickle cut just the way she liked it, into bite-sized pieces. Sean liked her—she had no idea why—but if he was looking to cheat on his wife, she didn't date married men.

CHAPTER FIVE

Max was awakened by the screeching sound of a siren, but stayed in bed a little while longer after a restless night worrying about Howie being hurt by her new partnership. In addition to her guilt keeping her awake, she'd also left the window open just to get some fresh air, but she'd never do that again. There was way too much noise outside. Using her elbows, she pushed herself up into a sitting position, adjusted the pillow behind her back, and sat there a few minutes, her eyes half-lidded, wishing she could sleep for another hour and sorry she hadn't gotten up in the middle of the night and shut the window. But she'd been too lazy, and now she was going to be dragging her butt all day.

She grabbed her cell phone off the nightstand to check for messages and as she scrolled through, she decided they could all wait until she'd had her first cup of java. Tossing her legs over the side of the bed, she stood and shuffled off to the kitchen, started the coffeemaker, then headed to the bathroom for a shower.

An hour later, she was feeling more refreshed than she'd expected and ready to take on the day. She was filling her cup with the hot liquid when her cell phone rang. Surprised to see the lieutenant's name, she clicked onto the call before the second ring. "What's up, Lieutenant?"

"It's Howie," the Lieutenant said in a low voice.

The first thing that went through her mind was that Howie was upset about the changeover.

"He's mad at me?"

"No. I wish that's all it was." He paused, and her insides stirred nervously, wondering what he was going to say. "God, I'm so sorry to tell you this, but Howie died last night from a heart attack," he said in a somber voice.

Max gasped. "Oh, no, no, no, no." Blinking her eyes shut, she looked skyward as tears ran down her cheeks. Guilt attacked her as she thought about every cross word she'd ever said to him. She dried her tears with a paper towel. "I have to go to Marina," she said in a wobbly voice. "She must be a mess."

"She said she's doing okay, but you know how she puts on a strong front for everyone." Hearing the emotion in the lieutenant's voice surprised her, because the boss and Howie rarely agreed.

"We may have had our differences, but we respected each other," he said.

"Did Marina tell you what happened?"

"She said she'd been packing to leave for the cabin, and Howie walked in complaining about being tired. He fell on the bed, and when his breathing became labored, she called 911 right away. By the time they got there, he was gone."

Max heaved a heavy sigh. "I need to go over there." She disconnected the call and let the waterworks erupt. She wished she could see Howie one more time so she could tell him she was sorry. Sorry for being so hard on him, and even sorrier they didn't have more time together.

Walking up the steps into Howie's living room, Max saw Marina, busily moving around the kitchen serving those who'd stopped by to express their sympathies. Howie's daughter was standing close by Marina, trying to coax her mother to sit down. When Marina saw Max, she stopped what she was doing and walked over. They immediately held each other tightly and cried.

"I am so sorry for your loss," Max said, drying her tears. "I loved him like a father."

Marina nodded. "And he felt the same way about you, Max." She wiped her tears with a tissue she'd pulled from her apron pocket. "How am I going to manage without him?"

Max hugged her again. "Oh sweetie, try not to think about it today. There's plenty of time to figure this out. Take the time you need to grieve with your family. That's all that matters right now."

Marina lowered her head and nodded, trying to compose herself. She released a heavy sigh. "Can I get you something to eat, sweetheart?"

"Marina," Max said, reaching for her hands and holding them, "you need to start thinking of yourself."

"I am, Max. That's why I need to keep moving, because if I don't, I'm going to fall flat on my face." Marina turned to head in the direction of the kitchen. "You stay right here. I'm going to get you some coffee cake."

As more neighbors walked into the house to comfort Marina, Max used that as her time to leave. She placed a quick kiss on Marina's cheek, took the coffee cake to go, waved, and made her exit.

During the ride back to the precinct, Max reminisced about the six years she'd spent being Howie's partner. She remembered their first meeting like it was yesterday, and it brought a smile to her face. At the time, she'd been a newly promoted detective.

Howie could be an overbearing mentor at times, and on more than one occasion, she had been annoyed at him for repeating things she already knew. After they'd arrested a suspect involved in a robbery, Howie had sent her to the interrogation room with the guy before joining her. The suspect seemed friendly enough, and that's when she exercised her independence and intentionally ignored Rule Number One about keeping a suspect secured at all times. In the midst of a friendly conversation, she'd decided to remove the guy's cuffs, and within seconds her rookie mistake had backfired on her. The suspect had tried reaching for her service revolver. Luckily, she was quick to react and remembered a grappling wrist hold that brought the suspect down to his knees, giving her enough time to re-cuff him just as Howie entered the room.

The expression on Howie's face told her she was going to hear plenty of his wrath. Later, when they'd discussed it, instead of Howie pulling rank, he'd used the incident as a teaching tool. From that moment on, she had respected his knowledge. His fatherly advice had become a huge part of their relationship.

She used her shoulder to wipe the tears running down her cheek. Max said a silent prayer, made the sign of the cross, and threw a kiss toward the sky. "That's for you, Howie," she said aloud. "I will miss you forever."

Lieutenant Wallace was the first to spot Max when she returned to the precinct. "How you doing, Turner? Are you okay?"

"No, but I will be."

"Do you need some time to regroup?"

"No. I'll be fine. I'm better off working." She took in a deep breath and released it. "So where's my new partner?"

"He's in the A/V room viewing the surveillance from the Barrett residence so he can catch up. I had Riley call in your warrant."

"Thank you, Lieutenant. Hopefully the new ADA will hurry so we can get it today, but for right now, I'm anxious to find out if Riley found anything unusual we might have missed. A fresh set of eyes is always a good thing." She waved as she walked away. "I'll catch you later." Max weaved through the crowded office, the boisterous chatter and phones ringing like the steady buzz of a bee. Along the way, several of her coworkers stopped her to extend their sympathies.

When Max opened the door, Detective Riley turned to see who was entering. "There she is," he said and handed her a container of coffee. "I don't know if this is still hot. It's been sitting here for a while."

She gladly took it. "Are you trying to butter me up, Riley?"

He laughed. "No. I wanted you to know how sorry I am over the loss of Howie." She nodded. "Actually, I'm lying. I was definitely trying to get into your good graces." His face reddened as bright as the color of his hair. "I know how close you and Howie were, and I want you to know that I understand if you're reluctant to take on a new partner. It's hard to fill someone's shoes."

"Thank you, Riley. That's very nice of you to say. It's true, Howie was a very large part of my career here at the precinct, but you have nothing to worry about. Just keep doing what you're doing."

"Thank you." Neal smiled. "Let me tell you where I'm at so we're both up to speed."

"Okay." She grinned at the enthusiasm in his voice. "What did you find on the surveillance footage?" she asked.

"I didn't see much of anything, except when the back lights went out, I realized someone was probably removing the lightbulb from the spotlights on the garage. I couldn't see anyone even though I replayed it several times. There weren't any notes in the file about cars passing by on the street either, so I jotted down the things I observed to discuss with you." Max gave an approving nod. "There was one car that *did* slow down in front of the residence. Fortunately, I was able to get a partial plate and, when I ran the numbers, it traced back to Jack Hughes."

Max enjoyed seeing the eagerness in his eyes. "Well, you've certainly had a productive morning. Hughes is our disgruntled boyfriend," she said. "Anything else?"

"Yeah, I took a quick ride over to the residence to familiarize myself with the location, and noticed the wooded areas that surround the house would make a good escape route," Riley said with excitement in his voice.

"Excellent, Riley. Good job." Max was already impressed. She removed the lid from the container and sipped the coffee. Despite its lukewarm temperature, it still tasted good. "Did the guest list arrive yet?"

"Not that I'm aware of, but I'm headed out to pick up the warrant for the Hilary Gardens surveillance, then I'll talk to the guy who placed the 911 call. He's the caregiver for his mother, so I offered to question him at his house. Bensonhurst and Santini are coming with me to run canvass in the neighborhood.

"And he's off and running!" Max said. "Thank you. Your enthusiasm is contagious. All right, I'm off to check the financials." They began walking in separate directions. "Hey, while you're at it, stop at the residence and see when the maid's two sons will be returning from Jamaica. If they're there, interview them."

"Absolutely."

Max returned to her desk and fired up her database. Keying in Jeffrey Barrett's name, she clicked on his bank information and did the same for Jack Hughes. Surprised by what she saw, she called Riley.

"This is Riley," he answered. "I'm at the carriage house, where the maid and her family live, talking to her sons."

"So they *are* home," Max said. "Howie was planning to check with the airlines to figure out when they left for Jamaica, but with his death . . . well, please ask them for a printed copy of their itineraries."

"They just told me they only visited for two weeks," Riley said, "but I'll ask for it. If they didn't save it, I'll call the airlines." He coughed. "Excuse me," he said and continued, "I was also planning to introduce myself to Dr. Barrett, but while I was talking to these guys, I heard the roar of a sports car engine. The guys jumped up to look out the window and announced Barrett was driving a bright yellow Lamborghini. I saw it myself."

Max humphed. "Boy, I can see how distraught he is over his wife's death that he's already replaced his car and he's out of the house so soon." The heavy sarcasm shot from her mouth. "I guess driving his wife's Mercedes is below him, huh?"

"I wouldn't jump to any conclusions here, Max. That car could be a loaner from the dealership."

"You're right. I suppose that's a possibility." A chuckle escaped her mouth. "Keep me straight, Riley."

"I'll do my best."

"I guess I'm surprised he's out and about already," she said.

"Everyone grieves in their own way," Riley said. "Besides, he may have patients to check on."

"Another good point. Hey, I've checked Barrett's financials, and it looks like he froze his accounts on October 3 to stop his wife from withdrawing anything from all their holdings. I want to talk to him about it." Max shook her head. "That's fifteen days before they renewed their vows. Do you know where he was going?" Max asked.

"Hold for a moment." She heard mumbling in the background. A few seconds later, Riley was back on the phone. "Maddie said the doctor went back to work . . . and she gave me the guest list."

"Terrific. Why don't you come back to the office and bring whatever you have and . . . did you get the surveillance from Hughes's building?"

"No, the warrant wasn't ready."

"She's a new ADA," Max said, annoyed. "Okay, come back to the office. Then tomorrow, we'll pay Dr. Barrett a visit."

"Sounds like a good plan, Max. See you in a while."

Noticing her boss walking down the corridor, she stopped him. "Riley's on his way back with the guest list from the party. Do we have any rookies who are free to help with the calls?"

"I'm sure we do. What about the warrant for Hilary Gardens?" Wallace asked.

"Riley said it wasn't ready."

"Okay, I'll have one of the guys pick it up later."

CHAPTER SIX

Tuesday morning, Max wanted Riley to know how grateful she for the reprieve after Howie's death,

"Thanks for helping me call all those guests yesterday. I'm sure that's not what you had planned for your first day on a new job, but I just couldn't go out after the trauma from Howie's death."

"That was not a problem at all, Max. I'm just happy to be out of NARC and doing something different with a partner I've always admired."

"Gosh, you're going to make me blush. Thank you."

He smiled. "You know, though," Riley continued, "based on the reactions I received from the guests I'd called, the women gave the doc high marks, the men gave a less flowery opinion of him, but overall they liked him. Funny, that wasn't the image I had in my mind when I sat down to make those calls, especially after reading the comments Howie left in the file."

"I had the same reactions from the women, who see the Barretts' story like a romance novel with a happily-ever-after. As for the men, I received the same thing as you. Only time will tell."

Walking from the parking garage, the two detectives headed toward Mount Sinai. It wasn't very often that Max got to enjoy the fresh air while on the job, so she looked upon the five-block walk over to the hospital as a rare treat. She didn't even mind the hustle-bustle of the crowded sidewalks, although she found herself suspiciously watching everyone who walked past. The familiar smell of exhaust fumes from a bus pulling away from the curb reminded her of the years she'd walked from the subway to school each day. She hated the smell, but it was all part of living in New York—although she did wonder what her lungs looked like after inhaling all those fumes every day.

They walked through the entrance, and Max pinched her nose from the strong medicinal and disinfectant smells that hit her the minute she exited the revolving door. "I hate the smell of hospitals."

"Yeah, it's not something I like either," Riley said. "I always think they're using chemicals to cover up the smell of decaying bodies."

"Geez." Max made a face. "That's a morbid thought." She released a low laugh. "Listen, before we get up there, I'd like you to pay close attention to Barrett's body language and reactions when I start asking him questions."

The volunteers' station was several feet away from the entrance. Huddled behind the circular desk, several ladies wore pink tops to help visitors identify them. Max approached an elderly woman. "We're here to see Dr. Jeffrey Barrett. Can you tell me where his office is?"

"I sure can, sweetie." The woman keyed his name into the computer. "He's in today." She made some notations on a small piece of paper and handed it to Max, then leaned over the desk and pointed with her pen. "The elevator is down this hall. Take it up to the third floor, get off, and take a left until you get to the nurses' station. You can ask for him there. Use this diagram in case you get lost."

"Thank you." Walking away, Max smiled. "I just love little old ladies with blue hair." She laughed.

The ride up in the crowded elevator car was quiet. The strong smell of Shalimar perfume reeked inside the close quarters, causing Max to hold her breath. She'd know that perfume anywhere. Her mother wore it all the time. Thankful when the doors opened on the third floor, Max and Riley got out in a hurry and made their way to the nurses' station.

"We're here to see Dr. Jeffrey Barrett." Riley said.

"Do you have an appointment?" the nurse asked.

"No, we don't."

"Well, Dr. Barrett is a busy man—" She stopped talking when Max presented her shield. "One minute, please." She spoke into a microphone. "Calling Dr. Barrett. Please contact the third-floor nurses' station." She pointed to a waiting room. "Why don't you have a seat? He should be with you shortly."

Fifteen minutes later, Jeffrey came walking down the hall with a sophisticated-looking blonde with long hair. Max thought she looked familiar but couldn't place the woman.

"Thank you, Dr. Barrett. Arianna is looking wonderful," she heard the woman say.

"The fact that her body is accepting the new heart exceptionally well is a good sign. She's getting stronger every day." Barrett walked the woman to the elevator and stopped at the nurses' station on his way back. Max could see the nurse's mouth moving and watched as Barrett turned to look in their direction. He headed toward them.

"Detective, do you have news for me?"

"Was that Senator Stansbury? One of our state senators?"

"As a matter of fact, it was," he said proudly, as though expecting them to be impressed with his clientele.

Max brushed it off lightly. "I thought so." She turned to her partner. "This is my new partner, Detective Neal Riley. Is there somewhere we can speak privately?"

"Yes," Barrett said. "Where is your other partner?"

"Sadly, he died Sunday night."

"I'm sorry for your loss."

Max nodded in acknowledgment.

"Let's go to my office." They followed him down the hall a short distance. Inside, his office was only large enough for a desk, a credenza with a bookshelf, and two wooden chairs in front of the desk. He gestured for them to sit, then made his way to his office chair and pulled himself closer to his desk.

"What news do you have?"

"I don't have any news, but we do have some more questions for you."

"What are they?"

"Well, I've been going through your financial statements, and I'm confused." Max pulled a piece of paper from her jacket pocket and looked at it. "Let's see. Forgive me for using a cheat sheet, but I don't want to forget anything. I get so busy sometimes I have to write things down. That ever happen to you, Dr. Barrett?"

"It happens to all of us," he said dryly and checked his watch. "I have to make rounds. Please, hurry along. I have a lot of patients."

"I don't mean to take up your time, but if you could just explain what I found, I'd appreciate it. On October 3, you placed a freeze on the joint checking and savings accounts, blocking Mrs. Barrett's access to any funds. I'm confused as to why you'd do such a thing two weeks before you renewed your vows."

Jeffrey released a sigh. "I told you, Helen and I were having trouble."

"Right."

"Well, I froze those accounts when Helen told me she was leaving"—he flicked his hand in the air. "I had to do something to convince her to stay."

"I get that, but see, here's the thing: if she was no longer in love with you and loved Mr. Hughes, enough to leave you for him, how did you manage to convince her to stay with you so quickly?"

"Well . . . I . . . I mean, we'd had a lot of years together."

"You seem a little ruffled, Dr. Barrett. Did I hit a nerve?"

"Yes, you did. I'm tired of you trying to point the finger at me. I did nothing wrong. I'm the widower here, remember?"

"And I'm the detective trying to solve your wife's murder. So what's the deal with the freeze?"

"I didn't want her taking our money to share with that asshole, Jack Hughes. I just wanted to remind Helen how much we meant to each other. As you can see, I lifted the freeze after she agreed to stay with me." He glanced quickly at his watch again.

"Uh, no, I'm not quite getting that," Max said. "You're making it sound like your wife only stayed with you because you lifted the freeze."

His face flushed with anger. "I have rounds, but before I go, was it really necessary for you to call all my guests from the party?"

"Yes, Dr. Barrett, it was necessary."

"What did you learn?"

"It will be in our final report at the end of our investigation."

"Are we done here?" he snapped, clearly annoyed with her answer.

"No, we're not, but I can schedule an appointment for you to come to the precinct. I came here to make it easier for you, but I think there are too many distractions. I'm also curious about why you came back to work so soon after your wife's death. And I hear you've replaced your Lamborghini already."

"What did you expect me to do?" he shot back. "Hide? Getting back to my routine is what I needed to do to stop sulking. You're working after losing your partner, Detective," he said in a clipped voice.

"Point taken, but he wasn't my spouse." Max shoved her hand in her pocket. "Okay. That's all for now. You'll be hearing from us."

He stood to usher them out of his office, then made an abrupt stop. "And what's happening with Hughes?"

"We're working on it." Max began to walk away, then stopped. "One more question Dr. Barrett. I assume you're having a memorial service for your wife. Can you tell me when that is?"

"Why?"

"I'd like to attend."

"If I do have anything, it will be by invitation only for close friends and family."

"If?"

"Yes, Detective. Now, if you'll excuse me, I have rounds. Have a good day," he said and briskly walked away.

On their way back to the parking garage, Max turned to Riley. "That was an interesting statement."

"I'll say," Riley said with a shake of his head.

"So what is your impression of him now?"

"I'm sticking to what I originally thought when I read the file," Riley said. "I guess all those people saying such flattering things should have been expected—he's the big man on campus. But today, meeting him for the first time, I was surprised his emotions fluctuated." Riley shrugged, "although his uneasiness came through loud and clear, especially when you asked about a memorial service."

"Yeah, he was pissed that I was quizzing him and had called his guests. What do you think? Guilty or innocent?"

"I think he's hiding something, but Jack's the one with the damaging evidence against him. This one, not so much. As far as I'm concerned, I loved that he got mad. He told us more than he intended—especially about him not wanting Jack to have his money. Now, it *really* sounds more like his competitive side doesn't like to lose than that he actually loved his wife." Riley scratched his chin. "I read one of Howie's comments in the file: he thought Mrs. Barrett might have been playing both sides." He nodded his head in agreement. "I'm beginning to think he might have been right."

"Me too, but I'm not totally convinced yet that Barrett had anything to do with her death. There might be something else going on in the background." She shook her head in confusion, "I just haven't put my finger on it yet." Max rubbed the bridge of her nose. "All right, our next stop is La Fontaine restaurant on Twelfth Street."

"Now I know we're not having lunch at that swanky place on *our* salaries, so what's there?"

"The Hughes guy and Mrs. Barrett had lunch there on Saturday."

"Wow, Mrs. Barrett certainly had a busy day," Riley said with a smirk. "Lunch with her former lover the same day she renewed her wedding vows, then finished the evening off by entertaining a hundred fifty guests?"

"Apparently so."

A *Closed* sign hung from the window when they arrived at the restaurant. Riley shielded his eyes from the sun, peered through the glass door, and noticed a young woman wiping down menus.

"There's someone in there," he announced.

Max knocked impatiently on the glass door, and the woman ignored her until Riley held his badge against the windowpane. Shortly after, Max heard the lock recess and the door open.

"We're Detectives Turner and Riley from the 51st Precinct, NYPD."

"Yes, Detectives. As you can see, we're not open yet."

"We're not here for food, ma'am, we're here to find out some information about two people—customers of yours." The smell of bread baking in the oven filled the air and brought back warm memories of Max's grandmother's kitchen. She inhaled. "Boy, that bread sure smells good. I haven't had homemade bread since . . . geez, since grammar school." Glancing around the restaurant, Max noted the elegant dining room with beautifully set tables, clearly too expensive on her salary.

"What can I do for you?" the young woman asked.

"We're investigating a homicide. I'd like to ask you a few questions about a Jack Hughes and a Helen Barrett. Do you know them?"

"I do," she replied meekly.

"So then, I guess you know she was killed on Sunday morning?"

She closed her eyes. "Yes, I saw it in the newspaper. What a shame. She was such a lovely lady."

"Yes, it is. We're investigating her murder. I saw a charge on Mr. Hughes's credit card for lunch at this restaurant for Saturday, the eighteenth—the day before she was killed. Can you verify Mrs. Barrett was here with him?"

"Yes, she was, but surely you can't believe he's the one who killed her."

"I never said that," Max responded in a clipped tone, her eyes making direct contact with the hostess. The sudden change in the woman's demeanor caused Max to be suspicious. "Is there something else you'd like to tell me?"

"No." Max noticed she shook her head too rapidly. "Nothing."

Max frowned. "I'm sensing something happened on that day. What was it?"

"I'd be happy to tell you what they ate as soon as I check the weekly receipts, but other than that, I have nothing to tell you."

"I'm not interested in what they ate. I want to know how they acted together."

"They were fine."

"What is your name?"

"Simone Grant. Why?"

"Well, Simone, I've been in law enforcement long enough to know when someone is hiding something."

"I'm not looking to get anyone in trouble," Simone said, her flighty hand movements telling Max she was nervous. "You're asking me to be disloyal to our customers."

"No. I'm asking you to tell me what you observed between the two." Simone ignored the question and continued wiping down the menus, which was fraying Max's already thinning patience. "Simone," Max said abruptly, "this is a murder investigation—the only one you're being disloyal to is Helen Barrett by not telling me what you saw and heard, so I'll ask again, what did you see and hear?" Max said it firmly, her voice a few decibels higher than the start of the conversation.

Riley intervened. "Of course, if you'd rather, we can arrest you for obstruction of justice for withholding information from the police." Simone remained silent.

When a chef walked out from the back, he looked concerned. "What's going on out here, Simone?" he said in his native French accent.

"This is my boss, chef François de la Fontaine." Max and Riley acknowledged his presence by introducing themselves. "They want information about two of our customers," Simone finished.

"So tell them what they want to know. Our business is to feed our customers, not protect them." He turned and walked back in through the double swinging doors of the kitchen.

Simone bit down on her lip.

"What do you have to hide?" Max asked.

"I like the people."

"That's okay. I'm merely trying to collect the facts so I can begin to eliminate suspects." Max's comment seemed to calm her down somewhat, and she started to talk.

"Okay." She fidgeted. "They argued. I have no idea about what, but the volume of their conversation started out very low, then Mr. Hughes's voice escalated, which began to disturb the other diners. The dining room was full, and when we noticed how upset our other customers were getting, we asked him to leave."

"Did you hear any part of their argument?"

Simone sighed. "Yes." Max was beginning to feel like she was pulling the girl's teeth out, trying to get her to respond.

"What . . . did . . . you . . . hear?" Max asked firmly.

"The only thing I heard was *kill you*."

Max turned to Riley, each getting a reading of what the other was thinking. "I'm going to need your reservations list for Saturday so we can contact those diners."

"I'm sure he didn't mean it the way it sounded," Simone continued to defend Jack Hughes.

"He probably didn't, but that's why we need the list, so we can talk to the others."

"Can I just go in and ask my boss if it's all right to make a copy for you?"

"Sure. Is there anything else you'd like to share?"

"Just that when I asked him to leave, he stomped out in a fit of anger." Simone turned toward the kitchen just as the chef carried out a white bag. Simone told him what they wanted.

"Madame," he said, "I'm sure you can understand my position. I ask that you give me . . ." He wiggled his fingers as though that would help the words come to him. "What is that piece of paper you get for permission?"

"A warrant."

"*Oui*. That is what I would like before I turn over the reservation list. I hope you understand."

"I absolutely do."

"Here," he said, handing her the bag. "I heard you talk about your childhood memory, so I buttered two rolls for you." Max opened the bag, inhaled the aroma of yeast, and took a roll before passing the bag over to Riley. He removed his roll and bit into it; Max broke off a piece of hers and popped into her mouth. "Oh my God, this is so delicious. How much do I owe you?"

"Nothing, Detective. Come in and have dinner with us sometime."

"I will. Thank you very much. And thank you, Miss Grant. We'll be back later this afternoon with the warrant."

CHAPTER SEVEN

"Holy crap," Riley said, walking back to the car. "The evidence against Jack Hughes is mounting quickly."

"I think we talk to the diners first to find out what they heard, then we go talk to him. I'll call in the warrant, then we'll go see Audrey, our ADA, to pick it up." Sitting on the passenger's side, Max was disappointed there were hardly any leaves left on the trees. She curled her lip. "Damn, I've always loved seeing Central Park with the colorful leaves, but it looks like that cold snap and the rain we had the other night did a number on them. I think snow is right around the corner." She crinkled her nose. "I absolutely hate having to trudge around in slush."

Riley groaned. "Yep, I agree. I think the leaves I raked up last weekend that the kids jumped in and flattened are the last of the season. Man, I was exhausted by the time I was done, but honestly, they did have fun."

She laughed. "That's what they're supposed to do. How many kids do you have?"

"Three rambunctious boys, ten, eight, and five."

Max smiled, but pangs of jealousy punched her stomach from wishing she had a family of her own. Still, she always wondered whether she was parent material given the tumultuous and painful childhood she'd had. She loved her nieces, got along well with them, but would that translate into good parenting skills? She didn't know and wasn't sure she wanted to find out.

"And your wife? Does she work?"

"Leslie has a decorating business that she runs out of our home. My in-laws live next door, so when she has a job, the boys can just go right over there and the grandparents will watch them."

"How convenient. Lucky you."

"So how about you?" Riley asked. "Do you have a family?"

"No. I'm married to my job."

"There's nothing like having a family, Max."

"I'm sure, but that's a subject for another day."

Riley pulled into the precinct garage, shut the engine down, and together they walked to the elevator and waited for the doors to open.

"Boy, I sure hope the disc from the Hilary Gardens is here. I'm anxious to see if Hughes was telling the truth," Max said.

"Do you really think he would have suggested we check the surveillance if he wasn't telling the truth?"

Max laughed. "I suppose not, but . . ."

"He'd be a damn fool to lie."

Heading to the A/V room, Max was the first to talk to Brian, the technician. "Did one of the uniforms drop off a disc from Hilary Gardens for me?"

Max turned when she heard the lieutenant calling out to her. He was holding the disc in the air. "Santini just dropped it off."

"Awesome, Lieutenant. Thank you. Want to stay and watch it with us?" she asked.

"I think I will."

"Let it roll, Brian," Max said. She handed the disc to him and eased down into a chair next to the lieutenant.

For the better part of the footage, there was nothing to see except the stillness of the hallways. "Geez, this is a pretty boring place," Riley said.

"So far, but for some reason, I think the show is just about to begin," Max said, and then she saw him. "Well, Riley, will you look at what this damned fool did?"

"Boy, I'll say." Leaning closer to the screen, Riley commented again, "He's leaving the building"—he squinted at the screen—"and he's exiting through the stairwell?" they said in unison.

"That's thirty-one flights down. I guess our so-called wounded lover didn't stay home after all. Brian, can you back that up again?"

"Yes, ma'am," Brian said.

She smiled at him. He was a nice kid, in his twenties and fairly new to the department. Coming from a corporate background, he'd witnessed firsthand how the NYPD worked their magic when his boss was caught setting up cameras in the vice president's suite to tape his after-hours extracurricular activities on his office sofa. That was what made him decide he wanted to be part of the police force.

"So Hughes said he was home all night alone?" the lieutenant asked.

"Yep, that's exactly what he told Howie and me on that first visit."

"The time stamp says ten o'clock," Riley said, jotting down the number. "Okay, so let's watch to see where this bugger goes, but also keep in mind that the Barretts' surveillance has Jack's car driving past the house at eleven o'clock that night."

"Yeah, but do you know for a fact that he was the one driving the car?" Wallace asked, lines wrinkling around his eyes from his frown.

"Probably, unless someone hijacked him on the way and stole his car. But, just to be sure, I'll check the database to see if he reported it missing to the auto theft unit." Riley stepped away and walked outside into the hallway, shutting the door behind him."

"How's he's doing?" Wallace asked Max when he heard the door close.

"Great. He's quick to notice things that even I've missed. I think he's going to work out just fine." She stopped talking when Riley reentered with a file in his hand.

"No reports." Riley handed the file folder to Max. "Also, Bensonhurst just returned with La Fontaine's list of diners from the afternoon Jack and Helen Barrett quarreled."

"Excellent. Let's divide the list and make the calls," Max said. Turning toward her boss, she frowned. "That new rookie," she said, "what's his name?"

"Sanchez. You want some help calling these customers?"

"That would be a big help. The sooner we can get this liar behind bars, the better off we'll be."

"I'll send him over to your desk."

"Thanks, Lieutenant."

"All right, Riley, how about you start off by calling Hilary Gardens to see if the elevators were down. Let's give Hughes the benefit of the doubt to see if he walked down those thirty-one flights for a legitimate reason."

Riley sat down at his desk and keyed in the number while Max noticed Sanchez on his way over to her desk. "Thanks for helping out," she said when he stopped next to her. She handed him one of the lists. "I'd like you to take this list and go back to your desk and call each person. What I want to know is if they heard an argument between two people on the afternoon of October eighteenth at La Fontaine and, if so, what specifically they heard. I wouldn't say anything about expecting them to testify because they may clam up. If we find their information useful, we'll subpoena them anyway."

"Okay. Sounds pretty clear-cut to me."

"Excellent. This has to be done today, so if anyone else tries to give you some work, ask them to talk to the lieutenant."

"Got it."

Riley disconnected his call. "The manager of the maintenance department over at Hilary said the last time they had difficulty with the elevators was the month of July." He humphed. "No one walks down thirty-one flights. I'll bet he thought that by taking the stairs, he'd bypass the surveillance cameras."

"I love it!" she chuckled. "Listen, I just gave Sanchez half the list of restaurant clients. Let's you and me divide what's left in half and talk to these people to see what they know. It looks like Simone gave us the complete list of reservations for the day, but I'd still like to talk to all of them regardless of what time they were scheduled. The customer could have changed the time, and Simone may have gotten sidetracked and forgotten to correct it on the log." They each sat down and started calling.

Max keyed in the number for the name on the top of her list. "I'd like to speak to Mrs. Warner."

"This is she. Who is this?"

"Hello, Mrs. Warner, I'm Detective Max Turner from the 51st Precinct, Homicide Division of the NYPD, and I'd like to ask you a few questions about having lunch at La Fontaine."

"Oh dear," the woman said. "I didn't see anyone get killed, if that's what you're asking."

Max couldn't help but smile at her comment. "We're investigating a homicide that may involve two guests who had lunch at La Fontaine on the eighteenth of October. I saw your name on the list and wondered if you did in fact have lunch there that day?"

"Yes. My friend, Trudy, and I did. I remember the date specifically because we were celebrating her birthday. Are you going to ask me about that evil man who started a ruckus in the dining room?"

"What man are you referring to?"

"There was a handsome couple who sat at a table closest to the bar. Trudy, that's my friend, she and I sat a few tables away from them. Funny, I kept glancing over at him because I honestly thought he was Jeff Foxworthy, but obviously, I was wrong. I just love that man."

"Did you hear any part of the argument?"

"It was obvious they were angry about something. At first the conversation was low. The woman was trying to calm him, but it wasn't working. We tried to ignore it, but then all of a sudden, the man's voice escalated and he was so angry, his words were all jumbled, but we did hear him say something about wanting to kill her. That had Trudy and me shaking in our boots. We almost left for that very reason, but the hostess came over and asked him to leave." She blew out a breath. "And thank God for that. There are some pretty weird people out there, Detective. Who knows what he would have done."

"Is that specifically what he said? That he wanted to kill her?"

"Hmm . . . give me a minute." She paused. "No, maybe not. The only words that I heard with clarity were 'kill you.' And after the hostess booted him out . . . well, not literally, but he stormed out of the place with clenched fists."

"And what about the woman? Did she also leave?"

"Not at that point. The poor thing was absolutely mortified. I could see her face was flushed, but she sat there for a while, I suspect trying to calm herself down. She waited about a half hour, then the hostess came over to the table and walked her out of the restaurant, you know, standing on the side of her that blocked our view." She sighed. "I've never seen anything so upsetting. It just ruined Trudy's birthday celebration. Did he kill her?"

"I'm sorry, but I can't answer that question. Would you mind giving me Trudy's telephone number so I can call and ask her what she heard?"

"Certainly." She recited the number.

"Thank you very much, Mrs. Warner. You've been extremely helpful."

"Well, I hope that man gets what he deserves. If he killed her, you can put a checkmark next to my name, because I'll testify to what I saw and heard."

"Thank you. We appreciate your assistance. I'd like to give you my phone number just in case you remember anything else that you think might be pertinent to the case."

Two hours later, Max rolled her chair away from her desk and covered a yawn with her hand. "How are you making out with the list?" she asked Riley.

"Out of ten customers, six dined later, two were dining at the time it occurred and recognized there was an argument going on but ignored it, and two claim they heard Jack say the words *kill her*."

"I found only two on my list who are willing to testify if needed." She checked her notes. "A Mrs. Warner and her lunch companion," Max said, picking up her phone. "Let's see how Sanchez is doing on his list."

By the time Sanchez was finished with his calls, Max and Riley had their warrant for Jack's arrest and were headed to his apartment building.

Max gave a forceful knock on Hughes's apartment door. He angrily pulled it open and groaned when he saw her.

"You couldn't call first to let me know you were coming? You had to surprise me?" He left the door open and walked in the opposite direction.

"That's far enough, Mr. Hughes," Riley said. Hughes stopped short and turned, a baffled expression on his face.

"Have a seat, because we have more questions," Max said.

"About what?" he snapped.

"Let's start with your lunch at La Fontaine the day before Helen Barrett died. Your last meal together. We have witnesses who will testify in a court of law that you threatened to kill her." Max's brow arched, almost daring him to lie again. Given Jack's quick temper, she and Riley were prepared to restrain him, if necessary.

"What? They're nuts. I did not." His face reddened with anger. "Yes, we had an argument, and yes, I was asked to leave, but I never said I wanted to kill her." His voice rose progressively higher as he spoke.

"Then tell us about that argument," Riley said.

"I was trying to win her back. She was making a mistake by staying with Jeffrey, and I told her that. But I wasn't shouting."

"These witnesses, all diners at the restaurant at the same time you were there, said you threatened her."

"My God"—he covered his face with his hands—"I loved her. I was beside myself and yes, I was very upset, but that's not something I would have said to her. Maybe I did shout . . . and didn't realize it. You have to understand, we had big plans for a beautiful future together."

"Then what did you say?" Max asked.

He rubbed his forehead. "I'm struggling to remember." He stared off into the distance for a while, then suddenly held up his hand. "I do remember." He nodded his head up and down. "I remember exactly what I said. I told her if she went back to Jeffrey *he* was going to kill her." He blew out a breath from his air-filled cheeks. "I swear, that's exactly what I said."

"I wish we could believe you, Mr. Hughes, but with so many lies, an already spotted record, and your anger-management issues, why should we believe you now?"

"I didn't lie to you."

"No?" Max replied. "Then why didn't you tell us you'd left your apartment Saturday evening? You even got annoyed at me for asking, and adamantly insisted you were alone," Max said, "so if you didn't leave, then why do we have you on video walking through the exit door on this floor and walking down thirty-one flights of stairs, getting into your car, and driving away from the building? How do you explain that?"

"I guess I forgot to tell you."

"I'm sorry, Mr. Hughes, I'm not buying it," Max said as he glared at her. "This is your last chance to explain yourself."

"Okay, so I had cabin fever and decided to go for a walk in the park. Nothing sinister about it, Detective. I needed to get out of the apartment. If you recall, ma'am, I was the one to suggest you view the surveillance. Do you think if I had done anything wrong, I would have suggested it?"

"So why didn't you tell us about your walk?"

"Because I was afraid you'd think I did something to hurt Helen. I swear to you, I did nothing. Not telling you was poor judgment on my part, but . . ."

"I'm afraid it's too late for any 'buts,' Mr. Hughes. We're charging you with the murder of Helen Barrett. Please turn around." Riley walked behind him, removed the cuffs from his belt clip, and slipped them around Jack's wrists, locking them into place.

"You can't be serious?" His face flushed with anger.

"I am. And by the way, we do have surveillance that has you driving past the Barrett residence late on the evening that they renewed their vows. Plus, we've checked with your commanding officer in the military, who informed us you were awarded the highest medal of honor for your expertise in explosives by the United States Department of Defense. They even revealed that you were so good at what you did, they put you in a senior supervisory role and referred to you as *the master*."

Max read Hughes his rights.

"You are dead wrong about this, lady," he mumbled, his face emotionless.

"Yeah, and so is Helen Barrett."

Late Tuesday evening, Cory Rossini walked into the Manhattan Detention Complex, which was nicknamed The Tombs. "I'm here to see Jack Hughes," he said to Darnell Richards, one of the guards. Cory knew Darnell from his frequent visits to the complex to see clients he'd represented in the past. He'd always liked Darnell, but the inmates had nothing nice to say about the man. As a matter of fact, the man Cory thought was a gentle soul had been described by his clients as a teddy bear with the soul of a lion. Cory noted Darnell's middle had expanded over the last several months, and his balding hairline had now become impossible to disguise. Darnell's ego, which had always been considerable, was probably wounded.

"Hey, Cory. Long time no see. Are you Hughes's attorney?"

"No. I'm doing private investigative work for a while. I needed a break."

"Yeah, I hear you. I feel that way sometimes myself, but this is all I know." He nodded toward the hall. "You know where Interview Room 8 is located. I'll get him for you."

Cory walked into the room and sat down on one of the chairs. Not much had changed since the last time he was there to visit with a client. The Tombs had remained in its usual state of disrepair. As Cory walked down the hall, prisoners reached their arms through the bars and begged for cigarettes while declaring their innocence. Cory noticed the same old chipped tables, the same old chairs, the seats torn with stuffing poking out, the same old dreary wall color in dire need of paint, and dented lockers around the perimeter. A strong scent of Pine-Sol masked the stench of urine deeply saturated into the cement.

Cory felt sick to his stomach knowing his friend was housed in this kind of environment.

Best friends since childhood, Jack was like a second brother to him, and his family had welcomed Cory with open arms, taking him on weeklong vacations and trips to the beach while his own parents worked. There was little doubt in his mind that Jack was no killer, and he was going to do whatever he could to prove it.

The sound of the door opening caught Cory's attention, and he stood when Jack walked inside wearing the customary orange jumpsuit. Cory watched as Darnell removed Jack's cuffs. He wanted to pull Jack into his arms for a guy hug to let him know he had his back, but he knew none of that was allowed.

"I didn't do this, Cory. I swear to you."

"You don't need to tell me that, buddy. How you holding up?"

"Right now, I'm just shocked over Helen's death. I don't even care what happens to me."

"Don't talk like that. You know she wouldn't have wanted this for you."

"I swear if I get out of here and that bastard hasn't been charged with her death, I may even kill him myself."

"Watch what you say in here," Cory warned in a low voice. "You never know who is listening." Jack slapped his hands against his thighs in disgust. "Did you talk to an attorney?" Cory asked, but Jack ignored his question, covering his face with his hands. "Did you?"

"Yeah, he was in earlier."

"What did he say?"

"I presume the same thing he says to every client—'I'll do what I can.'" Jack's frown caused deep wrinkles in his forehead.

"You know I'll be working in your corner to prove your innocence." The two men exchanged a glance.

"I know *you* will, but not if that bitchy detective has anything to say about it . . ." Jack's eyes filled with contempt.

"That bad, huh?"

"That bad." He nodded.

"What's her name?"

"What? You mean, you can't see her name etched in my forehead?" Cory grinned at Jack's snarky comment. "Detective Maxine Turner, and she's hell-bent on sending me to prison."

"What does she have?" Cory stared at him expectantly.

"Oh, that one has a whole shitload of charges against me that have been twisted to make it look like I did it." Jack crossed his arms and slid down to lean his back against the chair.

"Tell me the charges."

Jack filled in all the things he remembered. "And the first-degree murder was reduced to second, because if I did it, which I didn't, I would have had no way of knowing Helen would be driving the car. The other thing against me is my military experience with explosives."

The corners of Jack's mouth lifted in disgust. "The other guys in my cell block told me this female detective is worse than any male detective they've ever dealt with."

"Really?" Cory was curious why her name wasn't familiar to him, given his years of practice. He wrote her name down on a piece of paper. "Don't worry, I'll talk to her tomorrow and see what I can find out. Is there anything else I should know?"

"My arraignment is tomorrow."

"I know that. I'll be there, but I'll go see this detective first to find out why she's so confident it's you. Hang loose. We'll get this figured out."

"Thanks."

"Okay. If you think of things you want me to mention to your attorney, commit them to memory because they're not going to allow me to give you a paper and pencil."

"I hate to do this to you, Cory," Darnell interrupted, "but your time is up." Cory's disappointed expression had little impact on Darnell. "Listen, I did let you stay a little longer than I should have. The warden is watching all of us."

Cory sighed. "I know you did, Darnell." Cory turned back to Jack, who stood up and placed his hands behind his back so Darnell could put the cuffs back on his wrists.

Seeing the depressed expression on Jack's face, Cory gave it one more shot. "Don't worry about a thing. Know that I've got your back, bud. Hold on to that thought, okay?"

Jack did not acknowledge Cory's words of encouragement. Darnell yanked on his arm, and Jack slowly walked out of the room. An empty feeling of helplessness quivered in Cory's stomach. He needed to get Jack out of here . . . and back home where he belonged.

CHAPTER EIGHT

Max walked into the precinct the next morning feeling good about Jack Hughes being behind bars. Howie would have been proud of her for arresting someone so quickly. Her thoughts halted when the desk sergeant called out her name.

"There's someone here to see you."

"Who is it, Sarge?"

"I don't know, but he's anxious to speak to only you." He handed her the guest's business card. "He's waiting for you in interrogation room two," he said.

Max viewed the card and said his name aloud. "Cory Rossini, attorney at law?" She raised her shoulder in a dismissive shrug. "He must be new, because I don't recognize his name."

She looked at Riley. "I'll catch up with you after I talk to this guy." She entered the room, and when he turned around, fury attacked every nerve in her body. How dare he. How dare he show up here.

"What?" she said, facing him. "Making a fool of me in the stands at Yankee Stadium wasn't enough for you, or having viewers see us fighting on the Jumbotron? Are you here to feed your ego a little more?" He shook his head, ready to say something, but she continued. "Well,

Mr."—she looked at the card again—"Rossini, I didn't like you then, and I don't like you now.

"I would have thought, based on the fact that you're an attorney, that you would have had more common sense, but then again, maybe that scene was a marketing ploy to get more clients—at my expense, I might add." She smirked at the expression on his face. "That's it, isn't it? But then to make matters worse, you offered to buy me a hot dog. Seriously? Was that to show the more humanistic side of your personality? Are you running for political office or something?"

He shook his head.

"Well, let me tell you, that attempt was lame."

His handsome face turned roguish as he leaned forward in the chair and weaved his fingers together, obviously aware that saying anything was only going to set her off even more. And that damn smirk of his wasn't doing him any favors either. In fact, it only infuriated her even more, and the words flew out of her mouth faster than ammunition feeds into a machine gun.

"You know, I told my nieces I'd do my best to catch a ball for them as a souvenir. So they intentionally watched the game on television instead of doing their homework. When they saw both of us going for the ball, they were jumping up and down because they thought I had it. Need I express how disappointed two young kids were when I told them I didn't catch it?" Max angrily flipped her hair back over her shoulder. "Did you come here to gloat?"

He stared at her with intensity as though making some sort of decision.

"This is a joke to you, right? So let me express this in simple terms for you so you won't waste any more time. You cheated."

"Are you finished yet?" he asked with raised brows.

"Yes, I am. Now"—she gestured toward the door—"please leave!"

He cleared his throat. "I agree wholeheartedly with you. I was a louse. I didn't do it to make you look bad, or to embarrass you. I caught that ball for my niece who's dying of cancer, and although I felt guilty that I wasn't enough of a gentleman to give you the ball, I thought she was worth the ache in my gut. Furthermore, I'm not here for you. I'm here about Jack Hughes's arrest."

"Oh." Embarrassment flushed her cheeks, and it was obvious from the expression on his face he was enjoying every minute of Max trying to regain her composure. "Then you should have said so."

His lips smacked together in a tsk. "If you recall, I tried a few times during your tirade, but you kept bulldozing right over me."

Max cleared her throat. Uneasiness filled every part of her body. She simply stared without saying a word, and then she finally apologized. "You're right, your niece deserves that ball a lot more than mine."

He extended his hand. "Can we start all over?" She nodded and accepted his hand. "Hi, I'm Cory Rossini." His killer smile made her heart flutter.

"Hi, I'm Detective Max Turner."

"It's nice to meet you, Detective Max Turner."

"Thank you." She didn't return the sentiment.

"Now, can we talk about Jack Hughes?"

"Are you his attorney?"

"No, I'm a private investigator."

She held up his card. "Your card says you're an attorney."

"I was," he said, reaching into his pocket. "I gave you the wrong card." He pulled out another card, this time looking at it before handing it to her.

Max's brows furrowed into confusion. "You're no longer an attorney?" She watched him shift uncomfortably in his seat. "Why?"

"I just can't practice law for the next five months."

"So you were suspended."

"Yeah. But that doesn't have any bearing on what I know to be right. Jack and I have known each other since childhood. I know this guy better than I know myself, and I'm telling you he didn't do this," he said. "What exactly do you have on Jack to prove his guilt?"

"Now, you know I can't discuss that with you. You'll have to discuss it with his attorney of record." She checked her notes. "His name is Bill Cates."

"Cates? Why would he be using Cates?"

"Don't know. He requested a public defender. Cates is representing him pro bono."

"No, that can't be right. Jack's got plenty of money. He's a famous artist."

"I think you'd better talk to your friend, Mr. Rossini." Max noticed his jaw tense. "What I can tell you is we have an airtight case."

"I find that hard to believe. From what I've been told by my peers, you have an impressive record for arrests. I just hope Jack isn't filling a quota for you."

Her hand lifted in the air into a *stop* gesture. "Let me stop you right there." His distrust grated on her nerves and got her all fired up. She told herself to calm down—he wasn't worth it. "I'm not one of those detectives who needs to fill a quota. I'm someone who does my homework and leaves no stone unturned. If that makes me a hard-ass, so be it, but I've never accused someone of doing something unless I had the proof to back it up. If you're around long enough, you'll see that." Max stood. "Now, if you'll excuse me, I need to get back to work." Max abruptly walked out of the room and left him sitting in the chair. When she heard his feet hitting the floor behind her in deliberate steps, she knew he was on his way out too. She was still embarrassed about going off on him. Guilt for her actions sat in the pit of her stomach and rushed through every vein in her body. The fact that he smelled as good as he looked made her twice as angry. Because of his niece's condition, she'd accepted his apology, but having witnessed his passion for his friend, she hoped he wasn't going to be a pain in the ass.

Walking down the hall to her desk, she was surprised to see a stack of cards from her coworkers sitting on her chair. She was overwhelmed by the outpouring of sympathy extended to her.

"Are you okay?" Riley asked her. "You're as white as a ghost."

"I don't know what I am right now, Riley." She moved the pile of cards to her desktop and sat down in the chair. She wondered if she should tell Riley what she'd just done. She was going to bust if she didn't tell someone.

"What's wrong? Talk to me."

"Okay." She looked around to see who was close by. "Not here though."

Riley checked his watch. "How about we talk over lunch later?"

"Sounds wonderful."

Outside, Max lifted her chin and allowed the sun to hit her cheeks as she and Riley headed for Pat's Pizza Palace.

"Are you trying to get a tan?" Riley asked.

"I might as well take advantage of the sun."

"So talk to me."

Max took in a deep breath and blew it out. Her mouth twisted to the side. "I made a complete ass out of myself this morning." She rolled her eyes.

"Ha! That's an ongoing occurrence for me, so don't think you have the corner on that market. What did you do?"

Max hesitated.

"Your secret is safe with me."

"I went to a baseball game . . ." She filled in the rest of the details. "This morning, I ripped the guy's face off for taking the ball, only to find out it was for his dying niece."

Riley laughed. "Oh God. I'll bet that stung. So how did he find you?"

"It was a fluke. He was here because of Jack Hughes. They're apparently good friends, and he wanted to know about Jack's charges."

"You know what I think, Max?" Riley laughed some more. "I think you've met your match."

"Yeah see, that's the thing. I think you're right, but I'm embarrassed I ripped him a new one because the truth is I can't help but feel an attraction to the guy."

They each bought a slice of pizza, then filled their cups with ice and soda, and ambled toward the row of window seats. After biting into his pizza, Riley asked, "So what did he have to say about Hughes?"

"Oh, you know, the usual bullshit. We have the wrong person in jail, and he intends to prove it."

"Is he Hughes's attorney?"

"No, he was an attorney, got suspended for something, and now he's a private investigator."

"That suspension sounds ominous, but I guess we'll be seeing him quite a bit until trial if he's trying to prove his friend's innocence."

"Yeah, I guess so." Max had mixed emotions. Regardless of whether she was attracted to Rossini or not, she had no intention of falling under his pretty-boy spell.

"What time is the arraignment?" Riley asked.

"Two o'clock." Max felt an undeniable tingle of excitement at the prospect of seeing him again.

"I'll check him out for you."

Max snickered. "What is it about all you male partners wanting to be gallant knights?"

He gave a nonchalant shrug. "You're my partner now. We have to look out for one another."

"Now, don't go getting all sensitive on me. You don't need to check him out. I have no interest. I can't afford to be distracted by any romantic notions."

"Okay. Whatever you say." Riley wiped his mouth with his napkin. "Are you ready to head to the courthouse?"

Max took one last sip of her soda, covered her lips with a coat of lipstick, and pushed back in her chair. "Let's do it."

"Please rise for the Honorable Dale Clark." Once the judge was seated, the court clerk made the first announcement. "Docket number 09-N-571-023," he called out, "People of the State of New York versus Jack Abrams Hughes."

"Assistant District Attorney Audrey Beckwith for the State of New York," the ADA said.

"Bill Cates, attorney for the defense."

Max hadn't been surprised when she'd learned that Bill Cates had been assigned to Hughes. He'd been assigned by the court to represent a lot of criminals these days. He'd won a few cases, but too few to have any criminals knocking down his door for ongoing representation.

Max knew most of the attorneys in the county because she was often the arresting officer and had to testify against their clients, but she hadn't recognized Cory's name and wondered what type of law he'd practiced before his suspension. She watched Jack turn around to Cory, who was sitting behind him, and give his friend an appreciative smile, clearly showing the deep affection they felt for one another.

The bailiff, a beast of a man who'd been coined Mr. Clean, stood in front of the defendant. "Will the defendant please rise and state his name for the record?"

"Jack Abrams Hughes, your Honor."

"Does the defendant waive the reading of the rights and charges, Mr. Cates?"

"We do, your Honor."

"How do you plead, Mr. Hughes?"

"Not guilty."

Audrey stepped forward. "Your Honor, the State is filing a 731A Notice stating the charges against the defendant are supported."

"Would you like to make a statement regarding bail, counselor?"

"I would, your Honor. The State asks that the defendant be remanded until such time as the court has set a date for trial. We believe the defendant is a flight risk."

The judge nodded to the defense attorney. "Mr. Cates, would you care to speak your piece?"

"Yes, your Honor. There's no good reason for remanding the defendant. Regardless of what counsel thinks, this man is going nowhere. He's an upstanding citizen. He's an accomplished artist who has contracts with deadlines he must meet. If the court is concerned with him taking off, he's more than willing to turn over his passport. Denying him bail jeopardizes his business. I ask that the court allow him to continue practicing his craft."

Judge Clark stared at the defendant before hitting his sound block with the gavel. "The defendant is hereby remanded to Riker's Island until such time as a date is set for hearing."

Cory swallowed hard as he watched Jack's head lower in disappointment. His hand reached out to touch Jack to lend his support, but the bailiff noticed and scolded him.

"Thank you, your Honor," Cates said.

Riley scanned the room as they began to leave. "Is that your guy over there in the gray suit, the one who's walking with Cates?" Max noticed Cory and Cates had stopped a safe distance away and were talking. She assumed it was about the charges against Jack.

"He's not my guy," Max defended, although knowing he was only a few feet away had her heart pounding as loudly as the judge's mallet.

"Just a figure of speech, Max. He's a good-looking guy," Riley said.

"Yeah, don't judge a book by its cover."

Cory waved when their eyes made contact. She nodded an acknowledgment, but quickly averted her eyes and looked straight ahead, thankful he couldn't tell his presence excited her. How she could even face him after her ridiculous outburst was beyond her.

Max found herself thrown off guard again when she exited the courtroom and saw Cory leaning against the wall, their eyes made a connection. She quickly averted hers, but when she looked back, he was still staring in her direction. Max told herself to tamp down her ego, he was probably waiting for someone else, but when he began to make his way toward them, she prayed she'd be able to mask the anxiety dancing in her stomach. "Did you forget something?" she asked when he stopped in front of them.

"I did." His eyes shifted to Riley.

"Allow me to introduce my partner, Neal Riley." The two men exchanged a handshake.

"What's on your mind?" she asked.

"Do you have a minute to talk?" he asked, glancing at Riley again, who took the hint and moved on.

"I'll see you back at the precinct, Max," he said and walked away so quickly she didn't have time to protest.

"What can I help you with?" she asked.

"I'm dying for some coffee. Will you join me at Starbucks?"

"For what reason? So you can tell me again how Hughes is innocent?"

"No. I'd like to call a truce." His face cracked into a smile.

"We did that already, but we are still adversaries in regard to this case."

"That's fine—we don't have to be on the same side, because I'm confident you're going to find out Jack is innocent all on your own. That's not why I wanted you to join me."

"Why then?" She noticed he was losing patience when he'd sucked in his bottom lip. Why was she giving him such a hard time? "Thanks for the offer, but I really can't spare the time." She walked away wondering why she was having trouble accepting the fact that she hadn't been able to stop thinking about him.

CHAPTER NINE

"Hey, Max," Riley said when he saw her reviewing a file. "C'mon, work-day is over. A few of us are going over to The Alibi for drinks and a bite to eat. Want to join us?"

"I don't know. I've got a lot of work to do, and honestly, I'm not feeling right about celebrating."

"We're not celebrating. My wife is out shopping with the kids, and I don't feel like making my own dinner, so c'mon, it'll do you some good. I know you loved Howie, but you can't let his death keep you from having a little interaction with others. And who knows, you may just be glad you came."

"I know." She blinked her eyes and heaved a sigh. "You're right. Okay, I'll go."

Max had always enjoyed The Alibi, a local bar that had been anointed the unofficial hangout for law enforcement and officers of the court. It had started years earlier when several cops surrounded a young man who'd had too much to drink and was getting overly handsy with his objecting date. After arresting the guy on the spot and cuffing him in front of everyone, it was understood that such clientele was not welcome at The Alibi. Although the owner was upset in the beginning, he soon relaxed when he saw how busy the place became.

Having a hangout the cops could call their own kept the guys coming back regularly; they could let their hair down and unwind away from prying eyes. Despite the fact that Max didn't like hanging out in bars, she had to admit this was one place that made her feel comfortable. And it did fill the void of her lonely existence. Did she wish she had someone in her life to hang out with? Of course she did, but when things didn't happen in the love department, she'd accepted it as her fait accompli.

"Good. What were you reading in that file? Your face was so intense."

"Oh, I didn't realize until now that Howie had left notes from some research he'd done on Barrett. He was convinced the doc was guilty and said we'd need to take a good look at him. According to the notes he left, he'd found something, and placed a question mark next to Barrett's name with a note saying 'Talk to Max,' but he didn't elaborate." Max closed her eyes and shook her head. "You have to know this is going to drive me nuts until I find out what he meant."

"Whatever it was, we'll find it." Riley grabbed his briefcase and then headed out the door. "See you in a little while."

The small bar buzzed with peers from other precincts. Max had forgotten Wednesday night was karaoke night. Although she wouldn't get up on the stage and sing, she always enjoyed listening to her peers sing their little hearts out. Obviously, not all of them could sing, especially Eddie Perry, who worked in the two-one and was now crooning to a Maroon 5 song. He tried hitting a note higher than he was able to reach, and Max and Riley did all they could to refrain from laughing.

"You have to give the guy credit," Max said.

"Yeah. I guess you do." Riley saw some friends enter and waved them over to the table.

They removed their jackets and draped them over the backs of the chairs. Riley introduced Max. "This is my new partner, guys." They each gave her an appreciative smile. "This is Jake, Steve, and Bob. They're all NARCs."

"Good to meet you," Max said and was flattered by their attentiveness until she noticed their wedding bands.

A waitress came over and took their drink orders just as Eddie was finishing up his song. A few seconds later, "Love Me Tender" boomed through the speakers, and a baritone voice echoed through the microphone. Max glanced toward the stage and was caught by surprise. It was Cory who was singing and staring directly at her. It seemed the guys with the largest egos always felt if they smiled and winked at the ladies, they'd have them all clamoring to go on a date with them. Although she and Cory had come to an agreement about what happened in the stadium, Max felt a lingering anxiety about how quickly their tempers flared during the disagreement. Cory Rossini would have to do a lot more than sing a love song to her to get her attention.

She leaned over toward Riley. "I wonder what he's doing here?"

"Why? He's an officer of the court . . . or was, but I'm sure he's still okay being in here."

"I've never seen him here," Max commented.

Riley laughed. "And you come here so often that you'd know how frequently he's here?" She blew him a raspberry. "I must say, though, judging from this serenade, this guy's got it bad for you, Max," Riley quipped.

"No he doesn't." She flicked her hand in the air. "He's just trying to get on my good side so I'll be convinced Hughes is innocent."

"Boy, are you ever the cynic. Cut the guy some slack, will you?"

Riley's friend Bob turned around to watch Cory. "I'd give the guy a chance—before I try and cut in on his territory."

"Oh guys, stop. He doesn't have any claim to me, and Bob, I don't go out with married men."

He removed his wedding ring. "I'm not married now." Max rolled her eyes with disgust. "Relax, Max, I'm just kidding. I'm a happily married man with five kids, and I think you should talk to this guy."

Riley chimed in. "He's trying awfully hard to get your attention," he said in a sing-song voice. "If you'll give the guy half a chance, you never know what you'll find out. You may just find out you were all wrong about him."

When the song was finished, Cory received an enthusiastic round of applause and chants for him to sing another.

"Thank you very much," he said into the microphone, "but there's a beautiful young lady sitting over there"—he pointed—"and I don't want to miss my window of opportunity." Everyone turned in Max's direction and expressed their approval with loud whistles and clapping. Feeling the heat rise up her cheeks, Max lowered her head just before Riley and his friends vacated the table. She immediately covered her eyes with her hands, refusing to look up until she heard the chair scratching across the floor and inhaled the pleasant scent of Cory's woodsy-scented cologne. There was no way out; he was at her table. He poked her foot with the tip of his shoe.

"Hey." He threw his hands up when she uncovered her eyes. "It was the only way you were going to agree to have a drink with me." Max cleared her throat, ready to say something, but Cory's hand went up to stop her. "Seriously, you gotta give me extra credit for going through so much trouble to get your attention. You have to know I wouldn't be doing any of this if I weren't interested, but if you can look me in the eyes and tell me you aren't interested, then I'll get up nice and slow and walk away and never bother you again. So what do you say?"

There was a pause of silence between them that seemed liked hours rather than seconds. Looking into his eyes, she took a breath and opened her mouth to speak. "Yes, I'm interested, but if you ever embarrass me like that again . . ."

He interrupted her. "So what are you drinking?" he asked with a toothy grin. Music blasted from overhead. "Why do you try so hard to discourage me?"

Max didn't have an answer for him and simply shrugged. He pointed to her half-finished drink.

"Thank you," she said, "but I don't care for another drink."

He listened to the music for a minute. "I love this song. Will you dance with me?" he said, pushing back in his chair, his voice slightly tentative as if testing the idea.

"I can't. I'm going to be totally embarrassed having people see that I accepted your offer."

"Why? You're never going to see these people again anyway."

"Yes, I will," she said, giving him a playful tap on the arm. "I work with them."

"Oh, that's right," he said and winked at her. "C'mon." His hands moved in closer, removing any chance she could refuse by pulling her upright and onto the dance floor. He wrapped her in a tight embrace as they swayed to the music.

Melding into him, the warmth of his body next to hers was overwhelming. She wondered if he could feel her heart pounding against his chest.

"Look, I know I flubbed it up really badly that night," he said whispering in her ear over the loud music, "but I'd had a bad day and thought the game might help. The ball did help that, until we started arguing, and I got defensive. I knew I shouldn't have, but then afterward, I couldn't stop thinking about you, and that's when I realized I wouldn't have met you if I hadn't gone." He looked down at her, a serious look on his face. "So finding you a second time . . . it's kismet, Max, and we're supposed to give ourselves a chance at a relationship." She held her hand up behind her ear, pretending she hadn't heard what he'd said, but she'd heard every word of it and it warmed her heart.

He continued anyway. "I knew I was being a jerk, but the words were out before I could pull them back. When I saw your reaction, well, I became even more sarcastic. And when you wouldn't let me make it up to you with the offer of a hot dog, the guilt bothered me for days." He shrugged. "It's my Catholic upbringing. I'm sorry." His face scrunched into a pleading frown. "Do you think you can forget about that meeting and pretend we just met in your office?"

She smirked. "You mean the meeting when I practically ripped your face off? That meeting?"

"Yeah, *that* meeting." He laughed, indicating she hadn't fooled anyone with her chutzpah. "Honestly, that's what attracted me to you even more. You have spunk. I really like that in a woman. What do you think?"

Her heart turned over at his willingness to express his feelings. How often did a guy actually express his feelings so honestly? Like never.

"You know, if you'd agree to have dinner with me tonight," he said, a sparkle in his eyes every time he smiled, "you'd make me the happiest guy on the planet. So what do you say?"

She could no longer hide the excitement she was feeling. "I'd like that very much."

His surprised reaction told her he hadn't expected her response. "Awesome!" he said, squeezing her tighter. "Do you like Italian food?" he asked like a wide-eyed schoolboy who'd just sunk his first three-pointer.

"I do."

"I have a favorite restaurant in Little Italy."

"Oh, really? I'll bet I know which one. Angelo's."

"How did you know?"

"Because it's *my* favorite."

The music stopped, and Cory guided her back to the table to retrieve her belongings. "You know, we have more in common than you think."

Max didn't respond. She was afraid and cautious about telling him he was getting to her, yet she couldn't hide her interest. He was so different from any of the guys she'd ever dated. Hearing him verbalize his feelings was an added bonus and drew her in like a magnet. She wanted to know more about him.

"Are you ready to leave?"

"I am." Max reached for her jacket. He took it and held it out for her. She slid her arms into the sleeves and couldn't believe she'd found someone who wasn't intimidated by her. Someone who wanted to treat her like a lady. When Riley saw them walking toward the door, he gave her a smug wink.

"My car or yours?" Cory asked when they walked outside.

"I usually take the subway and leave my car home. We could do the subway if you'd prefer so we don't have to buck this traffic."

"I don't mind driving, but I'm embarrassed to say my car is a piece of junk."

"I don't care about that. It's hard to have a nice car in New York with the way these people drive."

"You know, you really impress me," he said. "Judging from the way you carry yourself, it might come off to some guys that you're a prima donna who's used to the finer things in life, and then I tell you about my beat-up car and it doesn't faze you in the least."

Max grinned. "Before you consider me for canonization as a saint, let me assure you that I do enjoy the finer things in life. This just means the car you drive doesn't change my opinion of you."

He chuckled as he unlocked the door and held it open for her. "I hope your opinion of me is improving." Max merely smiled, liking the fact that he was confident but not the egotistical guy she thought he was.

Cory shoved in behind the steering wheel and reached for her hand, brought it to his mouth, and kissed it. "Where have you been all my life?" he asked, cocking his head to one side, obviously waiting for her to respond. When she didn't say a word, he became concerned. "Am I coming on too strong?"

"Nope. You're doing just fine," Max said. "I don't know where this is going, but I'm willing to admit that I misjudged you. And for the record, I'd had a crappy day when I went to the game too. The only reason I was there was because my brother-in-law, who'd been given the ticket, didn't have enough for the entire family, and so my sister made me take it." She didn't tell him Julie had insisted Max take it because she'd been acting like a celibate nun and needed to get out more.

"A sister, huh? Do you have other siblings?"

"No, but I have a cousin who's a priest."

"I'd thought of becoming a priest in my younger days," he said, straight-faced.

"Really?"

"No." His face scrunched. "I'm just kidding. Do I look like the priestly type?"

"Well, it probably would take a lot of work on your part," she teased back. An easy smile played at the corners of his mouth, and she was glad she'd accepted his invitation. She liked his humor. Nevertheless, she was still slightly guarded because she wanted to be sure he didn't have an ulterior motive for getting to know her. She was thankful he hadn't mentioned Jack's name or anything about the case, because if he had, she'd have been out of there in a heartbeat.

It wasn't long before they drove down Mulberry Street.

"I can't believe we like the same restaurant," he said, looking over at her. "Now see, there's even more proof that we're meant to have a relationship. Pretty soon, you're going to agree with me that I'm irresistible and you can't live without me." He jabbed her with his elbow. "Am I right, or what?"

"Is that a fact?"

"You like the way I just mapped out our future?"

"Yes, I did notice that."

"I'm just having fun with you, but you should know I don't give up easily."

"I'm a big fan of stick-to-itiveness."

His head rose in the air. "See, now, that's another thing we have in common." He cleared his throat. "So when was the last time you were here?"

"It's probably been a month or more since my last visit." She'd decided not to mention that she'd gone there alone, and how happy she was to have someone with her now. Frequenting the same restaurant without a date made her feel others might think she was damaged goods. "How long has it been since your last relationship?" she asked when the thought came to mind.

"A couple of months. Why? Are you worried you're a rebound?"

"The thought did cross my mind."

"Well, don't give it another thought. My attraction to you has nothing to do with anything other than convincing you I'm worthy of a second date."

Max was glad it was dark and Cory couldn't see the broad smile on her face. She told herself they were off to a good second start. If it was meant to be, it would happen. A snort escaped her mouth at the irony of her sudden acceptance of fate.

"What's so funny?"

"Oh, you see all kinds of things walking the streets of New York," she lied. "I just have to shake my head in dismay and wonder if these people ever look at themselves in the mirror."

"That's for sure."

Cory searched for a parking spot but didn't find one and drove to the nearest parking garage. After exiting the vehicle, he rushed to her side of the car, opened the door, and helped her out.

"And he's a gentleman too?" Cory shut the door.

"He is. I was taught by the best: my grandfather."

"Well, my hat is off to your grandfather."

He waited for the parking ticket then grabbed Max's hand for the walk to the restaurant, causing her heart to flip over. She sucked in a deep breath and blew it out, trying to hide the sexual tension building inside.

"What's your favorite dish there?" he asked while strolling down the street, inching around a clump of people blocking the sidewalk.

"Wow, that's a hard question to answer, but I'd have to say the lasagna or eggplant Parmesan. My favorite dessert is cannoli," she said, salivating at the mention.

"Mine too."

"Did you make it to the San Genaro Festival in September?" she asked.

"Are you kidding? My family came over on the boat from Naples. That's our time to celebrate our patron saint with the entire family. I really like tasting the foods from all the restaurants that set up booths outside their storefronts. The array of different platters of every size, shape, and color not only looks festive, but the food tastes good too. It reminds us of Naples." He looked down at her with a sheepish grin, "Of course, no one cooks like my mama."

"It sounds like you might be a mama's boy."

"Absolutely. She's the one who taught me the importance of expressing my feelings, but she doesn't interfere in my life unless I need a good kick in the ass. And as for the festival, it's still fun trying to get through the crowded streets, tasting the foods, and dodging the droves of pickpockets." He shook his head. "Yeah, we definitely come every year."

"Your family sounds like so much fun," Max said wishing she had a story like his to tell. She'd always loved walking down Mulberry Street in Little Italy. For outsiders, it was a place with so many Italian restaurants that it was hard to choose. For the New Yorkers, though, they already had their favorite places to eat and knew where to get the best espresso or cannoli afterward.

"How about your family?" he asked, maneuvering her through the crowd. "Do they come?"

"I've been here with my sister and nieces, but it's rare because I'm always working."

"Well, maybe you can join my family next year." Cory tilted his head back, inhaled the smell, and moaned. "God, I love that smell."

"Me too. These restaurants are a real tease," Max said, placing her hand on her stomach. When they passed Ferrera's, another well-known restaurant on Mulberry, the waiter, who was rolling up the yellow-striped awning smiled at Max. Continuing on to Angelo's, Max was curious about reservations when she saw a long line of customers waiting for tables to free up outside on the patio. "We don't have reservations, do we?"

"Actually, I made them before I asked you," Cory said.

"Pretty confident, weren't you?"

"No. I wasn't at all, because I figured if you'd said no, I'd grab one of my friends, or come alone. Either way, I was going to eat here, but I'm thrilled you came with me." She smiled without saying anything, but he knew she was too.

Max glanced at the large awning covering the entire front of the building, waving from a gentle breeze. Seeing the stark-white lettering against the dark blue background announcing the location as *Angelo's of Mulberry St. Ristorante Italiano* always prompted the same reaction in Max—a screaming appetite. She lifted her nose in the air and inhaled the aromas of garlic and olive oil wafting out through the opened mahogany doors. "Mmm," Max said, "that smell gets me every time."

"Yeah, me too," Cory said with a smile. "I'm hungry." Passing by those waiting for a table, the pair walked toward the host.

Immediately recognizing Cory, the man in the dark suit greeted him. "Mr. Rossini. It's always a delight to see you. I have your table ready," he said and removed two menus. Walking ahead, he continued talking. "I had to practically sit on top of it so no one would take it."

Cory laughed. "Thank you. I appreciate it."

"My pleasure. Enjoy your dinner."

Max smiled at her favorite waiter on their way back to the table. "*Buonasera*, Enrico," she said. He leaned in and kissed her cheek.

"*Buonasera*, signorina."

"Enrico, will you take care of these lovely people?" the man in the suit asked.

The waiter extended his arm for Max to latch on to and walked her to the table. Cory tagged along right behind.

When they were seated, a waiter poured water into their glasses. "The usual wine, Mr. Rossini?" he asked, handing them menus.

Cory held up his finger, asking the server to wait.

"Yes?" he asked, looking at Max.

"I usually have Pinot Noir, but I'll try your usual, whatever that is."

"You don't have to do that."

"I know. What kind of wine is it?"

He put his finger down and nodded his approval. "Thank you." He answered her question. "A Sangiovese."

"That works too." Max leaned in closer to ask a question, whispering that she wasn't familiar with the man who'd greeted them. "Who is he?" she asked.

"He's the owner's nephew and works when Carmine is away on vacation."

"Aha. I guess I've never been in here when the owner was away."

Max glanced around and admired a new mural on the wall that made her feel as though she were in Italy. Arches with Italian pottery graced the niches of the restaurant, and short awnings extended on each side of the dining room to simulate an outside bistro.

"Did you notice that that mural was new?" She pointed.

"Yeah, I haven't seen it before."

The waiter returned with their wine and a basket of focaccia and poured olive oil into the dipping bowls. "Are you ready to order?" Enrico asked.

"We haven't even looked at the menu yet. Just give us a few more minutes."

Cory picked up his glass. "Shall we toast?"

"Yes, but let me do the toast," Max said.

"Okay."

"May this evening be a new beginning," she said, tapping her glass against his.

Cory's mood was buoyant. "And may there be many more," he added before digging into the bread basket. After breaking the bread into pieces, he dipped it into the oil and bit into it. She did the same.

Enrico stayed a safe distance away, checking often to see when they were ready.

"I think Enrico wants us to order our food," he said.

"Yeah, I'm sure. Okay, I'll look at the menu."

Max looked up from her menu and caught Cory studying her with such tenderness, she thought her heart might explode. She pretended she hadn't seen him, but his sensual expression made her body tingle with desire. She cautioned herself to slow her thoughts down. A relationship with him was not going to be based on lust—it had to be much more.

Cory knew she'd caught him staring at her, but he couldn't help himself. She was a beautiful woman, and it was perfectly natural to have those longing thoughts. A man would have to be dead not to want her. Not only was she sexy, but she was stylish, intelligent, someone he could have a meaty conversation with, when she wasn't blasting him for something she didn't like. Max was a woman he'd be proud to have on his arm. He laughed aloud.

"What are you laughing about over there?" she asked, brushing a blonde lock of her hair away from her eyes.

"Actually, Max, you make me feel like a lovestruck teenager, and I'm flabbergasted by it because we've just met." He paused. "Now that I've found you, I'm not going to give up until I give what I hope is a budding romance everything I've got. I know this is crazy, but you know how everyone always says, when the right one comes along, you'll know it? Wow, they were right."

Max actually giggled. "You're adorable, Cory, and I have to tell you I'm so flattered by your attentiveness. You've made me feel very special." Max went back to reading the menu until she felt the heat of his stare blazing through her again. She looked up. Seeing his broad smile warmed her core. She had to give him credit for being original, and the fact that he wasn't afraid to share his feelings had her seeing him in a different light. She'd never imagined he'd be like this and hoped he was being sincere and not playing her for a fool. Riley's comment about her being cynical came to mind. She was, but her job had trained her to be. But oh, that smile on his face and the deep cleft in his chin . . . it was enough to melt anyone's heart.

Cory cleared his throat. "I'm having the veal saltimbocca," he announced. "How about you?"

"I think I'd like ravioli tonight." The minute Max closed the menu, Enrico was there in a flash to take their orders.

"So tell me about yourself," Cory said.

"What would you like to know?"

"I have a ton of questions. Have you ever been married, have kids? Where are you from?" He took a sip of wine, waiting in anticipation for her response.

"No, and no. I'm a native New Yorker and never plan to leave. My life is my work. I have a sister, two nieces, and a cousin." Max was mesmerized by his green eyes. They sparkled with excitement every time he smiled at her. It made her feel like he really liked *her*, and that was a good thing, because she was really beginning to like him.

"All work and very little play makes for an extremely dull life?"

Max laughed. "Sometimes, but I guess I'm just too wrapped up in my work." She didn't want to say anything more. "How about you?"

"I was born and raised here."

"Did your parents meet here in the city?" she asked.

"No, they went to school together in Naples. When my grandparents decided to migrate to the States, my father wouldn't leave without my mother, so he proposed marriage, and they had their honeymoon onboard the ship en route to the States."

"Aw, what a beautiful love story. How sweet is that?"

"Yeah, my parents are still very much in love."

"That's rare."

"It is, and I hope to carry on the same legacy after I find the woman of my dreams. I've never been married, don't have any kids—not that I don't want a family—and I don't currently have a girlfriend, but we won't talk about that."

"Okay, that's fair enough. You don't have to tell me if you don't want to," she said, sensing it might be a sensitive subject.

"It isn't that I don't want to tell you about my last relationship . . . I just thought women preferred not to hear about that stuff on a date."

"Is that what this is? A date?" she teased.

"Yes, this is definitely a date. Are you okay with that even though we both thought there wasn't a chance in hell it would ever happen?" He chuckled and reached for her hand, giving it a playful squeeze.

"Yeah." She nodded. "I'm okay with that. I'd like to get to know you better too." She studied him for a while, unable to believe she was with him, or how wrongly she'd judged him. He caught her staring at him and winked, causing her heart to spiral out of control.

The waiter set a plate down in front of Max, while another waiter served Cory. Taking her first bite, she released a satisfied moan. "Oh my God." She continued chewing. "You have to taste this," she said, scooping ravioli on her spoon and placing it on the corner of his plate. He did the same with his veal, and they both tasted and swooned over the flavor of the dishes.

After finishing his meal, Cory relaxed back in his seat and stared at her. "I really like you, Max Turner, and I'm having a hard time taking my eyes off you," he said. "And it's probably because I want to make sure you're still sitting across from me."

Max chuckled. "Cory, I must say I can't help but love the way you express yourself. It warms my heart." Elation bubbled through her for the first time in a very long while.

"So there's a chance we can do this again?" he asked, watching the busboy remove the empty plates while Enrico approached. He nodded to the waiter, who headed back to the kitchen.

"I'd say there's a really good chance." Her sister, Julie, came to mind, and she laughed inside, knowing Jules would absolutely gloat over being right about forcing Max to go to the game.

Five minutes later, Enrico returned with two coffees and a cannoli cut in half, one piece for each of them.

"You little stinker," Max said. "So that's what that nod at Enrico was for?" She looked at her half of the cannoli and put her hand on her stomach. "I'm so full."

"Me too, but you must know there's a separate compartment for dessert, so there's plenty of room."

"I'm going to get fat."

"Yeah, I'm sure that little chunk is going to add another twenty pounds at least," he teased.

Finishing her coffee, Max sat back and groaned. "I need to run around the block."

"Is that what you want to do next?" he asked.

"I hate to be a party pooper, but I have work to do tonight." Cory's face was the picture of disappointment.

"Really?" He frowned. "It's not something that can wait until tomorrow?"

"Why? What did you have in mind?"

"I thought we could stop for a nightcap and dance a little."

"Well, I'm not a dancer, as evidenced by our last whirl around the dance floor."

"Really? I hadn't noticed," Cory said.

"Yeah, I'll bet." She gave him a look to let him know she was aware he was lying. "If you want, you can come up to my place for a nightcap."

"Does that mean you won't be working, then?"

"No, it just means I'll start right after you leave." Max eyed him pulling the money from his money clip to pay the bill. She released a sigh. Was he too good to be true?

Cory made a silly face that made her laugh. "I'd really love to see your place, but honestly, with the way I'm feeling toward you, it's probably not a good idea." She nodded and they stood up at the same time, walking through the dining room. Trailing her, he reached forward and took her hand. "I really meant it when I said I like you . . . a lot."

Max smiled inwardly as they exited the restaurant. When she turned to look at him, she noticed his expression and stopped. "I like you too, Cory, but that expression of yours tells me you have something on your mind. Just say it."

"I might scare you away."

"I don't scare that easily," she said as they walked outside still holding hands. He stopped and pulled her toward him and kissed her with such tenderness she didn't want him to stop.

"You blow my mind," he said, his eyes grazing over her face.

His kiss had her feeling a delicious rush of that first-date excitement and surprise. She hadn't expected that kiss, but she was so glad he had made the move. It had been a long time since she'd been out on a date, and this one was ranking high on her list of do-agains.

"You taste like a bowl full of cherries," he said, then noticed her expression. "Are you okay? Have I offended you because I kissed you on the first date?"

She released a low giggle, shaking her head, then reached for the collar on his leather jacket and pulled him toward her for another kiss. "There. Now we're even."

"Do you really have to work tonight? I honestly don't want this night to end."

"I'm afraid so." She didn't want the night to end either, but he was right about not coming to her apartment, not when they were both feeling so amorous. They would have thrown logic out the window and most likely jumped right into the sack. "So I guess my job doesn't bother you?" she inquired.

"Why should it? We're basically doing the same thing. The only difference is, I can't arrest anyone."

"But what happens after your suspension is over?" she asked when he opened the car door for her.

"I don't know if I want to go back to practicing law."

"Would you mind telling me why you were suspended?" she asked.

"I hadn't planned on telling you about it on our first date, but I believe in being honest, so yes, I will tell you." He started the car and drove out of the garage. "Where do you live?"

"In the West Village on Perry Street."

"Wow! That's a pretty classy side of the city. I would imagine you love living there."

"Absolutely. The restaurants, the culture, the artistic people . . . it's amazing, and I can't imagine living anywhere else. I've lived there forever, in a rent-stabilized apartment building, so I'm not going anywhere. Where do you live?"

"In the East Village on St. Marks Place."

"Oh, I love that neighborhood. All the quirky shops are great to wander into. But you didn't answer my question. Are you trying to stall so you don't have to tell me?"

"No, ma'am. I'm driving you home, remember?" She tipped her head to the side, waiting for him to tell her. "I borrowed money from a client's retainer fund," he said remorsefully.

Max's eyes opened wide with surprise.

Noticing her surprise, his hand rose in the air, and he offered an explanation. "Please wait before you jump to conclusions. It wasn't like I borrowed the money for my own gain. The niece I caught the ball for was diagnosed with cancer, my brother-in-law was unemployed as a result of downsizing, which meant there was no health insurance to pay for surgery, and without it, the surgeon wouldn't do the operation. It's always about the money." His face quirked. "I couldn't sit back and watch. And it wasn't like I could ask my parents for help, because my father lost all his money when the market crashed in 2008." He sucked in his lips. "I'd even considered selling my place, the brownstone my grandfather left to me after he died, but it's been in the family ever since they came to the States. He was a hard-working man who saved the money so he could give his family a better life. Having no money of their own, my parents lived with them until they started a family. There's so much history behind those walls, I couldn't do it. It's the only family legacy that remains. Please understand that I don't think what I did was right. My family means the world to me, and I make no excuse for my stupidity, but I don't want to lie to you either." He blinked.

"Did you pay it back?" she asked.

"Of course. I wouldn't have even borrowed it if I thought I couldn't pay it back. I'd already depleted my 401K as a partial payment to the surgeon." He glanced her way. "I thought the partial payment would have been good enough to get him started, but because there was no health insurance, he wanted all the money up front."

"I hate hearing stories about some of the horrible things doctors do, especially when it comes to money. I understand . . ." Max's face tensed, and then her hand lifted up like a stop sign. "Don't even get me started on doctors," she said, then took a deep breath and blew it out. "What I don't understand, though, is how they even found out you'd borrowed it?"

Cory pursed his lips and stared into the distance before responding. "The woman I was dating at the time turned me in to the partners." Max didn't mask her surprise. Cory's head nodded in agreement. "Yeah . . . she wanted more than I was willing to give to our relationship. For example, after only dating three months, she started pushing the marriage card. I wasn't in love with her, and knew I couldn't give her what she wanted, so I broke it off." A sour expression covered his handsome face and he shrugged.

"How did she know where you'd gotten the money?"

"Actually, she was the one who'd suggested it. She knew I was frantic with worry about Stacy, and . . . well, the rest is history. When they came knocking on my door, I told the State Bar the truth about why I did it. Even though they knew I'd already paid the money back, they didn't care and told me I was lucky that I was only getting suspended and not a jail sentence." He shrugged again. "Hey, I deserved it. That's why I accepted my punishment and made lemonade out of a bad situation. I took the test for private investigator." He looked over at her. "Did I ruin things between us?"

Cory's comment tugged on her heartstrings. Knowing he was a responsible person told her he was the kind of man she wanted in her life. The kind of man who wasn't afraid of owning up to his mistakes, a man who bared his soul and made her feel like she was the center of his universe. And above all, he treated her as his equal. That told her he knew who he was and didn't need to bully anyone to make himself feel better. "Not at all. In fact, I like you more, because I admire a man for telling the truth and taking his punishment with dignity and grace."

"Thank you."

Cory turned onto Perry Street. "You can drop me off anywhere on the street and I'll walk to my apartment. Trying to find a parking space is out of the question."

"Don't be ridiculous," Cory said with furrowed brows. "I'm not letting you walk to your apartment. What kind of guy do you think I am?"

She chuckled. "It's really okay, Cory." She patted him on the shoulder. "It's no big deal."

"Well, it is to me. I'm old school," he said and whipped right into a space that was just freeing up. "How about that?" he said. "The gods must be on my side tonight."

"I'll say. Maybe we should be going to Harrah's in Atlantic City instead of calling it a night."

"I don't always have this much luck. It must be because you let me take you to dinner."

"Yeah, I'm sure that's it," she teased. "I have magical powers." She winked at him.

He cut the engine. "You do indeed. You're my lady luck."

Max pulled her keys from her purse, and Cory walked her to the door. She inserted a key into the lock and opened the door. "You're sure you don't want to come inside?"

"Thanks, but maybe another time. I don't want to forget I'm a gentleman."

Max couldn't stop smiling. She was bowled over by his charm and respect for her. "Thank you for a wonderful evening. I really had a good time."

"Me too." He pulled her into a tight hold and kissed her again. "Good night, my sweet angel."

CHAPTER TEN

Cory Rossini couldn't wipe the smile off his face the next morning when he slid into his beat-up old Honda Accord. He didn't even mind the early snowfall that had hit New York with a vengeance. He inserted the key into the ignition of his car and cranked up the engine, revving it until he could no longer see his breath, then backed out of his garage and headed for Broadway, slowly easing his way into the traffic. Snow in the city was a major inconvenience, but right now, he didn't care because he couldn't stop thinking about Max Turner and how much he was beginning to care for her. He shook his head. Last night had proved it. She was one fiery chick and just the kind of woman he wanted—an equal partner. A woman who made him work hard to gain her respect. He didn't have any problems with that. None whatsoever. He'd been afraid he wouldn't be able to undo that God-awful first meeting, but that was a thing of the past, and he couldn't wait to see her again.

Watching the snowfall cover his windshield, his thoughts turned to Jack and his lies. Shaking his head in confusion, he couldn't believe what he'd heard. What the hell was going on with him that he'd lied to the detective who had the proof to back it up? Then, his argument with Helen, with more witnesses who swore they'd heard him threaten to kill her.

Exiting the car, he released his frustration, his breath rising in the air like a steady puff of smoke. With all that he'd heard about Jack, he wondered why he was even trying to free him. He truly wanted to believe Jack, especially after his longtime friend had assured him he was innocent. Cory had believed every word Jack had said, yesterday. Now, he wasn't so sure.

And if Cates was Jack's court-appointed attorney, he suddenly understood why Jack had used his one phone call to contact him instead of hiring an attorney. It sounded as though Jack was having financial problems. If that was the case, why hadn't he told Cory?

Tension filled him. He intended to find out all this information the next time he visited Jack.

Cory shivered when he exited the car and wished he'd dressed for winter. He massaged his frozen fingers, which felt as though they'd fall off any minute, and flexed them a few times, trying to get the blood to circulate. Wrapping the scarf tighter around his neck, he quickened his pace and headed for the warm building, wondering why he'd felt it necessary to come to the library instead of checking the *New York Times* society page in the comfort of his home to find out who Barrett's friends were. The truth was, he liked knowing he could get it done quicker and without interruption in the library because he had to shut off his phone. When he was working on something this important, he preferred complete silence because it forced him to focus.

Cory knew some of Barrett's friends from the country club, but wasn't sure of the others in the circle. Questioning them would start his investigation. During the timeframe Jack was involved with Helen, he had shared many stories with Cory about the other side of Jeffrey Barrett's personality and how badly he'd treated his wife.

Cory remembered Barrett being obnoxious in high school, and it appeared nothing had changed in his adult life. Cory reminded himself that leopards never change their spots. He shook his head, remembering the many times Barrett had displayed his pure rudeness. It made his stomach tighten. It was no secret that Cory was no fan of Barrett's, but hearing about the guy continually belittling Helen in public, even showing up drunk at a function where she was being honored for her volunteer work in the community, made him suspicious. Why Helen had suddenly decided to forgive the jerk and stay with him was indeed a real mystery. If these so-called friends of the Barretts had witnessed any of those incidents, he prayed one of them would be willing to talk to him about it so he could convince Max to check out what he'd been saying all along—Jeffrey Barrett killed his wife.

Cory spent a few hours jotting down the names from the *Times* society and style pages that mentioned the Barretts. He contacted only a few because there'd be no way he could talk to all of them, and unfortunately, he didn't have their phone numbers, which were probably unlisted. Olivia Nolo was the first on his list. According to the article, she was Helen's best friend. He remembered Nolo from the country club, but he'd never spoken to her.

Cory shuddered when he thought about the horrific way Helen Barrett had died. He truly believed Jeffrey was responsible. He'd never known the man to be clever, but if he had come up with a murder scheme this good—one in which no one would ever suspect him because they knew how he felt about his damn car—he deserved a gold medal. But was it foolproof? Not as far as he was concerned. Now, if he could just convince Max that Barrett had more of a motive to kill Helen than Jack did.

"Nolo residence."

"Good afternoon, my name is Cory Rossini. I'm a private investigator working with the NYPD on the Barrett homicide and wondered if I might speak to Mrs. Nolo." He could hear voices in the background. It wasn't long before a different voice came on the line.

"This is Olivia Nolo. How can I help you?" Cory repeated his conversation. "Sure, you can come over, but I don't know how much help I'll be."

"Anything you can tell me will be a big help. I'm in the city, about thirty to forty minutes south of you. May I leave now and come to your home?"

"Certainly. See you soon."

Cory realized that saying he was working with the police was a surefire way of gaining admittance to people's homes. For a second he felt a pang of guilt over telling a fib, but he pushed the thought aside. Cory wondered whether she'd tell him what he wanted to know, especially since her husband, Steven was also a doctor who worked at Mount Sinai with Jeffrey. He was sure Helen's best friend would know all of Helen's deep dark secrets, and chances were she'd find it hard to believe Dr. Barrett didn't kill his wife. At least that's what he was hoping.

Although the air was crisp outside, the sun shone through the cloudy sky and glistened like diamonds atop the fresh snow on the sides of the roadway. The thought of Max breezed through his mind, and the way they seemed to click last night. After their first two disastrous meetings, he'd never expected her to react to him the way she had, and now, he couldn't stop himself from fantasizing about a future with her. He sighed and warned himself he was jumping the gun. They barely knew one another.

Leaving the city, Cory headed for 9A north toward Riverdale, an area once known as a residential area for upper middle class. That was no longer the case. Now, it reeked of money with estate-like mansions. Although the mansions were set back, a few were visible through the bare trees that would later turn into a lush green landscape with the onset of spring. Cory wasn't surprised so many of Barrett's friends lived here. Even with the snow falling, the drive was pleasant, a nice respite from the Midtown gridlock. He grinned as he took it all in until the annoying voice on his GPS squawked that he'd reached his destination. He pulled into a short driveway with a call box and a decorative black wrought-iron gate trimmed in gold. A gold coat of arms hung on each side of the gate. Cory pushed the button and awaited a response.

"How can I help you?" a voice with a deep timbre echoed through the speaker.

"Good morning. This is private investigator Cory Rossini here to see Mrs. Nolo. She's expecting me."

The gates opened and Cory drove up a long tree-covered road toward the home. Behind the massive trees, a huge plantation-style home appeared in the clearing, with large white columns and black shutters. Cory suddenly wished his car weren't so junky. He intentionally parked behind some trees so that it was out of sight and cut the engine before slowly walking to the entrance and pressing on the doorbell.

A woman in a white uniform greeted him, pulling the door open for his entry. She called out to her boss. It wasn't long before Olivia Nolo descended the stairs, wearing a Nike outfit as if she was ready to do some serious exercising. Her long dark auburn hair was pinned to the top of her head, exposing a slightly average-looking face. There was nothing special about her body shape. He figured she hadn't yet hit the plastic surgeon circuit. A rolled-up purple mat in her hand told him she was probably heading out for a yoga class.

She stopped at the bottom of the stairs and greeted him. The minute she spoke, he understood why their home looked like a plantation. She had a thick southern drawl. Funny he hadn't picked up on that during their phone conversation. "How may I help you?" she asked.

"Is there somewhere we can talk?"

She led the way to the sun parlor, a room that was encased in glass with tall planters scattered throughout giving it a tropical feel and helping one to forget that the glass enclosure was covered with snow. She gestured for him to sit on the sofa. "Now, what's this about?"

"I'd just like to ask you a few questions about your friendship with Mrs. Barrett."

"Sure. She was my best friend. I already knew Helen, but my husband met Jeffrey after, when he interviewed Steven to fill a vacancy on his transplant team."

"And how did you meet Mrs. Barrett?"

"We met at The Little Tykes Academy, a small preschool." Mrs. Nolo gave a shake of her head. "She started that school after finding out she couldn't have children.

"Oh, I'm sorry. I wasn't aware of that."

"Well, it's not something people broadcast, Mr. Rossini," she answered gruffly. Looking down at her jacket, she flicked something off with her forefinger. "Anyway, I'd been looking for a volunteer job to work with children. Since I had a degree in education and heard she was staffing, I applied and got the position. That's also how we found out our husbands were both at Cornell Med. It didn't take long for us to become fast friends. I loved Helen as much as I could love any sister." She wiped a tear from her eye.

"Were you aware she was seeing Jack Hughes?"

"What kind of question is that?" she asked with a frown. "Of course I was."

"What did you think about their relationship?" Cory asked, rubbing his hand across his chin.

"It wasn't for me to say. It was what Helen needed at the time. She was a big girl, Mr. Rossini, and didn't need her friend chastising her for living her life." Her expression turned melancholy.

She continued. "But Jack had a short fuse when he didn't get his way, and she put up with it."

"Can you elaborate on that?"

"She was willing to do anything to fill the void left by Jeffrey's selfish ways and large ego."

Cory squared his shoulders, pangs of anger pounding inside him after hearing her comment. If Jack knew he'd been classified as a fill-in, he'd kill Jeffrey with his bare hands, but Cory saw no reason to share that information with him.

"How well do you know Jeffrey Barrett?" Cory asked.

"Jeffrey? He's always been like a brother to me. There were times I wasn't in his corner because of the way he treated Helen, but honestly, something happened, and if you could have seen him all aglow the night of their reception, you would have seen his sincerity. I was so happy to see Helen experience the bliss she'd wanted for so long." She bit down on her lip then continued, anger seeping into her tone. "The bliss that was taken away from her by that monster, Jack Hughes—" She took in a deep breath and released it.

"Jack didn't do this," Cory defended.

Olivia Nolo's lips pursed. Rising swiftly from her seat, she cut the interview short. "I think it's time for you to leave," she countered, and then called out to her maid. "Please show our guest out."

Cory rose from his seat feeling angry she was supporting Jeffrey. If the rest of Barrett's circle of friends felt the same way she did, Jack didn't stand a chance, and unfortunately, Barrett was sure to have more of them on his side than Jack would.

Determined to find someone who was willing to spill the beans, Cory headed for Bay Ridge, Brooklyn, an area that was chockful of small-town charm with quaint streets, similar to a waterfront resort that catered to families. Seeing signs for Owl's Head Park brought back warm memories of his entire family spending time there during the spring and summer months. He'd have to remember to put Bay Ridge on his list of things to do with Max. He was sure she'd already been there, but she hadn't been there with him.

Cory spent the remainder of the afternoon contacting the other names on his list of Barrett's friends, confident that one of them would reveal something that would help Jack's case. That never happened. By four o'clock, tired and disappointed, Cory finally decided to give up and head back to the city.

Cory got into his car, turned over the engine, and thought of Max. He knew speaking to her would help his lousy mood after his search for a defense for Jack had failed. Reaching for his phone, the familiar ring chimed for an incoming call. When he saw her name flash across the screen, it brought a wide smile to his face. He clicked onto the call.

"Hey, beautiful."

"What the hell are you trying to do?" her voice screeched through the receiver. "I've been getting complaints all fucking day from Barretts' friends that you've been harassing them. And as if that wasn't bad enough, you made it sound as though I sent you. You have some nerve using the NYPD's name."

"I merely said I was working with the NYPD—and I am, so to speak. They didn't need to know in what capacity or that we're on opposite ends of the spectrum."

"Stay the hell out of my way," she fired back. "If you use my name, the department's name, or any form of the NYPD again, I'll be forced to seek legal recourse."

He couldn't believe she was reaming him out again, especially after the kind of day he'd had. His temper flared, and he shot right back: "Listen, Max, I've had a bad day today, but more importantly, did you honestly think I'd stop trying to free an innocent man just because we had dinner? And for the record, I wasn't harassing them. I have every right to investigate your witnesses the same way you do mine. You're making this personal." He heard her huff out air. "I'm beginning to think that maybe our intuition about each other was right the first time around." He disconnected the call and tossed his phone on the seat.

CHAPTER ELEVEN

Julie Shelton stirred the tomato sauce simmering on the stove while the twins set the table in anticipation of Aunt Max's arrival. Resting the wooden spoon inside the empty puree can, now half filled with water, she turned to sit down at the kitchen table. She leafed through the family photographs, looking for a picture of their mother on this twentieth anniversary of her death. Julie stopped when she found a photo taken in front of the fieldstone fireplace in the living room of the small bungalow where they were raised, the monster adoptive father's face cut out of the picture. Even though his face was gone, the painful memories still remained.

The memories flooded through her mind, sharp and painful. A rush of guilt tightened in her chest over not realizing that Max was also being abused. A tear rolled down her cheek as she remembered how she thought that keeping her mouth shut about what he was doing to her meant she was protecting Max. Even Max's slight bruising hadn't been a signal, because it was always explained away as her frequent clumsiness. It wasn't until Max had found the courage to confide in one of her girlfriends, Ellen Summerfield, that their stepfather's secret was revealed.

Ellen had told her mother, and Mrs. Summerfield had orchestrated their escape. As the older sister, Julie always felt she should have known something was wrong. That she didn't would haunt her forever.

Julie slid her finger over the glossy image, briefly turning back the hands of time as she remembered that day. They'd each smiled for the camera, even though they'd been dying inside, but they'd done it for their mother, who'd stopped long enough to take the picture before heading out for work that evening. She'd had two jobs just to keep the family afloat. Unfortunately, those jobs were such that she slept during the day and saw her children in passing before she started her next shift. Julie resented the fact that David Lee Turner not only took their virginity, but took their mother away from them too while he stayed home and entertained himself at Julie and Max's expense. As a result, their mother saw very little of her girls. The monster had been laid off too many times to count. Seemed like he was *always* between jobs.

Julie wiped the moisture from her eyes with a napkin sitting on the table. A muted image of David Lee Turner's face appeared in her mind. She remembered his smug expression after their mother had been killed by a hit-and-run driver, which gave him legal guardianship of them to do whatever he wanted—and he did. If it hadn't been for Ellen's mother, she didn't know what would have happened to them. Fortunately, the woman reported him to the police, and David Lee Turner was sent to prison for the rest of his life, where the bastard was killed by an inmate. Julie prayed his death was slow and painful. Just the thought of him made her shudder. Refilling her glass with wine, she tried to push the horrid thoughts from her mind. She prayed that one day the ugly memories would fade away if she focused her attention on the good that had come out of their past: her bond with Max was so tight, nothing could ever come between them.

"Mom," Ellie's voice screeched as she elongated the letters, "Jenny said she's not going to let me wear her Halloween costume."

Although Julie was thankful for the interruption, her daughters' constant bickering drove her nuts. She closed her eyes and splayed her hands over them, counting to ten. Then she made her way over to her daughter and rubbed her ribs to stop the child from crying. "First of all, girls, I'm the boss of who wears what, and secondly, Jenny, why are you so mean to your sister?" she asked.

"She was mean to me." Jenny pointed a short skinny finger at her twin. "Like the time you . . ."

Julie cut her short. "For God's sake, this is your sister," she said, pointing to Ellie. You should have more respect for her." Julie doubted her words had penetrated permanently. She knew the words had gone in one ear and out the other. Nevertheless, she scolded them, hoping they'd learn to love each other the way she did Max. "Keep it up and neither one of you will be going out for Halloween," she said in a threatening voice. "And you know those new iPads you got for your birthday? They'll be on their way out, too and given to children who appreciate their sisters. Is that clear?"

"Yes, ma'am," they said at the same time.

"Now hug your sister and tell her you're sorry." Jenny rolled her eyes. "Girls, I've really had enough crap today to last me a lifetime. Don't push it!"

"Who's giving you crap?" Max said, entering the kitchen as the two girls stopped what they were doing and ran to her. "What's going on that you're making your mom crazy?"

"She started it," Ellie said, pointing to her sister.

"Stop," Julie yelled. "Now go watch some television until dinner is ready." Julie opened her mouth and gave a silent scream when the girls stomped their feet on their way out to the den. She walked over and gave Max a tight hug. "I love you, sis."

"Tough day, Jules?" Max asked.

"Yes, they're driving me to drink over stupid Halloween costumes. Cripes, do I have to listen to this crap for another freakin' week?" Julie held up her glass of wine. She took a sip, then set it down on the counter. "Want one?"

"Of course." Julie handed her a wineglass and nodded toward the bottle. Max raised her nose in the air and inhaled. "Mmm, it smells like we're having meatballs and pasta for dinner."

"We are. Hungry?"

"Starving," Max said, suddenly noticing Julie's new hairdo. "I love the new do." She stepped back and eyed her from a distance. "Yeah, I've always loved you in short hair."

"I know you have, and today, I do too. After looking at myself in the mirror a few times since I got home from the beauty salon, I'm really glad I let her cut it all off." Julie played with the spiky hairstyle. "I resisted for a long time, but trying to maintain my sanity while refereeing two nine-year-olds made me realize that short hair seemed to be the only sane thing to do." She laughed.

Max looked closer. "I really like the blond-on-blond streaks too. It brightens your entire face and accentuates your hazel eyes."

Julie grinned. "Thanks. I'm glad you like it."

"How does Mike like it?"

"He hasn't seen it yet. I didn't tell him I was having it done today, and now I'm a little nervous, because he hates short hair."

Max laughed. "Well, you have nothing to worry about, because you look like a hot mama! With that new look and your amazing figure after having twins, that man will be all over you. And just to show my support, I'll take the girls out for ice cream after dinner so you two can be alone."

Julie, two inches taller, stood and wrapped her arms around Max, giving her a tight squeeze. "You're my hero." she said, her eyes beginning to glisten with moisture. "If it wasn't for you always telling me things would be okay, I don't think I would have survived." Max's eyes welled up too.

"Through thick and thin, we've pulled each other through the storm." It wasn't until Max noticed the photographs sitting on the counter that she understood Julie's melancholy mood. "Ah, now I see what's happening. Why do you have the pictures out?"

"Today is twenty years that Mom's been gone. I just wanted to refresh the image of her face in my mind, but the only thing looking through those photos did was stir up old wounds."

"We're tough, Jules; we can handle this." Max kissed her cheek. "We've survived, and look at us now. Don't go back there. It's not worth it and only digs up all those bad memories of something we can't change. It happened and it's over." Julie's eyes lowered and she gave a slow nod. "Jules, maybe now is the time to go for therapy. You can let this destroy your life, or you can find ways to release that hatred by talking to a professional."

"Maybe you're right." Julie let go a heavy sigh.

"And speaking of being right!" Max said with enthusiasm, aiming to break through her sister's mood. She immediately had Julie's full attention. Max set her glass down and stepped back to look at her sister. "I need your advice," she said timidly.

"Excuse me?" Julie quipped and looked behind her. "I could have sworn you just said you needed my advice?"

"Very funny, Jules. You're really going to make me grovel, aren't you?"

"Yes, ma'am," Julie said smugly, crossing her arms against her chest.

"Okay. Yes, I'm asking for your advice."

"This is pretty amazing, because I thought you told me to mind my own business after that disastrous evening at Yankee Stadium."

"Are you having fun?" Max said, placing her hand on her hip and blinking her eyes.

Julie giggled. "Honestly, I am having a helluva good time." She giggled some more. "Okay, talk to Dr. Julie, mother of two rambunctious twins and wife of Mike Shelton, husband extraordinaire."

"Yeah, well, this is about that guy."

"The obnoxious one?" Julie screeched.

"Yes," Max said with a wide grin. "That one, who, by the way, is a private investigator, and I don't think he's so obnoxious anymore."

Amused, Julie shook her head. "You're kidding, right?" Julie stared at her sister, waiting for her to explain, but Max's face only morphed into a cringe. "Okay, but now you have to tell me what made you decide he's not so bad after all."

"Hey," Max said, raising her palms in the air, "what can I say?"

Julie pulled two stools out from under the bar, poured herself another glass of wine, and topped off Max's glass. "You have my undivided attention."

Max filled her sister in on everything that had happened between her and Cory, including the slight tiff. "And now, I'm just not sure how to react."

"Sounds like he's giving you a dose of your own medicine." She snickered. "I'll just bet you were dying after you practically ripped the guy's face off with your wrath yesterday." She threw her head back and laughed, because she knew Max's aggressive tendencies all too well, and she knew Mr. Ball-Cheater had received the bitter taste of her venom. "I can just see the look on your face when you realized he was talking to you as the detective who arrested his friend and not for a date with you." Julie giggled. "I'll bet you wanted to crawl under your desk and disappear into thin air."

"Oh my God, you know it!"

"And what was he doing while you zipped along from one thing to the next?"

"Smirking! But of course, that only made me madder. And by the next time I saw him in court, and then again at The Alibi, I had completely changed my mind about him being a jerk. I'm suddenly finding myself daydreaming about him and wondering what it would be like to have a relationship with him." She threw both palms in the air. "Am I a nutjob, or what?"

"No," Julie said. "It's all part of the infatuation stage in a relationship."

"And get a load of this one," Max said, touching her sister's arm. "He took me out to dinner and he expected nothing from me." Max intentionally left the part out about Cory borrowing the money from his client's fund, for fear Julie would only wind up judging him.

"You mean like the after-dinner dessert?"

"Right. I'm either not that appealing or he's one helluva guy. He's so different from anyone I've ever dated." Max sipped her wine.

"It sounds like he *is* one helluva guy." She tilted her head to the side and gave Max an affectionate smile. "I love seeing you bubble with excitement over a guy." What she didn't say was that she was concerned Max's work persona might turn him off. "How about that? If I could only have one wish, it would be for you to have the same kind of happiness I share with Mike."

Then Max's face fell. She returned to their blowup over the phone this afternoon, asking Julie what she should have done differently.

"What I am concerned about is whether or not you're going to be able to separate your work from your personal life. When you said you called to share your disappointment with him about interviewing friends of the family, whose case you're both working on, I might add, what set you off?"

"The fact that he had the witnesses—potentially *testifying* witnesses—believing I had sent him for further questioning pushed me over the edge, and I expressed my opinion rather abruptly. None of them had anything nice to say about Jack, so he pushed a little too hard proclaiming the guy's innocence. And it ticked them off." Max reached for the bottle of wine and poured more of the red liquid into both glasses. "Couple that with one of those friends wondering if this new line of questioning made me unsure about whether I had the right guy in jail. It made me look like I had done a bad job of investigating." Max stared at Julie. "See what I mean?"

Julie crinkled her nose and gave a slow nod. "But he wasn't really lying, because he *is* working the same case, just not on the same side. Yes, he embellished it a little too much." Julie shrugged while Max nodded her agreement. "It sounds like he held you accountable for something he did by playing the blame game. He might have been embarrassed."

Max released a deep sigh. "Am I crazy for missing him? It was only one date." She gave Julie a quizzical look. "I am kicking myself for not handling it better." Casting her eyes downward, she told Julie what was bothering her. "He hung up on me, and I haven't heard from his since. What should I do?" Seeing the slight smirk on Julie's face, Max knew exactly what was happening. "You're gloating, aren't you?"

"I'm not gloating," Julie said with a wide grin, exposing her teeth. "Do I look like I'm gloating?"

Max gave her an arched brow. "Okay, well maybe a little. So, let's see. What do I think you should do?" Julie scratched her head while she pondered a thought. "First of all, it only happened today, right?" Max nodded. "Well, I think you're jumping the gun here that he may never call you again. He's probably just as ticked off, and I'm sure embarrassed that he messed things up with you by fibbing his way into seeing those potential witnesses. I'd invite him out to talk about it. You have to communicate. Right now you're both speculating about what the other one is thinking." Julie's eyebrows rose and wrinkled her forehead. "You both need to apologize—you, for coming at him like gangbusters, again, and him, for making the witnesses think you'd sent him. He didn't handle the call so well either. At least you'll have tried to mend fences. And I'd find it hard to believe he wouldn't want to mend them, given the long list of attributes you've mentioned. I have to admit, he sounds like the perfect mate for you. Learn to agree to disagree." Julie leaned her head to the side. "You've lived alone for so many years, Max, you've never had to be flexible, but here's an opportunity to grow and learn from your mistakes."

"Thank you, Jules," Max said grabbing her hand. "Your advice is usually spot-on."

Julie's hand slapped against her chest. "You mean you really do follow my advice?"

"I listen to your advice, I just don't always follow it." Max razzed, giving Julie a playful punch on her arm.

"You know what, sis?" Julie said grabbing Max's fist and holding it tight. "I can't wait to meet the guy who has captured your heart. He must be pretty special." Julie stood and hugged Max. "I can't imagine having anyone other than you as my sister."

Max hugged her right back. "I love you too, Jules. I don't know what I'd do without you."

The whirring sound of the garage door had the twins running for the door shouting, "Daddy's home!"

Max quickly rose from her seat and put her glass on the counter. "I guess that's my cue to finish the salad."

"And mine to get dinner on the table," Julie said.

CHAPTER TWELVE

Bloodcurdling screams echoed through his ears, images of bodies peppered the landscape, pins and needles shot up his arms from the vibration of the *tat-tat-tat* of the ammunition feeding into his machine gun. He wanted to stop killing. He'd tried to run, but his friend pulled him back so the commander wouldn't see his weakness, but doing so caused his friend to wind up in the line of fire, catching the bullet meant for him. He died right at his feet. He remembered being slouched over his friend's body, sobbing like a baby, only to be scolded by his commanding officer, who told him to suck it up—this was war.

He crouched down into the darkened corner, his knees squashed against his chest, his hands slapping against his head, begging God to stop the scene playing out in his mind. But the stench of the decaying bodies, the blood and sweat, the shrill scream from a goat in the line of fire had him back in Kandahar, Afghanistan, reliving the ambush like a video on constant replay.

The sound of the door opening caught his attention momentarily. He slowly eased himself deeper into the corner to avoid being seen from the light flooding into the room. He held his breath to avoid another ambush. The intruder took a mop and left as quickly as he'd come in.

His commander's voice told him he had work to do, and he'd better get himself out there and do the job he'd been trained to do.

He took a deep breath and stood upright, dried his tears, and gingerly opened the door to see if anyone was passing. When the coast was clear, he slipped out into the hallway, trying to meld into the crowd filled with visitors anxious to see their loved ones.

He checked the time and was pleased he'd get there shortly after she was brought down from the recovery room. He walked past the room and noticed she was already back in her room with her mother leaning over her, planting a kiss on her forehead. He hadn't planned on the mother being there so early, but he'd wait across the hall. When the older woman left the room and headed for the elevator, he felt a sense of relief.

With the coast clear, he entered the private room where Candy Morrison was just beginning to stir. Reaching for her chart, he noted she'd been given Propofol during surgery, a drug anesthesiologists used to put their patients to sleep.

The young girl blinked her eyes open, saw him, and moaned in pain. "Nurse, it hurts." She cried soft tears.

"I know, sweetheart," he said, rubbing her arm. "I'm going to make you feel all better in a few minutes. You just hang on."

"Thank you," she said weakly.

Glancing at her, he noted she was a cute little thing. He hesitated before reaching inside his pocket, but then he heard his commander's voice shouting out his order to "Carry on." He jerked into action immediately, removed the vial and hypodermic needle from his pocket, pulled the plastic cap off with his teeth, and drained the bottle, filling the entire shaft with Propofol. Then, he inserted it into the port in her vein. "This will make you feel better and help you sleep for a long time. Sweet dreams, little one."

He stood and watched her decline, the numbers quickly lowering just before she flatlined and his heart rate escalated at having killed another. When the monitor began to beep, he narrowly escaped the room just as a team of medics raced inside. He bolted into a public restroom down the hall, locking the door behind him. Glancing at his reflection in the mirror, a mass of confusion suddenly overcame him and he was once again watching the villagers weep for their family members. He brought his hands up to the sides of his face and covered his eyes to block out the image, but it only served to give him a more vivid picture. He punched his head to stop the playback when his commander told him to stop being a wimp. *This is war!* He stood at attention and saluted the man. "Sir, yes, sir!" he shouted and pulled himself together.

He removed his scrubs and rolled them into a ball, then shoved them into his tote bag. He threw the bag over his shoulder and exited. When he walked past the room, he smiled when he heard those three magic words, *time of death*. He grinned at having done his job, and slowly walked down the hall, observing his surroundings to see if both parents were aware their daughter was dead. His heart beat faster when he heard the mother scream for her daughter. He stopped a short distance away and watched as she struggled with reality. Now, they knew what it was like to suffer.

Cory stood under the shower and let the water pelt against his body as he tried to erase the empty feeling roiling in his stomach while he replayed yesterday's unpleasant conversation between him and Max. He wasn't sure if she was ever going to speak to him again. Cory braced his arms against the wall, hoping to forget that he'd fallen harder for her than he'd expected. He wondered if she'd lost any sleep after his hurtful comment. He wouldn't blame her if she didn't forgive him. He was disgusted with himself. What was wrong with him?

That abrupt response had replayed over in his mind a million times since it had happened, and now, he was wishing he'd just admitted what he'd done and not cut her off before she'd had a chance to finish what she was saying. But it was too late for regrets now. He sighed, turned the water off, and exited the shower. After he toweled off and got dressed, he walked to the kitchen to fill a mug with the strong black coffee he'd made earlier. The toaster popped up a badly burnt English muffin. He attempted to pull it out and recoiled from the heat burning his fingers. Rushing to the sink, he shoved his hand under cold water. He was a mess. Dammit! What had this woman done to him? Feeling helpless, he guzzled down the bitter coffee, grabbed his briefcase, and headed out the door, leaving the burnt muffin on the floor.

Walking through the entrance to Mount Sinai, Cory's stomach growled and told him he'd function better if it were full, which was probably the first smart thought he'd had this morning. After breakfast, he'd start snooping to see what he could find out about Jeffrey Barrett in his work environment. He hoped Max had done as thorough an investigation on Barrett as she had on Jack, mainly because when a wife was murdered, nine times out of ten, statistics proved it was the husband. He wasn't falling for that loyal-husband bullshit Barrett was putting on for the police and all his friends. There had to be some of Barrett's so-called friends or colleagues who didn't like him. Everyone had enemies, and Jeffrey Barrett would be no exception.

The thought of Jack living in a six-by-nine cell at Rikers Island made Cory shudder. He was worried about his friend, especially with the lies he'd been telling. Did he not realize what he was facing if convicted? Was he so depressed that he just didn't care anymore?

Having represented clients who'd inhabited what was commonly referred to as *the box*, a cramped enclosure in a long line of cells on the cell block, he knew quite well the kind of living quarters Jack had. Cement walls on three sides, a narrow window for light, a cement slab with a thin mattress hanging off the wall as his bed, a sink, a toilet, and bars on the front giving full exposure to anyone walking past, even the inmates across the narrow hall. And that disgusting smell, so bad, it remained with you for weeks after. He shook his head. If Jack was convicted, that would be his home forevermore. And as if that weren't enough, it would not be long before he'd be declared someone's bitch. It was a status thing for prisoners to stake a claim on the newbie. Sure, Jack would fight until the end if anyone came near him, but with so many gangs in prison, he wouldn't stand a chance. Cory felt a rush of anxiety wash over him. He was not going to let that happen to his friend.

Cory was disappointed he hadn't found one of Barrett's friends who didn't believe Barrett's declaration of renewed love for his wife. He'd have to do a lot more digging to prove Barrett was guilty. The problem was that Jeffrey Barrett was a powerful man and highly regarded by the administrators of the hospital, but Cory hoped someone on the transplant team would help him get a better read on the man. Surely there were surgeons who had problems with the top dog, especially if they'd been competing against him.

Cory walked over to one of the elderly volunteers he'd recognized from when his niece was here at Mount Sinai for her surgery. She smiled, remembering him too. He leaned over toward her. "So what's the special on the cafeteria menu this morning?"

"I wondered if I'd ever see you again." She patted his arm. "How is your niece?" she asked.

"She's learning to deal with it."

She placed her fist on her heart, and Cory nodded a thank-you. "You haven't forgotten that Friday is sticky bun day, have you?"

"Are they any good?" Cory asked, engaging her in conversation.

"They're okay, but not as good as the ones I used to make back in the day."

"I'll check them out," he said with a wink that made her blush. "You have a good day," he said over his shoulder. "Thanks for your help."

Downstairs, the cafeteria had only a handful of people sitting at tables. With tray in hand, he meandered through the aisles and stopped to scoop scrambled eggs and a spoonful of potatoes onto his plate. Scanning to see where the sticky buns were located, he wandered over to the pastry station and stopped in front of them. Using the serving piece intended, he slid the bun out from under the heat lamp and onto a smaller plate. Then, using his spoon, he scooped up caramel and butter sauce to pour over the top. Whiffing in the sweet smell had his stomach grumbling. Yeah, there was no way he was passing these up. Maybe the sweetness would help his sour mood.

Making one last stop, he filled a container with coffee, splashed in some cream, added two packets of sugar, and headed for a table. Sitting down, he stabbed at the eggs, shoveling a forkful into his mouth. He hadn't realized how hungry he was.

Two women in scrubs sat down at a nearby table. They seemed to be having a lively debate. He could only hear bits and pieces, but he thought he heard something about heart transplants. He strained to listen. The conversation segued into a debate about a recent transplant. That was his lead-in.

Seeing him stare, one of the women cast her eyes in his direction. "I'm sorry. Are we disturbing you?"

"Sorry for staring. No, not at all." He stood. "I'm actually investigating a case about heart transplants and could really use your help. May I join you?" Cory planted two business cards down in front of them. Sensing their apprehension, he tried to put their minds at ease. "Listen, I swear to you, I'm one of the good guys. I'm a private investigator, and I'm working a case about this very thing. If an injustice has been done, then I'm going to see to it that it goes to trial and the right perpetrator goes to jail." He looked at them, his face forming into desperation. "Please, help me." The women looked at one another. "Listen, I know you don't know me, and I swear"—he held up his hand—"all I need is for you to lead me down the right path and I'll do the rest." He lowered his head, his eyes never leaving their faces. "What do you say?"

The two women nodded their approval but continued to look cautiously over their shoulders. The brunette whispered in her friend's ear and stared at her. When the other woman nodded her acceptance, the dark-haired woman spoke. "Mr. Rossini, we'll talk to you, but it has to be outside."

"Anywhere you say is fine. I'm just happy you're willing to talk to me. Do you have to get back to work?"

"No. We just finished the night shift, and my husband gets the kids off to school, so I'm good. How about you, Catherine?" she asked.

"I'm good too."

"Okay, give me one minute to get a box for this sweet roll," he said, "and I'll meet you outside."

Cory walked back over to the cashier carrying his bun and asked for a Styrofoam container, then made his way outside, where one of the ladies stood waving her hand so he'd see where they were sitting.

Catherine was the first to speak. "Before we say anything, we need complete anonymity."

"Okay, but how will I be able to prove what you're telling me is true?"

"Oh, don't worry about that. You'll be able to prove our story just by seeing the documents."

"All right. Then I promise not to mention your names. Tell me what you know."

"Several months ago, Karen and I were working the transplant floor. We had come in early, like we do every night, and we're pretty certain a heart transplant was given out of sequence to a senator's daughter. It's been haunting us ever since."

"What do you mean exactly?"

"We believe that a heart that was intended for another child was given to the senator's daughter instead. You know, VIP crap."

"That's a pretty serious allegation. What makes you so sure?"

"Because every time we bring it up during breaks with the other nurses, we're told to shut up, to keep our thoughts to ourselves before we get into trouble." Catherine humphed.

"Isn't there an organization that has strict guidelines in place to govern those transplants?" Cory asked. They looked at him with an unwavering stare. "I seem to remember reading an article about the government changing the guidelines to prevent something like this from happening."

"They did change the guidelines, Mr. Rossini, but some people think they're exempt from following those rules."

"Who was the surgeon to perform this surgery?"

"Sorry, but that's all we're going to say. Check with the hospital administrator. Her name is Valerie Morrison. The date we're talking about was July 2."

"Was it Dr. Barrett?"

Catherine's expression told him he was on to something big concerning Barrett, but how did this relate to Helen's death? Maybe not at all, but it would be one more nail in Jeffrey Barrett's coffin if it did. The two women rose and walked away without looking back. Cory wasn't sure this would help his search for the truth, but since the event spurring this allegation had taken place in the heart center at the hospital where Barrett worked, he had to believe Barrett was involved somehow. Anything that made Barrett look less saintly was a good thing. And if he couldn't prove it without a warrant, he'd beg Max to get involved. Surely, she didn't want to put an innocent man behind bars. If she wasn't willing to check it out because it might ruin her reputation, then he would know what kind of person she was and he'd go higher up the chain of command. The information he now had was too good to pass up. He decided to do a bit more snooping. Stopping back at the volunteers' station, he approached a gentleman.

"Can you tell me who the hospital administrator is and where I might find the office?"

"Can I see some identification first?" Cory flipped his leather ID holder open to show him. Presenting his ID was something new to him. Usually just handing out his business card as an attorney was proof enough, but he'd learned to do it automatically. "Do you have an appointment?" he asked.

"No, but I was told she'd be the person to see on a certain matter."

"Okay, that would be Mrs. Morrison, and she's on the fifth floor," the man said, sliding his finger down the chart. "Want me to call her for you?"

"I would appreciate that. Thank you," Cory said, and handed him his business card. He tapped his fingers on the counter while he waited for the volunteer to get off the phone.

"You're in luck, Mr. Rossini. She just finished up a meeting and said she can see you now."

"That's terrific," Cory said. "Thank you."

"Elevators." He pointed in their direction. "There'll be a sign directing you."

"Mrs. Morrison," Cory said handing her his business card. He was surprised to see that she was almost as tall as his six feet. Her dark hair was pulled back in a tight bun, and her eyeglasses dangled from a chain around her neck like a librarian.

"What can I do for you, Mr. Rossini?"

"Did you know there are rumors around the hospital that a transplant occurred out of sequence?"

"Mr. Rossini," she said, "I'm afraid you're in the wrong department. I have nothing to do with the transplant center, but Melanie Chambers does. She's the organ procurement and transplantation coordinator." She jerked her head toward her cell phone located on the side of her mahogany desk when it rang. "Excuse me, please. I need to take this." Cory nodded. After she greeted the caller, she gasped. "I'll be right there."

Surprised, Cory watched as she grabbed her coat off the hook and headed for the door. "I have to leave," she said, her voice filled with panic. "Check with my secretary." He walked to the door behind her and watched when she stopped at her secretary's desk and leaned in closer to the girl and said something. When the secretary's hand clasped against her chest, he knew something was wrong. Seconds later, the administrator rushed into the elevator, hitting the button a number of times before the doors closed.

Concerned, Cory stood by the door watching the secretary compose herself for a few moments. She immediately made a phone call, wrote something down, and walked toward him.

"Mr. Rossini." The young girl, whose adolescent face looked as though she was barely out of high school, addressed him. "I'm sorry, but Mrs. Chambers can't see you this morning." Checking her calendar, he could see it looked pretty full. "Unfortunately, I don't have anything available until the twenty-eighth at two o'clock."

"Are you serious?"

"I'm afraid I am. Between staff meetings, patient interviews, and conferences, she's booked solid. If your meeting is urgent, I can find someone else for you to talk to, but that's the best I can do." She looked up at him. "Will that work?"

He nodded. "I'd rather talk to her, so I'll wait. Wondering about Morrison's abrupt departure, he asked, "Is Mrs. Morrison all right?"

Her eyes glistened. Throwing her shoulders back, she stood a little straighter before responding. "Yes. She'll be fine." She handed him the appointment card and told him to have a nice day.

He knew something drastic had happened and wondered how he was going to find out. Maybe keeping the appointment would lead him in a different direction, but for sure, something fishy was going on, and he wasn't going to stop until he figured out what it was. Regardless, he'd keep the appointment and hope it somehow related to Helen's death. Determined to put his free time to good use, he decided to visit Jack first, maybe stop by the library for some more names of Barrett's friends, then he'd find out if the senator was in her Midtown Manhattan office to get her reaction to what he'd just heard.

On the drive over to see Jack, he couldn't get Valerie Morrison's reaction to the phone call out of his head. So he wouldn't forget what transpired, he took out his phone and spoke into the recorder, detailing what had happened in Morrison's office. He was going to find out why Jack had lied to the detective about his alibi.

When Jack entered the room, Cory noted he was looking tired and drawn. With everything closing in on him, he couldn't blame the guy, but it hurt to see him carrying around such pain.

"I sure do appreciate you going out of your way to come see me, Cory."

"That's what friends do for each other."

"Have I told you how much I hate this place?"

"You don't have to. I can see it on your face every time I come here. But you're the one who put yourself in this predicament, Jack. What did you expect when you lied to the detective about where you were?"

Jack gave an aggravated wave of his hand. "Look, no matter what I said, Cory, she wasn't going to believe me. She was anxious to close her case, so she made me the scapegoat.

"How can you blame her when she caught you in a lie? You said you didn't leave your apartment, yet they have you leaving your building, your car driving past Helen's house, and then, on top of all that, you had an argument with Helen in a public setting with witnesses who will testify that you threatened to kill her? What was that all about?" Cory crossed his arms and rested them against his chest, his face seething with anger.

"I didn't say that to Helen. What I said, but no one seems to have heard, or doesn't want to admit, is that I thought Jeffrey was going to kill her." Jack shut his eyes briefly. "You know how much I loved her, Cory. I could never say something like that to her."

"Jack, I really want to believe you, but it's been one lie after another. So where the hell did you go?"

"I drove to the park for a walk until I got a call from the First Alert call center that Mom had fallen."

"What happened to your mom?" Cory said, concerned. Mrs. Hughes was like a mother to him.

"She tripped on a step and got a cut on her cheek. She's okay."

"If you were going to your mom's, how did you wind up going past Helen's house?"

"I took a shortcut from the park. There was a lot of traffic, and I didn't feel like sitting in it. I wanted to hurry to see if Mom was okay."

"So why didn't you explain that to Detective Turner?"

"Because that woman already had her mind made up. She wasn't going to believe anything I had to say, so I just gave up."

"Jack, what the hell is wrong with you? We're talking about your life here."

"I don't care anymore. It's as simple as that."

"You have to care!" Cory rubbed his hands together, suddenly remembering something else. "By the way, there is another matter we need to discuss." It was obvious by Jack's expression that he was already tired of Cory's tirade. "You know, I've been completely confused about why you chose Bill Cates as an attorney, and even more surprised that he was court appointed, so I racked my brains trying to figure out how this happened, and it suddenly occurred to me that you might be having financial problems. Is that it?" Cory narrowed his eyes, waiting for Jack to say something, but he didn't have to. His expression said it all. "For God's sake, why didn't you tell me? I would have helped you."

"You had enough on your plate taking care of your parents and your niece. I couldn't tell you."

"I still wish you had," Cory said. "This whole thing is becoming one major mess after another. I know you're no killer, and when I find enough evidence to prove it, you'll be free, but I need your help here. Having you fall apart at the seams does us no good, and lying makes it even worse." Cory's lips tightened. He needed to get out of there before he blew a gasket. He loathed liars, and just because they were like brothers didn't give Jack a free pass. "Look, I have a lot to do today, so I'm going to head out, and I'll be back again soon. No more lies, Jack. You got that?"

CHAPTER THIRTEEN

Valerie Morrison encouraged the cab driver to hurry to New York Presbyterian Hospital after receiving a frantic call from her sister-in-law, Molly, that her sixteen-year-old niece had died. Valerie rushed inside the elevator and took the ride up to the floor where her brother and Molly were waiting. She exited as soon as the door opened, stopping at the nurses' station for information.

"My niece, Candace Morrison—" She didn't have to finish her sentence. The nurse pointed to the family waiting room, and Valerie briskly walked inside. Molly was leaning against Valerie's brother, Dean, sobbing hysterically.

"I'm here, Moll." The woman turned and sobbed on Valerie's shoulder, giving Dean an opportunity to express his grief to the police, who were firing questions at the surgical team.

"She's g-gone," Molly screeched out in a stuttered sentence. "I never should have agreed to this." Molly blew her nose. "She just wanted to look pretty."

"Tell me what happened."

"No one knows what happened to her except she's dead." Molly lowered her head into her hands. "I never should have agreed. This is all my fault."

"Moll, what was she having done?"

"A nose job. The kids at school were making fun of her and calling her names, so I agreed."

"This is the first I'm hearing about this. At sixteen?" Valerie shrieked, quickly wishing she hadn't said those words because Molly was already blaming herself. "I'm sorry, Moll, I didn't mean to question your parenting."

"I told you this was my fault."

"Stop. You were just trying to keep your daughter happy, so don't do that to yourself." She pulled the woman into a tight hug. "Tell me what happened."

"She came out of surgery and went into the recovery room for about an hour. They brought her to the room as soon as the meds wore off. She was fading in and out of sleep, so I left the room to go down to the cafeteria to get coffee, when I received a call. It was the head nurse telling me there was an emergency and to get back upstairs. When I entered the room, a team was gathered around her bed trying to resuscitate her. She had flatlined, and no one seems to know what happened."

"You'll request an autopsy, won't you?" Valerie asked.

"Yes. I'm told it's mandatory in cases like this." Molly wiped her tears on a tissue, looked at her husband, and released a painful regret: "My sweet Candy is gone." She elongated the end of the word as her knees buckled out from under her and she fell to the floor. The staff's fast response time had Molly awake in seconds with the aid of smelling salts. Molly pushed the nurse's hand away. "Let me up. I'm fine."

Valerie heaved a nervous breath, her hands shaking from the shock. "Thank God you're all right."

"I'd like to keep you for observation, Mrs. Morrison," the doctor said. His name card read *Dr. Disconti.*

"Why? So you can kill me too?"

"Molly," Dean, said taking her hand in his, "please let's not jump to conclusions. We don't know what happened. Let these guys do what they do best. Please?" He wrapped his arms around her and walked her to the gurney being wheeled into the room. "Let them do their jobs." Molly protested. His hand flew in the air. "Please, we don't know what happened to Candy. I'd like to think the coroner is impartial and he knows what he's doing, so let's trust him. And if he finds negligence, we'll sue their asses off. Now, please, let them check you out. I can't lose you too." A tear slid down his cheek. She nodded and wiped it with her fingers.

"Will you stay close by?" Molly asked him.

"Of course. When was the last time you ate anything?" he asked.

"I haven't eaten all day. I don't think I could eat anything."

He watched as family members rallied around Molly Morrison. He moved closer to get a better view, pretending to be reading a notice on the wall when he heard the woman sobbing hysterically. She was being wheeled out of the family waiting room on a gurney.

"It'll be okay, Molly," he heard her husband say.

He smiled to himself and followed the gurney down the hall until he saw the elevator doors open. He rushed inside and pushed the Down arrow, congratulating himself on a job well done, anxious to continue his quest.

CHAPTER FOURTEEN

The frigid cold surprised Cory when he exited his home, his cheeks stinging from the wind whipping around his body. He picked up his pace and rushed into the garage for his car, surprised the temperatures had dropped so drastically. Unlocking the doors, he slid behind the steering wheel as quickly as he could and turned the engine over, moving the lever for the fan to high, hoping the car would warm up quickly. He backed out of the garage and headed for the senator's mid-town office, surprised she was working on a Saturday and thankful he didn't have to drive to Albany. Traffic was always worse on the weekends in New York City, but he managed to make decent time without sitting for hours in the mid-town gridlock. Seeing the building ahead, he eased through the traffic and pulled into the parking lot. Inside he stopped to check the directory for her suite number. Seeing her name, he took the elevator up to her floor and exited, walking down the hall to the sign that read *27th State Senate District Office, Senator Kay Stansbury*. Walking up to her secretary. "I'd like a moment with Senator Stansbury," he said.

"I'm sorry, sir, but she's busy at the moment. What can I do for you?"

"I need to speak to the senator."

"Can you tell me what this is in reference to, sir?"

"Sure. I'm a private investigator," he said, showing her his identification and slipping his business card over to her, "and I'm investigating her daughter's transplant." The secretary's eyes opened wide.

"What's wrong with her?"

"I didn't say anything was wrong—" He stopped talking when the senator came rushing out of her office with a handful of papers flapping in the breeze. He noted that she was even more beautiful than she appeared on television or in the newspapers. "Senator Stansbury," he said, catching her off guard.

She jerked her head toward him. "I'm sorry. Do you have an appointment with me?"

"No, but my name is Cory Rossini, and I'm a private investigator," he said, handing her his card.

"I have an urgent matter to handle here," she said, waving the papers.

"That's fine, I can wait."

"And what exactly do you want with me, Mr. Rossini? I'm terribly busy right now," she said.

"Too busy to talk about your daughter's transplant?"

She took a cursory view of the business card. "Who's investigating the transplant?" she asked.

"I am, ma'am."

"Who's paying you, Mr. Rossini?" She made a sudden stop. "Are you working for the newspaper?"

"No, ma'am."

"Then what firm are you with?"

"My own firm. I promise, I won't take up too much of your time."

She sighed. "I'm investigating another case which is going to trial, which may be related to your daughter's transplant."

Cory watched a series of emotions sweep across her face. She released an impatient sigh and pointed toward her office. "Wait in my office while I take care of this."

Making his way inside, he wondered what her urgent business was all about, but even though he strained to listen, all he could hear was mumbling. Looking around the room, he noted the office had an elegant flair. Not that he should have been surprised. The senator was a classy-looking woman, and this décor fit perfectly with her persona. He'd been in many political offices during his time serving as an attorney, but her office was decorated unlike the typical politician's. He thought it was nice that she'd put her own mark on it. It was a stylish, comfortable room with a plushy gold carpet. Upholstered brown and beige striped straight-back chairs complemented the brown sofa, with a rectangular coffee table centered in the grouping. In the corner of the room was a glass-topped circular desk, with a black wooden base that looked striking against the gold carpeting.

Of particular interest to him were the framed photographs hanging on the wall. Hearing a noise, he kept a watchful eye on the door. He was hoping to find something that would help the case, when he suddenly noticed she'd left a desk drawer open. Inquisitive, he made his way over and saw some photographs loosely sitting on top of a pile. Afraid she would walk into the office any minute, he took a quick look at the top photo. The senator and Jeffrey Barrett were alone on a boat, standing close and smiling at one another like two lovers. Maybe it was his imagination working overtime, but he felt certain there was something going on between the two, and not just idle chitchat. He scooped up the pile and shoved them inside his jacket pocket. Not long after, he heard the senator's footsteps click against the wooden floor in the reception area, and he scrambled to pick up a framed photograph of her daughter sitting on the top of her desk.

"That's my favorite photograph of her," she said, walking into the room. "Arianna had just turned three." Her smile weakened. "That was taken in 2012, the year we discovered she had heart disease."

"Dr. Jeffrey Barrett performed the surgery on your daughter, didn't he?"

"Yes, he did. He's an amazing surgeon."

"Based on what the newspapers say, he's the best. How long had you known him?"

"I didn't. We met when he performed my daughter's transplant earlier this year. My daughter's cardiologist, Monica Feinstein, suggested I let Dr. Barrett take over for the transplant. It was kind of last-minute. Normally, I would have wanted to sit and talk with him, but there wasn't any time. My daughter had been sick for two years, so when a heart became available, I based my decision on his reputation in the field, read the press reviews of his notoriety, and I placed my trust in his ability. Today, I thank God he saved my daughter's life."

She took the framed picture from his hands and placed it back down where she'd had it, then made her way behind her desk, immediately noticing the opened drawer. For a second her facial expression seemed confused, possibly trying to remember if anything was missing, but when her demeanor changed, he knew she'd figured it out. She closed the drawer with her hip and was suddenly unable to look him in the eyes, lowering her gaze to her file drawer instead. Squatting down, she removed a file and placed it on the edge of her desk, her eyes looking everywhere except at him. "I know you didn't come here for a social visit, Mr. Rossini, so get to your point quickly," she said using a clipped tone.

"Are you aware of the gossip circulating about your daughter's transplant? People are saying you received special treatment because of your status."

She released an exhaustive sigh. "I'm not surprised. Everything I do is questioned or gossiped about," she said wryly. "That's the nature of the beast. It's all part of the political arena. The opposition loves to start rumors so it's documented before the next election, then they can use that in negative commercials."

"Doesn't that concern you?"

"Why should it?"

"Because these rumors aren't coming from your political opponents, they're coming from within the hospital."

"Wait just a minute, Mr. Rossini. Just because I'm a senator doesn't make the seriousness of my daughter's illness any less of a priority than anyone else's health. We were lucky a heart became available when it did." She fumbled with her earring. "Was there anything else that you wanted?"

"No. I wanted to see what you thought about the rumors."

She turned abruptly. "Well, now you know. Listen, I have to leave to check on my daughter. I'd appreciate it if you'd show yourself out." She picked up the file and placed it into her briefcase. "Good day, Mr. Rossini." She gestured her hand toward the door.

"Thank you, Senator."

Walking back to his car, Cory couldn't shake the feeling that the senator was hiding something, based on her sudden nervousness. If Barrett did perform an illegal transplant, the egotistical doctor was going to be drowning in a sea of troubles.

Home in his townhouse, Cory removed his coat and left it on the banister, exhausted from his long day. He made his way to his bedroom, and changed into something more comfortable. When his stomach growled, he remembered the care package his mother had given him the last time he'd had dinner with the family. He pulled the refrigerator door open and removed the plastic container, popping the lid only to see a solid covering of mold.

"Well, I guess I'm not eating that." Disappointed, he carried the container to the trash can and dumped it out, and then took to searching the cupboards for something to eat. It suddenly occurred to him he couldn't remember the last time he'd shopped for food.

Donning his coat, he walked the few blocks to his car and drove to the supermarket. Entering the store, he reached for a small food basket and walked down the dairy aisle for milk, butter, and eggs when he noticed Jack's mother. Surprised to see her, Cory hugged the short woman.

"It's so good to see you, Cory," she said. "Have you been to see Jack?"

"I've been to see him twice so far, Mrs. Hughes. I wish it were more, but I'm busy investigating his case."

"You know my Jack could never do something like this."

"I do know that, and that's exactly why I'm working as hard as I can to get him freed. So tell me, how are you feeling after your fall?"

"What fall?" she asked with confusion. "Where did you get that idea?"

"I can't remember where," he lied, "but someone said you fell. Well, I'm glad you didn't fall, and it's a good thing you wear that First Alert around your neck."

She jerked her head back and stared at him with perplexity. "Cory, what the heck are you talking about? Are you getting sick?" Her hand automatically touched his forehead.

"No." He chuckled and feigned confusion. "I don't think so. I guess you don't have one of those either, huh?"

"No, I don't."

"Well, okay." He released an embarrassed chuckle. "I must be working too hard, because I could have sworn you did have one. My parents do, so I guess I assumed all our parents wore them. And since you don't, please give it serious thought, because living alone without anyone around to help if something were to happen can be pretty scary." Pangs of anxiety attacked his stomach. Now, Jack was lying to him too. "Well, I need to get going. You call me if you need anything. I don't care what time it is."

"You're such a sweet man. I love you just like you were my own."

"I know that, Mrs. Hughes. Call me."

She waved him off. "Don't be silly. I'll be fine."

"I need to get back home to make some calls," he said and headed for the checkout, his gut so loaded with fury that he wasn't even hungry anymore. Tomorrow, he'd go to see Jack first thing in the morning to find out why he'd lied to him. Inside his car he was fuming. "What the fuck are you doing, Jack?" He spat out the words as though his friend were standing in front of him.

CHAPTER FIFTEEN

Cory waited in the visitors room for Jack to appear the next morning. When the door opened and Jack entered, Cory watched as the guard removed his cuffs.

"And to what do I owe this great honor?"

"We need to talk, but first I'll get coffee from the machine. You still drinking it black?"

"Yes. What's the matter, Cory? You seem on edge today."

Cory didn't respond; he just continued to the vending machine and filled two containers, capped them, and returned to where Jack was sitting.

Jack removed the lid from the container and sipped the hot beverage. "Okay, you've got something on your mind, so spill your beans."

"I want to know why you lied to me about your mother's fall."

"Oh, that."

"Yeah," Cory shot back, "that." His nostrils flared from anger. "Did you think I wouldn't find out?"

"No," Jack said, shaking his head. "I guess . . . Christ, I don't know what I thought," he answered in a flustered voice.

Cory continued. "I ran into her in the supermarket last night, and she thought I'd lost my marbles asking her about the fall and the First Alert. If you lied to me about that, what else have you lied about?" His lips pursed. "The evidence the detectives have against you may be partially circumstantial, Jack, but they have enough proof and witnesses that they could put you away for a long time." Cory blinked. "And now, you're fuckin' lying to me—your best friend," he said through clenched teeth. "I won't defend a liar, Jack. Friends or not." He rose from his seat prepared to leave.

"Are you shittin' me?" Jack simply stared at Cory, seemingly waiting for the words to come from his mouth. "I'm not dealing with this loss very well, and half the time, I don't know what the hell I'm doing. My mind is locked on all the ways I should have shown my love to her . . . the things I should have said and done that might have convinced her to stay with me . . . and now, it's too late. You have to know how much I loved Helen."

"Yes, I do, and I also know how much you hated Jeffrey," Cory fired back. "You knew Helen wasn't allowed to drive his car, so why wouldn't you have set those bombs to go off to get him out of the way?"

Jack appeared shocked by Cory's words, and when the reality finally hit, he lowered his head down onto the table and sobbed, releasing the unshed tears he'd held in too long. Cory's anger turned to pity, but he could not let up, not if Jack was guilty. He needed to know that right now. When Jack finally raised his head to look up at Cory, the pain in his eyes ran deep. "I promise," he begged, "I will never lie to you again." Cory handed him his handkerchief. "C'mon, man, we're family," Jack's tormented voice blurted out. "Everyone makes foolish mistakes, and I can't bear to think that I've lost you too." Cory couldn't help but wonder if this was how the scene with Helen had played out when Jack found out she was leaving. Jack dried his tears while Cory stared in silence.

"Did you set those bombs?" Cory asked as though pleading a case in a court of law.

"Christ, no!"

"Did you set them intending to kill Jeffrey, and then when Helen walked out and got into the car, you couldn't warn her in enough time? Is that what happened?"

"No." Jack's fist pounded the table. "No, no, no." His shoulders shuddered. "Did I drive past her house? Yes, I did. Why? Because I thought I could convince her to stay with me."

His hands rifled through his hair. "Why didn't I admit that to you? Because I knew you'd tell me what an ass I was, and you'd be right." He blew his nose. "And all that shit about how they claim I threatened to kill her, I swear I did not. It was exactly as I told you it was." He held up his hand. "But dammit, I don't know how I'm going to prove it."

Saddened by Jack's display of emotion, Cory watched his breakdown, the guilt raging in his own gut. He'd never seen Jack so upset before, and he automatically sat down next to him.

"I'm not going anywhere, bud." He sighed and allowed Jack to release his pent-up regrets.

Cory walked back to the parking lot worried about Jack and why he was lying so much. Had he killed Helen?

CHAPTER SIXTEEN

"What can I do for you, Mr. Rossini?" Max said into the phone when he called her the, her voice still frosty from his outburst and abrupt call disconnection the other day. He'd not given her a chance to say anything. Still, she wished she hadn't missed him so much.

"I've discovered some interesting facts about the Barrett case I think you need to know. I'm on my way over."

"I'm busy right now."

"Fine, Detective. If you'd rather not know about it, I can continue doing my own thing, but don't come crying to me when it blows up in your face." He clicked off the call abruptly, deciding Max Turner was the most stubborn woman he'd ever met. He smiled when his phone rang so quickly after disconnecting and her name flashed on the screen.

"Dammit, Cory, you didn't give me a chance to tell you what time I would be free. Weren't you taught that it's rude to hang up on people? Not to mention it's immature."

"Then what time is good for you? Is that mature enough for you, Detective?"

"Listen, Cory, you've told me other things about this investigation that proved to be wishful thinking on your part. If this proves to be viable and I've missed something, you'll have my undivided attention."

"Then when can I see you?" he asked.

"Give me an hour." They disconnected the call, at the same time.

Cory was smiling to himself afterward. It was obvious Max Turner didn't like being on the receiving end of impatience. The truth was, she had every right to be mad at him, but if her anger included any expectation of him stopping his investigation because they'd had dinner, she was sadly mistaken. He didn't need any more female grief. He'd already had more than his share.

Max twisted her mouth and chewed on the inside of her lips, curious about what Cory had found. Had she rushed to judgment too quickly on Jack's guilt? No, dammit, she hadn't. When had she become so insecure about her arrests? Max blew out a frustrated breath. This guy was doing a number on her heart. Allowing that to happen was a big mistake. She had work to do and couldn't afford to let anyone or anything get in the way of solving her case. She raised a dismissive shoulder, set the timer on her phone for an hour, and then delved back into her research until her alarm alerted her that Cory would be in her office shortly.

Nervously closing the file folder, Max shoved it into her drawer, then raced to the restroom to primp. Swells of nervousness waved in her stomach after not seeing or hearing from him since they'd sounded off on one another. In hindsight, she knew her tone the other day was uncalled for, but once the words were out, it was too late. Cory had every right to continue his investigation, but his harsh words were uncalled for too. Julie's suggestion came to mind. She'd wait to see how he acted before inviting him to dinner.

Applying a coat of gloss to her plump lips, she licked off the taste of cherry and remembered Cory's comment about her tasting like a bowlful of cherries. Fluffing her hair, she took one last critical look at herself in the mirror and headed back to her desk. That's when she heard his manly laugh—one of the many things she liked about him. She could see Riley nodding in her direction, and Cory turned to look. Her stomach flipped over at the sight of him. He was tall and masculine with a tight body that didn't have an ounce of fat. This man did things to her mind no other man could claim, and she wasn't quite sure why. Well, that wasn't quite true—of course she knew. He was a turn-on, handsome, he smelled good, and just being near him gave her butterflies. Was she just too damned lonely, or was her mind playing tricks on her, telling her they might actually be good together?

Max heaved one more breath to quell the anxiety attacking her insides and walked up behind him, warning herself about combining sentimentality and business. It was too easy to throw caution to the wind where he was concerned. It wasn't that she couldn't have a life and still work, just not if it jeopardized her cases.

Max wasn't quite sure how to act around Cory after that last set of calls. Should she show that she was happy to see him, or treat him like anyone else who had an appointment? Or should she be mad he'd hung up on her? She shook her head, unable to believe she was acting like a schoolgirl with him, questioning his motives, her motives. It was enough to give her a full-blown headache.

Cory smiled when he saw her, and her heart melted. She extended her hand in greeting and told herself to act normal. *Damn him* was all that came to mind.

The trio entered the interview room, each taking a seat around the Formica table.

"So what do you have that we don't?" she asked.

"A lot of coincidences that don't add up—maybe too many."

"Okay, shoot," Riley said, and pulled out his pad.

"I went to the hospital to snoop around. While I was in the cafeteria, I overheard two nurses conversing about a suspicious transplant that involved Senator Stansbury's daughter." Max's brows rose. Cory filled them in on the details about his findings. "Then at their suggestion, I went to see the hospital administrator to converse with her about the rumors, but she told me she had nothing to do with transplant patients and asked her secretary to schedule an appointment for me with the organ procurement and transplantation coordinator, a Melanie Chambers. But the interesting thing about my meeting with the administrator is she received a call and said she needed to take it. After she greeted the caller, she gasped, grabbed her coat, and ran out of the office. Before rushing off, she told her secretary something. She also showed signs of disbelief, then the administrator rushed into the elevator. It may not be anything, but it's worth checking. I asked the secretary about what happened, but she wouldn't tell me. I could tell she'd been crying, but she put on a professional face and told me Morrison was fine."

"Interesting. So when are you meeting with this Chambers woman?" she asked.

"Unfortunately, she didn't have anything available until October twenty-eighth."

"She's a busy woman."

"So it would seem." Remembering the photographs, Cory smiled. "I've saved the best for last," he said, holding up the photographs from Senator Stansbury's office.

"Holy crap," Max exclaimed, "where did you get these?"

"I went to see the senator at her Midtown location to ask if she was aware of the rumors I'd heard about her daughter's transplant.

All I had to say to the secretary was that I was investigating her daughter's transplant and her finger was on the buzzer to her boss.

But the senator had come rushing out of her office with something that needed immediate attention anyway. When I told her why I was there, she sent me to her office to wait. Needless to say, I snooped around." Max's eyes widened in surprise, but he continued anyway. "I found these in an open drawer sitting right on top." Cory watched their expressions as they flipped through one picture after another. Leaning over to see which photograph they seemed to be lingering on, he tapped the edge of the photo.

"Now, I ask you, do you see how close these two are wrapped in each other's arms? And feast your eyes on those loving smiles. What does that tell you?" His head dipped as he arched his brow. "For sure, it's this photo that has me more than convinced there's more going on with this case than just Helen Barrett's death." Cory leaned back in the chair, feeling smug about his find.

"I can't believe you stole these photos from her desk drawer!"

"Hey, it was open and they were out in plain sight. That's allowed if it relates to my case, isn't it?"

"Oh my God, Cory," she shrieked. "That's only if you're a detective." She lowered her voice. "That was definitely a gutsy move. These probably won't be admissible in court given the way they were obtained."

He shrugged. "So we'll find another way to prove it."

Max was having difficulty fathoming that Cory was gutsy enough to do something like steal the photos. "Okay, go on."

"Anyway, I pressed on a little harder and asked how long she'd known Barrett, and she still lied. She said they'd just met as a result of her daughter's surgery, but if you'll notice in this particular picture," he said, removing one from the pile, "the date stamp is June 2011, which proves she was lying. She knew him prior to her daughter's surgery." Cory chuckled. "When she walked behind her desk and noticed the photographs were gone from her opened drawer, her entire demeanor changed, and it was obvious she was shaken. She knew I had the goods on her. I didn't expect her to say 'You stole the photographs of me and my lover.' But they clearly are romantically involved, and she's definitely lying. My questions remain: What is being hidden about her daughter's transplant, and why is she lying about it and her relationship with Barrett?"

"Both good questions," Max said and left Riley to scrutinize the photo, but the image spoke for itself. "You're right, they're cuddling," she said, "and it's obvious they're on a boat." Max fired up her computer and keyed in something. "Okay, this appears to be noteworthy. The senator's reelection is this year. That means, if this picture was taken in June of 2011, that's the year she was elected to office."

Riley put the photo down. "You're right, Cory. This woman is definitely standing a lot closer than a candidate would. They look like they're ready to jump each other's bones."

Cory continued. "Further into our conversation, her cheeks flushed, and she tried to hide it by bending down to pull a file out from her drawer. She stumbled over her words, unable to focus on anything except getting away from me as fast as she could."

Deep wrinkles creased Max's forehead. "Maybe she was afraid if she told you she had been seeing him, it would raise stronger suspicions about the gossip."

"But she knew I was aware of the truth. Why lie?"

"So you think she's responsible for Helen Barrett's death?" Max said, pushing back in her chair.

Cory nodded. "It wouldn't be the first time two lovers were in cahoots and wiped out the third party."

"What else did you find?"

"Nothing else at the moment." Cory slid his teeth over his bottom lip. "Are you going to investigate this further or not?"

"Yeah, we'll check it out." Max could tell by Cory's expression he didn't like her lack of enthusiasm.

"Look, you can be pissed at me all you want, but I'm giving you valuable leads that might be crucial to your investigation and you're acting nonchalant?" he fired at her.

"And we're very appreciative. I said we'd check it out, and we will."

"I guess I expected a bit more of a reaction from you. Seriously, if you think I'm wasting your time, I can go directly to Jack's attorney instead."

"You're certainly entitled to go wherever you think is appropriate, Cory. Thank you for your time. I appreciate your help, and yes, we will investigate it."

Cory stood. "I don't understand why you don't think Jeffrey had anything to do with his wife's murder."

"We'll get back to you. Thanks for stopping by." She watched Cory's determined walk out of the office. She knew he was pissed, but she brushed it off because she was just as annoyed with him as he was with her. What was even more frustrating was how she'd missed the relationship between the senator and Jeffrey—a major oversight on her part. Maybe she was letting her feelings with Cory interfere with her investigation.

"It's hard to believe Barrett was involved with another woman after the way he took his wife's death," she said to Riley.

Riley offered her solace. "Maybe Barrett's a very good actor. Or maybe it's just a photograph that is being misconstrued. But Cory's right. Why lie about it? I'm sure we're going to find out a whole host of things we never expected. We're just starting our investigation, and besides, shit happens."

"And, on that note, let's call it a night and use what little time we have left of the weekend."

"I couldn't have said it better myself," Riley said.

CHAPTER SEVENTEEN

"How about you keep investigating Barrett and the senator," Max said as their last assignment Sunday evening, "while I talk to the boss. See what else you can find out. I want to get the good doctor in here for questioning to find out what he didn't tell me." She tapped her finger against her mouth. "If Barrett was having an affair with her during his marriage, I'll bet the dirt-bag is still screwing the woman."

"No doubt, Max," Riley said watching as she walked away.

Twenty minutes later, Max was back and noticed Riley holding a magnifying glass over the top of one of the photographs.

"What are you doing?" she asked.

"I want to get a closer look at this photo. There's no doubt they're on a boat." He squinted and adjusted the magnifying glass midway. "Aha!" he said. "Wait a minute . . . it looks like there's *another* boat in the background behind them."

"What?" Max asked.

"Take a look for yourself." Riley held the magnifying glass over the photograph.

"I see what you mean."

"I'm going to find out more about whose yacht that is in the background." He sat down at the computer and typed in the name of the yacht. "Well, I'll be a son of a bitch," he said. "*Mister's Mistress* is owned by none other than Jeffrey Barrett."

"Even the name screams affair. As soon as I return from talking to the boss," Max said, "we can start our suspect board. Evidence is building up pretty rapidly now, and I don't want to sidestep anything important."

"Then while you're talking to the boss, I'm going to get a list of marinas near their homes and visit to see where they dock their yachts."

"I'll be anxious to hear what you've found. You know, Riley," Max said, "we may be getting ahead of ourselves, but if the senator is the jilted lover, isn't it possible she hired someone to plant those explosives hoping to kill the doctor? There's too many questionable things at play here," she said, shaking her head. "All right. See you in a little while."

After leaving the lieutenant's office, Max's quickened pace was exaggerated by her frustration at missing something that was right in front of her nose. Her own worst enemy, Max set an often too-high standard for herself. If it was true that Barrett was having an affair with the senator after his pathetic display of grief, she was really going to be pissed.

Riley had a smug expression on his face when he walked back to his desk. "Barrett's a member of the Bayside Country Club and Marina. It's an exclusive private club, and that's where he docks his yacht."

"Is the senator a member?" Riley shook his head. "Do they allow outsiders to dock their yachts there?"

"The attendant said they don't. It's only for members of the club. So I checked out the other marinas close by, and she's docked at The Peninsula, a few miles up the road."

"Now, isn't that interesting. She's not in the same club, yet they met at sea, maybe for a party. He anchors his yacht and climbs into hers?" Max paced in short succinct steps while thinking. "Refresh my memory. Were there any other boats besides Barrett's and the boat they were standing on?"

"Not that I could see in that photograph."

"Regardless, Cory's right about her hiding something. It may turn out to be something completely innocent, but it deserves our attention." Max rubbed her hands over her chin, thankful Cory had discovered another aspect of the case. The more she thought about it, the more she realized the things Cory had revealed about the case had given new meaning to the term *bedside manner*, but she still wasn't sure how this Valerie Morrison's unexplained departure fit into the scope of things. She decided it might be worth pursuing.

CHAPTER EIGHTEEN

Cory woke up earlier than usual on Monday, anxious to get a hold of Greg, the son of his grandfather's former business partner in the clothing industry. Sitting down with his coffee, he wondered how Greg was going to react to him calling after so much time had passed.

After word had gotten out about him borrowing the money from a client, it had spread around the club like a fire. When Avery Paulson, one of the partners at the firm, and a club member, let it be known what Cory had done, Cory had pulled away from everything, including his friends, and focused solely on his family and his niece. It was the embarrassment of his friends knowing what he'd done. Although those who knew him really well would know he hadn't done it for his own gain.

Regardless, it was Jack now who needed the help, and he had to put his pride aside and wait to see what Greg's reaction to him would be. If anyone would know about Jeffrey and the senator, it would be Greg. His wife was known as a busybody and knew everyone's business.

He flipped through his phone directory, clicked on Greg's number, and waited for him to pick up.

Hearing Greg's voice, Cory felt his stomach turn over.

"Well, I'll be a son of a bitch. I was just talking about you the other day."

"I hope it was good."

"Of course it was good. Where you been, buddy?"

Feeling uneasy, he forced himself to act normal. "So good to talk to you."

"You too. What happened?"

"What do you mean, what happened?"

"To us?"

"I haven't been in touch with anyone, Greg."

"Yeah, Cory, but we're friends. You know I don't hold anything against you because of what happened. I know the kind of person you are. Hearing about your niece's cancer, I totally understood, but I wish you'd come to me first. I would have lent you the money."

"Thank you, I appreciate that, Greg, but getting others involved was the last thing I wanted. But I do need your help for Jack. I'm working a case, and I was hoping someone who's still a member of the club might be able to help me."

"Shoot," Greg said, "I'm still a member and I spend a good deal of time there. What do you need?"

"I'd prefer to discuss this in person."

"No problem. Sounds ominous. How's tonight? I made reservations at the club for the family, and everyone, including the wife, bailed on me. Why don't you join me for dinner?"

"I haven't been to the club in a long time, and . . ." he stammered.

"Cory, you don't need to say a thing. You know what I say about all those two-dollar millionaires? Screw 'em," Greg said. "I'll meet you by the entrance at six-thirty tonight." After they'd disconnected, warm thoughts of his childhood played over in Cory's mind. He and Greg had been friends since high school, where he, Jack, and Greg had played on the football team and then hung out after college until Greg got married and had children. Since neither Jack nor he ever married, they no longer had much in common. Cory smiled at the thought of having a reunion with Greg. It was going to be nice to catch up with someone he'd known since childhood.

Stepping out of the shower, Cory toweled off and walked to his closet to pick out a suit. Going to the club after his scandal felt uncomfortable. Even his stomach was playing racquetball at the thought of seeing those familiar faces again after all this time. Choosing the gray suit with a striped shirt and coordinating tie, he buckled his belt and slipped his feet into his tasseled loafers. He ran a comb through his hair and slipped his jacket on. Taking one last look to make sure he hadn't forgotten anything, he checked himself in the mirror, then walked outside and locked his front door. Tonight, he'd give his 2009 Mercedes a workout. He hadn't driven it since he'd left the firm. It brought back too many painful memories. He wondered what Max would think when she saw it. Judging from her reaction to his old junker, he was certain she could care less. Besides, he'd learned quickly that the car wasn't worth that much money when he tried to trade it in to pay for his niece's surgery. It didn't even come close to what the surgeon was charging, and by that time, his girlfriend's idea had already taken root in his mind. Sitting behind the steering wheel again reminded him of how much he'd been missing. Going to the country club for dinner was always a treat.

He'd thought he had a huge circle of friends at the club, but he'd quickly learned they weren't as invested in him as he was in them. One man in particular named Dominic Williams, who also happened to be friends with Barrett, had struck up a friendship with him. Cory didn't like any of Barrett's friends, but Dom quickly won him over, frequently having a beer with him after a golf game. Unfortunately, Dom was one of the people who'd turned his back on him. As for the rest? He remembered most of them as consistently getting drunk and making asses of themselves. These days, they weren't even close to the kind of people he wanted to associate with on a regular basis. His grandfather always said you were judged by the company you kept.

Nevertheless, he'd be lying if he said he didn't miss the interaction. Shaking his head, he wondered if he could ever rejoin the club. He decided that was a thing of the past, but if he ever did go for membership again, it would certainly never be at the Bayside Country Club and Marina. He wasn't sure he could ever feel comfortable there again.

Cory pulled up to the circular driveway in front of the country club and got out of his car at the parking attendant's station, deciding to wait outside for Greg. One thing he really liked about the club was the creativity of the landscaping crew and how they maintained the rolling hills of green velvety grass. In the very early spring, they even arranged large pots filled with flowers to remind members that warmer weather was right around the corner. Despite the bare trees of October, the club was still posh and beautiful.

Checking his watch, it suddenly dawned on Cory that he'd neglected to ask Greg what kind of car he drove, but it probably wouldn't have mattered anyway because Greg was the last person who'd ever park his own car. It was no secret Greg enjoyed the finer things in life, and paying someone to take care of what he considered menial tasks was right up his alley. Cory walked around, trying to kill his impatience, when he recalled a conversation with Greg about his own wedding. Notorious for being late, Greg had made a joke about showing up later than the bride. Apparently his wife didn't think it was so funny because she *really* smashed a piece of the wedding cake in his face at the reception.

Although most people just rolled with Greg's tardiness because it was part of his persona, it drove Cory nuts. Nevertheless, he regretted not having kept in touch. But his embarrassment, and the speed with which people abandoned him after his legal issues became public, left him wary and afraid to test any more friendships.

Just as Cory was about to ask the attendant what kind of car Greg drove, a white Lexus sedan with gold trim pulled up to the station. Greg waved to him before getting out of the car.

"Hey, buddy, so good to see you. You don't look any worse for wear after what you've been through."

"Thanks. You're looking pretty good yourself."

"It's the good life," he said, patting his belly. "So let's go inside, have a drink and a decent meal. My wife should have given me a warning when we met that she didn't like to cook."

"Yeah, but I'm sure she has other meaningful attributes."

"She does, and she's a helluva good mother." Greg acknowledged a few of his friends, who'd quickly turned away when they saw Cory with him.

The maître d' walked them to their table. "Good to see you, Mr. Rossini."

"Thank you, Jerome. I appreciate the welcome. It's good to see you too."

"So what's our Monday night special, Jerome?" Greg asked.

"Meat loaf. That's your favorite, isn't it?"

"It sure is," Greg said, pulling out his chair to sit. Cory sat down across from him and deliberately ignored his surroundings.

"Martini?" Greg pointed to Cory.

"Sure. That sounds good." They unconsciously watched the man walk to the bar.

"Okay, let's get down to business. How can I help you?" Greg said.

"I'm working on a homicide investigation for which Jack is being charged."

"I'd heard about Jack and I was sick over it, but not sure what to think, because I knew he had an intense dislike for Barrett, as most of the 'real' people do."

"Surely, you don't think Jack is capable of killing anyone?"

"I didn't mean to imply that," Greg said. "Tell me what you want me to do."

Cory filled Greg in on some of the things he'd been doing in his new career.

"Let me ask you something. What do you know about Jeffrey Barrett and Senator Stansbury?" Cory asked, finally.

"They've been an item for a long time."

"Do you know this for certain?"

"I do."

"How long have they been together?"

"Maybe two years, but time flies, so I may not be remembering it correctly." Greg looked at Cory with disbelief. "I can't believe you didn't know that."

"I never paid attention to that pompous ass or his friends. Where did you first hear it?"

"My wife." Greg stopped talking. "Okay, that's it." He pointed a finger in the air. "You don't have a gossipy wife." He suddenly jerked his shoulders and looked around to see who was close by and lowered his voice. "I'd better be careful. These women are as tough as a lynch mob." They'd almost finished their martinis, so Greg ordered another round, then continued. "Anyway, after Nancy told me, I figured it was just that—idle gossip—until one day we were sailing out to sea. I guess it was the end of June when I saw the senator's yacht hightailing it like she was in a race, and lo and behold, Barrett wasn't far behind on his own yacht. We continued on our way only to return a while later, and sure enough, they'd dropped sea anchors and were lashed side by side with boat bumpers, pretty damn far from the shoreline."

Cory snickered. "That's a clever way to cheat—no witnesses so far out. But how did you know it was her yacht?"

"Stansbury's yacht is fairly easy to spot because she named it after an act near and dear to her heart that she helped get passed. I happen to know the guy who painted the name *Heroes* on the boat."

"Heroes?" Cory asked.

"Yeah, the Helping Heroes Keep their Homes Act. I wasn't about to blow the whistle on Barrett, not because I like him, but I don't need the drama. I figured his wife would find out sooner or later. As for the other members who saw him and the senator together, I don't know if they ever asked him what was going on."

"Excellent information, Greg. I can't tell you how much I appreciate it."

They ordered their dinner when the waiter appeared. Greg ordered the night's offering of meat loaf and Cory ordered a steak. "So how's the family?" Cory asked.

"Good. The kids are getting big. They're at the age when they don't want to hang out with the parents anymore." Greg shrugged. "It gives my wife and me more time together, and that's a good thing."

"I imagine it is, and frankly, I'm a little envious," Cory said.

"Why is that? No involvement with anyone?"

"No. I haven't found anyone who wants to marry me," Cory said with a touch of humor.

"Now, I can't imagine that being true. Are you dating anyone special?"

"I'm working on it."

"Anyone I know?" Greg asked.

"I don't think so, not unless you've been in trouble lately." Greg frowned. "She's a detective, and she's working on Barrett's case, and, man, she's mighty fine." Cory wiggled his brows.

Greg laughed. "Now that sounds serious."

"What? The case or us?"

"Both."

"It could be." Dinner was delivered and the two men dug into their food.

"It's so good to see you, Cory. Wait until I tell Nancy I had dinner with you. She's going to be so envious. She's always liked you."

"I've always liked her too, Greg."

"Do you think you'll ever renew your membership here at the club?"

"Not this one, that's for sure. Not with the way those who I thought were my friends turned their backs on me. They'll never get another chance to hurt me."

"Yeah, but I'm the only one of your friends who really matters, and I didn't turn my back on you." The waiter delivered another round of martinis, and Greg held his up and toasted, "Here's to more great nights of getting together. I've missed you, Cory."

"I've missed you too, Greg. As soon as Jack's freed, we'll go out and tie one on like old times."

"I'll drink to that," Greg said, "and maybe next time this Madame Detective will actually be your girl."

"I'll definitely drink to that one!"

CHAPTER NINETEEN

He moved with the grace of a panther, reached up and covered the security camera lens with a cloth, and carefully taped around it so the fabric wouldn't fall off. He then unscrewed the lightbulb near her car in the parking garage, stopping for a few minutes when he heard noises. Remaining quiet, he thought about the important job he and his team had to do. He crouched low to the cement floor in his black ninja suit that covered everything but his eyes. His training had prepared him for this. Excitement surged through every part of his body, and he loved it. This is what he was meant to do—be part of an elite team of specially trained naval forces.

Killing those who threatened the United States was satisfying. He relished knowing that he'd stopped the enemy in its tracks. He loved the element of surprise, of sneaking up on enemies and watching their faces morph into panic.

When the noise stopped, he scanned the area to make sure he was safe to move around. Then he made his way to her car. He'd been following her mother for days, but decided the impact of the daughter's death would have more of an effect. "An eye for an eye," he whispered.

Yes, the enemy's daughter would have to pay for her mother's sins. It was better this way.

He impatiently checked the time again. She had already been shopping for two hours at this silly midnight sale. He could feel his pulse pounding through his veins. His excitement escalated and made him antsy. He tried to calm down, because just one mistake could shoot his plan to hell. *Patience,* his mind shouted, *patience.*

Snaking his way around to the passenger's side of the vehicle, he saw his commander's hand rise in the air, giving him the go-ahead. He reached up and held the weather stripping apart with his fingers so he could slowly slide the tool down along the window, hoping he was going slow enough to make contact with the door mechanism. He felt the clunk of having the tool in just the right place, the pounding in his ears magnified by the tight-fitting hood covering his head. This is what made him tick. He pulled back on the tool until he felt the lock pop, opened the car door, and hurried inside, shutting the door quickly. He removed a screwdriver from the belt around his waist, felt for the screws on the dome light, and performed his magic, removing the lid and the bulb.

Now that the interior light was disconnected, she'd never see him crouched down on the floor in the back. Smiling, he couldn't wait to make contact. To curb his excitement, he focused on his own breathing, reminding himself not to move too fast because he could ruin everything. He knew better than to become overanxious and blow the ambush.

The silence was deafening. Apparently, everyone else was involved in getting the best deal at this hour. He shifted to a more comfortable position just as the car door opened and she entered, talking to someone. For a split second he panicked but quickly realized she was on her cell phone. Slowly, he managed to bring himself back into the right frame of mind.

She eased herself down into the car seat, flinging her package into the backseat, just missing him by an inch or so, while she continued to talk. She pulled the seat belt over her chest with her right hand while holding the phone with her left, snapping the end into place. She continued her conversation as she shoved her key into the ignition and started the car, pushing the heater lever over to high, trying to force the fan to blow out warm air.

"Yeah," she said to whomever was on the other end of the call, "you should have seen that bastard's face when he realized I wasn't giving in. If security hadn't intervened when they did, I don't know what would have happened. He was madder than hell." She laughed. "And you know me, I wasn't about to give in to his demands. He probably bullies his wife too." She paused. "Been there, done that. No man will ever have that power over me again. Ever!"

His excitement peaked when he rubbed his fingers over the sharpness of the blade. He rose swiftly and caught her off guard, sliding the knife from left to right, enjoying the sound of her skin coming apart. Her scream was horrifying. Blood shot out from her throat, spraying the front windshield. When the last gurgle escaped from her mouth, the phone dropped to the floor and her body slouched to the right. He positioned her upright while her friend's screams screeched through the phone and bounced off the windows like surround sound.

Mission accomplished. He smiled, ready for his next assignment as he slipped out of the car and vanished into the darkness.

CHAPTER TWENTY

Cory wished his mind would stop replaying his last encounter with Max. Since he hadn't heard from her, it was obvious she wasn't over his sharp rebuttal yet. He heaved a sigh. God, he wished he hadn't been so caustic. He really hadn't meant to fly off the handle the way he had, but after having one barracuda in his past, his instinct was to retaliate. Max shouldn't have to take the brunt of what Lyndsey had done to him. He sighed, unable to stop that annoying feeling dwelling inside him that he'd been a complete jerk about it. He hoped sharing the information Greg had given him about Barrett would break the ice. That's if they were still talking.

Jack's attorney came to mind. Sure, he could have given the information to Bill Cates, but he didn't have a lot of confidence in Cates's ability to exonerate Jack, and that was why it was important to feed this information to Max before she got all tangled up in the discovery process. Any little bit of information he could give her that would result in one less piece of evidence to use against Jack was well worth the effort.

Pain throbbed in his right knee every time his foot hit the pavement as he jogged toward the hospital, trying to dodge the raindrops. Having had knee surgery just two months earlier, he'd been advised not to jog, but without a raincoat or an umbrella, he had little choice. Sure, he could have flagged down a taxi to drive him the five blocks from the parking garage to the hospital, but chances of getting one in this sudden downpour were next to nil. Normally, his umbrella would have been in the backseat of his car, but he'd lent it to his sister the last time she'd visited him.

He stopped in the doorway of a store and pulled his sports jacket up over his head to use as a shield and then jogged the remaining distance to the front door of Mount Sinai.

Inside the hospital's vestibule, he removed his jacket and shook the raindrops off. Then he slid his arms back inside the sleeves and walked through the second set of double doors. Seeing a sign for a restroom, he made a beeline inside and used paper towels to dry his hair and the cuffs of his trousers. He combed his hair with his fingers and made his way over to the volunteers' station. He leaned against the tall counter, and an elderly man approached, his pale face mottled by the bright red blotches that covered his bulbous nose. "I have an appointment with Mrs. Chambers," Cory said. "Can you tell me what floor she's on?"

The man eased himself down in front of a terminal and keyed in the name. "Let me get that information for you," he said. "You said you have an appointment with her?"

"Yes." He presented his identification.

"I don't see your name on the appointment list."

"Mrs. Morrison's secretary was the one who made the appointment for me."

"Let me call upstairs and find out," he said, dialing the number. While he spoke, Cory sat down and waited until the volunteer gestured at him. He returned to the counter.

"Her office is on the twelfth floor, Room 12N561, and the elevator bank is that way, sir." He pointed, then turned to answer another visitor's question. Cory heard the man's voice fade into the background as he headed toward the elevator. He stopped to push the lighted button just as everyone else who was waiting for the elevator had, as though it would cause the car to appear faster. When the doors finally opened, a man in a lab coat entered ahead of him and gave a casual nod of his head to a surgeon in the back who was dressed in scrubs. Cory stepped inside the already packed car, with visitors and hospital staff crammed in like sardines, half wondering if he should wait for the next one. Checking his watch, he opted to remain, knowing the next car wouldn't be any better.

The doors closed and he held his breath against the smell of an overabundance of strong perfumes and heavy nicotine users. Wedged between two men, nausea roiled in his stomach from the sharp mixture of smells. He pinched his nose to block out the offensive odors, not caring if he offended anyone, and just wished the damn elevator wouldn't stop at every floor along the way.

When the doors finally opened on his floor, he elbowed his way out to catch his breath. He'd definitely be taking the stairs after this meeting, although he could feel his knee beginning to swell, reminding him he'd tried to do too much too soon after the surgery.

Seeing offices on each side of the hall, he looked for the department name until he found it and walked inside the reception area. An older woman served as secretary. She looked up from her computer wearing brown-rimmed glasses perched on the bridge of her nose.

"Are you Mr. Rossini?" the woman asked. Cory nodded and handed her his business card. "I'm Donna Gordon, Mrs. Chambers' secretary. "I'm sorry to tell you Mrs. Chambers had to leave, but Kelly Sweetstone is covering for her."

"Okay." Cory shrugged. "So long as she can answer all my questions, that's fine. Although that's why I'd accepted a later appointment with her."

"I know, but these things happen. Kelly's more than qualified to fill in for her. Why don't you have a seat." She gestured. "She'll be out in a few minutes." The secretary no sooner finished her sentence than the door opened and Kelly Sweetstone walked in.

She extended her hand in greeting. "Mr. Rossini, I'm Kelly Sweetstone. Thanks for stopping by. We're always happy to have the general public ask questions. Please, come in and have a seat." She walked behind the desk and sat down. "So what's on your mind?"

"Thank you for seeing me on such short notice," he said. "What happened to Mrs. Chambers?"

She closed the binder on her desk. "She had something she needed to take care of." She shrugged. "So how can I help you?"

She rubbed her hands up and down her arms and shivered. "It's cold in here today." Reaching for a sweater on the credenza, Kelly slipped her arms inside the sleeves and raised her shoulders. "Ah, that's much better. Sorry. So tell me why you're here and how I can help?"

"I'm doing an investigation on heart transplants that was prompted by a recent transplant performed on the senator's daughter—there's talk that the process might have been circumvented and she got special treatment because of her status."

"That's absolutely impossible. There are strict guidelines," Kelly stated firmly.

"Then can you help me to understand how one person might be bypassed for another?"

She shook her head in dismay. "I apologize for my reaction, but this happens every time a family member of a high-profile figure receives what the public thinks is special treatment. As you can imagine, we must have a backup plan for every organ that is requested by one of our surgeons, mainly because, at a moment's notice, something could go wrong." She looked at Cory full on. "Let me tell you the process. When a candidate's name is next on the list, that person is called into the hospital to be prepped for surgery, as is the backup candidate, just in case something goes wrong with the primary candidate. In each case, the candidate who is to receive the organ may be rejected because of a mismatch."

"Even though it was originally thought to be a match?" Cory asked.

"Absolutely. There are many contributing factors that go into the decision. For example, many tests are performed to evaluate a perfect match. Blood tests are taken and analyzed right up to the very last minute to determine if it's a good donor match and to avoid any chance that the donor organ will be rejected, which is always a possibility. In addition, diagnostic testing is done to check the lungs and overall health status of each recipient: X-rays, ultrasound procedures, CT scans, pulmonary function tests, and even dental examinations. Don't forget, even though these people have been under our care, they're still exposed to relatives visiting who may not even realize they're coming down with something. Our patients are very vulnerable to contagions." She angled her head. "So, as you can see, it's not a cut-and-dried process. And, even after all this is done, there's always the possibility that the heart could still be rejected and both the patient and the heart are lost." She stared at him, apparently waiting for a response.

"And there would be records of these tests being performed to prove the person wasn't a match and why?" he asked.

"Of course," she said with a strong conviction.

"What if the results were fudged to make the other recipient look like a bad candidate when they weren't?"

"Mr. Rossini. Do you realize what you're saying?"

"Yes, I do."

"Do you have any idea how many employees it would take to *fudge* a report?" She gave a tilt of her head. "We're talking several, maybe more than a half dozen people."

"It is possible, though, isn't it?"

"Why would someone do that when they know they'd be risking their job and their reputation?"

"What if it weren't six people but only the lab technician who fudged that report, knowing the heart would be given to the next person in line. Maybe the technician is a member of the senator's family?"

Her smirk widened. "I don't mean to be rude, Mr. Rossini, but you're reaching."

"Maybe, maybe not. Rest assured, though, I will get to the bottom of this."

Cory couldn't fault her for refusing to admit that fudging the records could happen. Comments like that left the hospital vulnerable to a lawsuit.

"So there you have it. The whole process." She gave a slight shrug.

"Thank you for your time."

"I hope you find what you're looking for, Mr. Rossini."

"I will."

CHAPTER
TWENTY-ONE

Max walked back to her desk. "Oh my God, I smell hot dogs. I'm famished."

"Then that works out well, because I ran outside and bought us lunch from the vendor on the corner." He handed the bag over to her.

"Bless your heart, Riley." She shook her head. "I don't even freakin' know what day it is."

"My sentiments exactly," he said. "With the hours we've been putting in, the days are all running together. So as not to keep you in suspense any longer, it's now 2:10 p.m. on Tuesday afternoon." He grinned. "Want the date too?"

"No." She snickered. "I think I can figure that out." Max unwrapped her hot dog and took a bite. "I know I'm going to be tasting this all afternoon, but I don't care, because there isn't anything like a street vendor's hot dog with lots of mustard and sauerkraut." She took another bite and moaned. "Thank you."

"My pleasure."

"So what did you find out about the financials?" she asked Riley.

"Not a thing," he said, taking a sip of coffee. "Other than the freeze Barrett had on his account, there's nothing else that's obvious. But we also have to take into consideration that these people have all kinds of money; it could be an offshore account that's being used to pay someone off for cooking the records, for all we know. Now that we're pretty certain there was a relationship between the parties, they each have enough clout to do anything they want, pay out any amount of money, and still not get caught. Neither one of them are slouches when it comes to exposure. They're smart, educated people who know their way around the system. And what they don't know, financial advisors will know and would recommend what would get them the least attention."

"Make sure you check everything," Max said. "Grants, scholarships, foundations he may be involved with, like Big Brothers Big Sisters. I know he sponsors several organizations in the city . . . the names of those escape me at the moment, but let's do a thorough search on all of them and the preschool Helen Barrett founded. It's called The Little Tykes Academy," Max said, glancing down at her notes, "over on East 35th." She twisted her head from side to side in an effort to relieve the tension in her shoulders that was now working its way upward into a splitting headache. Pulling her desk drawer open, she grabbed the bottle of ibuprofen and dropped four pills into the palm of her hand. She tilted her head back and slugged down the pills with the stale coffee sitting on her desk. She made a face. "Christ, that tastes like sludge."

"How long has that cup been sitting there?" Riley asked.

Max shrugged. "Hell, I don't know. I didn't even know what day it was, how do you expect me to know how long the coffee's been sitting?" She laughed.

"Why don't you go relax for a while in the break room, maybe walk outside to get some fresh air? It might help that headache of yours," Riley suggested.

"Thanks, but I'll be okay as soon as the ibuprofen kicks in." She rubbed her temples. "We may be grasping at straws, but that's what we'll do until we get to the bottom of this. If they're paying hush money, we're bound to find something in their books." Riley was jotting down notes as she spoke. "For sure, the senator is going to want the residents of New York to know she's fighting for some worthy cause with the kind of money she has at her disposal, so if she's paying hush money, she could be using those funds," Max said.

"Then we're talking money laundering if they're using a foundation to pay people off." She nodded. "If these two were co-conspirators in the death of Helen Barrett," Riley said, "and if what those nurses told Cory is true about that transplant being an illegal act, Barrett and Stansbury are in a lot of trouble."

"Yes, and if they're guilty, those two smart, educated people are going to spend a whole lot of time behind bars." Max rubbed her hand over her eyes and covered her mouth with a yawn. "Excuse me. I was up late last night."

Riley's brows rose. "Oh yeah? With anyone I know?"

Max laughed. "Yeah, me and my notepad."

"Geez, Max, you lead a boring life."

"Tell me about it." She gave a half smile. "Okay, enough of this silly talk. I have a few more questions I want to ask Barrett, so let's get him in here."

"I'll send the uniforms to pick him up," Riley said and keyed in the number.

Max noticed Jeffrey Barrett walking through the front entrance in his scrubs looking rather perturbed. She greeted him. "Thanks for coming down to the precinct, Doctor. We have a few more questions we'd like to ask."

"I thought you were done with all of that."

"Well, we thought so too, but we have some new information we need to investigate, and we'd like your help."

"You realize you pulled me away from an important meeting."

"I'm very sorry about that, but I'm trying to solve a homicide."

"And I'm trying to save lives," he spat out.

"Touché, but mine trumps yours. Sorry you don't see it that way. Don't you want to know who killed your wife?"

"Of course I do. But I've also got a job to handle."

"But you have other doctors who can handle your work when you're not around, just as you had arranged when you planned your honeymoon, so relax and please cooperate."

"Every surgeon has a large enough workload already, let alone having to cover for me too. Do you get that, Detective?"

"Oh, I get it all right. Unless you're a Jack Kevorkian, there's never a convenient time for someone to die." Max gave him a pointed frown. "We all have these minor inconveniences every once in a while, but you learn to roll with the punches. Now, can I get you a soda or some coffee?"

"Neither. Let's get this done so I can get back to work."

"Certainly. So how are you doing, Dr. Barrett?"

"I'm still grieving, but my work has helped me deal with it. It's the alone time that has my mind working overtime. Thankfully, the right person is behind bars and will be for a long time. I couldn't ask for more."

She pointed to the door. "Right in here." She gestured. "You sure you don't want anything to drink?"

He rolled his eyes. "No. I'm fine. Can we get on with this?" Jeffrey sat down in the chair and stared at them expectantly.

"We just discovered something that's a little confusing for us, and I'm hoping you can clear up the mystery."

"You want to know about Senator Stansbury and me?"

Max feigned confusion. "What about her?"

"You weren't at her office on Friday, now were you?" The two detectives watched him shift uncomfortably.

"No. I was at the precinct all day." She turned to her partner. "Did you visit the senator on Friday, Riley?"

"No. I was right here too. But we're interested in knowing more," he said. "Are you saying someone from our department paid her a visit? What did they want?"

Barrett scratched his cheek. "I guess I was mistaken. Just disregard what I was saying and go ahead and tell me why you brought me down here."

"But now you've piqued our curiosity, and we want to know more about you and the senator," Max said.

He huffed out air. "Well . . . all right." He shook his head in disgust, realizing he'd left himself wide open for scrutiny. "I didn't really know the senator until I operated on her daughter."

"Okay." Max walked around the room while questioning him. Jeffrey followed her with his eyes. She liked using this method for questioning. It made the suspects anxious, and very often they'd blurt out the truth just so the detective would stop.

"We really just met."

"Okay. So who was asking her questions?"

"I don't know who he was, but she said he was tall with dark hair. I thought it was someone from this office."

"They never gave her a business card?" Max asked.

"She said they did, but she doesn't know what she did with it."

"That's interesting. As for who could have gone to see her, that could be a million people in this office, Dr. Barrett. So the senator called to tell you?"

He shifted in his seat. "Yes . . . well, no. She called me to ask a question about her daughter's transplant, and while we were chatting she mentioned someone from the NYPD came to see her. I just thought it might have been your team."

Max pretended to be confused. "Did he say he was from our office?"

He shook his head. "No, I don't know that. I guess I just assumed. Forget I even brought this up."

"So you know the senator and her husband on a personal level?"

"Yes . . . I mean no. She's not married."

"How do you know that?" she asked.

"Oh . . . I don't know. I guess maybe I heard it on the news or read it in the papers," he said.

"It's interesting how something like that sticks in your mind, isn't it, Doc?" Max said arching her brow. "She is a beautiful woman. I'll give you that. So why do you think this person, whom you don't seem to know, showed up in her office?"

"Detective, will you please stop that damn pacing?" he barked. "You're making me nuts."

"Sorry, but it helps me think better." She continued her pacing. "So what did this person want?"

"I don't really know why this person went to see her, and now I'm wishing I hadn't said anything at all."

"So let me see if I have this right. You don't know her on a personal level, yet you know she's not married, and she called you to say someone was snooping around? Do I have that correct?" Max stuck a folded piece of gum into her mouth and chewed. "You were having an affair with her, weren't you?"

"No. I wasn't," he snapped back. "Where the hell did you get that idea?"

Max held up the photograph. It was obvious he was trying not to react, but his initial wide-eyed expression gave him away.

"Where did you get that?"

"I have access to a lot of things, Dr. Barrett. Do you know when it's dated?"

"I have no idea."

"June 2011. That was the year she ran for office."

"Then it had to be a campaign party. I told you, I contributed to her election."

"You did? I actually don't have that in my notes. When exactly did you tell me that?"

"Oh, I don't know, but I know I told you."

"Do you think you meant to tell me, but it slipped your mind?"

"Yeah, that might have been it. Geez, you know how that goes." He stopped for a minute and bridged his hands over his eyes as though thinking.

"I have a few problems with that, Doc. First, you said you'd just met her; second, if this was a campaign party, where are all the other guests, and why are you both in bathing suits and standing so close together? We think you're lying and the two of you were having an affair." She handed him the photograph. "Take a good look."

"No, Detective, we were not. What I actually think is that you have a dirty mind."

She snorted. "You're a clever man, Doc. I find it interesting the way you twist things around and push blame on the other person to get out of answering a question." She arched her brow. "Now, answer the question. Why are you standing so close to the senator?"

"Christ, Detective, I don't know. I don't even remember anything about it. I'm just suggesting it was a party because I wouldn't have been there otherwise. Obviously, there were other people onboard if someone took the photograph."

"The senator could have a captain who sails her around who could have taken the photograph."

"Here's what I'd like to know," Riley interjected. "If she was having a function, why would you have sailed out to meet her yacht?"

"What makes you think I sailed out to meet her yacht?"

"Your yacht is in the background." Riley pointed. "See it?"

"Who the hell remembers that far back?" His hands flew in the air. "I probably missed the scheduled departure because of work and caught up to them." Max and Riley looked at one another.

"I think it's fascinating that you have an answer for everything."

"That's because I'm telling you the truth."

"Were you invited to her victory party after she won?"

He ran a nervous hand over his face and stared into the distance. "I honestly don't remember."

"You can tell me you weren't having an affair with this woman all you want, but I'm convinced you were, Doc."

"No, dammit. She was a referral from Dr. Feinstein."

"Doc," Max said, "you must know that lying to me is not doing you any favors, because I'm going to find out sooner or later anyway. You know that, don't you? You being in this photograph that's dated in 2011 proves that you're lying."

He gave her a blank stare. "I guess I forgot."

"Did you also know there are rumors circulating in your own hospital that you showed partiality to the senator's daughter and gave her the transplant that was intended for someone else?"

"Look, I'm sure you know how well documented these transplants are—check the records. You're the one who's going to look foolish, Detective." He stood. "Am I done here?"

"Not quite yet," Riley said. "Do you have a military background?"

"Yes, but what does that have to do with anything?"

"What did you do in the military?"

"The military paid for my medical education, and I served at their pleasure."

"Is that where you and Jack Hughes first met?"

"No. We've known each other since high school." He huffed out a breath. "I don't see what any of these questions have to do with my wife's death."

"Well, you see, they do," Riley shot back. "We believe the person who planted those bombs had military training."

"Right," he said dryly. "So, now you think I'm a suspect. Jack Hughes had military experience with explosives." The detectives just stared at him without saying a word. "May I go now?"

"For today, sir," Max said. "But I wouldn't leave town if I were you."

Barrett shot her a hostile look and walked out of the room.

"He's lying," Riley said.

"Yeah, something's not right. Okay, I'm going to call Cory back in. Maybe we should investigate this together."

Riley smiled. "You like him, don't you?"

"I respect him for his work ethic, except when he lies his way into a witness's house. But we also need to protect our reputation. What if his suspicions are right about Barrett having an affair with the senator? I don't think the lieutenant would be pleased that I missed something so significant."

"But you do like him, though, right?" Riley ribbed her.

"For chrissake, Riley, *yes*, I like him—a lot." Riley didn't comment, but his appreciative smile told her he was on board with the idea. "Regardless, the major thing here is I think he's brought something important to the table with this case—things we can't ignore."

Max walked back to her desk and punched in Cory's phone number. He answered on the second ring, and she started talking the minute he picked up without first saying hello. "I think the things you've presented are significant enough that we should seriously discuss them together. Why don't you come over so we can talk?"

"Excellent, Detective. When would be a good time?"

"Can you make it in the next half hour?"

"Cory Rossini to see Detectives Turner and Riley," he said, standing at the desk sergeant's counter waiting for the stern female to tell Max he had arrived.

"Sit over there." She gestured. "I'll let you know when they're ready."

Cory was surprised that Max actually admitted he might have been right. He sighed and decided they'd definitely make a good team. All that was left to do was convince the stubborn woman that if she thought what they had was a slight infatuation, she'd better guess again—he was dead serious about getting to know her, hopefully even having a relationship with her.

Cory meandered over to the row of folding chairs and sat down, watching the sergeant's mouth move as she spoke into the phone. "Okay, Mr. Rossini," she called to him a few minutes later. "Officer Monteague will walk you to the interview room. You have a good day."

It was a few minutes before he would see Max's face. His heart had already increased its dance and was now doing a rumba. Despite her tough exterior, he prayed Max's heart was racing as fast as his. He told himself she was a cop and had to be very selective when showing her emotions. If he wanted her in his life, he would have to settle for the romance when they were alone together, because that's what counted.

"Good afternoon, Cory," Max said. "Thanks for coming over. Can you tell us what you've been doing since we last spoke?" He handed her a bouquet of red roses. Her surprised expression made him feel good. Riley smiled as he walked away.

"Thank . . . you," Max said, and swallowed hard. "Why did you give me flowers?"

"Because we've been at odds with one another recently, and I wanted to let you know how much you're starting to mean to me. Can we start over?"

The moment was lost when her peers began whistling and clapping hands. Max's face turned a brilliant crimson.

"Oh God, Max, I'm sorry. I didn't think . . ."

"It's okay," she said. "Give me one minute and we'll talk." She called out to a woman in the clerical pool. "Would you mind putting these flowers in water for me?"

"Sure," she said, smiling at Cory. Max turned back to Cory.

"Okay, let's talk," she said, and together they walked to the interrogation room, where Riley was already waiting. Inside, Cory walked to the coffeepot and filled a cup. Adding sugar packets and milk, he stirred the liquid and set down on the table. "I met with a friend of mine named Greg Barton. He's a member of the Bayside Country Club, and he informed me the senator and Barrett have been having an affair for at least two or more years that he knows of. The way they cheat is by sailing their yachts out to sea and anchoring."

"How interesting. Is that just idle chitchat, or did he see this first-hand?" Max asked.

"He saw it firsthand. What he said was he and his family followed Barrett out to sea, not intentionally, but when they'd finished sailing around they returned and both yachts were anchored right next to one another.

"And yesterday was my appointment with Melanie Chambers, the transplant coordinator at Mount Sinai. As it turned out Mrs. Chambers was out of the office and a Kelly Sweetstone met with me instead. She was pretty adamant about it being impossible for there to be any wrong-doing when it comes to transplants. She gave me a detailed list of tests that are performed before the surgery and what could go wrong." He arched a dark brow. "I even asked if it was possible to fix the records, but she denied the possibility."

"Why wasn't the actual transplant coordinator meeting with you?"

"I don't know," Cory said. "Her secretary said she had to leave. Again, no other explanation except 'these things happen.' But it seemed pretty interesting to me that she left in the middle of the day when she had an appointment. Maybe my imagination is getting carried away, but I just have an odd feeling about it."

"Honestly, she could have left the office for a perfectly legitimate reason," Max added.

"But I'm finding myself really wondering why two women in the same hospital leave suddenly during work hours," Cory said. "I really don't like the sound of that, Max." His lips tightened. "Isn't there a way you could find out?"

"We can check their names in the database and pull up relatives and associations. If you feel that strongly, we should definitely find out what we can. Again, it may be nothing."

"I know, but I just have this feeling in my gut. I want to know more about it and see if it relates to our investigation," he said and made a face when he tasted the bitter coffee.

Max laughed and continued. "It's been sitting there for a while." Cory pushed the cup aside. "We'll be checking everything we can to see if these things are related." Max brushed a wisp of hair away from her face. "But back to this Sweetstone woman at your meeting. Did she say the records couldn't be falsified?"

"That's what she said." Cory's mouth twisted into a smirk.

"That's a bunch of bull," Riley said. "I'm sure there are many ways those in the know could figure out how to bypass the rules without getting caught. At least, without getting caught right away."

Cory continued. "Near the end of our conversation, she finally admitted anything was possible, but that it was highly unlikely and that several employees would be putting their jobs on the line to do it."

"Maybe the doc is a cult leader like Charles Manson, and his followers march to his command," Riley suggested.

"Yeah, right," Max said. "You have to admit he's pretty damn hot looking, though. I might even join his cult." When Max noticed their expressions, she laughed, and her hand automatically shot up to a stop. "Just kidding, you guys. The truth is I can't imagine anyone being dumb enough to risk their job for him or anyone else. Unless of course, it was for a promotion or more money. However, if that was the case, then that's where our focus needs to be right now—on the financials and how and why this could have been pulled off." Checking the time, Max made a face. "I'm tired. Let's call it a night. We'll be working plenty in the coming days."

"Tonight, though," Riley said, "I'm glad we're not working overtime. It's my son's ninth birthday. I missed his birthday party last year, and he hasn't let me live it down since. I don't want the poor kid developing a complex."

"Well then, scoot," Max said, shooing him away with her hands. "And wish your son a happy birthday from me."

"Thanks for helping us out here," Riley said and grabbed his jacket off the back of his chair and headed out the door. "Have a good evening."

"Thanks, you enjoy the birthday party," Cory said to Riley. After the door closed, Cory turned to Max. "So what do you say? Will you have dinner with me so we can talk about what we're going to do?"

"Sure," she said, forcing down her excitement at the prospect of being with him again. "Let me tell the lieutenant what's going on. I could meet you at the restaurant. Where did you want to go?" he asked.

"How about Café Monarch?"

"Okay. See you there in a hour or so."

Cory watched the sway of her hips as she walked away, realizing just how much he'd missed her. He'd tell her tonight he was sorry for his outburst. Gathering up his files, he stuffed them into his briefcase and left the building.

An hour later, Cory spotted Max snaking her way between the tables to where he sat chewing on bread. Just the sight of her gave him goose bumps, something he'd never felt before with any other woman.

"I was afraid you weren't going to show," he said, standing to greet her.

She gave him a quizzical glance. "Why would I not show?"

Cory shrugged as he pulled the chair out for her and inhaled the flowery scent of her hair when she sat down. "A million reasons, I suppose." Max placed the cloth napkin on her lap, just as the waiter arrived and poured her a glass of red wine.

"I took the liberty of ordering you a glass of Pinot Noir. I was pretty sure that's what you wanted the last time we got together, even though you tried the Sangiovese."

"What a memory." She picked up the glass and smelled the bouquet and moaned. "Mmm, the nose on this wine smells like a candied apple." Drawing in a small sip, she swished it around in her mouth, swallowed, and grinned. "Total perfection," she said to the server who stood wait-ing. "Thank you." She held up her glass to Cory and toasted him. "To this case. May we enjoy lots more Pinot Noir. By the way, have you ever tasted Sea Smoke? That wine is so damn good, forget about pouring a glass—just give me a straw." The busboy replenished the bread.

"No, I haven't tasted it, but your enthusiasm makes it sound appeal-ing. Listen, I'm starved. Do you mind if we order first and talk while we're eating?"

"Not at all. It's been another one of those days where I almost skipped lunch and I would have completely if Riley hadn't gone outside and bought me a hot dog." Max suddenly stopped and laughed.

"You mean like the hot dog I wanted to buy you at Yankee Stadium?"

Nodding in agreement, she said, "Exactly."

"What do you feel like eating?" he asked when the waiter approached.

"I'm not sure. What are you having?"

"Steak."

"Mm, that sounds good. Then I'll have what he's having."

"How would you like that cooked?"

"Medium." After the waiter left she continued. "This wine is yummy."

"Good. Listen, Max, how about we call a truce?" he asked.

"A truce for what? The case, us, or . . . ?"

"How about a truce about everything?" His smile suddenly relaxed.

They both started talking at once. Cory backed off. "I'm sorry, you go first."

"Can we start with discussing our conversation about you talking to Barrett's friends? It's been bothering me that you didn't give me a chance to explain my frustration and why I was upset."

"Please do. I'd like to clear the air."

"When I called you that day, I'd just finished listening to a number of complaints about you, and before those calls, I was already feeling the pressure of not being able to close this case as quickly as I had hoped. It had nothing to do with your continued investigation. You can investigate as much as you want, but you used the NYPD to get your foot in the door, stretching the truth to fit your needs without considering mine or the department's, and you know better."

Cory nodded. She was right. He did know better. Releasing an embarrassed sigh, he inched his opened palm across the table, hoping she'd accept his invitation. She slid her hand inside his, and he released a contented smile. "I am sorry about that," Cory added. "I could give you a million reasons why I let my emotions cloud my judgment, but they'd only be excuses . . ." He paused momentarily, then continued, "I am sincerely sorry for using the NYPD as a means of getting them to talk to me."

"You made me look foolish."

"I swear, that wasn't my intent at all." He brought her hand to his mouth and kissed it.

"Okay, that's fine. At least I know you won't do it again."

"No, I won't." His eyes scanned her face, stopping to look directly into her eyes. "I've really missed seeing you, and I'm going to do my hardest not to cross that line ever again, because I do want to get to know you, but understand that I'm not perfect. I'm probably going to make some mistakes, but that doesn't mean I want to stop getting closer to you."

"I'm not perfect either, and I'm sure I'll screw up just like you." Max said. "It's refreshing to talk to someone who doesn't try to weasel out of something he did wrong, or try to place blame on others. I have a lot of respect for that. But in terms of getting to know each other on a higher level, I think we need to wait until this case is solved."

He paused, showing disappointment, but then reluctantly nodded his agreement and knew she wasn't going to give him too many chances to get this right if he wanted to move their relationship forward. "But you won't put a hold on us having dinner to discuss our progress with the case. Right?"

"Only if we keep it professional between us." She knew there was a fat chance of that happening, but so long as she kept her distance, things would be okay.

CHAPTER
TWENTY-TWO

"I can't shake this feeling I have about the heart center," Cory said sitting across from Max the next afternoon in one of the interview rooms.

"What do you mean?" she asked nonchalantly.

"Max." Cory took a quick sharp breath. "I've been talking for the last ten minutes and I'm sensing you haven't heard one word."

"I'm sorry. I was distracted. I've got a million things going through my brain right now. Please continue." Cory looked skyward, a little perturbed. "Really, I'm sorry," she muttered, feeling slightly embarrassed. After a few seconds of silence, she cleared her throat.

Amused, Riley laughed. "You two act like a married couple." He'd apparently thought his comment was funny because he chuckled, but neither acknowledged it. He broke the tension by changing the subject. "Were the names of the women you visited at Mount Sinai, or I should say attempted to visit, Valerie Morrison and Melanie Chambers?"

"Yes. What about them?"

"The more I think about your suspicions regarding wrongdoing, the more convinced I've become that something is amiss, so I'm headed to check these names in the database. We'll see if what happened to each of them separately is somehow related."

An hour later, Riley walked back over to where Max was sitting. "You're not going to believe what I've just found."

Max's eyes widened with anticipation. "Well, don't keep me in suspense. What did you find out?" Max asked.

He read from the screen. "Sharlene Chambers-Inghrams found dead in her vehicle on October twenty-eighth by a security guard in the Global Parking garage on West 40th. Bag from Macy's Department store on backseat containing child's skirt. Security attendant, Nate Williams, found body during second security check when he noticed vehicle still running. Victim's throat slit from ear to ear. Detective of record is Louis Lucio of the 17th Precinct. Case open."

"If this turns out to be a relative of Melanie Chambers, then you have a sixth sense," Max said to Cory. "How about the other one?"

Riley keyed in the other name. "Sixteen-year-old Candace Morrison. Autopsy report lists death as a result of an overdose of Propofol at NY Presbyterian Hospital. Patient had rhinoplasty surgery. Case open. Detective of record, Lawrence Howe, 22nd Precinct."

"Wow," Max said, making her way over to the small refrigerator. She pulled out three bottles of water, unscrewed the cap on one, and handed it to Cory. "We still don't know if either of these cases relate to one another, but it's worth checking with the two detectives."

Cory loved the way she multitasked. Seeing her nurturing side shine through was a total surprise to him because she had such a tough outer shell. He doubted many were capable of chipping their way through that rock. God, he was falling for this woman, although he had to admit sometimes her wavering moods were off-putting. Now that he was in his forties, he had little patience for sulkiness. Admittedly, his moods hadn't been so rosy lately either. They were still getting to know one another's quirks, and given a little more time, they'd get used to each other.

"If so," Cory said, "that would mean two deaths involving relatives of employees who work at Mount Sinai, plus Helen Barrett makes three, and it's the same place Jeffrey Barrett works," Cory said. "Are you seeing a pattern here?"

"I hate to burst bubbles here, guys, but this is New York." Max felt her ponytail slipping and pulled the scrunchie off, smoothed her hair back, and reapplied the elastic to pull her hair tighter. "There are three-point-five murders every day." Addressing their assumption, she offered her opinion. "Just because these two victims have relatives who work at the hospital, one of whom works in the heart center, does not necessarily make them a connection to Helen Barrett's murder," she warned. "Trust me, I'd like nothing better than to solve this case based on that information, but we all know that would be way too easy. Once we talk to the other detectives, we'll have a better idea. If it turns out the way I'm hoping, then we'll have our confirmation that it's more than a coincidence."

Cory checked his watch. "Geez, don't you guys ever get hungry? I'm starving. Can we break for lunch and then come back to talk about the next steps?"

Riley snickered. "You know, we're so used to skipping meals that it never occurs to us until we're suddenly so famished we're ready to eat everything in sight." Max was nodding in agreement. "I could use a little sustenance," Riley said. "I'll call Berg's Deli. They deliver."

"While we're waiting for the food to arrive," Max said, "I'll go out to my desk to call the two detectives and see what I can set up for tomorrow. I'll bring the food in here when it's delivered." She headed for the door.

"Wait," Cory said. Leaning to the side, he pulled a money clip from his pocket, peeled off a bill, and handed it to Max. Riley did the same.

CHAPTER TWENTY-THREE

The next morning, Riley walked into the office carrying two containers of coffee and a bag. He placed one of the containers down in front of her.

"Thank you." She removed the lid and sipped. "You look exhausted. What's up?" Max asked.

He released a groan. "We had a shitload of kids at the house last night for a pre-Halloween party, who giggled like hyenas on speed. Geesh! Had my wife told me we were planning to host an overnighter, I might have spent the night in the city. Need I say more about a sleepless night?" Riley removed the cover from his container, added sugar and cream, stirred, and drank. "I'm likely to need lots of this stuff today," he spoke through his yawn. "In fact, I may not make it through the day." He opened the bag and offered Max first dibs on a pastry.

Peeking inside the bag, she saw two orange-frosted donuts with multicolored sprinkles. She frowned.

"It's Halloween month, Max."

"Ah, how could I forget." She laughed and reached inside her briefcase for her wallet out and flipped him a twenty-dollar bill. "I hope it's just kids trick or treating and not the weirdos of the world dressing up in costume."

"Yeah, my kids are all revved up about having a weekend sitting around eating candy."

"You won't let them do that, will you?"

He scrunched his face. "Are you kidding? You think I want to spend my salary on unnecessary dental bills? My wife rations it so that it's spread out over the next month." Riley pushed her money back, but she shoved the bill into his jacket pocket anyway.

"This was to be my treat today." He protested, but it made no difference, because Max wasn't giving in. "Thank you," she said, "but you have a family of five. I don't even have a cat. Let this be my treat."

He sighed, pulled the money from his jacket, and shoved it into his pants pocket.

"Thank you . . . So listen," Riley said, "on my way into work this morning, I was going over a few things in my mind, and I'm curious about why you're still so certain Jack killed Helen, and not Barrett or the senator."

"At this point, Riley, I'm not sure who did it. Other than the solid evidence of Jack's threat that no one at the restaurant has disputed, his sneaky stairway behavior and lying, our case doesn't have much traction. The fact that Barrett's having an affair with the senator doesn't prove he killed his wife. True, it's a strong component, but it isn't enough to accuse him," she responded.

"But what if there's more to this than you're looking at?" Riley asked. "The very fact that Cory is so adamant about Jack's innocence says a lot about the guy. Couple that with the woman at the restaurant who wanted to protect Jack."

"I understand what you're saying, Riley, but remember that Cory and Jack are best friends, and Cory knew nothing about Jack's financial problems. And he sure as hell didn't know about Jack leaving his apartment that night, or that he had threatened Helen Barrett. If they're such good friends, why didn't Jack share any of that with him? Couple those factors with Jack's explosives training, and we have a strong case. Add on the fact that we're now friends with Cory, it makes it muddled. I don't want that to cloud our judgment. We deal in facts and evidence proving those facts. I need to play devil's advocate here."

"Yeah," Riley said, "but during our search of Jack's residence, we didn't find any bombs or the material to make one. I didn't find anything in his storage unit either, and the rest of what we have is circumstantial—except for his threat to kill Helen Barrett."

"In a court of law, it doesn't matter what Jack's comment was. All that matters to a jury is witness testimony. And since we have three who will testify to what they heard"—she stretched her arms straight out—"Jack's guilt is a slam dunk."

"Yes, Max, but then Jeffrey Barrett gets away with murder."

"May I remind you we didn't find any bomb-related material in the Barrett house either," she pointed out and tilted her head to the side. "If these new homicides show me they are somehow related to Helen's murder, we'll pursue every new lead with a vengeance. It's not like I'm hell-bent on putting Jack away. I couldn't do that if I didn't think he was guilty."

Riley chose what he wanted from the bag, and then Max pulled out the remaining scone. "Although I'm thrilled to work with you, Riley," she announced with an eye roll, "I have to say, you have a sweet tooth, and getting into these pants this morning was a bit of a chore."

"Yeah, right," he said with a twist of his mouth. He muffled a yawn with his hand, and she yawned in return.

"Geez," Riley said. "We're a good pair this morning."

She grabbed a napkin from the bag, placed the scone on top, and broke off a piece, placing it into her mouth.

They both looked up when Lieutenant Wallace stopped to talk.

"Hey, good morning," Max said. "Riley and I will be meeting with Detectives Lou Lucio from the 17th and Larry Howe from the 22nd today. They're handling the two open cases I mentioned to you yesterday. We need to find out what evidence they have," Max said.

"What makes that a logical move?"

Max responded, "If what we suspect about these two victims is true, that they're related to the administrator and heart transplant coordinator who work at Mount Sinai, then sitting down to put our heads together might prove worthwhile. Maybe they've found things we haven't that will point us in another direction, and then maybe not, but it's worth a shot."

"I agree," Wallace said. "All right, we'll catch up later." He turned and walked over to Bensonhurst and Santini's area.

Detective Louis Lucio was just finishing up an interview with a suspect when the team entered his precinct's main office area.

"I'll be ready in a minute," he said, holding up his finger.

Detective Lucio was a nice-looking, clean-cut man with a few pock-marks from teenage acne, short dark brown hair, and dark eyes. He was neatly dressed. Max noticed his jaw muscles flicker, a sure sign he was stressed, but that was the nature of the job. She and Riley were escorted to an interview room by one of the clerks. It wasn't long before Lucio walked into the room with a tall, thin man whose face was lined with deep insets from what appeared to be a chronic scowl. Max figured him to be Detective Howe. He placed his file folder down on the conference table. After introductions were made, Max led the discussion about Helen's death and detailed the evidence they had, passing her paperwork and photographs around the table for everyone to see.

"Christ," Lucio said, "it sounds to me like you've got your guy, so why the prolonged investigation?"

"Look, guys," Riley said, "our field manuals clearly state that our first question in any case should be *Is this related to anything else?* Either the answer to that question is a resounding no or there's a killer who thinks he's outsmarted us by picking victims and locations in different precincts so we'll never suspect they are related. I don't know which of those is true, or why those two victims were chosen, but that's why this meeting is so important to us."

Max glanced over at Howe, who might have read Riley as a smartass. Riley must have picked up on it too and nodded for Max to continue.

"So this is what we have so far on our case," Max said and continued sharing the pertinent information. Howe listened with a deep frown on his face. Despite his frown, Max ignored him and continued. "Mount Sinai is where our victim's husband works. He's well-known for his skill in heart transplants. You may have heard of him, Dr. Jeffrey Barrett. He was recently in the newspaper and I believe on the cover of *Time* magazine when he performed a transplant on Senator Stansbury's daughter." The men agreed with a nod.

"He's also the head of the transplant center. Because the names of your victims match two of the women who work there, we think these cases might be linked somehow," Max said. "Why don't you tell us about your cases? We might have the hub of a wheel with many spokes, and it would make all our lives easier if we found out we're working on the same case."

"Okay," Lucio said. "Here's a copy of my report on Sharlene Chambers-Inghrams's homicide," Lucio said, giving his head a slow shake. "This is a very sad story. The young woman was out shopping at Macy's during one of those Moonlight Madness sales that let the shoppers get a head start on the holidays. You know, one of those all-nighters where hordes of shoppers wait outside in the bitter cold for the doors to open at midnight?"

"We talked to her friend Dianne Orofino, who was the last person she'd spoken to, and Ms. Orofino confirmed that our victim called her at about two-twenty in the morning—even woke her up out of a sound sleep, but she said they were like sisters and she didn't mind. But the reason she'd called was to complain about a confrontation she'd had with another customer. We also learned from this friend that Sharlene's mother was supposed to go with her, but was tired and decided to stay home at the last minute, and watch the granddaughter instead."

"Do you have the mother's name?"

"I do." He slid his finger down the report and stopped. "Yes, her mother's name is Melanie Chambers."

"Oh boy," Max said. "If she's the Melanie Chambers in our case, she's the organ and procurement coordinator for heart transplants at Mount Sinai." Max smiled at Riley, knowing there was a connection. "Okay, please continue. Those sales bring out the worst in people. Do you know what the confrontation was about?" she asked.

"It was over an item of clothing." Lucio rubbed his cheek with his shoulder and continued to talk. "The store security also verified the incident. It seems like a tug-of-war commenced between our victim and a Carlos Perez. Store security intervened and escorted Mr. Perez out to the parking lot, but when we spoke to him, his alibi checked out.

"During the course of the two friends' chat, Ms. Orofino said there was a sudden stop in the conversation when the victim released a blood-curdling scream, then a gurgling sound, a loud thud, and a final deafening silence. The events were so horrifying, she started screaming and ran to her house phone to dial 911.

"Uniforms tracked Sharlene down by her cell phone." Lucio pulled photographs of the crime scene out of an envelope and placed them down in the center of the table for them to view.

"By the time our guys got there, the attendant had already realized something was wrong, because he'd made his second round of patrol and realized her motor was still running. He was standing by the car when our guys arrived. He told them he knew something was wrong when she didn't respond to a tap on the driver's side window.

"Flashing his light inside and seeing the blood, he called 911 as well." Lucio's report held everyone captive. "When I arrived on the scene and opened the door, it wasn't locked. The killer apparently wanted out of there in a hurry. The distinct odor of acrid blood hit me in the face. I could see this woman's head leaning back against the seat. Checking a little closer, her head was barely hanging on by a thread. This was the work of someone very angry. We're definitely ruling this a homicide."

Lucio took a slug of water to moisten his dry mouth. "It was apparent she'd put up a struggle because her body was in an awkward position, and there was blood all over the place, including massive spattering on the windshield. Two of her fingers on the right hand were severed and found on the carpeted floor, indicating she'd fought hard. Her cell phone was on the passenger's side floor. Her purse was nowhere to be found, so we had no idea who she was. We did find the registration in the glove compartment, and we checked the plates as well. The car is registered to a Melanie Chambers. It was much later that Sharlene's purse was found in a trash can down on the second tier of the garage. Everything was intact. Money and credit cards still in the wallet."

"And where was she parked?"

"On the fourth tier." Lucio pointed to the photograph of her neck. "This guy is no amateur. Look at this clean cut across the neck." He pointed to the picture with the ruler. "It's six inches in length and two inches below her jaw, which severed the carotid artery and other vessels that caused the hemorrhage." Max and Riley were nodding in agreement.

"Yeah, it's as clean a cut as a surgeon's incision," Riley said.

"No visible signs of break-in, no fingerprints, no fibers, no nothing, which usually indicates a slim-jim was used. After our investigators removed the door panels, they confirmed it was indeed a slim-jim based on the scratch marks on the X plate that holds the window frame." Lucio's lips tightened, causing a muscle to flicker in his jaw. "We had hoped to find prints on the dome light that had been disabled, but that proved fruitless. The killer definitely knows what he's doing."

"That poor woman," Max said. "What a brutal way to die."

"I'll say. Because of the horrific nature of the crime and the fact that nothing was removed from her wallet, and everything else was intact, we believe our killer has an ax to grind. Until today, we've had no leads, but after listening to your case, it's beginning to sound like they may be related somehow." Lucio picked up a bottle of water and unscrewed the cap, slugging back another drink.

"We've questioned the victim's estranged husband, who was fighting for custody of their three-year-old daughter. There was legal action going on between the two, but now that she's dead, he'll get his custody. Naturally, he was our first suspect, but he's in Florida shacking up with his current main squeeze." Lucio rubbed his hand across his jawline.

"The Chambers woman told us the father hadn't started paying support yet, so she was paying the freight since her daughter didn't have a job." He shrugged. "Our forensic investigators combed the fabric off the seats in the vehicle for fibers or hair follicles to no avail, and we're thinking it's because he must have worn a suit or something." Lucio held up his hands. "That's all I've got so far."

Next was Howe's turn. His face remained void of emotion while he spoke. "I don't know what to think about my case with this sixteen-year-old. I've gone back and forth with various witnesses, but no one seems to know anything. Surveillance has been viewed a million times, and we've interviewed nurses who had access to the recovery room, orderlies, and the nurse who administers the drugs—we came up empty." Howe looked up from the report to catch his breath, then continued. "Fortunately, they're all cooperating, but the nurses are really shaken, and rightfully so, because we're still looking at them."

Lucio said, "Who else has access to those meds besides the one nurse on that floor?"

"No one. We did find an empty syringe in the trash can in the public restroom down the hall from the kid's room. The lab is testing the inside of it to determine if it's the same drug that killed her. Not surprising, there are no prints. Our forensic experts have combed the room for clothing fibers, and they did find several pieces; maybe they'll contain the person's DNA. All are currently being analyzed by the lab, as is a small thread that turned out to be canvas. We're speculating it could have been from a duffel bag. Whether it's the killer's or not, we don't know, but we hope it shows something when it's analyzed."

Max's mind temporarily blocked out Howe's monotone voice, wondering how his peers worked alongside a man who showed little emotion. Forcing herself back, she sat up straighter in her chair.

Howe continued. "We've checked the meds against the surgeries performed at New York Presbyterian, but it all balances out. I can't imagine the nurses are covering for one another, but you never know. As for any link to your case, the child's parents don't work at Mount Sinai, so where's the connection?"

"Did you check the database for the kid's relatives?" Riley asked.

"How about Valerie Morrison? Does that ring a bell?" Max asked.

Howe immediately checked through his notes. "Okay, I did speak to her, but she arrived after the kid died. My notes say she's the aunt—sister of the victim's father. I think I'll go talk to her again." Howe pinched his nose. "I still can't get over the fact that these parents allowed a sixteen-year-old to have a nose job because some kid where she volunteers told her she looked like Pinocchio. It's just absurd." He shook his head again. "Parents today are too easy on their kids." Howe's perturbed voice rose.

"Do you know where she volunteered?" Max asked.

"I don't know, some preschool." He shrugged. "All I know is she read stories every week to the kids. Why is that significant?" Howe asked.

"Because our victim founded a preschool called The Little Tykes Academy. If she worked there, maybe it's connected somehow," Riley responded, trying to get a word in edgewise.

Turning toward Lucio, Max questioned him next. "Do you know if Sharlene's daughter was enrolled in a daycare facility?"

"Now, that's interesting," Lucio said. "I will check it out and get back to you."

"You might also consider checking with all the surrounding hospitals to ask if their drug usage is on target," Max suggested.

"Good point. We should both check on that," Lucio said to Howe, who nodded in agreement.

"Okay," Howe said, giving the table a knock with his knuckle, "it looks like we do have some similarities, Max, and I don't think we can ignore those nuances. All these cases have possible connections that start with your victim."

Max gathered her paperwork and stood to leave, tossing her empty coffee container in the trash can along the way. "Let's keep each other in the loop so we can compare notes as we go along. Thanks for meeting us today. We'll talk soon."

Riley and Max walked to the car. "I think we should examine the hospital medical records for patients who have grievances against Mount Sinai or Barrett." He switched his briefcase into his other hand. "When you consider how much time patients needing transplants have spent in the hospital leading up to the actual transplant, there's bound to be a lot of complaints." He unlocked the car and opened the back door, putting his briefcase on the backseat.

"This is an excellent time to do that, Riley." She checked her notes. "The Stansbury child had her transplant on July 2, so let's request files from April through October. If we don't find anything, then we'll go back farther."

"I'll call the ADA for the subpoena when we get back to the precinct and serve them on Mrs. Morrison. It's going to take forty-eight hours for their legal team to review and ask questions anyway," Riley said.

"And while you're at it, I also want warrants for Stansbury's and Barrett's offices, residences, and even their yachts."

"You've got it."

After easing into traffic, Riley brushed a hand over his face and released an exhausted sigh, catching Max's attention. "Boy, after last night's slumber party, I'm glad we didn't have the number of kids my wife said she wanted when we first married. I never would have survived."

"As my sister always says, every parent should experience a slumber party just once." She grinned. "It's all good."

"Yeah, real good"—Riley deadpanned—"when someone else has the party." He chuckled. "It was good for the boys, though."

When Max's phone rang, she smiled at seeing Cory's name flash across the screen, and her heart skipped a beat.

"I was wondering if you'd join me for dinner tonight?" he said. Without waiting for her to respond, he interjected a thought. "I mean, you have to eat, so it might as well be with me so we can talk."

"Okay, yes, I'd like that. Where would you like to meet?"

"Do you like Mexican food?"

"I do."

"Toloache. You okay with that?"

"More than okay," Max said, as Riley weaved the car through the traffic. "I have a busy day today, but will look forward to our meeting."

"I take it Riley's sitting next to you."

"That would be correct."

Cory gave a low chuckle. "Okay, I'll make the reservations for six thirty," he said. "Pick you up outside the precinct." She thought she heard him sigh. "I can't wait," he said and disconnected. His comment had her pulse pounding.

She set the phone down next to her then glanced over at Riley, who was grinning. She asked herself who she thought she was kidding. If Riley didn't suspect something, then he wasn't paying attention.

Max meandered outside the precinct door and was surprised to see Cory get out of a cab.

The wide smile on his face told her he was excited to see her. "I figured I'd let someone else do the driving tonight so I can give you my undivided attention." Her stomach felt like a million butterflies were doing jumping jacks. Just as she was ducking down into the vehicle, he snuck in a kiss. "Sorry, I've been holding on to that, and I couldn't let the moment pass."

Max kissed him back. "Me too."

He reached his arm around her, and she leaned her head on his shoulder. His nearness gave her a feeling of complete contentment, as though this was where she belonged.

When the cab pulled up in front of the restaurant, Max was reminded of how much curb appeal it had. The familiar wooden-framed French doors seemed to be an architectural staple since most of the restaurants on that street used them. In addition to giving the place a homey feel, it also gave passersby a view of the busy dining room. During the warmer weather when the doors were left open, the aroma of food permeated the air and lured customers inside. Of course, having Times Square just mere blocks away didn't hurt either.

Cory held the door open for Max to walk inside. She stopped to admire the brick walls dotted with white plaster, which provided the framework for the décor, an authentic touch of old Mexico. Arched window inserts above each table supported wine storage above them. The core of the restaurant had two rows of tables and a long bar on the opposite side of the dining room to meet everyone's needs.

After being greeted by the hostess, Cory requested a quiet spot. It was still early by New York's standard dinner hour, which was after nine o'clock. The hostess weaved through the restaurant and led them to the perfect table next to a crackling fire.

"So what's on your mind?" Max asked after the waiter took their drink orders.

He chuckled. "You are always on my mind. You've been working extra hard, and I thought this would be a good opportunity for us to relax together and let our hair down. Do you think you can relax and not think about work?"

"How sweet of you. I can absolutely do that. Thank you."

"I also thought it would be a good time for us to discuss our relationship." Cory held her gaze in an unflinching stare, obviously waiting for her reaction to his comment. "I know you're feeling something."

She laughed. "Cory, Cory, Cory, you're such a romantic."

"Are you saying that's a bad thing?" he asked.

"Not at all. You make me smile because you always seem to say the right things . . . most of the time." She stopped talking when the waiter set the margaritas down in front of them. They each took a sip. "That goes down nice and easy," Max said. "Maybe a little too easy."

"Max, I want us to be a couple," Cory blurted out.

She peered over the top of the menu. "You do?" Actually, she shouldn't have been surprised. He'd made no secret of the depth of his feelings for her. She set the menu down and steepled her fingers. "I'm truly flattered, honestly, I am, but how can you be so sure after only two dates?"

"Well, let's see. First, it's not just two dates, it's our third, and secondly, every time we're together feels like a date to me. Doesn't it feel that way to you?"

Hearing Cory's declaration made her heart swell—something she hadn't felt in years, but they had a long way to go yet. "Yes, I guess it does, well, except when we're at odds with one another."

"Yeah, but that's all part of the process. Seriously, you wouldn't want our relationship to be rosy all the time, would you?" He gave her an odd look. "Where's the fun in that? It's the discovery of each other's personalities, likes, and dislikes. That's what makes a romance solid, because by the time you fall madly in love, you've already learned the good, the bad, and the ugly. If you're still standing after all of that, then it's true love. That's what I want for us."

She could hear the sincerity in his words, and she certainly loved hearing all his wonderful compliments, but she was slightly apprehensive. "I told you before, I don't want to be your rebound girl."

"Oh Lord." He heaved a breath. "Max, please get this through that head of yours, you're not. I swear to you. I went with Lyndsey for three months—I wasn't in love with her, so how could you be a rebound? I'm not going to say I haven't dated other women, and I won't tell you I didn't have a long relationship while I was in law school, but that was more about being away from home and out on my own. Besides, Lyndsey wanted to wear the pants in our relationship. I believe in equal partnerships, and then after that breakup, the rest were just dates because I no longer trusted women. But what we're building is different. Whenever we're together, it feels like the beginning of spring when the air smells sweet from the budding trees." He reached for her hand and she felt the electricity of his touch surge through her like a delicious blitz of heat.

"I've never had anyone say such nice things to me, and sometimes it feels like I'm dreaming and it's not reality."

"Does it scare you?"

"A little."

"In what way? Like I'm being insincere?"

"I guess."

"Well, let me assure you that I have never"—he held his hand up to swear—"said these things to any other woman—not even the one in law school. Being with you feels natural to me, so why look further? I just want to cultivate what we have and keep it going."

"Okay. I concede and definitely agree we have something very special going on between us." She grinned a wide smile, no longer hiding the excitement. It was true, she was crazy about this man, and if she had only one wish, it would be to make him feel as secure with her as she felt when she was with him.

"The truth is I knew you were special on that first date," he said. "When a man knows, he knows. And regardless of how Jack's case turns out, I'm still going to be crazy about you. It'll break my heart if he is found guilty, but I'll just have to accept his fate." He stopped talking when the waiter appeared and interrupted the conversation. "Do you know what you want to eat?" he asked. She nodded and they ordered their food. They continued the conversation after the waiter walked away.

Max liked knowing he was crazy about her. If they could get along after this case, maybe they were meant to be together. If not, nothing ventured, nothing gained. "And I'm sure you want to know when I knew we had something special?"

"Of course." He shut his eyes tight as though afraid of what she was going to say. "Please tell me. I'm dying to know."

"When you told me the truth about what happened with your suspension. You went from zero to thirty in a matter of seconds."

"So I guess it is a good thing I didn't accept your invitation to your apartment that night."

"Yeah, it probably was."

"So what do you want to know about me?" he asked.

"You said you were very close to your family. Tell me about them."

He smiled warmly. "I have a great family."

"It sure sounds it." She took another sip of her drink.

"I come from an immigrant family who came to the United States from Italy. My grandfather was a blue-collar worker who never missed a day of work. When he first arrived at Ellis Island, he met my friend Greg's grandfather, and together they partnered in a clothing business with the few dollars they'd saved up before coming to the States. Their hard work and determination paid off, because their business thrived and provided both families a secure future. After my parents married, my father, whose dream was to work in a restaurant in the States, and eventually open his own, quickly learned starting at the bottom was not going to give him the kind of wages he needed to support a family, so he went to work for my grandfather. There's three of us. I have two amazing sisters who dote on me, and of course, I love it. My family and Greg's built a profitable company out of nothing."

The arrival of the food had both of them inhaling the smell. Cory didn't waste any time digging in. "All through my childhood, every Sunday and every holiday, the entire family, with all the in-laws and Greg's entire family in tow, gathered around my parents' table to have a feast."

"Aw, that sounds so wonderful. You're a good family man, Cory Rossini."

"Thank you. How about you?" he asked.

"I have my sister, Julie, who has twin girls."

"That's right. You did mention a sister," he said.

She nodded. "My sister and I are two years apart. Our father died when I was just a baby, and eventually my mother remarried. The man she married was a lout—drank, couldn't hold down a job. My mother worked two jobs, often the night shift, to support all of us. My mother was an angel, and I adored her." Max stopped talking and swallowed hard.

"What's wrong?"

"It's hard talking about it because I relive those days every time it comes to my mind."

"Then, Max, stop, you don't have to tell me anything."

"No, I do. If we're ever going to make this work, you need to know everything about me." She took a deep breath and blew it out, pausing to find the right words. After a few seconds, she knew there was no right way to say it and finally blurted it out. "My adoptive father abused me and my sister, although I had no idea she was going through the same thing until the ordeal was over." Cory's mouth dropped open. He reached for her hand and rubbed his thumb over her skin. "It started when I was eight years old." Cory shook his head in disbelief.

Her eyes lowered while she played with the wrapper from the straw in her drink, refusing to make eye contact. "Someday I'll tell you everything, but for right now, let's just say it was horrible." Max fought off her emotions, trying not to make a spectacle of herself in a public place.

"Our only blessing after that horrible time was knowing he would be in prison for the rest of his life, and *that* somehow helped us, because we knew he wasn't getting away with anything. But the real celebration was learning that he'd been killed by an inmate when he bragged about what he'd done to my sister and me."

"Oh God. That bastard got what he deserved!" Cory got out of his seat and squeezed in next to her in the booth. "I knew you were a strong woman, Max, but now I'm in awe of your courage." He leaned over and whispered into her ear, "I'm sure it wasn't an easy time, and trying to forget what happened must have been a struggle, but you made it, and today, you've developed into a beautiful human being. I think you're amazing!" He leaned back and stared at her for a moment. "I can't tell you what it means to me that you've shared this part of your life with me. I can only imagine how hard it was."

"Thank you for saying that." She gave him an appreciative smile. The heavy weight in her chest dissipated, and she was glad she'd told him. Not that she thought he'd have second thoughts about her, but because she was able to share it with him—something she'd never done before, and it made her realize he meant more to her than she'd been willing to admit.

Max cleared her throat and told him about the rest of her family. "My sister, Julie, lives here in New York, with her husband, Mike, and their rambunctious nine-year-old girls, who drive my sister crazy. And the only other relatives I have, besides my cousin, John, who is a priest, are the overseers of the convent we lived in after our stepfather's incarceration: Monsignor Bishop and Reverend Mother Francis Louise, who became my mother, for all intents and purposes."

"I'm surprised you didn't become a nun." Cory returned to his side of the booth and looked at her.

Max laughed. "Funny you should say that. I actually did go through the two-year candidacy, but every time I tried to let go of my past, it came back to haunt me. I bowed out and told the Reverend Mother that my calling was law enforcement. She understood without me even going into a long list of reasons."

"And your sister's okay too?" Cory asked.

Max nodded. "She's very happy."

Max cut into her chili relleno and took a bite when a mariachi band began to play, a welcomed intrusion after baring her soul.

"I'm curious," she said, "will you go back to practicing law after your suspension is lifted?"

"I'm ambivalent at the moment, although I plan to keep the title at least until I finish using my new business cards." He grinned. "Truth be told, I'm really enjoying this PI stuff, but that might be because I've met you. I'm a firm believer in fate. If I hadn't broken up with Lyndsey, if my suspension hadn't happened, then I wouldn't have met you." Now it was Max who was sliding her open hand across the table, and he latched on.

"I wish none of that had happened to you," she said. "But I am impressed with your acceptance and willingness to do the right thing."

"My troubles pale by comparison to what you've lived through, Max. I'm grateful I only got suspended."

"What happened to your clients?"

"Once they heard, they bailed, and I don't blame them one damn bit."

They walked out of the restaurant hand-in-hand and the close connection Max felt with him was overwhelming. "Want to come back to my apartment?" she asked. If he was shocked by her invitation, he didn't show it. "I still have some decadent brownies my sister insisted I take home with me from the pasta dinner the other night. I don't want to eat them all by myself." His mouth broadened into a wide smile.

"I thought you'd never ask. Does this mean we're going to become a couple?" Max didn't respond. A taxi pulled up in front. Passengers were just getting out to go into the restaurant. Cory and Max got inside, and Max gave the cabbie her address. She sat back and they snuggled close to one another. Max could barely handle the anticipation, and when they stopped in front of her building, Cory paid the tab then exited the vehicle. He walked up the stairs behind her and waited for her to unlock the door to the brownstone.

"Brace yourself. It may be messy."

"I'll keep my eyes closed. How does that sound?" Cory didn't give her a chance to respond because the minute the door closed, he had her in a tight embrace and his lips were devouring her mouth, sending a jolt of undeniable passion through her body. She felt weak in the knees, and all she wanted to do was pull him down onto her bed. He nuzzled her neck and his hot breath sent her senses soaring out of control. Their breathing increased to a pant. When Cory could no longer take it, he stepped back.

"I want you so bad, Max," he whispered.

"Me too." Her breathy words came out crystal clear. "Right now."

He pointed toward the hall. She nodded and he slowly backed her toward the bedroom as they each pulled at one another's clothing, leaving a trail of garments on the floor. The heat between them intensified. Reaching the room, Cory scooped her naked body up into his arms and gently eased her down onto the bed, kissing every part of her body, starting with her toes. And when he entered her, she begged him never to stop.

CHAPTER
TWENTY-FOUR

"We're off to the hospital to go through the medical records at Mount Sinai," Max said when Cory answered her wake-up call. He'd been sleeping so soundly when she'd left, she didn't have the heart to disturb him. Besides, she liked seeing him in her bed.

"Do you need help?" he asked.

"Thank you for offering, but it's not allowed. HIPAA will be all over us," she said, making sure she sounded professional so Riley would not suspect they'd spent the night together. "We're only allowed to have six months' worth of records, and only under complete supervision. I hope we find what we're looking for right away."

"By the way, you were wonderful, you know that?" Hearing his compliment sent currents of pleasure through her stomach and had her wishing she was lying next to him.

"Thanks. My sentiments exactly."

"Mmm, you're welcome," he said in a dreamy voice. "Am I going to see you tomorrow or will you be sleeping all day?"

"Both," she said. "By the way, I left a house key for you on the kitchen counter."

"Thank you for entrusting your apartment to me in your absence. Okay, we'll discuss tomorrow over dinner tonight—that is, if you're free and don't have a hot date with someone else."

"Oh, I'm as free as a bird. I'll pencil you in on my calendar," she teased.

"That's very kind of you," he joked right back. "Text me when you're ready and I'll meet you outside the precinct."

"That sounds like a wonderful idea," she said, noticing Riley was ready. "Listen, I'd better go. We're ready to rock 'n' roll over here."

"Have a great day."

"You too." Max sighed and disconnected the call. "Are you ready, hotshot?" Max asked Riley when she turned around.

"Yes, I am."

After finding the appropriate floor, Max and Riley exited the elevator and followed the signs to the administrator's office. Stopping at the secretary's desk, Max identified who they were and held up her badge. "We're here to review the hospital's medical records." Hearing a voice from behind, Max turned.

"I'm Valerie Morrison, the hospital administrator, and I haven't received a call from my legal department giving me the okay yet, " she said. Her secretary called out to her. She excused herself and picked up the receiver. Max heard her chastise whoever was on the other end of the phone for not letting her know. As soon as she disconnected, she dialed another number. Minutes later, she was on her way over to Max and Riley.

"Okay, Detectives. That call was from our legal department. I guess it's better late than never." She gave a slight nod and turned to the young woman. "Margaret, please escort these detectives to our conference room." Turning to Max, she continued. "The files are currently being transferred to the room."

"Thank you, Mrs. Morrison," Max said. "It's nice to have your cooperation." The pair followed Margaret to the elevator.

When they reached the room, the files were already on the table when Margaret unlocked the door. The room was a normal plain conference room with a long table and chairs around it. Pieces of art hung on the wall.

"As you can see, you have plenty to check, but allow me to give you a few pointers. The year any incident occurred is marked on the outside of the file folders. Then," she said, pointing to the front of the file boxes, "the alphabetical markers are in the front."

"Do you have an inventory of all the files?" Max asked.

"As a matter of fact, we do," she said. "Why don't you get set up while I return to the records room and make a copy of the complete list of our files." Margaret left the room.

"Why don't we split these files in half, Riley."

"That's fine."

Ten minutes later, Margaret returned to the room. "Here's the list. As you can see," she said, running her finger down the line items, "it's broken down by month, the name of the complainant, and the category in which their complaint belongs."

"Great! That really makes this task easier."

"Happy hunting," Margaret said, pulling out a business card. "Here's my card with my direct contact number in case you need to get in touch with me." Margaret reached out and handed a spiral wrist keychain bracelet to Max that had the room key on the end. "Take this in case you need to leave the room, but please remember to call me when you're finished for the day so I can pick it up and return the files to their proper place."

"Of course. Thank you. I won't forget."

As soon as the door closed, Max noticed Riley staring at the long row of boxes they were about to dig into. She grinned when she heard him sigh.

"Oh boy! This job is going to take a lot of caffeine," he said.

"So who wants to go for coffee?" Max asked Riley.

"Nicely played, Max."

"Well, I was giving you an option. Look at it this way, Riley: trudging down to the cafeteria gives you another half hour of freedom before you have to tackle the files. How's that?" When Riley didn't move, she prodded. "Should I give you more time to talk yourself into it?"

Riley groaned. "Point taken, Max. Tell me what you want."

"I'll take a large black coffee."

"Do you want anything else?" Riley asked.

Max had a good answer for that, but vocalizing it might have Riley blushing. "That's it. Thanks, Riley," she said as he walked out the door.

Max checked the boxes and leafed through the files until Riley returned about twenty minutes later with the coffee. "My God, we have a whole lot of work ahead of us today," she said.

"Okay, so tell me specifically what we're looking for."

"Anything having to do with patient complaints, medical malpractice, unresolved issues, and specifically those where Barrett was involved. For now, we'll just pile the Barrett files up on this table to review them together."

After three hours of bending over and checking the files, they each stopped at the same time. Max stretched her arms over her head and yawned, wishing their search was finished and they could move on to the next thing. "How freakin' boring is this?"

"Yeah, I have to agree with you on that one," Riley said.

"Judging from the pace so far," Max said, "we're never going to get these files reviewed by end of day."

Riley made a face. "And I'm not giving up my weekend off. I promised the kids I'd spend the entire weekend with them doing whatever they wanted."

"We're not," Max confirmed. "I've already put in a request for someone to finish what we started. Wallace was in agreement. We'll be taking off."

Riley blew out a breath. "If we work tomorrow, this would be the third weekend."

"I know. We need to clear our heads."

"Hear, hear!" Riley exclaimed. "That being said, I could really use a lunch break. How about we go down to the cafeteria for coffee and something to eat," he suggested.

Max chuckled. "I'm not crazy about the shuffling through boxes either.

Riley blew out a breath. "Amen."

She pointed to the closed door and nodded. "Let's go eat."

The pair exited the elevator on the ground level and followed the signs for the cafeteria.

Walking inside, Riley got in line with the throng of medical staff who were waiting in the grilled-foods line, while Max headed for the salad bar, filling her bowl with all her favorites. Reaching the condiments section, she removed two small containers and filled them with salad dressing. On her way to check out, she noticed Riley had a lot of food on his tray, and was surprised when he stopped at the soft-serve station to fill a bowl to the brim with frozen yogurt. She paid for her food, walked out into the dining room, and was looking for an empty table when she heard a familiar voice behind her.

"Detective Turner?"

She turned to face Jeffrey Barrett.

"Investigating. How are you, Dr. Barrett?"

"I'm getting better every day. What are you investigating?"

"Now, you know I can't tell you that. It's nice to see you."

"I don't want to bug you, Detective, but you'll let me know if you have anything to report, right?" he said sharply. Max just smiled and nodded slightly.

Riley was frowning when he approached the table, having noticed Barrett walking away. He gave Max a questioning look. "He wanted to know why we were here," she said, popping the lid off the small container of salad dressing that she poured over the leaves. "I asked how he was doing, and—"

Riley interrupted. "Wait. Let me guess. He wanted assurance that you'd contact him if you had anything to report."

"Exactly."

Riley chewed on a french fry. "When is the team serving the other warrants?" he asked.

"Monday morning." They made small talk until they finished their lunches. Then Max released a sigh. "Sadly, lunch break is over."

"Yeah, I know. It's back to the salt mines."

Back in the room, Max eyed the pile of tagged files. Sitting down, she opened the first file. "Okay, it looks like this patient's family sued Barrett for malpractice because he prescribed the wrong medication and the patient had a stroke. The suit was settled in the plaintiff's favor." Placing the file aside, she opened the next one. "Here's another malpractice," she said as her eyes scanned the information, "and it looks like the plaintiff lost." She pushed the folder over to Riley. "Let's get a copy of all the proceedings from this case, contact the attorneys of record, and see what we can find out. The plaintiff's name is Mifflin, and he claims he was not notified about the side effects of a procedure and now has issues with blurred vision. It says the court ruled in favor of the defendant."

Scanning the file, Riley remarked, "I'm surprised the court allowed the case to even go to trial. With the kind of malpractice doctors face today, they have all their patients sign their lives away before any surgery." He read down a little further. "Yep," he said, "that's exactly what happened. The guy had forgotten he signed the papers and lost his case, nor did he read the fine print. That's too bad," Riley said. "I really can't wait to see what we find when we do the searches on Stansbury and Barrett. I think we're going to open a huge can of worms."

"Yeah," Max said, "bring on the worms. I've asked to have four teams serve those warrants simultaneously before either of them has time to hide anything."

Checking the time, Max looked at Riley. "Shall we call it a day?"

"I love the sound of that song. Let's call Margaret and let's get out of here."

Parking the car in the underground garage, Riley cut the engine and turned to Max. "I feel like a kid excited the school year is over."

"Me too," Max said. "Now, get out of here," she told him. He saluted and rushed down the street to the subway. Before walking into Wallace's office, Max texted Cory.

Max was happy to see Cory standing next to his car with the door open for her when she exited the precinct. She rushed over and kissed him. "You're a sight for sore eyes, Cory Rossini," she said.

"Right back atcha." He backed out of the space and gradually eased into the traffic. "You look exhausted."

"I am."

"Well, I've planned a very quiet evening tonight."

"Oh good, because the last thing I want to do is to see anyone other than you."

"Well, then this should work out well." She gave him a curious look. "Dinner is waiting at your apartment."

"Who did you order from?" she asked.

"You'll see."

"Ooh, that sounds exciting."

He laughed. "Now put your head back and rest."

It seemed like only a few minutes had passed when Max felt a hand shaking her. She blinked her eyes open and stretched her hands over her head. "I guess I snoozed."

"You needed it."

Mounting the steps, Max unlocked the front door and inhaled the smell of Italian food. "Is it my apartment that smells so good?"

"I believe it is," he said as they both entered the kitchen. A red tablecloth was draped over the table, with a candle in the center dividing the place settings where two glasses of wine waited for them.

Max glanced around the room, surprised by the sight. "You know how to cook?"

"I do."

"You made me spaghetti sauce?"

"I did." He pulled out the chair. "Now sit while I finish." He handed her the glass of wine. "Salute," he said.

Max sipped her wine and watched in amazement as Cory made his way around the kitchen, a skill she totally lacked.

"Can I help?" she asked.

"Nope. You just sit and relax," he said as he ladled sauce over the spaghetti and set it down in front of her. Max leaned forward and smelled the food.

"Cory Rossini, you are full of surprises. You absolutely amaze me."

"That's a good thing, isn't it?" he asked, amusement curling the corners of his mouth.

"Uh-huh. You are a man of many talents, and I'm in awe."

"Thank you," he said with pride. "That's some endorsement."

Max chewed the spaghetti. "Oh man, if you ever need someone to cook for, I'm your girl."

"I was hoping you were my girl, but then you placed that hold on our relationship until after the case is done."

Max laughed. "Yeah, and you see how well that's going, don't you?"

"What? The case or the hold?"

"The hold." She blew him a kiss.

"So what's on your agenda for this weekend?" he asked.

"Sleep in late, then get up and lounge around the house all day. Maybe go out in the evenings." She grinned. "Do you want to hang out with me?"

"Starting when?" he asked with a curious tone.

"Starting right now."

Cory's gaze narrowed as her meaning sunk in. He shoved off his chair, walked over to where she sat, and pulled her upright.

"Who can refuse an invitation like that?" he whispered in a heady voice, and moved in close, his mouth crushing down on hers with unyielding passion, sending delicious shivers through her body that had unleashed a reckless side she never knew existed.

Max took a step back. "I think it's time for dessert?" she said in a breathy voice. Curling her finger in a come-hither gesture, she walked toward the living room, stopping only to remove her clothing one piece at a time in a slow, sensual motion exposing her body, one length at a time. Cory's eyes hooded as he watched her, his breath coming in quick succession until he could no longer wait.

"Oh God" was all that he could say before he moved in and devoured her body.

The smell of coffee brewing stirred Max from a sound sleep. She smiled, thinking back to an unforgettable night. She sat up in bed when she heard the shuffle of Cory's feet across the floor, and smiled when he entered with an erection, knowing the next two days promised to be even better.

CHAPTER
TWENTY-FIVE

Riley was already fast at work when Max walked into the precinct on Monday morning. "How was your weekend?" he asked.

"Absolutely amazing."

"Mine was great too. It was nice being able to spend time with the family. What did you do?"

"Stayed in bed all day, and hung out at the apartment. It was just nice to stay in my pajamas the entire weekend." That wasn't exactly true, but she wasn't about to tell Riley that.

On the ride to the Midtown senate office, Max keyed in Cory's number. Being away from him for a few hours seemed like an eternity, and she just wanted to hear his voice.

Cory's cheerful voice pulled her from her trance of reliving their weekend of lovemaking. Max smiled. Record searching by day, love-making by night was definitely a nice bonus for a boring search that had proved to be a waste of time. Apparently Bensonhurst felt the same way, as stated on a note he'd left. Regardless, it was something they had to do, and now that it was done, they could move on to the next task: the property searches.

"Good morning," she said and felt her heart pick up its pace. "Just wanted to give you a heads-up that we have our warrants in hand and four teams will all be doing their searches simultaneously. Needless to say, we won't be at the hospital today."

"I knew that, silly," Cory exclaimed.

"I know."

"Oh, I get it. You wanted to hear my voice."

"I did." She released an embarrassed laugh.

"Hearing your voice under any circumstance is wonderful," Cory said. "You know, technically speaking, I hate Monday mornings, but after the weekend I just spent with the most amazing woman in the world, I'm still feeling the glow. How about you?"

"I'd say you've got that right."

"Oh, good." She could hear him sigh. "Okay, darn it, it's back to business. So listen, since you guys are going to be busy today, and neither Barrett nor the senator can hang out while you're searching, they have to go somewhere, so I think I'll put a tail on him to see where he goes. I doubt he'll be hanging out in a hotel room watching television."

"Be careful," she said.

"Thank you. I will."

Now, more than ever, Cory was convinced she really did care about him, and this weekend proved it. There was no way she was faking her feelings, because if she was, then she needed to be on Broadway. He released a sigh. Being in love felt good. His thoughts stalled when those words rang through his mind a second time. Yes, he was in love with

Max Turner, and it felt damn good to think those words and even better to say them, but he'd keep it to himself for now for fear she wasn't ready to hear them. Cory pulled his gray fedora off the rack, plopped it on his head, exited his house and walked out to the sidewalk. After stopping at the corner, he crossed the street when the light changed, and he walked the last block to the garage where his cars were parked. He pressed his remote button, and the old wooden garage door creaked when it lifted outward.

He contemplated using the Mercedes but remembered Barrett would most likely recognize the car from his days at the club. He unlocked the door, got behind the wheel of his beat-up old Honda, and backed out of the driveway.

Hearing Peter Bradley Adams's voice singing his favorite song, "I May Not Let Go," Cory cranked up the volume and crooned right along. He wasn't letting Max go, no matter how long it took to cultivate this relationship. They were off to a good start, but taking anything for granted was not a good idea.

A long list of items needing his attention buzzed around in his head, one of which was finding an office for his PI firm or whatever he would decide to do with his career. There was no question he missed practicing law, but he wasn't sure what kind of clientele he'd have if anyone researched his name.

Jonathan Spencer, his former boss and partner, came to mind, and a sense of sadness swept over him, knowing how his suspension had affected Jon. Cory knew he needed to put his embarrassment aside and call the man, especially since Jonathon was the one who'd rallied the troops in support of Cory's return after his suspension. That day would forever be emblazoned in his mind as the worst day of his life. He remembered Jonathan's face when the partners voted against Cory, and after the vote, security, who'd been waiting on the sidelines, escorted him out of the office for the last time. Cory understood their position, because his actions were unconscionable.

A Pharrell Williams song blasted through the speakers and had him tapping his fingers on the steering wheel. The song helped him ignore the heavy morning congestion now moving at a snail's pace. Out of the corner of his eye, he caught a glimpse of a new billboard on the Bank of America building advertising his old law firm, Spencer, Burton and Blackwell, Attorneys at Law. He took that as a sign it was time to call Jonathan, and he automatically hit speed dial. His call went to voice mail. Just as he was about to leave a message, he heard the beep and Jonathan's number appeared on the screen.

"Hey, Jon, how are you?"

"Other than the usual colds, I'm doing well," Jonathan said. "Good to hear your voice. How are you?"

Nervous tension bubbled through Cory's veins, and awkwardness had him scrambling for something to say just to get through the conversation. Thankfully he saw a billboard with a couple on it, and Max came to mind. "I'm doing okay. I met a real nice woman whom I'm dating," Cory blurted out to fill the empty pause.

"I hope she's better than the last one."

"Oh yeah. She's a detective in the NYPD."

"That ought to keep you in line." He chuckled. "How's your niece doing?"

"She's doing okay. Losing a limb took its toll on her, but she's looking on the brighter side of things. It took a lot of work to get to that point, though."

"I'm sure. I miss seeing you, buddy."

"I miss you too, Jon. I hope we can get together some time soon."

"I do too. We're crazy busy right now."

"Who did you get to replace me?" Cory asked.

"No one. I wouldn't let them hire anyone after they voted you out." Cory heard him sigh. "I still wish you'd asked to borrow the money from me."

"In hindsight, Jon, so do I, but I can't take it back, and wishing is fruitless on my part. Knowing I saved my niece's life, though, has helped me to swallow the guilt a little easier. Nevertheless, it was a foolish mistake on my part."

"So what are you doing these days?"

Cory told him about his new profession, and Jon promised to send clients his way. After they'd disconnected, their conversation left him with a warm feeling inside, and he promised himself he wouldn't let so much time pass until his next call. Jon always made him feel better. He was just one of those feel-good guys.

Ducking his head under the edge of the windshield, Cory peered up at a specific building, wondering if the office space he'd seen last week was still available. He was disappointed when he noticed signage for an attorney painted on the glass. "Too late," he heaved out with a breath. Office space and apartments went quickly in the city. He'd known better and should have put down a deposit on the office, but he still wasn't sure about what he wanted to do going into the future. He shrugged and continued to scan the office windows when he noticed the name of the New York Foundation of Heart Transplants. He grinned because it was as though some higher power had hit him over the head with a perfect way to obtain Barrett's weekly schedule. Sure, he could follow him every night after he left the hospital, but doing an arbitrary tail was a waste of time. While in the gridlock, he used his phone and queried the names of cardiologists in the area and decided to impersonate one. Choosing a name, he hit *67 first before keying in Barrett's office number, which would prevent the scheduler from seeing his number.

"Mount Sinai Cardiology, this is Sara."

"Hi, Sara, this is Dr. Contis from Brooklyn Cardiovascular Care. Are you Dr. Barrett's secretary?" he asked.

"No, But I'm filling in for her. How can I help you?"

"I'd like to schedule an appointment with Dr. Barrett to discuss a patient of mine. I know this is a long shot, but would he have any free time today, like maybe an hour?"

"I don't think so, but let me check the schedule." Cory heard her typing. "Let's see," she said. "It's not looking good for today, Dr. Contis. He's only doing rounds this morning, and he'll be out of here by noon. *That* has been written in bold letters, so I don't dare try to squeeze you in. I'm sorry. We have other cardiologists available to talk with you."

"Thanks, but I really need to speak with Dr. Barrett about this case. I have no doubt he needs the time to unwind. This is a tough business. Hmm, okay, when is his next available appointment—I only need about an hour,"

"He'll be out of the office all week. I can schedule you for Tuesday, November 11, and . . . it looks like he has an opening at three o'clock. Will that work for you?"

"I'll make it work."

"Can I have your phone number, Doctor, just in case something unforeseen happens?"

"Sure. I'm at 929-995-6743, extension 24." Cory's mouth broke into a smug grin, pleased he'd remembered the times he'd had his secretary at the law firm call witnesses who played the catch-me-if-you-can card ducking a subpoena to testify. "Thank you, Sara. You have a good week." Cory disconnected the call and punched his fist in the air, pleased with himself.

Noticing it was only nine o'clock, he had a few hours to kill before Barrett would be heading out. He decided to put the time to good use by continuing his search for an office. He parked his car and walked out of the public parking garage to the street level and called the rental agency he'd used before.

"Mrs. Bellarsaro, please," he told the receptionist at Realty One. "This is Cory Rossini, and I was wondering if she had any free time to show me some more office space."

"I'm sorry, Mr. Rossini, she's out of the office today, but the good news is I have one of our top sales representatives here who can help you. You've actually caught us at a good time, because she just walked in and her calendar is clear this morning. Let me transfer your call."

"Outstanding," he said, feeling the adrenaline pumping through his veins. He hoped he'd find the right place today. He was feeling especially confident after hearing Jonathan's promise to send clients his way.

Ninety minutes later and Cory was signing a lease for his new office space on Broadway and eager to start his practice, even though the office was located on the fifth floor without an elevator. He shook hands with the rental agent and headed back to his car. Barrett would be heading out in another ninety minutes.

Luckily, he'd timed the traffic just right. The worst times to drive in Manhattan were before ten in the morning and after three. The ride over to Mount Sinai was typically a twenty- to thirty-minute drive. Barring no catastrophes, it would give him plenty of time to wait outside the parking garage for Barrett's exit.

Cory double-parked by the exit door of the physicians' underground parking garage and waited for Barrett to make an appearance. Time seemed to pass by quickly. He noted it was already a little after eleven. Several cars exited, but Barrett's yellow Lamborghini wasn't one of them.

A few seconds later, he groaned when he saw the driver of the vehicle he was blocking get into his car and kick over the engine.

"Dammit," Cory mumbled. "Ah, buddy, please don't make me move my car," he said, looking in the rearview mirror. There was nowhere for him to go except around an entire city block to return to where he was, which was way too risky because chances were Barrett would be long gone and all his effort would have been in vain.

Nope. He wasn't going anywhere until he saw Barrett. He continued to pretend he didn't hear the guy leaning on his horn. Instead, he increased the volume of his radio, knowing full well it wasn't going to take long before the guy pitched a hissy fit. A sudden loud thud to the rear of his vehicle had Cory turning around to see the guy's patience completely gone. He was ready to swing his bat right through Cory's back window. Panicked, Cory stepped on the gas and almost crashed into a Mercedes coming out of the garage. He slammed on his brakes, and swerved to the left, trying to avoid an accident. The standstill caused a symphony of horn blasting, even inspiring the driver of the Mercedes to roll down his window and spit out a few choice words that brought a smile to Cory's face. The angry driver was none other than Jeffrey Barrett.

"Lucky break!" he said, pulling the fedora down lower on his forehead and adjusting his sunglasses. He waved an apology to the menace behind him as Barrett pulled out onto the roadway. Cars raced in front of Cory, not allowing him to get behind the Mercedes, but with this much traffic, there was no way he could lose Barrett.

Max and Riley walked into the lobby of the senator's office with their team and approached the secretary.

"Is something wrong?" the young woman asked when she saw their shields.

"We're here to search Senator Stansbury's office," Max said, handing her the warrant.

"I'm sorry, but the senator is not here. You'll have to wait until she returns."

Riley spread his palms on the surface of her desk and leaned in closer. "That's not the way this works, ma'am. The federal warrant gives us the right to search at any time."

"Well, let me at least call her so she knows what's going on."

"You can do whatever you'd like after you unlock her office door," Max said.

"Now, you just wait a damn minute," the secretary said, cocking her head and slapping her hands on her hips defiantly.

"What is your name?"

"Beth Carson," she snipped.

"Well, Beth Carson, the answer is no, I can't wait," Max spit out, every bit as surly. "But if you'd prefer, I can kick the door down, and you know what, I'd really rather not have to burden the taxpayers' bank accounts with more taxes."

"Are you sure this is legal, ma'am?"

"It's detective, and please, be my guest and check with my boss at the 51st Precinct of the NYPD to verify if what we're doing is legal." She scribbled the phone number on a sheet of paper and passed it over to her.

"Fine!" Beth angrily pulled the keys from her pants pocket and unlocked the door, then walked to her desk, using deliberate steps, punched in a phone number, and waited for whomever she called to answer. Neither detective paid any attention to her and entered the office to begin their search.

Once inside the plush office, Max checked the drawers of the senator's desk, wondering if the photographs had been replenished. The drawer was neat and tidy, with no sign of any evidence. "Looks like she did a housecleaning job," she said.

"Are you surprised?" Riley asked.

"No, not really." Max's head jerked to the right while she scanned the room. "I suppose I would have done the same thing."

"Don't worry, we'll find something. Her kind always forgets and leaves something behind," Riley said, walking over to the bookshelf. He removed several books and leafed through the pages, trying to find hidden items, while Max searched through Stansbury's desk, "We'll find something incriminating."

Not five minutes later, Beth walked back into the office. "My boss is really . . ."

Max held her hand up in a stop gesture and called out to the patrolman. "For chrissake, Dietz, do your job!"

The girl froze in her tracks like a frightened child being reprimanded but didn't fail to send Max a contentious glare. "What form of transportation do you use to travel back and forth to work?" Max asked the secretary. Dietz appeared, seemingly ready to defend himself, but waited for the secretary to respond to Max's question.

"Subway. Why?"

Max turned to the officer. "How long have you been on this job, Dietz?"

"Two months, ma'am."

"Either escort Ms. Carson home or to the subway."

"But I have to answer phones," Beth protested.

"Not today you don't."

"But Senator Stansbury is going to be mad, maybe even fire me."

"Then I suggest you forward the senator's phone to a different department." Max turned to Dietz. "Officer?" He nodded and took the young woman by the arm and led her out of the room. When Max heard the front door close, she released a sigh of relief. "Have a nice day, Ms. Carson."

Max blew out an exhausted breath, and walked back into the senator's office. "Have you found anything yet, Riley?"

"No, not yet."

"I think we need to check on the top of those shelves. Do we have a ladder?" she asked one of the officers helping. "I want every inch checked . . ."

◆ ◆ ◆

Cory noticed Barrett's left signal flash just before he pulled into a drive-way on Willow Lane in Englewood, New Jersey. "Pretty clever, Barrett," Cory said, rushing to park his vehicle so he could take photographs of Jeffrey Barrett pulling up to a two-car garage door. Only one door lifted, as he impatiently inched his car forward into the garage. The clunk and whine of the door reversed and closed just as his taillights blinked off. Cory strained to see if another car was parked in the garage, but the doors shut so quickly, he couldn't tell.

A smile creased Cory's face when he watched Barrett emerge from the side door of the garage, carrying a bouquet of flowers, and walk up the few brick steps to the entrance and insert a key. Barrett walked inside and shut the door. "Well, well, well, what do we have here?" Cory said with smugness.

No matter how much he wanted the doctor to be responsible for his wife's death, Cory knew he had to keep in mind that Barrett might be house sitting. Cory didn't think the doctor was the type to extend himself in such matters, unless he was using the opportunity to shack up with the senator, and the flowers were certainly a hint Cory might not be far off in his thinking. Regardless, he wrote down the address of the home in order to inquire who the owner might be at the county clerk's office.

The house, an old Cape Cod with weathered clapboard walls and a fieldstone chimney, was a picture-perfect postcard image. Centrally placed on a large lot with medium-sized trees, it had a canopy that buffered the front windows and offered the residents privacy and shade in the summer. A mature winding path around the side of the residence led to the backyard, and from what he could see, it was mostly bare now, except for a scattering of deciduous plants with a lone leaf hanging on for dear life.

A half hour later, with no visible movement from within the house, Cory wondered what Barrett was doing. Cory had been warned by his friends that stakeouts were not only boring but could turn out to be a waste of time. Either way, he was going to wait it out, praying something would happen sooner or later. Thankfully, he'd brought his tablet to fill the idle time.

Noting there were barely any cars driving down this quiet street, he understood why Barrett had chosen this house. It was good place for a hideaway. Not so good for a bored investigator, though. Because it was still daylight, it was difficult to see inside the residence to figure out the rooms, but Cory assumed the lamp centered inside the picture window had to be the living room. Reaching for his camera, he aimed the lens toward the front window and focused it until he had perfect clarity and could be ready at a moment's notice if Barrett walked out of the residence. In the meantime, he reached for his tablet and played a game, glancing up every once in a while.

At four-thirty, the front door finally opened, and Barrett was the first to exit, the senator right behind, holding her daughter's hand.

"How about that?" Cory said aloud. "The mama bear, the papa bear, and the baby bear. Now isn't that special." He happily aimed his camera, taking several shots, excited he had more proof to show Max.

"Boy, that was a lucky find," Max remarked to Cory over the phone while viewing the photographs of the trio he'd sent her. "Barrett's got himself a ready-made family. What bothers me is why kill his wife? Why not just divorce her?" She held the phone out for Riley to see while he drove back to the precinct.

"Riley's just shaking his head," Max told Cory. "As for our search, not many finds at the office, but our investigators did find photographs in her Litchfield County home, confirming the affair too. And now we have proof for a motive."

"I'm happy to hear you say that, Max," Cory said, "and I know it's a matter of proving it beyond a reasonable doubt, but I have no reservations that you will."

"Now, all we need to find out is the owner of record. Will you take care of that for us?"

"Sure. If you have any clout in the Bergen County Clerk's Office, after hours, it would save me a trip back? They closed at four o'clock. I called a few minutes ago, but no one answered. I could come back tomorrow, but I figured since it's so near their closing time, I was thinking maybe someone might still be in the office. What do you think?"

"Let me talk to the lieutenant. I'm sure we can do something. Hold tight a minute." Max hung up from Cory and called Wallace. Within minutes, Max called Cory back. "One of the employee's is still at the clerk's office, and she's waiting for you."

"Fantastic!" he said. "I'm on my way. Thanks, Max. And what about Barrett—you said his financials looked okay?"

"Yeah, Barrett's did look okay at the time we reviewed them—no red flags, but we'll go over both of their accounts again. People this smart have all kinds of ways to hide money."

"Did you find the ledger for her campaign funds yet?" he asked.

"Not yet, but we will. If there's any wrongdoing, our forensic accountants will find it right away," Max said.

"Do you ever wonder how these people sleep at night?"

"All the time," Max said. "Okay, we're heading over to the senator's house. Let me know what you find out about the owner. Thanks for doing such a good job today."

"I didn't do it for kudos, I did it to free an innocent man."

"I know that. We'll talk soon."

"Did you find an accounting ledger anywhere in the house, Fisher?" Max asked the lead investigator the minute she walked into the senator's residence a short time later.

"No, ma'am, but Alex Camarino found a safe onboard the senator's yacht, but this warrant doesn't cover the safe."

"No shit!" She turned to Riley. "She has a safe on the yacht?" She chuckled. "But seriously, who the hell installs a safe on a yacht?"

Fisher seemed amused by Max's reaction to hearing about the safe onboard. "Rich people do, I guess," he said, the corners of his mouth quirking to the side. "Solving this one, Max, is going to get your name in lights."

"You think so, huh?" She released a low laugh. "Well, I don't need the notoriety, but solving this case would put a feather in my cap."

"That it will." Fisher turned to talk to one of the investigators, and Max continued to walk through the rooms. She then made her way over to the evidence and surveyed the items collected.

"Maybe Wallace can have someone get the warrant." She keyed in his number. "Hey, Lieutenant, I need another favor. A warrant for the safe we found on the senator's yacht."

"No kidding. Okay, I'll get it, but I want to see you and Riley in here to pick it up. We have a matter to discuss," he said before disconnecting abruptly.

"What's wrong, Max?" Riley asked.

"Wallace is pissed about something. He wants us to go to the precinct to pick up the warrant."

"Did we do something?"

"I have no clue, my friend, none whatsoever. I guess we go and face the music."

The minute Max and Riley entered the precinct, Lieutenant Wallace's voice boomed out their names. "Turner and Riley, in my office, now!"

"Uh oh," Riley said, "this sounds serious."

They did a quarter turn and walked into the room. Wallace stood erect with his arms crossed, arched brows above the unyielding expression on his face.

"What the hell is going on?" he asked. "I have all kinds of government officials on my ass." The muscles tightened in his jaws.

"Sounds like the senator complained about us doing a search."

"Well, she wasn't happy about it, but she was fuming mad that you roughed up her secretary."

"What?" Max screeched. "For chrissake, I did no such thing." Wallace didn't look convinced. Max extended her arm, pointing to Riley. "Ask my partner if you don't believe me." "That twenty-something broad was ticked off because I wouldn't let her stay to answer the phones. I asked her to leave several times and she refused. She was afraid the senator would fire her if she left for the day."

"She's just covering her ass," Riley said.

Wallace gestured for them to sit down. "Tell me what happened with the young woman."

Max gave him a rundown about what transpired, and Riley confirmed the story. "And if you're thinking Riley's covering for me, then please ask Officer Dietz. He'll tell you the same thing." Max bit on her lower lip to stop herself from flying off the handle. "Look, I'm sorry the senator thinks we were invading her privacy. And she should be, because we found plenty. So if she's mad, oh well. She's getting nervous with us narrowing in on this case, so she's decided to make a stink, but as we all know, it's the people who complain the loudest who usually have the most to hide. Check out this photograph," she said, handing Wallace her phone.

"Well, how about that," he said in a calmer voice. "Is this the picture from the PI you told me about?"

"Yeah, he's the one trying to free Hughes, and he tailed Barrett today, who's on vacation. He sent me this picture of the Three Bears exiting this house in New Jersey. They can no longer deny their relationship.

Finding out why they kept it a secret is the trick. There are way too many unanswered questions cropping up that are too intriguing to pass off as nothing. It's beginning to look like the case I originally thought was going to be easy is a lot more complicated."

"What exactly are you thinking?"

"That Barrett and the senator conspired to kill the wife, and there's something fishy about the senator's daughter getting the heart transplant. We'll also be checking the records of her campaign funds to look for any discrepancies there. Where there's smoke, there's fire."

"Okay, stay on them," Wallace said. "Do you have a team over at Barrett's residence?"

"Yes, sir. The investigators are at Stansbury's and Barrett's residences, emptying the contents of those safes as we speak. Riley and I are headed over to the Barrett residence right now." She turned, and stopped short. "Were you able to get us a warrant?"

"I did." He handed it over to her. "The judge said no more special favors for tonight, he's going out." Wallace's palm rose. "Where did you say you were headed?"

"Over to the Barrett's' residence."

"Okay, Give me the warrant back. I'll have Sanchez deliver it to the team over there so we can get all the evidence in house."

"Thank you. I appreciate your help." As she was walking away, Wallace stopped her again.

"How about the love nest? Did you find out who the owner is?" he asked.

"I haven't heard back from Cory yet. Thank you for helping out, and I'm sorry you had to take grief from the senator."

"I have broad shoulders." Wallace returned to the open file on his desk.

"Does this mean we're off the hook?" Riley asked Max on the way out.

"You, my friend, were never on the hook. I was the one on the hook . . . in the cold meat locker."

Maddie Thomas, the Barretts' maid, rushed to Max's car as soon as she stopped in front of the house.

"Detective Max," she cried out, "why you doing this to Dr. Jeffrey?"

"Just doing our job, Maddie."

"But he's a good man."

"I'm sure he is, but even good men do bad things. Tell me, have you ever seen him with another woman?"

A "No" cannonballed from her mouth.

"You answered too quickly, Maddie. Talk to me. Tell me what you know."

"I already told you everything I know. Besides, Dr. Jeffrey is a single man now."

"Right. So you *have* seen him with someone." Max found the picture on her phone and showed it to her. "Have you ever seen him with this beautiful woman and her child?"

"Please, no trouble."

"No one is trying to get you into trouble, Maddie. Don't you want to know who killed Mrs. Barrett?"

"Yes, I do," she cried out.

"So have you seen this woman with Dr. Barrett?"

"Once, a long time ago."

"Before Mrs. Barrett died?"

"Yes, once. Maybe two or three years ago."

"Thanks for your honesty, Maddie. You've been very helpful." Maddie began heading back to the house. "Oh, I'm sorry, Maddie, you can't go into the main residence while the team is investigating. They'll be searching your house next."

"But why? I have nothing to do with Mrs. Barrett's death."

"I know that. It's just a formality. Do you have some place to go until we've finished?"

Maddie's expression changed to one of annoyance, but she cooperated. "I go see my sister. She works for the Ridgeway family."

"Okay, we'll drive you over there." Max got the attention of one of the patrolmen. "Please transport Mrs. Thomas over to the Ridgeway residence. She'll tell you where to go."

She watched the woman get into the backseat of the car. "Thank you, Maddie." She simply nodded in silence. With the maid out of the way, Max entered the residence. When Jerome Bevans, the lead investigator, saw Max walking toward him, he gestured for her to join him.

"What did you find?"

"I thought you'd want to know that I just tagged a checkbook under the name of Souley Regains. Unless Barrett's holding this for a friend, it looks like he's using the fictitious name."

"Nothing would surprise me with this case. Thanks for the heads-up." She turned to walk away, then stopped. "How about passports? Did you find any of those?"

"One for the wife and the husband, but it doesn't look like there were any others," he said, sliding his finger down the list of items.

"Thanks. Talk later, Bevans." Then she turned to the door and called for Riley.

"What's up, Max? You're smiling," Riley asked when they walked outside. Max got into the driver's seat and started the engine, pulled the gear into place, and drove out of the driveway.

"Yep, Riley, this plot is getting fatter. I can't wait to check the evidence to unravel this puzzle. Bevans found a checkbook, and it didn't have either of the Barretts' names on it." Riley's eyes widened with surprise. When her phone rang, she looked at him. "Will you get that for me?"

"Detective Turner's line. Can I help you?" Riley smiled and turned to her. "It's Cory with some good news."

"Put him on speaker so we can both hear it at the same time." Riley punched the icon. "Okay, Cory. Give us some good news."

"The house is owned by a Madeline Thomas."

"Hmm," Max said, a puzzled expression on her face, "Madeline Thomas, Madeline Thomas. Why does that name sound familiar?"

"Isn't Thomas the maid's last name?" Riley asked.

Max gasped, "For chrissake." She smacked her leg. "Maddie is short for Madeline." Max pulled over to the side of the road. "Hang on for a minute, Cory. I want to turn around and go back to talk to Maddie to see what she has to say." Max turned the car around and drove back past the residence toward the Ridgeways' mansion while Riley keyed the name into the database for the address. "Okay, you can keep talking." Riley gave her directions by using his finger to point out the turns toward the mansion while she continued her conversation with Cory.

"It's a beautiful home in a pretty high-class neighborhood for someone on a maid's salary," Cory said. "Do you think she knows about this house?"

"Anything is possible, I suppose, but I'd be surprised if she did. And since you're giving us such good news, here's some for you. Our team found a safe on the yacht."

"No way!" Cory's voice rose a few decibels, breaking into laughter. "I'm certain they never expected you to search the yacht. You're brilliant, you know that?"

"Yeah. If only that were true. Now, here's another weird thing. They found a checkbook under an assumed name." Hearing Cory's voice for the third time today made Max happy. "Are you headed back to the city?"

"Yes, I am. Where are you headed?" he asked.

"We're headed back to the precinct after I make one last stop to see Maddie, then we'll start examining this evidence tomorrow."

"Are you going to ask her if she knows about the house?" he asked.

"In a roundabout way. Okay, thanks. We'll chat later."

Max pulled into the driveway, stopped at the gate, and pushed the black button on the call box. A security guard answered.

"Hi, I'm Detective Max Turner from the NYPD. And I'm here to see Mrs. Thomas, who was dropped off about ten minutes ago. May I see her, please?"

He was gone for a few minutes before coming back. The gates opened, and Max drove through and down the long winding driveway to the main entrance, where Maddie was waiting on the front steps of the residence.

Max stopped the car a few feet away from the steps.

"What do you need?" Maddie asked.

"One last question. Do you own any real estate?"

Maddie looked puzzled. "Like a home?"

"Right. Like a home?"

"No. Not even the house in Jamaica. If not for Mrs. Barrett, I never have a place like this to live. She was always good to me, buying me things all the time, but not the doctor. He's good to me now, though." Maddie looked confused. "Why do you ask?"

"Why do you think he's good to you now?"

She shrugged. "He knows Mrs. Barrett always take good care of me."

"I just wondered."

CHAPTER
TWENTY-SIX

Tuesday morning Max entered the evidence room. "Good morning, Jasper," she said when she saw him. She'd always liked Jasper. He was a short, average-looking man she figured to be in his early fifties. He had salt-and-pepper wiry hair that, despite a short haircut, made him look frantic.

"How you doin', Maximus?" Max always enjoyed it when Jasper called her a silly name.

"Good, Jasper. How are you doing?"

"If I was any better, I'd think I had died and gone to heaven."

"That's always good to hear. I need the Barrett evidence boxes."

"All right. Just sign here on the dotted line, and I'll let you know where you can find them inside the cage." He keyed the information into the database and wrote something down on a piece of paper.

"We're way in the back, I see," Max said. "I thought you put the newer evidence in the front."

"I changed the system," he said walking out from behind the counter to the door of the cage. He removed the large key ring from his belt and unlocked the gate, allowing them access. "Aisle 29, row 233, boxes 1–20. I'll call my guy and tell him to get the boxes down and deliver them to the room."

"Awesome. Thank you. I'm sure you did a great job."

"I did." He grinned. "Wait until you see the new room. It's a lot more comfortable and better looking," Jasper said with pride.

Making her way into the room, she was surprised to see the new look. It was now set up much like a library meeting room, with three rows of mahogany tables that extended the width of the room, a nice change from the Formica tables they'd had before that always reminded Max of a prison visiting room. Max sat down on one of the benches when she heard Riley's voice.

"You're getting an early start," he said before setting down two containers of coffee.

"We have our work cut out for us today, so why don't you hang your coat up, then stop at your desk to get your laptop, a pad, and something to write with, because we'll be spending most of the day in the evidence room."

Riley snorted. "You're a piece of work this morning," he said. Riley looked around the room and groaned. "Methinks this is starting out to be another one of those highly caffeinated days, but not you . . . I think you've already had way too much caffeine."

She released a snicker. "Yeah, you're probably right," Max said. "I started at six o'clock this morning." Riley frowned. "Hey, I couldn't sleep," she said, raising her palms in the air. "It's a lot to undertake, but I'm anxious to get this show on the road."

"I can see that." He grinned.

"So after you hang up your coat, can you grab your laptop on your way back so we can check the database?"

Riley stopped short. "Yes, ma'am." He saluted the same way Howie had done a million times when she was getting overly aggressive.

Max got the message loud and clear. She hadn't remembered telling him that was the way Howie had let her know she was getting too bossy and wondered if he was feeling the same way. Maybe she needed to downshift just a little.

When Riley walked out of the room, she slid down in the chair, slipped out of her shoes, then lifted one leg up onto the other. Shutting her eyes, she inhaled deeply, blowing her breath out in a slow steady stream. Riley was right. She was getting way ahead of herself. She continued to control her breathing until she heard him walk back into the room.

"I just checked out Souley Regains, and there seems to be only one in the Bronx, but he's been dead since 2012."

Max humphed. "I figured you were going to tell me something like that." She slipped back into her shoes and stood. "I'm really curious to find out if it was Jeffrey Barrett who opened this account to hide the money from his wife, or if it was Helen who figured this was a foolproof way to stop her husband from taking it away from her."

"Don't you think the doc would have noticed money missing out of their account?" His hand gestured. "Hell, I'd be all over it if it was my wife."

"Yeah, but I can almost guarantee you Mr. Rich Guy doesn't handle his finances. He pays someone to do that."

"All right. Then if that's the case, why wouldn't the accountant bring it to his attention?"

Max's face was covered in skepticism. "Maybe Helen Barrett wasn't the sweet little thing people seem to think she was."

"Meaning?" he asked.

"Meaning maybe she had something going on with the accountant and she schmoozed him into keeping it quiet," Max said.

"Hey," his shoulder rose in a shrug. "I guess anything is possible. But it could have been the good old doc who opened the phony account too." Riley's brows rose. "Especially if what we're thinking is true about people being paid off to adjust medical records. He wouldn't take the money out of his own account when he knows we're watching."

"I suppose. I do want to know what's going in and what's coming out of that account."

"Yeah, and I checked the bank information on the house. It was a cash deal."

"Hey," Max said, "I just thought of something. What are Maddie's sons' names?"

"Mandu and Fejoku."

"No Souley, huh?" Riley shook his head. "Is their last name Thomas?" she asked.

"If I'm remembering correctly, I don't think so." His finger slid down the information in the file. "Nope, their last name is Curtina."

Max's face screwed up. "So where the hell did this name come from? Did they do an eenie meenie miney mo from a list of obituaries?"

"Ha. I gave up a long time ago trying to figure out the human mind," Riley said. "But I'm curious about what made you think the name was somehow associated with Maddie."

"Because the name sounds Jamaican." Max tilted her head back and pondered a thought. "I'm thinking of a few possibilities. Maddie is denying owning real estate. Helen Barrett bought it for her, or maybe the good doc bought it, and used her name, figuring she'd never know about it."

"There's no way she could afford the upkeep on the house," Riley said.

Max's hand flew up. "There's no point in speculating, I'm going to call the woman and ask her."

Max punched in the number while continuing her conversation with Riley. "I really don't think Maddie would lie to me about that when she was so concerned about having a job after Helen Barrett died." Max stared at Riley.

Maddie's voice caught Max off guard. "Maddie, Detective Turner here. I have another question for you. Are you married?"

"Yes. My husband, Souley, he lives in Jamaica with my other children."

"And his last name is Thomas?"

"No, Regains. I use Thomas for my work visa." Max gave Riley the thumbs-up sign. "Why do you keep asking me these questions, Detective Max?"

"I was just curious. Okay, thank you."

"But what does this have to do with Miss Helen's death?"

"Probably nothing, but the question was on my mind and I thought I'd ask. Thanks." She disconnected the call. "All right, this is beginning to make sense," Max said. "Helen Barrett probably opened the account . . ."

"Because she feared for her life or for monetary protection?" Riley said. "Because those are the only two choices."

"No, they're not. She could have bought it for Maddie because she was running off with Jack and knew Barrett would fire her."

"Okay, good point, but why not give Maddie the checkbook when she set up the account?" Riley asked.

"Where do you suppose this Souley would have cashed a check in a third-world country?" Max asked.

Riley shrugged.

"When will you be calling Barrett down to the precinct to talk again?"

"Maybe sooner than you think," Lieutenant Wallace said, hearing the question upon opening the door. "Barrett is here and wants to talk to you, Max. He's already given me quite an earful. He said he had to cut his vacation short to come here."

"Want to come with me, Riley?"

"I wouldn't miss this for the world."

"He's in Interview Room 1."

"Let's go make him squirm a little," she said, walking toward the room.

"It's your show, boss," Riley said and opened the door to the room. Their entrance caused Barrett to stand erect.

"Detective Turner, what the hell is going on? You're searching my home, my office. What is it you're looking for and why?"

"I'm surprised to see you here when you're so busy." Max jabbed an insult in after all the times she'd been scolded by him because he didn't appreciate her interruptions.

"You pulled me away from my vacation," he repeated.

Max ignored his remark. "We're still investigating the case, Dr. Barrett, and searching for evidence is mandatory. Just remember, nothing is ever sealed in stone until we've dotted all the i's and crossed all the t's in a case."

"How many ways can I tell you? I did *not* kill my wife!" he said with emphasis.

"Dr. Barrett, you must know that we have to check out every avenue. Regardless of what you think of Jack Hughes, I want to be sure I'm sending the right person to prison."

"Is there any doubt?"

"I'm working on that."

"Can you share that with me?"

"Dr. Barrett," Max said, slanting her head to the side. "You keep asking me to share confidential information with you when I've already told you I won't disclose anything until I finish investigating the case. At that time, you'll be given a full account of what we've done. Just know that by the time we're done, the guilty party won't have a chance in hell of beating the rap. Not everything is cut and dried, as laypeople would like to believe. In a high percentage of cases like this, it's the spouse who's typically the guilty party."

Arrogance covered his expression. "So now you're saying even though you've put Jack Hughes behind bars, you're still checking me out?"

Max and Riley stared him down.

"Dr. Barrett, Jack Hughes is awaiting trial—he hasn't been convicted. Anything can happen between now and then."

"I can't emphasize enough—"

"I know." Max cut Barrett off and nodded in agreement. "But I have to wonder who you're trying to convince. Me or you?" She'd heard enough of his so-called devotion to his wife.

"What is that supposed to mean?" he snapped.

"That, if you're not guilty, then you have nothing to worry about." She stopped and stared at him. "Right?" Barrett's eyes were averted. "Look, I won't keep you, Doc. I'm sure you have plenty of patients to take care of, and you don't need me taking up your time, especially when I don't have much to tell you. I'll catch up with you when I have more questions."

"I really wish you could share some of those details with me now, but I guess if you thought I were guilty, you would have arrested me already." He gave a surly grin.

"That's an interesting thing to say."

"I guess I just need something to make me feel better, but I have to trust your investigative skills to figure this out. Thank you for seeing me."

"You're welcome. Try to relax, Dr. Barrett. There's no point in you losing sleep over this. We'll let you know when we have something substantial to share."

"Thank you," he said at the door.

As soon as he was gone, Riley commented, "Nicely handled."

"Yeah, I was pretty proud of that too. Here I was expecting him to be boisterous, like the lieutenant said, yet he was like a little lamb."

"He's getting nervous. I'm sure he's worried we're getting close." Riley fired up his laptop and logged on to the database.

"Well, according to the bank papers," Riley said, zipping through the various screens to see the documents for the real estate transaction on the New Jersey residence, "it looks like the attorney of record is a John Paterno, who's located in the Bronx. I think I should call him to find out more, but maybe we should talk to Cory first to see if he knows the guy."

"Good idea," Max said. "If he does know him, he'll probably be able to get more information out of him than we would. Why don't you give the lieutenant the scoop on what happened with Barrett, and I'll start searching the database to see what I can find out about Paterno."

"Thanks, Max. I was beginning to think you didn't trust me enough to update the lieutenant."

"Good grief, Riley. Why didn't you say something? That was never my intent. I guess taking the lead is just a force of habit. Sorry. I swear, Riley, it isn't that I don't trust you. I'll try to refrain from being so militant."

Riley held up his hand in gratitude. "Thanks." He strode toward the lieutenant's office with energetic steps.

Max reached for her phone and called Cory. "Do you know an attorney by the name of John Paterno? He's in the Bronx."

"John Paterno . . . oh boy." Cory released an expletive.

"Is that a yes?" Max didn't like the sounds of this Paterno, from the noises coming through the phone. "Shady guy?"

"To say the least."

"Tell me about him."

"I met him a few years ago at a Lions Club business meeting. He's as crooked as the day is long. Unfortunately, no one has ever been able to prove it. He has a host of friends in the real estate industry, from title companies, to adjustors, to loan companies, giving loans to people who can't sustain a mortgage. That's the kind of crap that happened before the 2008 market crash and caused all kinds of havoc and foreclosures, but he manages to pull those closings off without a hitch. I had a client who had bad credit, was losing his house, and John got him into another mortgage before the bank took possession of the residence, because he wouldn't have been able to buy another home or anything on credit for the next seven years."

"But who gave him a mortgage?"

"One of Paterno's friends holds the mortgage, and after the closing, he sells the mortgage to a bank, and that's how the vicious circle begins again. If he's the attorney of record, then you can be sure he couldn't have cared less about who was signing the papers, so long as he got his money," Cory said.

"He's obviously not concerned about his law license either," she said. Her attention was drawn to the door as Riley came in. "Okay, Riley just walked into the office after talking to the boss. Will you contact Paterno to see what he can tell you about that closing on the New Jersey house? I want to know who was there and who signed the papers."

"Of course I will." He sighed. "I'll get back to you."

"That's fine. In the scheme of things, we've got plenty to do, so please keep it on your list of things, because I'll forget." Cory laughed. "Listen, I have to go. Catch up with you later." The smile on Riley's face made her curious. "How'd you make out, Riley?" Max asked, clicking off the call.

"The lieutenant wants us to get the twosome gruesome in here as soon as we finish checking the evidence from their safes."

"I don't have a problem with that, so let's get back to our evidence so we have enough to charge them."

CHAPTER
TWENTY-SEVEN

Entering the Interstate 495 east on Wednesday morning, Cory eased into the traffic and headed for Rikers Island to see Jack. He had expected the traffic to be heavy, but with the colder weather, not as many people were out riding the highways. It wasn't long before he veered off onto Interstate 278 east. Thinking about all the things he had yet to do took his mind off the trip, and before he knew it, he was exiting the highway and driving right up to the entrance where a large white sign read *City of New York, Correction Department* with the words *Rikers Island* underneath and *Home of New York's Boldest*. The sign always gave Cory an unpleasant feeling, especially after he'd borrowed money from his client's fund. The firm's partners could have easily voted to send him to jail. He could have been in a cell right next to Jack if his firm hadn't agreed to the suspension instead.

Walking inside the facility, he showed his credentials and headed for the security line.

"Who ya here to see?" the guard asked.

"Jack Hughes."

"How you doing, Mr. Rossini?" He heard Malcolm Wright's familiar voice in the distance. "Going to see one of your clients?"

"Yes, Jack Hughes. How's my guy doing?"

"He's not looking too good these days. He doesn't associate with anyone during meals and stays to himself even when he's outside."

"Thanks for sharing that with me. I'll see what's going on with him."

Jack stood when he saw Cory. "You're a sight for sore eyes, Rossini. Thanks for stopping by." They shook hands. "Got anything new to tell me?" Cory could see Jack's complexion was sallow. He was tired and thin. "I hope you know how much I appreciate what you're doing for me, my friend, but honestly, I don't know how I'm going to pay you."

"You're not going to pay me. You look like death warmed over."

"The food in here sucks, and the last thing I want to do is socialize with these idiots. The next thing you know, they'll think they own me, and you know what that means? Did you bring me any magazines? The ones here are outdated by three years, and I've already read them from cover to cover."

"Uh, no, I didn't bring any magazines, but I will on the next visit. I didn't even think of it. Jack, you have me very concerned. Why aren't you eating?"

"I told ya, bud, it's disgusting. Not edible at all, and it doesn't even look like food."

"Let me get us some sodas at the dispensary," Cory said. Seeing Jack like this broke Cory's heart and gave him all the more drive to get him out of this place.

Jack took a long pull on the straw. "So tell me what's going on with the case."

"I don't want you getting overly psyched, because you never know—"

"What the hell kind of disclaimer is that?"

"I'm just managing your expectations."

"Why don't you let me take care of that? Now tell me what's happening."

"All right." Jack stared at him with anticipation. "Well, we've learned that the senator and the doctor have been an item for a number of years."

"Hell, I could have told you that."

"Are you shittin' me? You knew that and never thought to mention it?"

"No. I'm sorry. I thought everyone knew."

"You could have saved us a lot of trouble."

"Who's *us*?" Jack asked.

"I've been working with Detective Max Turner."

"And you're not the least bit worried she's using you to get information about me?"

"No." He frowned. "She could be saying the same thing about me. We have an understanding."

Jack eyed Cory suspiciously. "Oh hell, you're sleeping with her, aren't you?"

"Jack, just stop it, and start telling me what you know."

Jack made a face, but continued. "Just that they've been shacking up for a long time."

"We just wish we had more evidence that could link the affair to his wife's murder."

"Then that gets me off the hook?"

"Relax, Jack. This is going to take time. We're all doing as much as we can, but we don't have anything concrete. Did Helen tell you about the house in New Jersey?"

"Yeah. We actually stayed there." Cory closed his eyes and lowered his head in controlled disgust. "I'm sorry, Cory. I seriously never gave it a thought."

"Then tell me about the house."

"What do you want to know, where it is?"

"No, I found the house by tailing Barrett. Why is it in her maid's name?"

"So that bastard is using the house with the senator?"

"It appears so."

"Helen bought the house for her maid."

"Lucky woman. Do you know why she bought it?"

"I don't have a clue." Jack's hands rose. "Helen never answered that question."

"And you never thought to mention that to me, either?"

"All I've thought about in this hellhole is that I'll never have Helen in my life, and I might be convicted for a crime I didn't commit." Jack lowered his head and shook it. "I'm sorry, buddy."

"Yeah, I'm sorry too. Look I understand what you're going through, but honestly, Jack, I can't help you if you don't let me. So how are they treating you here?"

"Ah, as well as can be expected, I suppose. They think I'm a criminal. They don't know me." He tipped his head to the side. "When am I getting out of here?"

"I'm working on it, and we're getting closer all the time. There's a lot more to this case than we ever expected. Just know that we're making progress, and every day is one day closer to your freedom." Cory stood and shook Jack's hand. "Stay strong."

Max and Riley made their way through the evidence for the second day as methodically as possible.

"I'm really anxious to see what they found in the safes."

"Yeah, me too."

Riley no sooner sat down than the files were delivered, and they both dug into the boxes.

"Let's each take them in order and make comments on the sheets."

Three hours later Riley was just opening the number five box. "Well, lookie, lookie at what I found, an evidence bag with a key." Pressing his fingers against the plastic bag, he noticed writing. "Chase Manhattan Bank in Chelsea. It looks like a safe deposit box key. The bag says it was found with Helen's belongings in the safe. Apparently, Jeffrey didn't know it was there or otherwise I'm guessing he would have removed it. I wonder what we're going to find."

"I like how the evidence is pulling together nicely. I'm about ready to check the box from the senator's safe." Excitement sailed through Max as she opened the box and examined the information written on the evidence bag. "Ooh, here's the ledger they found on the yacht." She laughed. "I have to give her an *A* for effort, but how could she think we might not even search the yacht? Silly woman." Max leafed through the pages. It all seemed rather normal, except an entry to M. C. Party Planners for one hundred thousand dollars. Max slid the book over to Riley. "Feast your eyes on this entry."

"You mean having one of those political parties costs that much money? Geez, my wife suggested we hire a caterer for a big barbecue for our niece who's graduating eighth grade. I said yes, but man, if that's how much they charge, Costco, here we come." He slid his finger across the entry.

"Yeah, but your party wouldn't include a security detail, would it? I'm sure that amount includes more than just the food and the service for the caterers."

"Okay, that makes sense. I wasn't thinking of security, plus the photographers . . . there's a lot of pieces to the pie." He keyed the name into the database. "There's nothing listed for an M. C. Party Planners."

"Maybe it's a new business and not listed yet."

"No, Max, I checked that too. It's not here."

"Okay, so maybe it's a payoff and M. C. Party Planners is a front for money paid out, and one more thing to check. The evidence just keeps mounting. I think that's a very good question to ask the senator," Max said. "Check Souley's financials again while you're at it. See if there are any payouts for large sums of money."

"Holy shit, there's a million dollars in this account, and yes, there's an entry for a check made payable to M. C. Party Planners, after the Barrett woman's death," Riley said. "So it looks like Stansbury and Barrett both paid this company $100k?"

Max's eyes opened wide. "Christ, that's even worse. We need to find a canceled check from her accountant, and a paid receipt from the party planner. I'm sure she wouldn't have paid the planner in cash."

"Unless the caterer didn't want to claim it as income," Riley said with raised brows.

"Yeah, but that's a helluva lot of money to have on hand or hide from the IRS," Max said.

"Ooh, this guy is good," Riley said with a whistle, looking at the cancelled check from Souley's account on the computer screen, "and I'll just bet if I compare Barrett's signature from his personal checking account against this one, the signatures will be identical. What do you think, Max?"

"I think you'll be right."

"Bingo!" Riley said. "And we have a match."

"I'm loving it! Keep 'em coming," Max said. "Here's what has me confused," she added. "If Helen bought the house, how did the doc find out about it?"

Riley pondered the thought, his fingers covering his mouth until his facial expression changed. "Wait, didn't you tell me Barrett had his wife followed by a private investigator when he suspected the affair?"

"That's right, he did!" Max said, snapping her fingers. "I wonder if she was using it with Jack?"

"Why wouldn't she? She closed on that house six months prior to her death, and since Maddie didn't know anything about it, I'm sure she wasn't going to let it sit idle. We need Cory to find out what Jack knows," Max said and keyed in his number. When she heard his voice mail kick on, she felt a flutter of excitement in her stomach. "Hey. Can you check with Jack to see if he knew about the love nest and get back to me? Thanks."

"You know," Max said, "if Barrett is using this checking account, he's had to use some form of identification."

"Right. A passport and a driver's license," Riley said, the words rushing out like a song. "But he'd be recognized in New York." He laughed. "But not in New Jersey?"

"Yes!" Max punched her fist in the air. "We are closing in on this guy, Riley. Damn, it feels good, but we can't back down on the pressure now. There's little doubt in my mind that Barrett won't be using this account as his getaway funds for when the lovebirds take off."

"I love it when we knock the egomaniacs off their pedestals. They actually believe they can outsmart the police." Riley released a low laugh. "You know, I'll bet that safe deposit box has plenty to say."

"For sure," Max said. "I think I'll call the boss and ask him to send someone over to the bank to remove the contents of the safe deposit box and bring it back while we continue to check out these boxes."

"My God, Max, we're getting so close, I can taste it."

"I hope so, Riley. If this all works out the way we think it will, then we've done our job." Max speed-dialed the lieutenant's number to fill him in on the ledger entry and the Souley Regains payout.

"Have you checked Stansbury's financials?" Wallace asked.

"Not yet."

"One other thing. The guys said they found a note in the home in our victim's belongings that's crucial to your investigation."

"Did they say what it was?"

"No. Bensonhurst left me a short message, but his voice faded out." Max felt a jolt of excitement. "It's got to be in the box, so pay particular attention to the contents."

"Okay, Lieutenant. Thanks for the heads-up." Disconnecting, she turned to Riley and told him to look for a note.

"I hope it's solid information that we can use."

Max placed her hand on her forehead. "My stomach is jiggling around like a washing machine," she said. "I love getting to this point in a case, because things start falling into place, and putting the bad guys away for a long time is a short putt away." Max stopped talking when Wallace rushed into the room.

"Here it is," he said, waving the white paper in the air before placing it in Max's outstretched hand.

Max and Riley read it aloud, their mouths gaping afterward. "Helen Barrett says she has incriminating evidence against Stansbury and Barrett." Max kissed the note. "Thank you, Helen Barrett." High fives were raised around, including Wallace, until a sudden sinking feeling attacked Max's gut. "But what if we don't find anything else that gives us specifics about what evidence she has against Mr. Bigshot and his sidekick?"

The lieutenant was shaking his head. "Uh, I don't think I'd discount Helen Barrett just yet. If she dropped this bomb, you can be sure she's planning a dramatic ending that's going to blow up in their faces." Wallace was nodding his head with certainty. "Something tells me if she suspected something was going to happen to her, she was going to make damn sure they paid for what they did to her. If she went this far, you're going to find what you need."

"But where?" Riley asked. Max picked up the evidence bag with the key.

"In Helen Barrett's safe deposit box!" Max shouted.

"Hot damn," Riley said. Looking over at Max, he couldn't keep from saying, "We're good, you know that, Max?"

Wallace cut in, "You certainly are."

"So why wasn't this note in the evidence box?"

"Bensonhurst said he hadn't logged all the items in last night and left it in the locker until this morning," the lieutenant said.

"I guess that means there are more items that need to be logged? Or has he finished?" Max asked.

"No, he confirmed this is everything. When I didn't see you two at your desks, I brought the box over to Jasper for him to tag, and he said you were in here."

"Lieutenant, did you happen to see another note, addressed to Maddie Thomas?"

"I really didn't look thoroughly. This just caught my eye and I pulled it out."

"Okay, I'll look later, but in the meantime, let's get our lead suspects in here tomorrow for questioning."

"Not to worry, I've already scheduled a car to pick them both up. Go home and get some rest so you're bright-eyed and bushy-tailed."

"Awesome! Thanks, Lieutenant."

Max reached for her phone when she saw Cory's name on the screen. "I've been to see Jack again," he said with a humph. "He confirmed everything: the affair, the house that Helen bought for Maddie, which they actually stayed at a few times, and that Maddie and Helen went to the closing. From what Helen had told him, he was certain Maddie didn't know what she was signing, but for sure, Helen wanted to know that Maddie was well taken care of after she left Jeffrey, because she knew he would probably fire her."

"Well, that confirms our suspicions," she said, but thought it odd that Jack hadn't ever mentioned any of this to Cory. She decided not to make a big deal out of it so long as they had confirmation that what they'd been thinking was correct. "How did you make out with Paterno? Did you have a chance to take care of that yet?"

"I did. Paterno's on vacation, but his paralegal informed me she does all of his closings. He signs off on the paperwork before the closing, but she meets with the clients. She specifically remembers that two women, one a Caucasian, the other a dark-skinned woman with an accent, signed the papers, which, now that we know the truth, we don't have to send photographs of the two women."

"No kidding!" Max shoved a piece of gum in her mouth, leaned over, and threw the wrapper into the trash can under her desk.

"I sure hope Maddie hasn't been snowballing me."

"Why would she do that?"

"I don't know. I guess it's the nature of the beast. I'll give her the benefit of the doubt until I find out otherwise, but that would just blow me away."

"Listen," Cory said. "Stop and think about what you're saying. If the woman knew that what she signed was a home in her name, don't you think she'd have her entire family here? Why would she let them continue to live in poverty in Jamaica? And here's another point. People who've lived in poverty all their lives and suddenly become wealthy overnight are going to spend it like it's water because they suddenly feel carefree."

"You're probably right, but I can't rule her out just yet."

CHAPTER
TWENTY-EIGHT

"What do you want now?" Senator Stansbury said with contempt in her voice when she saw Max on Thursday afternoon. Standing beside the senator was an older gentleman with black horn-rimmed glasses, a long black coat, and a hat. Max assumed he was her attorney.

Senator Kay Stansbury was pleasant to look at. Tall and statuesque. The paper had coined her the blonde bombshell of the city, which wasn't quite fitting for her demeanor. Her gait was graceful as she walked toward Max. After she removed her coat, the man draped it over his arm, then placed it over the back of one of the vacant chairs. He removed his outer garments and placed them on a different chair. Dressed in a tailored taupe-colored suit with a white blouse, the senator wore coordinating brown leather pumps and seemed the picture of professionalism. Her blonde hair was pulled away from her face into a low bun that showcased her graceful neck and high cheekbones.

"This is my attorney, Mathias Jacquard, who travels with me." Max acknowledged his presence with a nod.

Riley extended his hand in greeting. "And this is my partner, Neal Riley."

"Would either of you like coffee, water, or soda?"

"No, thanks. Let's get this over with," Stansbury said. "I have a district to run."

"Yes, ma'am." Riley said and directed them down the hall. "We'll be going to Interview Room 2." Riley flipped the light switch on when he walked inside.

"Could this room be any more beat up?" the senator squawked when she saw how bad the room looked. The long Formica table was chipped on the corners and laced with graffiti obviously left by previous collars.

"I do suppose it could be a lot worse, but your office has cut some of our funding," Max said with deference. "I understand you're used to much better, but the Taj Mahal it ain't. It's the best we can do under the circumstances. Please have a seat."

Her attorney pulled out the chair for her, and she leaned over and brushed the cushion with her hand to remove whatever might have been left behind by the previous occupant.

"I can get you a bag to sit on if you're afraid of getting something on you." The senator made a face, grabbed her coat, and covered the entire chair before sitting down.

"Because of my client's political position, I have advised that she defer your questions to me."

"All right. I'm going to turn on this recorder for security purposes—both yours and ours." Max pushed the button down and began Mirandizing her.

"Today is Thursday, November 6, 2014. And present with me, Detective Max Turner, is my partner, Detective Neal Riley, Senator Kay Stansbury, and her attorney, Mathias Jacquard. Senator, will you please state your name again, address, phone number, and occupation for the record." Mr. Jacquard gave her the go-ahead with a nod.

Once she finished, Max began the questioning. "Thank you. Senator, we've asked you to come down here this afternoon because of questions we have about previous conversations and evidence we've found during our searches."

"What evidence?" shot out of the senator's mouth.

"We'll get to that in a second." Max opened her notepad. "Okay, Senator, I'd like to get right to the point. In a previous conversation with the private investigator, you told him that you'd met Jeffrey Barrett when your daughter's cardiologist recommended using him after your daughter, Arianna's condition worsened. Can you tell me when that was?"

"I realized afterward that I misspoke when I said that. I actually met him during my campaign. He contributed to my election and attended my victory party."

"You did not know him before then?"

"No. I did not."

"When did your affair with Dr. Barrett begin?"

Just as she was about to respond, her attorney cut in. "My client refuses to answer that question. That's no one's business."

"It is when we have a murdered wife and pictures proving the affair. How do you suppose that's going to look to a jury?"

Jacquard leaned over and whispered something in the senator's ear.

"No, I'd like to respond." He shook his head unfavorably, but she ignored him and continued. "We lied about our affair because we figured you'd suspect we had something to do with Helen's death."

"Unfortunately for you, that's exactly what we think. Lying about it only made it worse. Okay, so here's what's puzzling. After Helen's death, you two picked up right where you left off. How do you explain that?"

"Helen had an affair first."

"How do you know that?"

"Because Jeffrey told me."

"Was that before or after you'd started screwing her husband?"

"I resent your tone, Detective."

"Oh gee, I'm sorry. Answer the question."

"Jeffrey approached me. It didn't start out as an affair. And yes, we met during my campaign in 2011. After I'd been elected, we maintained contact as friends, and one day, he called and asked me to have a drink with him to discuss his wife."

"What if I told you Helen Barrett wasn't having an affair and didn't start having one until 2013?"

"I'd say you were misinformed."

"Because Jeffrey told you otherwise?" Max's brows rose. "Is that right?"

"Well, yes. He's an honest man."

"Hmm." Max took a quick glance at Riley. "And you both sailed out to the middle of the ocean where you thought no one would recognize either of you so you could have complete privacy?" The senator sucked in her breath. "I guess you didn't think we'd find out about the Peninsula Marina?" Max snickered. "Did you not think you'd be recognized when you named your yacht after a bill you got passed, and with Dr. Barrett's yacht being called *Mister's Mistress*? That was like hanging a neon sign outside. You're lucky your constituents weren't paying attention. Did you honestly think no one would notice, or that you could get away with it?" Max frowned. "Or did you think that you're somehow smarter than us?" She shrugged. "So, Senator, so tell us about it."

"Jeffrey was distraught when he found out Helen had been cheating on him and thought I might be able to help him understand what was happening with his wife." Max did not comment, but the expression on her face clearly upset the senator. "Detective, you make it sound like this was some sordid affair when it wasn't like that at all. Yes, they were married, but they'd been doing their own thing for some time."

"But that was according to Jeffrey. Wasn't it?" She nodded in agreement. "Yeah, and you make it sound like he was justified. The problem now, though, is Helen is dead, and I can't get her side of the story, but the good news for us is she's talking from the grave." The senator's body stiffened in shock. "She was a smart cookie and certainly a lot smarter than either of you. And you know how I know this?" The senator gave her an empty stare. "We found a note from Helen Barrett stating she had incriminating evidence against you and the doctor. What do you suppose she's going to tell us?"

"I haven't the faintest idea."

"Kay," Jacquard said, "I'm telling you to shut this conversation down now."

"Quite frankly, Mathias, I'm so tired of looking over my shoulder. I just want to live my life, and I can't do that with this crap hanging over my head."

"All right then," Max said, "let's talk about how you felt when Jeffrey decided to remain with his wife, even going so far as to renew their vows."

"Obviously, I wasn't happy, but that's the chance you take when you date a married man."

"Just like that, huh?"

"I'm not proud of it, but it is what it is, Detective. I'm a healthy forty-one-year-old woman who still has needs and wants."

"Are you saying you understood Dr. Barrett's need to stay with his wife?"

"No, but I did accept it."

"I don't believe you, Senator."

"Well, you can believe what you want, but I swear, I haven't seen him intimately since before the renewal of their vows."

"Really? You're really going to sit here and look directly into my eyes and tell me you haven't seen him intimately? Really?"

"Yes, really," she replied emphatically.

Max pulled a photograph out from the file and slammed it down on the table in front of her. "Then how do you explain this photograph from Monday night?" Max said, pointing to the date stamp. "A nice little threesome going about their business as if nothing ever happened—the happy little family living in a love nest in New Jersey away from the crowds of people who might recognize them. I'd say that was pretty naïve of both of you to think we wouldn't put a tail on you." Max frowned, waiting for a response, but none came. "If you are that naïve, then maybe it's a good thing for the residents of New York that you'll be losing your stripes at a jury trial."

The senator's shoulders squared, but she was visibly upset and shaking. Her eyes darted around the room.

"Do you want to tell me now?" Max asked.

"My client refuses to answer your question on the grounds it may incriminate her," Jacquard intervened.

"Senator, you can tell me now or you can face a jury and let them decide your fate. You're looking at quite a few years behind bars. That means you will be nothing more than a faint memory to your daughter."

Jacquard rolled his eyes. "She's just trying to get you riled up, Kay. Don't fall for it." The senator nodded slowly and then began to fidget in her seat, cupping her four fingers over the others. She snapped her head toward the door when it opened and a uniformed officer walked inside with Jeffrey Barrett in tow. The minute Jeffrey realized it was the senator he took two steps backward as though ready to run in the opposite direction.

"Uh-oh," the officer said looking surprised. "Geez, Max, I'm sorry. The desk sergeant said the room was free."

Upon seeing him, the senator gasped and called out his name. "Jeffrey." His eyes dropped downward. "Jeffrey!" He ignored her. "What's wrong with you?" she asked, but again, he remained silent. The senator turned to her attorney, a baffled expression on her face. Jacquard said something to her in a low voice, and she quieted down, but a mask of confusion covered her face.

"Max, I need to see you for a minute," the officer said.

"Can it wait?"

"No. I don't think you'll want to wait for this information."

"Okay." Max held her finger up. "Please excuse me for a minute." She shut off the recorder. Just before exiting, she turned to Riley. "Will you take Dr. Barrett to another interview room while I speak with the uniform?"

Riley jumped up and led the doctor down the hall. When Max finished talking with the officer, she returned to the room and tried to gauge the senator's reaction to everything that had happened in the past fifteen minutes. It was obvious anger was swelling inside the woman's chest because the triangle at the base of her neck was visibly pulsating like a stuttering dial tone.

"Thank you for waiting," Max said to them when she returned to the room and placed a manila folder down on the table. Riley returned a few minutes later and sat down. Mr. Jacquard leaned toward his client and again whispered in her ear. As much as the woman tried to hide her panic, it was very obvious she was scared. Max pressed the recorder button down and continued, "Senator, I thought you'd like to know, the officer who was just in here with Dr. Barrett picked him up at his residence and brought him down for questioning. Unfortunately for you, Senator Stansbury, he found the doctor packing his suitcase. He was planning to leave town without you." Max tilted her head to the side and raised her brows. "Do you still think Dr. Barrett is an honest man?"

The senator gasped. "I'm telling you, Kay," Jacquard warned. "Don't listen to her."

"Do you know what else he had in his possession?" Max waited a few seconds for effect and noticed an increase in the pace of the senator's breathing. "A single one-way ticket to the Republic of Macedonia in the name of Souley Regains. And oddly enough, he had a passport with his picture using the same name. It sounds to me like he was jumping ship and letting you take the fall for whatever Helen Barrett was referring to in her note. Knowing that, do you still want to stand by him and let him do this to you?"

"Jeffrey wouldn't do that to me. He loves me, and he loves my daughter. I'm his ticket to the one thing Helen couldn't give him—children."

"Fine. You can believe that fantasy all you want. Just don't say I didn't warn you."

"I don't need a warning, Detective. We're in love, and that trumps everything."

"All right, then let me ask you this. Did you call him when my officers were at your house to bring you down here for questioning?"

"What exactly are you getting at?"

"If you told him that you'd been summoned for questioning, I'm sure he knew he'd be next and figured he'd better bail out before we found out too much. Too bad for him, we caught him in the act."

"Jeffrey wouldn't do that to me and Arianna."

"You're a fool if you believe that. Answer the question. Did you call and tell him you'd been summoned to come down here to the precinct?" Max said with a raised voice.

The senator gave a slow nod. Tears gathered in her eyes. "You're trying to trick me into saying something against the man I love. I know him well enough to know he wouldn't bail on me. We've been through too much together, and our relationship is rock solid now that Helen is out of the way."

"Kay," her attorney urged in a strong voice, "if you don't shut up, I'm going to walk out that door. Just remember, he has nothing to lose but money and prestige. You have a daughter."

"Senator, you have a choice here," Max said.

"Then show me some kind of proof that you're telling me the truth."

Max opened the file folder and pulled out the plane ticket and passport Jeffrey had in his pocket and showed it to her.

"That son of a bitch," she said sharply, abandoning any pretense.

"So now, are you ready to tell me how you two conspired to kill Helen? Because I'm beginning to think maybe it was you who killed Helen." Stansbury stiffened at the challenge. "Listen, I can understand you being the jealous mistress who figured getting the wife out of the picture would clear the path for you to be together, but I never figured you for a dummy."

"I did not." Her words shot out emphatically. "I had nothing to do with Helen's death. Nothing." She held her hand up in a swearing position. "Not a thing."

"Are you saying Jeffrey may have?"

"I don't know." She raised a dismissive shoulder.

"But you're having second thoughts now that you know he was bailing on you, aren't you, Senator? Honestly, I totally understand and wouldn't blame you one bit. I'd be angry too, especially after all the time you'd invested in this man and then he turned around and dumped you for his wife." Max shook her head to make the senator think she could relate to her situation. "The man you intended to marry who gave *her* the sensuous wedding night he'd promised you. I'll bet that just killed you, didn't it?"

The senator took a quick intake of breath.

"Kay, I'm warning you. Don't fall for this crap," Jacquard warned.

"I'll bet you even pictured them in the act, didn't you? And that's when you decided to wipe her out. With her out of the way, Jeffrey would have to come back into your arms, and the three of you could live happily ever after in some far-off exotic place that has no extradition treaty with the United States. You'd both be free and clear to do whatever you wanted without any worry. Isn't that right, Senator?" The woman remained silent, biting down on her lip so hard it started to bleed. "You actually trusted this man with your life and your child's life?" Max paused for a second, hoping the impact of her statement would spur the senator to tell the truth. "It's a shame the plan backfired."

"No. There's got to be some explanation as to why he only had one ticket. We had big plans."

"There is only one explanation, because he's already implicated you. He said it was your idea."

"What? He's lying."

"That's enough." Jacquard stood and pulled the senator by the arm. "You have nothing but circumstantial evidence. We're out of here."

"I don't think so, Mr. Jacquard. We have more than circumstantial evidence. I'll be holding the senator for seventy-two hours."

"No," she screamed. "You can't do that. My daughter. I have to get home to her. The sitter will be leaving shortly."

"Then I think you'd better call her father with your one phone call and make other arrangements."

She burst into tears. "Her father is dead." Mr. Jacquard tried to console her while Max buzzed for a uniform to take her into custody. A few seconds later, the door opened. "Take the senator to a holding cell."

"Wait," she said. "I'll tell you what I know."

"Kay, I'm advising you not to say a word."

"Mathias, shut the hell up! I can't do this anymore."

"Then I'm out of here. You know you've just lost your place in the political arena."

"The hell with the political arena. My daughter means more to me than my political status. I'm sorry, but I have to do this."

"You're playing right into their hands," Jacquard said.

"Mathias, you saw Jeffrey. He didn't respond to me nor did he make eye contact. I'm sorry you don't agree with what I'm doing, but I have to, for me and Arianna, and hope the court will take pity on me because I finally told the truth." The door slammed, and the woman heaved a forceful breath.

"Do you want something to drink before we begin?" Riley asked.

"Yes. My mouth is parched. But before I talk, will you speak to the DA so he'll go easier on me?"

"Your cooperation will go a long way, and the DA will know you admitted to your responsibilities. What he'll do with that information is anyone's guess. I can't guarantee a positive result, but you'll be far better off admitting the truth than if you lie. Do you still want to talk?"

Stansbury stared into space. She inhaled deeply and blew it out. "I do. What kind of role model would I be for my daughter if I don't confess to my wrongdoing? My only hope is that someday she'll understand that I did it for her."

Regardless of what Kay Stansbury had done, Max couldn't help but feel sorry for her. She nodded for her to begin. "Go ahead, Senator. Please tell us what happened."

"My daughter, Arianna, is six years old. She was born with a defect in her heart that eventually got worse, though we didn't know about it until two years ago. She was near death until Jeffrey saved her life. The transplant was actually on her birthday, you know?" She stopped to dry her tears. "What would you have done if it was your daughter, Detective?" Max stared at her but remained silent. The senator began to cry harder. "I'm sorry. I couldn't let my daughter die because she wasn't next on that list of transplants." She took a sip of water and tried to calm down. "Jeffrey and I thought we had the perfect plan of what to do and when to do it, and then he got careless one night when we were talking on the phone. He didn't see Helen hiding behind a pillar on their back patio listening to his side of our conversation. For months, she kept threatening she'd go to the authorities. Jeffrey decided to beat her at her own game and froze her out of all their monetary holdings, and refused to release the freeze. That's when Helen decided to take matters into her own hands and began to blackmail me. Seeing that she wasn't going to back down, I convinced Jeffrey to unfreeze the accounts and pretend he was in love with her again. The renewing of vows was his idea, but he had to convince her he was sincere . . . and he did a good job."

"And she obviously believed him?"

"Apparently. And afterward, when he looked so happy, I wasn't sure what was ahead."

"You started to worry?"

"Yes. I have to be honest. It could have been worse, but I was happy I still had my daughter."

"Is that why you killed Helen?"

Stansbury held up her hand. "I swear to you," she said, shaking her head, "as God is my witness, I had nothing to do with Helen's death."

"You know, he's blaming you for killing Helen," Max lied.

"What?" Tears gushed down her cheeks like a broken dam. "I don't understand why he would do this to me. Why would he give my daughter a heart transplant, then turn around and do all the things you've said?" The senator looked dazed. "None of this makes any sense," she said. "You're making this up so I'll confess, aren't you?"

"No, Senator, I wish I were making it up. You saw him when he came in here. He ignored you—didn't even look at you. You have to know this wasn't something he just arbitrarily decided upon as an afterthought. Oh no," Max said, shaking her head. "This was his plan all along. By giving you something, such as your daughter's transplant, he lured you into believing he was committed to you and your beautiful daughter so you'd never suspect he was capable of doing such a thing." Max shook her head. "Yeah, I've seen creeps like this before." Max noticed Stansbury's tears lessening as the conversation continued. Her face was tense.

"So do you want to tell us about your grand plan and how you managed to pull it off?" Riley asked.

"Jeffrey took care of everything."

"Okay," Max said, although she didn't believe her. "Then can you explain an entry on your campaign funds ledger for a hundred thousand dollars paid out to the M. C. Party Planners?"

"What about it?" she asked. "I don't handle my money. I have an accountant for that."

"Then why do you suppose that entry is in your handwriting?"

Stansbury's mouth gaped.

"I'm astounded you're so surprised, Senator. You're a bright woman. Did you think no one would ever suspect what you did was illegal?"

"People do foolish things in the name of love." Stansbury crossed her arms and rested them against her chest.

"That's a lot of money for a catered affair." Riley said.

"I'm sure you can understand . . . ," she said.

"All right, Senator." Max's eyes narrowed. "Enough," she said gruffly. "Let's get down to specifics. Isn't it true that the entry for M. C. Party Planners is just a fictitious event created by you and Dr. Barrett?"

Stansbury licked her parched lips.

"Here's your chance to tell your side of the story, Senator. You've already seen that covering for him is a worthless cause," Max warned. "After examining yours and Dr. Barrett's financial accounts, we found two entries for a hundred thousand, both paid to M. C. Party Planners. Yours is an entry on your campaign ledger, and Dr. Barrett's is from his Souley account. We believe that you paid the original one hundred thousand as hush money out of your campaign funds to the individual who covered up the illegal heart transplant, and the second payout from Dr. Barrett's account was made because the individual was blackmailing you . . . or maybe it was paid to kill Helen Barrett? How am I doing so far, Senator?"

Stansbury's eyes cast downward as she played with the lid from the bottle of water sitting on the table in front of her. Max's silence caused the senator to look up. Max's patience was waning. "Listen, if you're just going to ignore my questions, then there's no reason for us to waste time. We have a lot of work to do." Max turned to Riley. "Will you call for a uniform to transport the senator to her cell?"

"Okay, I'll answer your questions, but I hope this is going to keep me from going to jail."

"I told you before, I can't guarantee anything, but I will tell the district attorney that you did cooperate."

Noticing she'd finished her bottle of water, Riley passed another over to her and one to Max.

"The money, Senator? What was the money you paid out for?" She didn't respond. "What was Dr. Barrett's payout?"

"I don't know."

"Did you use your campaign funds to make that payment?" Stansbury simply stared at Max. "Your lack of a response tells me that's exactly what you used.

"Was the money used to blow up the car with Helen Barrett in it?"

"Not as far as I was concerned. I have no idea if Jeffrey had planned to do that. I don't know why he let her drive his car when he wouldn't even let her ride in it." She shrugged. "Honestly, it was surprising to me."

"I'm going to ask you this again. Did you use your campaign funds to pay out the one hundred thousand?" The senator continued to stare. "Okay, Senator, I'm going to take your silence as a yes." When the senator neither admitted nor denied, Max knew she had her answer.

"Was part of your payout to M. C. Party Planners to kill Helen?"

"I told you, dammit, I had nothing to do with that."

"Then tell me who the owner of this company is."

"I . . . don't . . . know." She blew her nose. "My aides took care of that function for me."

"So if the aides took care of that for you, why was Jeffrey paying the funds out of the Souley account?"

"How should I know?" Max noticed her eye twitch, a known physical indication from the body language experts that she was lying.

"Senator, you're lying."

"Talk to Jeffrey. I gave the money to him and he handled it all."

"From your campaign funds?" Max said. The senator looked directly into Max's eyes. "Okay, Senator, I'm once again going to take your nonverbal response as a yes." Max took a breath before continuing. "Does the M. C. stand for Melanie Chambers, the transplant coordinator? Did she need money, and you caught her at a vulnerable time?"

The senator remained silent.

Max refused to play her game. "I'm going to ask you *one* more time, Senator, did you two conspire to kill Helen Barrett?"

"I told you, no. I might have wished she was dead, but I didn't have anything to do with it. I don't know why he gave her the keys to his car, and I sure as hell don't know if he killed her. What I do know is that he wasn't about to give up his millions to her and have to start all over."

"Oh, really?"

"Can I go home to my daughter now?"

"I'm afraid not, Senator." Max nodded to Riley, who removed his handcuffs from the back of his belt as he stood.

"Senator Kay Stansbury, please stand and put your hands behind your back." It was obvious the fact she was about to be arrested hit her hard, because she was sobbing. "You are under arrest for attempted murder, conspiracy to commit murder, fraud and conspiracy to commit fraud, as well as hindering prosecution and false statements to law enforcement. You have the right to remain silent . . ."

"You can't do this. I'm a senator of the United States of America."

"Actually, Senator, I can. Just because you're a senator doesn't give you a license to break the laws. You not only broke the rules of your office, but there's no excuse for your behavior. Rest assured, these charges are only a beginning." Max nodded to Riley, who opened the door and called a uniform into the room.

"You tricked me, Detective. You made me think you were my friend just so I'd spill my guts. You know how vulnerable I am right now."

"First of all, you are an adult. Second of all, I did no such thing. And if you recall, I have a recording of the conversation to prove it."

Stansbury clamped her mouth shut and stared at the floor. "I have to make arrangements for my daughter's care," she said in a remorseful voice.

"And you'll have your chance. Right after you change into your orange jumpsuit." Max nodded to the uniform to take her away.

Riley turned to Max. "So what's your take on her involvement with Helen's killing?" he asked.

"I'm not convinced she took part in it, but that remains to be seen. That's one down and a few more to go. Let's go see if the attorney for Dr. Wonderful has arrived."

"By the way," Riley said after the senator was carted away, "having the uniform come in here with Barrett was classic."

"Oh, I didn't plan that." She gave Riley a hard wink, and he laughed.

"Good afternoon, Dr. Barrett," Max said after walking into the interrogation room, thankful that Riley had taken all the necessary steps to prepare him for questioning. She eased her way over to the recorder, clicked the remote, and stated the names of those in attendance.

"You're in a lot of trouble, Dr. Barrett. Do you know that?" Barrett gave her an impetuous glare. "Where were you going when our officers came to your house?"

"My attorney is on his way, and I'll answer no questions until he's present."

"That's certainly your right, but cooperating with us now is in your best interest."

"I've done nothing wrong."

Max snickered. "Then you have nothing to worry about. Right?" she said matter-of-factly. "We had this same conversation on Wednesday morning. You came down here to find out how much I knew?" He glowered at her. "You can pretend you're innocent, but that isn't what your dead wife said."

"Excuse me?"

"Did you know that juries have a tendency to give more credence to a victim who speaks from the grave than if they were listening to them in person?"

He snickered, crossing his arms. He leaned back as though closing his mind off to the conversation, but after a moment, he took the bait. He snorted. "So now you're going to tell me you had a séance and she spoke to you?" he mocked. "What kind of fool do you take me for?"

"You don't believe me, huh?" Max shoved a piece of gum into her mouth. "You know what I think, Doc? I think you underestimated your wife. No one could ever accuse Helen Barrett of being a dummy. In fact, she was a woman who knew you so well that she suspected you might try to do something to her, and because of that, she left a handwritten note in Maddie's duties binder." His eyes narrowed with skepticism. "She did!" Max held up her hand. "And you know where it was? Right in the pantry! Maddie didn't even know it was there. I guess your wife knew you would never have any reason to be looking in that binder, but there was a chance Maddie would at some point."

Barrett's eyes smoldered with fire.

"From what Mrs. Barrett told us, I'm afraid this party is over for you and the senator." His lips twisted into a cynical grin. "Yes, Doc." She nodded her head up and down. "Aren't you even curious about the note?" She waited for a reaction, but he maintained the cool exterior so inherent to those in the medical field. "Okay." Max shrugged. She walked to the door, opened it, and called out to another detective, "Will you please escort Dr. Barrett to a holding cell?"

"With pleasure."

Max moved out of the way to allow him to cuff the doctor and watched as an angry Barrett stared her down, daring her to defy him. She knew that look all too well from her adoptive father. She stood erect, unflinching as she stared right back at him without breaking her focus. She watched as he was escorted down the hall to the holding cells and then turned toward her partner.

"Okay, Riley, we have a lot of work to do within the next seventy-two hours. Our first stop is to give the boss an update. There's a lot more than meets the eye on this one."

"Yes, ma'am, but let me bring you up to date on the M. C. Party Planners," Riley said, catching up with her long stride. "Lucille Brennen, who was in charge of the senator's entertainment during the campaign, has no knowledge of this catering company and said they never catered any of the senator's functions. She didn't hire them, but she did say she was out for a few weeks with a leg injury. She suggested checking with Gwen Miller, the senator's accountant. Oh, and bringing up whether or not they both paid out that money does beg the question of blackmail. Good going. Despite Stansbury's silence, I'd bet my paycheck that she used her campaign funds."

Max glanced at the clock on the wall. She was tired, but her anxiety to solve this case was pushing her forward. "I'm not concerned," she said, "because I know our guys will find it when they go over her accounts with a fine-toothed comb." Riley was smiling at Max for no apparent reason. "What?" she asked.

"I was just thinking about how lucky I am to be working with you. You're like the Energizer Bunny—so full of knowledge, you've helped me tremendously, and I know I'm going to be a better detective." He smiled. "So thank you."

"It's called paying it forward. Howie taught me, and whatever knowledge I can impart on you helps me pay the debt back to him."

"I guess being part of the upper echelon gets you better cases," Riley said.

She laughed. "It's seniority."

"I think you're being a bit humble here. You're a damn good detective, Max, and I'm honored to be working with you."

"Thank you. I enjoy working with you too. I like your youthful energy too—that's something that was missing for me for a few years. God rest his soul, Howie was a wonderful partner, the father I always wanted, and a very knowledgeable mentor. I learned so much from him, and I'll always be grateful for that. He was a good detective, but he had slowed down considerably toward the end." She patted his shoulder.

"Your enthusiasm and excitement motivates me. So I have to thank you too, for giving me that extra sparkle."

Riley's face turned crimson, and it brought a smile to her face. "Thank you, Max. I'm flattered by your compliment."

Seeing his embarrassment, she changed the subject. "I'd like to stop at the lieutenant's office to see if he'll approve overtime. I want to utilize every minute of those seventy-two hours to prove them guilty."

"Want me to wait here?" he asked.

"Hell no. C'mon, let's talk to him together." Trying to keep up with her, Riley walked faster.

"What's happening, Max?" Wallace asked when he heard her voice. She and Riley both entered his office.

"Good news, Lieutenant. I just arrested Senator Stansbury. She spilled most of her guts after finding out that her cohort was trying to skip out of the country without her. Barrett however, clammed up and is waiting for his attorney, and since the clock is ticking, we need a warrant for the heart transplant records for the years 2012–2014."

"And?" Wallace's brow rose. "What else?" Max looked at him expectantly. "And you want me to approve overtime?" She scrunched up her face. Wallace groaned. "All right, let's do it. I know I don't have to tell you the captain is going to have my ass on this one, but with it being a high-profile case, we do what is necessary. I'll have one of the guys get your warrant and serve it."

"Thank you, Lieutenant." They exited his office, and Max caught Riley's grin. "And what's that grin for?"

"I was just thinking, *and that's how it's done.*"

"Right"—Max flashed a toothy grin—"and *that's* how it's done!"

CHAPTER
TWENTY-NINE

Max groaned and blinked her eyes shut when she saw attorney F. Leigh McGuire strut his stuff into the precinct late Thursday afternoon. "I have to go, Cory," Max said. "Barrett's attorney is here."

"Who is it?"

"None other than F. Leigh McGuire."

"Ooh, he's an arrogant son of a bitch."

"My sentiments exactly. I've had previous dealings with him, when I was a rookie. He was representing a known gangster that I arrested and charged with first-degree murder. The DA, Ryan Sullivan, argued the case, but he was no match for this skilled attorney."

Cory snickered. "If you want someone who can twist the truth, then he's your guy."

"He was so good, he got the case dismissed. But you know what? He taught me to be prepared, and I won't lose to him again."

"Good girl. Okay, catch up later?"

"I hope so. I'll call you either way."

Max was definitely prepared this time. She couldn't wait to compile all the evidence she had on Jeffrey Barrett, the Mr. Tough Guy who thought he was above it all. She loved being confronted by men like him and his lawyer so that she could prove she had no problem holding her own.

When the uniform brought Barrett to the interrogation room, she'd been expecting his belligerent attitude. She found it interesting how quickly he'd changed from the forlorn widower to a caged lion; his reproachful eyes and creased forehead signaled his change of demeanor when he sat down. She'd give him just enough rope to hang himself. His expression told her he was used to being in charge. He bulldozed over the first words out of her mouth.

"I don't have time for this game you're playing, Detective. I was scheduled to perform a transplant that had to be reassigned to another surgeon. If that patient dies, that's on you."

"And a very good afternoon to you too, Dr. Barrett." She nodded to his attorney as a polite acknowledgment.

"If you don't start asking me questions," Barrett bellowed, "I'm going to walk right out of here." He scowled.

"You think so, huh?" Max's hand shot to her hip as her voice boomed, "Then let me remind you that I'm running the show in this room, and if you set one foot out of this office, there are several uniforms right outside just waiting for you to step out of line." Turning to his attorney, she said, "I'd suggest that you instruct your client to speak when spoken to. Am I making myself clear?"

McGuire's hand clamped onto his client's arm while he spoke to him in a low voice. A few seconds later, Barrett seemed more resigned.

"Senator Stansbury and your deceased wife have implicated you in a grand scheme to buck the transplant protocol, Dr. Barrett." He gave her a skeptical frown. "I find it very interesting, Doc," Max said with a chuckle, "that you don't believe anything I tell you. Trust me, I don't make claims unless I have documentation or a witness to prove it." He remained silent, but his smirk did not go unnoticed. "So tell me, what do you have to say about that?"

"Not a thing. They're both nuts. I knew the minute I'd met Kay she was going to be a big pain in my ass. I loved my wife with all my heart, but she did have bouts of insecurities and did things just to hurt me."

"Is that why you froze her out of all the monetary accounts?"

"I told you why I did that. I was trying to convince her to stay with me."

"Hmm, that's not what the senator said. She implicated you in every way."

"What did you expect her to do?" Barrett fired back.

McGuire put his hand up. "Detective, how exactly did Senator Stansbury implicate my client? Your report doesn't show any documentation to prove her allegations. She's a disgruntled woman who made a play for my client, and it didn't work."

"That's not exactly true, Mr. McGuire." Max pulled out the photographs of the love nest. "Your client, Senator Stansbury, and her daughter were caught walking out of a home in New Jersey just last Monday."

"That hardly proves your claim. You realize the child is under his care?"

"Of course, I do, Mr. McGuire, but I highly doubt that care includes a sleepover in a home that belongs to Madeline Thomas, Dr. Barrett's maid, do you?" She showed him all the photographs they had from their searches. "When we first questioned the senator and the doctor, they both made false claims about everything, including when they met, but now we have the proof."

"You've obviously had Dr. Barrett under surveillance. Do you have any photographs of them in bed together?" McGuire asked.

"If I may intrude here, Mr. McGuire," Riley spat out, "you're passing this off as nothing by making an excuse for everything we have. Dr. Barrett may have you on his side right now, but I can assure you, we have enough evidence to put him away for a long time. Make no mistake: we will be taking advantage of the hours we have left to hold your client while we gather more incriminating evidence, even if we have to get an extension."

"And what are the charges?" McGuire asked.

Max stepped in. "First-degree murder, fraud, conspiracy, and that's just for starters. We're not talking menial offenses here, Mr. McGuire, we're talking major felonies."

"And my client explained this to you, Detectives. This woman has tried every way to get my client into her life but hasn't been successful other than having him care for her daughter."

"Is that a fact? With all due respect, Mr. McGuire, that's a fabrication and you know it." Max displayed Helen's handwritten note.

McGuire read the note. "Again, Detective, this proves nothing. You know the Barretts were having marital problems. Mrs. Barrett probably wrote this out of spite after my client froze their assets and simply forgot to get rid of it after she agreed to remarry my client."

"I highly doubt that, Mr. McGuire, but just so you'll know, we found a key to a safe deposit box, and I suspect we're going to prove that the renewal of vows was simply a sham."

"That's ridiculous!" Barrett shouted. "Helen and I were madly in love that morning."

"You mean, so in love that you couldn't wait to buy another Lamborghini the day after her death, when you could have used her Mercedes that was unharmed in the carriage house garage? So in love that you went back to work that same day? Is that the love you're talking about?"

"You don't know what either of the Barretts felt," McGuire fired back. "You're playing a guessing game."

"Well, you've got me there, Mr. McGuire, but this note confirms Mrs. Barrett wasn't sure she could trust her husband, and this was her way of evening out the score. In addition, Mr. McGuire, did Dr. Barrett tell you he was skipping out of the city for the Republic of Macedonia, a country that has no extradition treaty with the US, and that he was impersonating Souley Regains on his passport as well as with a checking account? A checking account Helen Barrett had opened as insurance for her maid, Maddie, and her family's future. She even purchased a home in New Jersey to go along with that insurance—the love nest where the doctor and the senator were shacking up."

"Maybe the maid gave him permission to use it."

"Mr. McGuire, Madeline Thomas has no knowledge of any of this."

It was obvious McGuire's patience was running thin by the way he kept glancing over at his client, then back to her. "You have to know, as a world-renowned surgeon, my client is recognized no matter where he goes if he uses his real name. He must use a false identity if he wants to enjoy himself when he travels. I'm sure you can understand that."

"Well, hell, that explains everything!" Max's hand bounced off the table. "Unfortunately, using the Souley Regains identity wasn't just for travel purposes, because Dr. Barrett used this identity for other things as well, like paying out a hundred grand to a fictitious company that was to have catered a political event for the senator, an event that never actually took place. Can you imagine our surprise when we found what we first thought to be a deposit from the senator's campaign fund into the Souley account for this exact dollar amount, but now we're questioning whether it was a double payment to M. C. Party Planners? We believe Dr. Barrett paid the M. C. Party Planners for killing his wife, and the senator paid the same party planner for fudging the records for the illegal heart transplant, all one day apart. How do you explain that?" she asked.

"I presume you have proof of this, Detective?"

"Not at the moment, but I will. You can count on it, Mr. McGuire."

"Detective, tsk, tsk. You know better than to play this game with me."

She chuckled as he held up her hand. "Oh, trust me. This is no game to me. By the way, Mr. McGuire, do you know who this Souley guy really is?"

"A made-up name, I presume."

"Nope. It's the husband of Mr. Barrett's maid, who resides in Jamaica." McGuire glanced at his client again, making it obvious he hadn't been told about the things Max was presenting as evidence. Pursing his lips, McGuire held his hand up. "Detectives, can we reconvene a little later? I haven't had much time to discuss your allegations with my client."

"Of course." She pressed a buzzer, and two uniforms entered and cuffed Jeffrey Barrett and escorted him out of the room. "Enjoy your evening, Dr. Barrett." Max smirked, and Barrett's expression threw daggers at her.

"Leigh," Barrett yelled out. "Get me out of this hellhole."

"Jeffrey," McGuire warned, and nodded at the detectives on his way out. "Good day, Detectives."

Max flopped into the chair and blew out a large breath. Riley was grinning from ear to ear. "You know, Riley, I used to hate it when attorneys would try to make me look bad when I was arresting their clients, but not anymore."

"Why is that?"

"Because that sharp attorney who just walked out of here is the one who taught me a valuable lesson. I lost a case because he was fast on his feet and managed to shoot holes in my evidence. The case was lost, and the Mafioso I was trying to get convicted was released."

She groaned and pushed herself out of the chair again. The two almost ran into Lieutenant Wallace as they headed out the door.

He was smiling at Jeffrey Barrett in handcuffs, walking down the hall with a uniformed officer and not looking very happy about it. "Well, it looks like you got your man?"

"Not completely. There are still some other things to check. We're off first thing in the morning to get the heart transplant record boxes picked up."

"I didn't get a call from their legal department confirming that."

"But your secretary did and called me."

He shook his head, "Boy, I don't know what I'd do without that woman. She runs a tight ship."

"Yes she does!"

"Go sic 'em, tiger."

CHAPTER THIRTY

"You know you're wasting your time, don't you?" a well-dressed woman said when Max and three uniforms walked into the department and handed her the subpoena for all the boxes containing the heart transplant records.

Checking her nametag, Max realized she was talking to Melanie Chambers, who apparently had returned to work. "I hope you're right, Mrs. Chambers," Max said. "But that's what we need to find out. Will you be around if I have questions?"

"All day, Detective. I have a lot of work to do."

Max's heart ached for the woman, knowing what she must have gone through after her daughter had been killed, but it didn't change the fact that she may have colluded with Barrett. She'd be charged just like any other criminal. Max observed signs of strain and depression on her face. But it was her dark eyes that got Max the most. They appeared sunken, with dark circles underneath.

"This is nothing personal, Mrs. Chambers. We're just doing our jobs—the same way you do yours. We'll return these boxes as soon as we're done with them," Max said and turned to leave.

Melanie stepped back and simply stared as the uniforms placed boxes on his hand truck to carry out of the building. Melanie shook her head in disgust as Max walked away. "What a waste of taxpayers' money," she said. "And what if I need something from the records?" she called out to Max.

"I'm sure you have a backup measure in place." Max turned her attention to the uniforms helping. "Guys, make sure you get all the boxes from June 2012 to the current day." Max gave Melanie a slight wave. Following the cart of boxes down the service elevator and into the parking lot, Max watched the uniforms load the boxes into a police van, when she noticed Riley on a call. He disconnected and walked over to her.

"I just spoke to the lieutenant, and he said a member of the Organ Procurement and Transplantation Network is en route to JFK International from Virginia to get involved with the transplant records. They think we're on a fishing expedition."

Max's lip curled. "We can't worry about what they think! Based on Helen Barrett's note and the senator's confession, we have a host of people involved in this conspiracy, and we're going to jail every one of them. There's no way just one or two people are involved in this ruse. You remember the saying *no man is an island*? Well, I'm pretty sure there are a few people shaking in their boots with our investigation."

Riley nodded. "I agree, and I can't wait to go through these records. Are we going to have help?"

"Probably not."

Cory came to mind, and she wished he could help them go through the records, but she knew better than to ask. The fact that Cory had led them down the right path, opening avenues they probably would have found eventually but not as quickly without his help, had her a bit resentful. He deserved to be around for the final stages. She knew that was irrational thinking on her part. With all the evidence they needed to go through, she wouldn't be able to see him for a couple of days. A churning feeling punched her insides, but she pushed it aside—she had more important things to worry about than her personal life. If she was supposed to have a relationship with Cory, then it would happen on its own. It wasn't like she was going to fall apart if it didn't work out. Hell, who was she kidding? For the first time in her life, she'd found someone who was perfect for her. Losing him would be devastating. They'd just have to learn how to work through their respective schedules and careers. She snickered, asking herself when she had become a lovesick puppy.

Max pulled into a space and cut the engine while the van pulled up to the entrance of the precinct.

"Where do you want us to unload these boxes?" the driver asked.

"Bring them to one of the interview rooms." Max walked past them and headed toward the lieutenant's office.

"I'll get started while you talk to Wallace," Riley said.

Max nodded and stuck her head inside the lieutenant's office. "Got a minute?"

"Yeah, sure. What's up?"

"We have a shitload of boxes and the better part of two days to complete our search. Who's free to help?"

"I've been checking all morning and haven't been real successful. We managed to get Fred Jones, and of course the doctor from the OPTN, but his flight doesn't get in until later."

"I just don't know how we're going to get it all done."

"I wish I could pay someone to come in, but we're already paying overtime for you and Riley. I don't think I can squeeze any more into the budget. The captain's already complaining that we haven't closed the case yet. Why don't you see what you can get done on your own? If things get tight, I'll see if I can get approval for another expenditure." His head tilted in sympathy. "I'm sorry, Max. I'll keep trying to find someone. In the meantime, you've got Fred."

"How about the rookie?" she asked.

"He's involved in a robbery across town."

Max sighed. "Okay, you know where I'll be." She left his office disappointed and tired of hearing about the damn budget constraints. She'd known better than to ask, but she did it anyway. Sometimes, she was her own worst enemy. Her negative thinking was making things worse. She needed to focus. What she feared most was not finishing their investigation before the seventy-two hours were up and Barrett fleeing to some foreign country. She had to make sure she had solid facts before McGuire shot her case to smithereens. She quickened her pace toward the evidence room. She didn't have time for negative thinking.

Riley and Fred were well into reviewing each file folder. "Did they give you any trouble?" Riley asked.

"No," she said, waving to Fred. "But Melanie assured me we weren't going to find anything." Max slipped out of her heels, ready to get to work. "She doesn't know how relentless we are, does she, Riley?"

"She sure doesn't, but she will."

"I really felt for her today, though. She looked terrible."

Fred looked up but didn't ask the obvious question. Fred Jones had worked out of the precinct the longest of anyone.

"Thanks for helping us," Max said.

"Happy to lend a hand."

"And we're happy to have you." Max smiled to herself as she spoke. She'd always liked Fred, who was a fine gentleman with impeccable manners and kind words to say about everyone. Hearing about Fred's journey to the NYPD was an interesting tale. In his younger days, his dream was law enforcement, but his strong Catholic family had other plans for his future and shipped him off to a seminary. After his ordination, he'd been assigned to a church to serve as pastor, but his dream of being a member of New York's finest intensified, and he ultimately hung up his robe and enrolled in the police academy.

Fred concentrated on the file in his hand, his index finger on the side of his nose, reminding Max of Santa Claus. With white hair that glistened under the overhead lights and his rotund body, he was an easy double for Santa, and she could almost picture him flying through the air on his reindeer-driven sleigh.

"Is anyone else coming to help us?" Riley asked.

"No." Max draped her coat over the chair. "The boss has been trying to find someone who's free, but with budget constraints—"

"Yeah," Riley cut in. "What is he waiting for? For the full seventy-two hours to be up without us finding enough to nail Barrett?" Max gave Riley the stare, and he knew to stop complaining in front of Fred.

"Let's just think positive. The lieutenant has already extended the budget with our overtime. We're going to find something soon."

"Boy, some of these cases are pretty sad," Fred said, changing the subject while pulling out a file folder. "The candidates hang on until the eleventh hour only to find out there was something wrong with the match. I can't even begin to imagine what these families go through."

"I'm sure. How are these boxes labeled?" she asked.

"Basically, by month and year—same as the other records."

"No magic formula, huh?" Max said.

"Afraid not."

Max looked through her notes to see when the senator's daughter's surgery took place, then sought that box out first.

"Are you cheating?" Riley asked.

Her face cracked into a toothy grin. She removed the lid from the box, pulled out the Stansbury child's file and leafed through the papers. She wanted to understand the time frame of the girl's surgery. "I can't wait to find the file of the bypassed candidate so I can prove to the OPTN and McGuire that Helen's note was factual." Checking the dates on the lineup of folders, Max noticed that there were two surgeries listed for that day.

"I can't see how Chambers wasn't involved if she has the final say, but is it possible the technicians were the ones to fudge the records?" Riley said.

"That's always a possibility," Max said. "This case is like a ten-million-piece puzzle and sometimes the pieces fit, sometimes they don't. I guess no one said it was going to be easy."

Max turned back to the file and scanned the dates of care for Arianna Stansbury. She wrote down the particulars. "Okay, the kid's first bout with problems started in August 2012 . . . her surgery was on July 2, but if they were correct, there should be another file." She flipped through the tabs on the file folders looking for dates. "But it's not here." Max checked her notes. "So if that's the case, then where the hell is the file?" she asked aloud.

"What are you mumbling about over there?" Riley asked.

"I'm missing a file. Can you guys stop what you're doing and help me search through these boxes for any files dated July 2014? I'm going to give the staff the benefit of the doubt here and say I think it's been misfiled."

Twenty minutes later, Riley was the first to speak. "There's nothing in these file boxes."

"Yeah, I've searched in my boxes and the only thing I've found is the Stansbury kid's info. If she was the only candidate for that day, then why the rumors about a transplant being out of order? I would think there would have to be another file." Max was beginning to fume.

"I can't find anything either," Fred said, shaking his head.

"You guys continue; I'm going to make another trip to the hospital."

Max walked over to Stephanie, whom she'd seen earlier doing the filing. The young girl was a cute, stylish redhead with a bridge of freckles across her nose. She was very young, and her demeanor screamed *first job*. The young woman was still filing. She looked up when she heard Max's footsteps.

"Hi, Detective. Did you forget something?"

"My boxes are missing a file for July 2, 2014." Max felt like a skyscraper standing next to the short young woman, as she looked down to speak to her.

"All the files should have been in those boxes," she said. "We have strict rules about everything being filed in their proper places at all times in case one of the surgeons wants to refer back to a case study."

"Yes, I'm sure you do, but in the real world, not everyone follows the rules." Max was getting tired of hearing how flawless the staff claimed to be, but there was a chink in their armor with this missing file. "Is it possible the last person to view it inadvertently filed it in the wrong box?"

"That would be highly unusual. Regardless, I'll look for the file and get back to you. Is there anything else I can do for you?"

"Actually, there is. Do you have an index of patient surgeries and the names of which surgeons performed the transplants?"

"Yes, but you should have had that index in the year-end box."

"Ah, I guess that's what I missed. I went straight for the gusto instead of looking through the boxes. Where would I have found it?" Max asked.

"Each year-end box should have a red file folder with a tally sheet for the entire year that lists every surgery with detailed information of what happened at what time, who performed it, the patient's condition during the surgery, everything you need to know. And it should be initialed by the staff member handling the procedure."

"Even the patients who've expired?"

"Absolutely. Hang on while I get you another copy. Excuse me for a minute."

Max called Riley, asking him to check the December 2014, box. "Is there a red file folder at the end, or maybe it's the front, of the year-end 2014 file box?"

She could hear Riley moving boxes and rifling through the file folders. "Oh, wait a minute," he said. "Here it is." There was a pause. "Okay, what do you want me to do with it?"

"Open it. Does it have a year-end index list of surgeries for 2014?"
"Yes."
"Then tell me what you see for July 2," she said.

"One surgery for Arianna Stansbury, but . . . hmm," Riley said. "Something's funny here. It looks like this document was created in Excel, but there's an inconsistency just above the Stansbury kid's name. That's not the case with any of the other dates, and there are multiple pages of transplants that took place. Obviously, something was deleted, but the cell itself was not. It's been left blank. I would have thought with a center that's supposed to be spot-on with rules and regulations, their printouts would be the same."

Max's heavy lashes flew up in surprise. "Really?"

"Yes, ma'am."

Stephanie walked back into the room, and Max held her finger up. "Hang on a minute, Riley."

"Here's the index, Detective."

"Thank you, Stephanie, but my partner did find it. Sorry for making you go through the trouble. If you don't mind, can I keep this second copy?"

"Of course."

"You know, though," Max said acting embarrassed, "I am confused about something."

"What's that?"

"If what we have been told about the primary and secondary candidates both being prepped for the transplant just in case the primary doesn't meet the requirements for one reason or another, you'd keep that record, wouldn't you?"

"Oh God, yes. Melanie would have a coronary if something happened to it."

"So then the primary's name would still appear on the index with details about why that person was rejected?"

"Absolutely," she said with certainty.

Max pointed to the empty cell above the Stansbury's kid's name. "So why would there be an empty cell above her name?"

Stephanie's eyebrows rose. "I suspect Melanie deleted something and neglected to fix the chart."

"Melanie does these reports?" A confused frown cast over Max's face. "With everything she has to do?" The girl nodded. "I would have thought . . ." Max stopped.

"Exactly," Stephanie said with bitterness in her voice. "She said it had nothing to do with me."

"Oh, so you maintained these reports?"

"I did."

"But you don't do it now?" Max jerked her head back with a questionable look.

"Because Melanie took it over in July." Stephanie flung her hand in the air with displeasure. "I asked if I'd done something wrong, but she assured me it was nothing that had to do with me, but the proprietary nature of the senator's daughter's surgery." Stephanie's mouth twisted to the side. "Yeah, like I can't be trusted."

"Then why didn't she let her secretary do it?"

"Donna? Who knows." She looked over her shoulder. "God, I hate this job," she said, and then a sudden look of worry had her blowing air from her mouth. "I'm so sorry. I never should have said that."

"Hey, listen, you don't need to worry about me. I can see your frustration, and it's okay. I'm not going to squeal on you," Max assured.

"Thank you. I appreciate that."

"Is Melanie in her office so I can speak to her about this index and the missing file?"

"I'm afraid not. She's gone for the rest of the day."

"Oh, crap. She told me she was going to be around all day if I had questions."

"Donna probably could answer your question, though."

"Hmm, Donna." Max leaned in a little closer. "She's a little too stiff for me. I'm not sure I could work under her. Besides, you're much easier to work with."

Stephanie smiled widely. "Thank you!"

"Okay, so will you search for that file for me?"

"I will," Stephanie said. "Hey, do you have any openings for secretaries at the police station?"

"We're always looking for clerks. Our office isn't set up like this, though. We have a typing pool, so you'd be working for anyone who handed you a typing job."

"I actually like the sound of that."

"If you're serious, I'll put in a good word for you."

"Would you really?"

"Absolutely. You're the only one who's gone out of your way to help me. That shows me you're dedicated to your job." Max meant what she'd said, but showing Stephanie she wasn't the enemy, she was hoping she'd get more information from her. Max lowered her voice when she saw Donna Gordon walk past them.

"Is there something I can help you with, Detective?"

"No, thanks. Stephanie has been extremely helpful."

"That's what we like to hear," she said, walking back to her office.

"You know I'm really surprised Melanie isn't here after she told me she would be. Did something happen?"

"I don't know, but she left suddenly. Something to do with her in-laws." Stephanie shifted from one foot to the other. "That's all I know."

"I'll have the supervisor of our clerks give you a call. Let me have your phone number. One more thing I should tell you about working at the precinct. It's a lot busier than what I've seen in this office." Max smiled. "Expect a call from Sabrina Hammond."

"Oh wow. That would be wonderful. Thank you so much."

"I imagine Melanie isn't the easiest person to work for either."

"She used to be, but something happened, and that's when everything changed around here."

"In what way?"

"Nervous and jerky, and even more so when Dr. Barrett walks into her office unannounced. But that's how we all act around him. He's the big guy on campus here . . . sort of like a god." She chuckled. "He's not very nice. He's demanding, and I'd better shut up. Well, I'll search for your file first, then I'd better get back to my filing before the Wicked Witch of the East comes back."

Max laughed. "Thanks for your help. Call me when you find the file, and I'll send one of our guys over to pick it up." She winked at the young girl. "Thanks for your help."

"And thanks for yours."

As soon as Stephanie walked back into the records room and shut the door, Max returned to her conversation with Riley. "Did you get all that?"

"I did. What do you make of it?"

"I think something's rotten in Denmark!"

"Melanie?"

"For sure," Max said on her way to the elevator. "There's a cover-up here."

"You think it's Barrett?"

"It's beginning to sound that way."

On the drive back, Max called Riley again. "Did the lieutenant manage to pull the rookie off his assignment to help us?"

"Yeah, he's in here now."

"Oh, good. So let him continue looking through the files, and I'd like you to call Lucio to see if he has any information on where Chambers' in-laws live. If she is there, I want her picked up for questioning."

"Will do."

"I think she's running scared," Max said.

"I should hope so, knowing we're examining the records."

"All right. I'm on my way," Max said.

Along the way, Max drew a mental picture in her mind of the connections to all the players and how she thought they fit into the equation. When her cell phone rang, she noticed it was Riley and clicked onto the call just as she was pulling into the parking garage.

"I have good news to share," he said. "I've traced Chambers' in-laws to Staten Island, so I called the locals, and sure enough, she is there visiting. And she's being picked up by the police as we speak. They've agreed to drive her to the precinct."

"Excellent. Okay, I'm here, Riley. Be up in a minute."

Max walked into the lieutenant's office and told him about Melanie and the missing file.

"I've heard. She should be here in the next couple of hours. We don't have time to waste."

"Yes, sir," she said as she saluted.

"Listen," Wallace continued, "you and Riley look like you haven't slept in a week. Why don't you take the night off? I'll have the night shift pick up the slack so you're ready to rock 'n' roll first thing tomorrow morning."

"No way," Max said. "I appreciate your concern, but this is one case I have to work until I get that bastard behind bars." Her voice was weary even to her own ears. "I'd love the help, though, to save time, because we're at a pivotal point." She turned to see Riley at his desk and motioned for him to come over. "The lieutenant has suggested we go home for the night. If you want to go home for some rest, that's fine, but I'm staying."

"Nope," he said, "if you're staying, so am I."

Wallace knew he was wasting his breath. "Then, get the hell upstairs and take a nap." Max nodded and headed up the stairs to the second floor, where the department had a room with bunk beds. Inside the room, she looked at Riley and said, "I'll take the top bunk."

Three hours later, Max was barreling down the stairs after some much-needed rest and a shower, ready to get back to work. She was anxious to see the look on Barrett's face when she charged him. She already had plenty of charges against him but felt whatever Helen had in her safe deposit box was going to clinch the deal and send that pompous ass off to prison. She was feeling very motivated. There was also no doubt in her mind now that the role Melanie Chambers had played was the key evidence to the entire fiasco. She wasn't so sure how Valerie Morrison fit into the scheme of things, though.

Riley was already sitting at his desk, talking to Santini and Bensonhurst, when Max walked over. Max glanced at the clock to check the time and it was one-fifteen Saturday morning.

"Here she is," Riley said and handed her a container of coffee.

"You're pretty awesome, Riley, you know that?" He blushed. She addressed the two detectives. "Thank you so much for helping us out."

"It was our pleasure," Bensonhurst said. "I'm sorry it wasn't sooner, but we're also dealing with a heavy workload."

"That's okay. I understand completely. So . . . don't keep me in suspense. What did you find?"

"I have a feeling your grin is going to be even brighter when you find out what we've got for you." Just hearing those words had her heart beating faster. "Today, you're going to get the distinct privilege of charging that asshole Barrett."

"Yeah," she said, encouraged, "tell me."

He held out four envelopes. "This is what we found in Helen Barrett's safe deposit box. One is addressed to the NYPD, one to the OPTN administration, one to the hospital board of directors, and the final one just says 'Maddie.' We opened the letter that was addressed to the NYPD."

"Ok." Max blew out a breath. "And?" She gestured with her hand. "C'mon, don't tease me. What's in the letter?"

"That Barrett and Senator Stansbury arranged an illegal transplant for the senator's daughter, and paid Melanie Chambers to alter the records so it would look official."

Max looked skyward. "Thank you, God!" Bensonhurst smiled at Max's reaction. "Then that's probably why the file was missing from the box," Max said, looking at Riley.

When Max noticed Wallace walking toward them with a big smile on his face, she knew it was more good news.

"Melanie Chambers has just arrived. They'll be bringing her upstairs in about ten minutes."

"I think I should take naps more often," Max said.

"Yeah, a lot can happen."

"For sure. Sounds good." Max watched as the elevator doors opened. Melanie Chambers was being escorted in their direction.

Strong enthusiasm surged through Max, knowing they were getting close to solving the case. There was more to do, but having Helen's letters was even better than she'd expected. Max and Riley followed Melanie into the interview room.

"Good afternoon, Mrs. Chambers," Max said, noticing the woman's eyes were swollen from crying. The guard removed her cuffs and she rubbed her wrists, giving the man a dirty look while chastising him.

"You know," she said, "you didn't have to make those cuffs so tight. I'm obviously not going anywhere." He shrugged and left the room.

Max gestured toward the chairs. "Have a seat, Mrs. Chambers." She did as she was told. "Can I get you a cup of coffee?" She simply nodded in agreement. "How are you doing?"

"I feel degraded and disrespected. I'm an upstanding citizen in this city, and there's no reason I should be treated any other way."

"I'm terribly sorry. I'll speak to my lieutenant about your complaint." Max glanced at Riley. She thought this interview was going to be a piece of cake, but it wasn't looking so good. "Before we start," Max said, "Detective Riley is going to read you your rights, and I'll be recording this session so we all remember what was said."

"Fine."

After Riley finished Mirandizing her, Max asked, "Would you like your attorney present?"

"No."

"Okay. That's fine. I just wanted to be sure you understood your rights. Do you know why you're here?"

"I heard. But I had nothing to do with what Dr. Barrett did or didn't do."

"Then why did you take off after my partner asked for the heart transplant records?" Riley asked.

"You mean, like going to my in-laws' house?" She gave an exaggerated eye roll and a disgusted snort. "I didn't know I needed permission to help my elderly in-laws, whom I fear won't be around much longer. I've already lost two relatives; I don't need to feel any more guilt than I already do."

"Two relatives?" Max inquired.

"Yes. My daughter and my granddaughter. I'm sure you've heard what happened to my daughter."

"Yes, I did, and I'm very sorry for your loss." Max could see the pain in her eyes. "I don't know what happened to your granddaughter, though."

"Her father, the one who never wanted her since she was born, got the custody of her after my daughter was killed."

"I'm very sorry to hear that. I had no idea."

"Why would you have known? You don't know me." The words shot out of her mouth with a vengeance.

Max cleared her throat. "All right. We're getting off on the wrong foot here, Mrs. Chambers, and that was not my intent. I understand you feel hostility, but we need some help here regarding an illegal transplant performed on the senator's daughter, and we know, as the lead coordinator, that nothing happens without your approval. Based on that, we believe you are involved in Barrett's scheme." Max tilted her head, waiting for a response.

"I don't have to agree with what the doctors want, but I work for them, and they pay my salary. It is not for me to decide whether they're right or wrong. I don't have the education they do."

"So . . . are you saying if they asked you to do something, regardless of whether or not you agreed with it, you'd go along simply because they are your bosses?"

"Isn't that what I get paid for?"

"Even if you knew it was illegal?"

"Detective, do you even have any idea what I've been through?"

"No, so tell me what went on. Help me to understand why you would take part in something like this."

"I was led to believe there was nothing wrong with changing the protocol if in the end it all worked out."

"I'm not sure I understand what that means. Are you saying he asked you to put the Stansbury child before another patient?"

"What I'm saying, Detective, is anything that occurred as a result is on Dr. Barrett's shoulders. I did what I was told to do, and now I'm in here."

Seeing she was getting nowhere fast, Max decided she was wasting valuable time. Taking one last shot before sending the woman to her cell, she continued.

"What can you tell me about the missing file?"

"If there is a missing file, you should know, as with any work environment—"

Max's hand shot up. "Stop," she said. "Look, you've already implicated yourself, so why are you going to lie about where you've hidden the file?"

Chambers patted her hair, apparent self-consciousness taking over before responding. "The clerk probably made an error and forgot to give you the box."

"Okay, then let's discuss the index of transplants on the sheet for July 2, which shows a single entry, with a blank cell above it. Did you delete an entry and hide the file somewhere so we wouldn't be able to find it?"

"I have no idea. It must have been Stephanie's error."

"That's not what I'm hearing, Mrs. Chambers. I was told you took over the data input in early summer and no longer allowed anyone else to touch it because of proprietary information concerns."

"Sorry, but I don't have a good answer for you," she replied.

"All right, one last question. Are you saying Dr. Barrett was in charge of the Stansbury child's heart transplant, and he more than suggested your assistance in the scheduling?"

"That's exactly what I'm saying. May I go home now?"

"I'm afraid not, Mrs. Chambers. You've just admitted your involvement in an illegal transplant. Just because you work for the man doesn't mean doing something illegal gets you the employee-of-the-year award. It makes you just as guilty." Max buzzed for a uniformed officer. "Please cuff Mrs. Chambers, and kindly refrain from making those cuffs too tight."

Max gave Riley the go-ahead, and he began, "Mrs. Chambers, you are being charged with falsifying medical records, and aiding and abetting an illegal transplant."

Melanie was sobbing again as she was escorted out of the room.

"I feel for the woman," Max said as she watched her taken away.

"Are you crazy, Max? Why would you feel sorry for a woman who knowingly committed a crime? Plus, you know she's lying."

"Because she's a poor, lost soul who feels she was forced into committing a crime, that's why. It's obvious to me that she needed the money and wound up losing the two things that mattered most to her."

Riley started laughing. "For chrissake, you must be in love. I've never seen you act like such a marshmallow." She crinkled her nose at him. "How about we let this fun continue and get the good old doctor up here so we can charge him too?"

"Sounds like a plan. I'll get the coffee, you get the doctor," she said and left the room.

When she returned to the room, Dr. Barrett and his attorney were sitting at the table. Having been in custody overnight, Barrett's normally clean-shaven face was now covered in dark stubble. Regardless of his rumpled and unkempt appearance, the man still had great sex appeal, and it was easy to see why he was able to seduce and manipulate two women, although it was clear that Helen was having the last laugh on him.

You've wasted enough of our time," McGuire snapped. "If you haven't come up with any charges against my client, then kindly let us get on with our lives."

Max opened her file. "Not so fast, counselor. Dr. Barrett, please stand." She nodded for Riley to cuff him. "Dr. Jeffrey Barrett, you are under arrest and charged with the first-degree murder of your wife, Helen Barrett, conspiracy to commit fraud, fraud, criminal facilitation of an illegal heart transplant, and medical malpractice."

"You're out of your mind," McGuire said.

"You think so, Mr. McGuire? Well, now it's up to you to prove me wrong. With the evidence we have, your client is going away for a very long time. You probably ought to get busy trying to win your case," she snapped at him. "Oh, and just so you know, I'm sure we're going to have a lot more to add to his list of charges."

"Oh, don't you worry about that, Detective."

"I did not kill my wife," Barrett growled. "I swear to you, I didn't. I really wanted it to work between us."

"Sorry, Doc, no one is buying your sad tale of woe, because the evidence speaks for itself. Like I told you before, Helen's been talking to us from the grave. You must know, the one who laughs last laughs longest." Barrett's body tensed, his fists tightening at his sides. "I'm surprised you didn't hear her in your cell, Doc." His eyes narrowed into a glare. "The note Mrs. Barrett left in Maddie's job binder stated she had something on you and the senator. The key we found in the house safe sent us to a safe deposit box. It provided us with all kinds of evidence. Inside the box, we found three letters to the authorities stating that you and the senator colluded and gave an illegal heart transplant to the senator's daughter."

Barrett's lips thinned in anger, and she thought he might explode. McGuire kept his hand on his client's arm, and Max noticed that every once in a while, he'd squeeze it as an apparent attempt to keep Barrett's temper in check.

"What we want to know are the names of your staff members who you convinced to break the law with you, and the name of the child you bypassed because of your selfishness."

"Jeffrey," McGuire said, "you will do no such thing. I'm the one who'll get you off."

"I have nothing to say," Barrett said. "Besides, they must have been old letters."

"No, no, no, Dr. Barrett. Mrs. Barrett dated them the morning of October 18, the day of your vow renewal, and the bank records show she'd signed in around that time." Max waited for Barrett to say something, but he ignored her. "Okay, so it looks like you're not going to tell me. Not to worry, Dr. Barrett, we will find out."

"Detective," Barrett said, "I loved my wife. That's all I'm going to say."

"Yeah, that's why you gave her the keys to your car, the auto she wasn't ever allowed to drive. It's pretty clear you killed her. Money does bad things to people when they're as greedy as you, Doc. You thought having her blow up in a car was quick and dirty. You even collected on her insurance policy—triple indemnity." Jeffrey remained straight-faced. "And then you ran out on your girlfriend and let her take the rap. What a guy! Now she's going to be in prison until her daughter's too old to remember her. And just so you'll know, we now have two women who spilled their guts and told us this was your idea. I guess your plan backfired, Doc, and we caught you. So tonight, when you're sleeping on that thin mattress in your cell, I want you to think about what Helen was feeling, knowing you'd pulled another ruse on her by giving her the keys to your car. But then, that was the whole idea, wasn't it?" Max snickered. "And you know what else I think, Doc?"

"No, but I'm sure you're going to tell me."

"I think it's interesting that out of all the charges against you, the only one you're challenging is Helen's death."

"Good luck trying to get these charges to stick, Detective Turner," McGuire said. "I poked holes in your last case with me, and I'll do it again."

"Not this time, Mr. McGuire." She turned to Riley. "Get this piece of crap the hell out of here. He makes me sick to my stomach."

CHAPTER THIRTY-ONE

Cory sat at a table in The Alibi and kept his eyes glued to the door, anxiously awaiting Max's arrival, anxious to be alone again. Seeing all the customers, he couldn't really say *alone* with a bar full of people, but he'd block that out the minute she stepped through the door. Cory fiddled with his glass of beer, wiping the condensation off the sides with his fingers. He knew she'd enjoy the glass of red wine he had waiting for her after the hectic day she'd had.

He wanted to get started on a long-term relationship with her if Max would have him. But maybe she wasn't one of those long-term-relationship types of women. Actually, she was different from most of the women he'd ever dated. The fact that she was no shrinking violet kept him on his toes. He'd never dated anyone in law enforcement before. He chuckled as he thought back to their first two meetings. Man, she'd really given him a mouthful, and then when he'd told her he wasn't there for her, the speed with which her face flushed made him want to laugh. Fortunately, he'd maintained his composure, but that didn't stop him from howling inside. Thank God he'd shown good judgment.

Cory rubbed the end of his nose with his fingers. He could smell his citrusy cologne, and it made him smile because she'd told him it drove her wild. Perhaps it wasn't fair for him to tease her like this, but she was a big girl. The truth was he hoped the smell would drive her over the edge and they'd make love again. He remembered automatically reaching for the bottle while he was getting dressed and thinking about her, so maybe his subconscious was ruling him after all. He sure as hell didn't mind a bit. He wanted to show Max how much he cared for her and to convince her that, at their age, holding back from such pleasure was silly. The sooner she saw they were a perfect match, the sooner they could get this show on the road. They had so many things in common: they had similar personalities that complemented one another; they saw through those trying to bullshit them; they had similar vocations; and besides, they were cute together, something he knew his mother would say when he showed her off at the family dinners, but he wasn't sure she was ready to take that next step. Cory couldn't believe he'd fallen this hard for her. What was it about Max Turner that had him making these long-term plans?

Just thinking about her made his trousers tighten. He tried to calm down, telling himself it wasn't a good idea to get aroused in a public place. Just then, she walked through the door. He raised his hand in the air so she'd see him, because there was no way he could stand to greet her in his condition. He tried acting nonchalant, hoping his lack of manners would go unnoticed, and it might have, except she caught his gaze traveling over her entire body, which made her smile. Her jeans and tight red sweater outlining her full breasts and trim waistline had his mind racing, and he ached to be touched by her soft hands. He cleared his throat and pulled a napkin down onto his lap to shield the evidence of his desire.

"Hi," she said, sitting down across from him. "Good to see you." She released a heavy sigh. "Boy, it's been a long couple of weeks."

"You're telling me. So what's the good word?"

"The senator's been charged, the doctor's been charged, Melanie Chambers has been charged, and—"

He interrupted, "What about killing Helen?"

"I can't answer that yet, Cory. The senator swears she had nothing to do with it, but I'm not so sure about the doctor. There's no question he's trying to hide something, but why don't we wait to discuss everything when Riley's present. The team is working as we speak, and to tell you the truth, I'm exhausted from everything to do with this case. Can we just have a good time tonight without mentioning it?"

"Absolutely, but why did you suggest meeting at a place with all your peers?"

"It was a weak moment." She shrugged, then she slipped out of her shoe and slid her warm foot under his pant leg, rubbing it up and down. At first Cory was startled, but after she'd stripped for him last week, he shouldn't have been surprised. He loved her spontaneity, but he didn't want to take their relationship for granted just yet. She hadn't given him any indication she wasn't in agreement after all the times they'd spent together making love, but—he stopped himself. What the hell was he doing? Why was he looking for problems that didn't exist? *Go with the flow, man,* he told himself. Max's voice interrupted his thoughts.

"How about we go somewhere else?" she asked.

"That works for me. Where would you like to eat dinner?" he asked.

"You know what I would really enjoy more than anything? Going somewhere for takeout and relaxing in front of a fireplace. The only problem is I don't have one of those."

"But I do. Want to go to my apartment?"

"If you're inviting me, the answer is yes."

"Terrific." They both slid to the end of the booth, and just as she was about to stand, he held out his hand and pulled her up the rest of the way.

Max waved to a few of her peers when they walked past the bar on their way to the door.

◆　◆　◆

Outside, the brisk air filled her chest, and she pulled her jacket tighter. "I hate the cold. Have I told you that?"

"Actually, no, you haven't, but . . ." Cory pulled her close in a tight embrace and lifted her chin, his lips devouring her mouth with eagerness that filled her with fiery warmth. He felt her relax and melt into him. His muscular arms felt like a warm blanket. "Did that heat you up?"

"Oh, yeah." They shared a laugh at her reaction. "Now, I'm all toasty inside, like a cup of hot chocolate covered with whipped cream."

"Don't tease me now," he warned and reached for her hand, giving it a tight squeeze as they walked toward his vehicle.

When she saw his car again, she broke out into a fit of laughter when he opened the passenger door and it creaked.

"Hey! Why the laughter? It's not like you haven't seen or ridden in this clunker before. You knew it was my work car." He laughed with her and immediately began to point things out as he opened the door. "Listen, you see all these dings? I got these fair and square." He walked around to his side of the car, got inside, and patted the steering wheel. "This little beauty was my grandfather's car, and I'd advise you not to look a gift horse in the mouth because the heater in this old buggy will have you begging me to turn it down in a few minutes." He inserted the key into the ignition and started the car. He turned toward her and scrunched up his face. "Ah, please tell me you haven't turned into a prima donna now that you've solved the case."

She laughed. "Hardly. I'm just busting your chops."

"So are you saying this is the *real* you after all?"

She reached for his hand and kissed it. "Yes, I guess it is. What you see is what you get. I just want a peaceful evening snuggled up next to you."

"I really like this Max tonight. You're very different."

"Actually, I've thought a great deal about you, and I want us to get to know one another a lot better. It's been a long time since I've felt this comfortable with anyone, and I've decided I'm being silly. We're not teenagers anymore, and I've really missed you, so there's no reason not to take advantage of how we feel. So what do you think?"

"I think it's music to my ears," he said with a cheeky grin. "What kind of food shall we order for our first official date as a couple?"

"Chinese takeout?"

"Sure. I love Chinese. Okay, why don't you order before we get to the house and ask them to deliver it?"

"I believe you told me you live in the East Village on St. Marks Place. Is that correct?" she asked.

"Wow," Cory said. "I'm really impressed with your memory."

Max's mouth skewed to the side. "Seriously? I'm a homicide detective. It's my business to remember these things."

"Now, why didn't I think of that?" he smirked.

In a jovial mood, Max continued to razz him. "So seriously, you mean your neighbors actually allow you to drive down that street with this car without stoning you? Or is that where the dings came from?" Despite the straight face, she did everything she could not to laugh, but when his eyes narrowed on her in a fixed stare, she could no longer hold it inside.

Cory gave her a raspberry. "And as a reminder of what I told you before, my brownstone was left to me by my grandparents. I didn't earn the money to afford it. I was left the townhouse and this car by my grandparents, so there's a lot of sentimental meaning to what I have. Every time I walk into my home, I feel the warmth of their love." He glanced over at her. "Now, say you're sorry for teasing me."

"Do I have to?" she teased.

"Yes."

"All right," she said, dragging out the sounds. "I'm sorry."

"Thank you. You will be rewarded for such behavior," he said with a faint glint of humor in his eyes. He leaned over and kissed her cheek. "Now, let's focus on food."

She saluted, pulled out her pad, and looked to him with anticipation. "Yes, sir. I'm ready."

"I love your carefree persona tonight. Let's do this more often when we're together."

"I'll take note of that. I guess an occasional devil-may-care attitude is good for the soul." She leaned over and kissed him.

"Then that should work out just fine."

"So where am I ordering from?"

"There are a lot of restaurants in the Village, but the one I like best for Chinese food is RedFarm over on Hudson Street."

"Do you have a preference about what you want to eat?" Max keyed in the name and waited for the phone number to appear, then clicked on the screen to place the call.

"No. Surprise me."

"Okay. What is your address and apartment number?"

"Two-ten."

"No apartment number?"

"It's a single-family residence."

"That's a big house."

"Yeah, and one day I'll have a house full of kids." He winked at Max who smiled as she keyed in the number to order their dinner just as Cory was pulling into a vacant space in a two-car garage. "A garage too, huh?"

"Yes," he said, pointing to a Mercedes sedan parked in the other bay, "to keep my other car nice." He cut the engine and walked to her side to open the door. As he helped her out, she chuckled.

"Honestly, Cory, I told you before, I really don't care about any of that stuff. What you drive or where you live does not define who you are, nor does it change the way I feel about you. I'm just happy to be in your company. Besides, riding in clunkers is my specialty." She winked at him when he looked her way, and she noticed a glimmer of moonlight in his eyes.

"Growing up, before my mother married the monster, our entertainment was strolling through the Village," she said. "We always enjoyed watching the crowds, and one of my absolute favorite streets was St. Marks Place."

"Oh, you're just saying that."

"No, I'm not." She held up her hand to swear. "There was a beautiful townhouse on that street that got me every time. It was covered with ivy and reminded me of a fairytale. I'd rush ahead of my mother and stand in front of that house and pretend I lived there." She sighed. "Do you know which house I'm talking about?"

"I do. I've stood in front of it many times myself. I might have been too young to enjoy it as much as you, but I always fantasized that I would someday live there," he said, and locked the garage door before latching onto her arm to walk the three blocks to the ivy-covered townhouse.

"Oh wow," Max said standing in front of the house, mesmerized that it was still as beautiful as she'd remembered. Inside, the house was lit up. Porch lights and the glow from the streetlights showed only a little of its beauty in the darkness, but her memory served to fill in the blanks. "Do you know the people who live here?" she asked.

"I do. Would you like to meet them?"

"Oh, I wouldn't want to bother them."

"They won't mind at all. You'll get to see the inside that way." Max hesitated, but he egged her on. "C'mon. They really won't mind."

"Well, if you're sure."

"I am."

"What if our order comes while we're visiting with your neighbors? They won't be able to find us," she said with concern.

"We won't be that long." He took her hand and pulled her toward the steps.

Max clutched her chest, the excitement strumming through her body. "I'll bet my mother is smiling down from heaven right now, seeing me walk up these steps." When Cory pulled out a set of keys and shoved one into the lock and opened the door, another gasp escaped her mouth. "You have a key? Are you house sitting?" He shook his head, and her eyes opened wide with shock. "You do *not* live here."

He held his hand up and grinned. "I swear, I do."

"Oh my God!" She was suddenly struck with unexpected warmth that rippled through her as she remembered her childhood. Tears welled in her eyes. "I can't believe it. This was your grandparents' home?"

"It was," he said with a smile.

"I remember them well. They'd sit on the steps during the summertime with their grandson." She stopped talking. "Oh my God." She repeated the words, "with their grandson." She turned to look at him, and her heart was pounding from the coincidence. "Was that you?"

"That had to be me. Did the little boy ever hand you a lollipop?" he asked.

"He did. He gave my sister one too." Max shook her head. "What a small world! How do you know it was you?"

"Because my grandparents only had one grandson. C'mon, let's go inside before we freeze to death."

Before Max mounted the steps she stopped to admire the recessed entryway straddled by gothic carvings on pillars that connected to the ornately engraved overhang. Cory smiled at her reaction and reached for her hand to pull her inside.

"So I've known you for a long time," Max said.

"So you have." He chuckled.

"Okay, moratorium is officially over, we've courted way longer than we should have."

"I thought that was over a while ago."

"Well, not officially, but it is now." She winked at him.

"Good, then it behooves us to stop this fooling around and get down to business right away." He opened the door wide and stopped her with his hand. "Allow me to give you the same disclaimer you gave me. My house looks like a bachelor's pad. My bed isn't made."

"Who cares? It's only going to get messed again anyway."

He shook his head. "God, I love that mind of yours."

Stepping into the foyer, she drew in a deep breath and stared at the long hallway. There was a parlor on the left side and a long winding stairway up to the second floor. The walls were a beige plaster with dark wood framing the openings to the rooms.

"Let me have your coat," he said. Max unbuttoned it, and he helped remove it from her shoulders, placing it on the sofa next to them.

"Cory . . . I'm so excited to be here with you in my fairy-tale house."

"I am too," he said, pulling her into his arms. He teased her by brushing his lips over hers. When they separated, he stepped back and their eyes locked. Emotion snaked through her like an electric current.

"Make love to me," she whispered in a breathy voice.

Cory nodded and scooped her up into his arms and carried her to his bedroom. As he eased her down onto the edge of the bed, they stared into each other's eyes while they quickly removed their clothing, tossing the pieces onto the floor. Completely naked, she watched his eyes rake over every part of her body.

"You're so beautiful," he whispered and slowly lowered his mouth to her breasts, his tongue gliding over her nipples and sending her over the edge. She quivered as she lay back onto the mattress, trembling with desire as his hand seared a path to the moisture between her legs, his hardness electrifying her as he brushed against her thigh, building her sexual desire beyond anything she'd ever experienced. She begged him to hurry, but he wasn't in any hurry—not until he tasted every inch of her. Waves of ecstasy throbbed through her as his slow, gentle touch had her surrendering to his seduction, the heat scorching her insides until she was intoxicated with desire. And when he finally lowered his body over hers, she gasped and instinctively arched toward him as he dove into the depths of her body, rocking into a tempo that bound them in perfect harmony. She writhed and moaned until they could no longer hold back and together they soared into complete erotic pleasure.

CHAPTER
THIRTY-TWO

"Breakfast is ready," the deep timbre of Cory's voice called out as she exited the shower.

She wrapped the towel tightly around her body and walked out to the kitchen. "Hmm, it smells good. I love that you cook, but I have to confess, I don't."

"That's okay. I'll teach you," he said, pulling the chair out for her. "Hungry?"

She laughed. "After that workout and the amazing smell of bacon and coffee, I'm famished." He poured coffee into a mug and handed it to her. "I should probably get dressed first, no?"

"Not on my account. I love seeing your creamy skin wrapped in a towel. It's giving me ideas, but I'll try to behave because I know you need to get to the office."

"Oh darn. I forgot about that."

"Yeah, I'll bet." He laughed. "Today is going to be a banner day for you, so I'll tuck my needs away and let you do what you have to."

"My banner days started after the first time we made love." Cory moaned his approval. The happiness she felt was exhilarating, something she'd never experienced before. She shook her head. "Who could have ever imagined this?" Certainly not her. "This is so amazing, Cory, I feel like I'm dreaming." She felt giddy and giggled. "And all this from the guy I thought was a creep."

"Yeah, I didn't like you very much either, but there was something about that smile of yours that day I walked into your office that set my heart afloat. And now, we're a couple?" He wanted to hear her say it.

She nodded in agreement. "Yes, we're a couple."

He stopped what he was doing and pulled her upright and kissed her so tenderly, it brought tears of happiness to his eyes. "You've just made me the happiest guy in New York."

She took a fast glance at the clock, then pulled the towel off her body and let it drop to the floor.

"You're going to be late."

"I'll eat on the run," she said.

"Aw, but this breakfast was supposed to be a celebration."

"Honey, this *is* a celebration!"

On the ride into work, Max couldn't stop smiling. As a matter of fact, her cheeks hurt from smiling so much. Rushing toward the subway, nothing seemed to faze her this morning, not the sirens, not fighting her way through the crowded sidewalks, or any of the things that normally pissed her off first thing in the morning, but that was because she couldn't focus on anything else except the glorious time she and Cory had spent together last night. Max was amazed, after all this time, that she was finally smitten with a man who understood her needs, her work, and best of all, her heart. If anyone were to ask her right now if she was in love with Cory Rossini, she'd deliver a resounding yes.

When she got to the office, she greeted Riley and said, "I'm heading over to see Maddie Thomas. I need to share some good news and see one of these people happy for a change. Do you want to come with me?"

"No." Riley smiled. "I want you to have that pleasure all to yourself. She seems to have taken a liking to you."

"I hope so. I'll see you later."

"Did you get the copy of the deed to present to her?"

"I sure did."

Max rode the elevator down to the parking lot, thrilled to be the one giving Maddie Helen's long-overdue gift. The trip seemed to take forever, and she was thankful when she pulled into the circular drive. Max shoved the gear into park, cut the engine, and made her way to the carriage house.

She walked up the path, rang the doorbell, and waited for Maddie to answer. A few minutes passed before a young man appeared at the door.

"Hi, are you Mandu or Fejoku?" His only response was a smile. Max hadn't expected them to be so tall, since Maddie was a short woman. Her son was tall and lean, dressed in jeans and a T-shirt. He didn't respond. "I'm sorry. I'm Detective Max Turner," she said, showing him her badge, "and I'm here to see your mother. Is she in?"

He opened the door and allowed her entry into the home. The room was sparse, with cardboard boxes stacked three high up against the wall.

"I'm Mandu," he said in a low voice.

"Very nice to meet you."

"Mama," he called out. "She's back." Max could only imagine what he meant by that. She assumed Maddie had been expressing her discontent.

Maddie rushed into the room, a frantic expression on her face until she saw Max.

"Detective Max, I wonder if I ever see you again."

Max leaned in and hugged the tiny woman. "It's so nice to see you again, Maddie." Noticing Maddie's new hairdo, she commented. "I love the haircut. Short cropped hair looks good on your pretty face."

Maddie ignored the compliment and blurted out her sadness. "Dr. Jeffrey—" She began to cry. "He kill my Mrs. Helen."

"We think so, Maddie, but that's not why I'm here. Is your other son at home too?"

"Yes, why?"

"I'd like to take you somewhere."

"I'm sorry, I need to pack," she said, waving her hand at the empty boxes. "I have to move."

"I know, but this is very important." Max held up her hand. "I swear you won't be disappointed."

Maddie resigned herself. "Okay, I pack later." She called out to her sons and together they piled into the car. "Where we go?"

"You'll see. Where are you moving?" Max asked.

"Mrs. Stallman, down the street, she say I can work for her, but she doesn't have a house like we live in now, but we can stay in her basement."

"I'll help you find something, Maddie."

"Thank you, Detective Max."

The entire ride to Englewood, Maddie rested her arm on the doorframe and looked out the window at the scenery. When Max turned down Willow Lane, the confusion on Maddie's face set in.

"This is a very beautiful street," she said.

"It is indeed." Max pulled into the driveway.

"Who we visit?" Maddie asked, perplexed, as they walked to the front door. "You live here, Detective Max?"

"No, Maddie, you're going to live here."

"What?" she shrieked. "Oh, no." She frowned. "This is too far from Mrs. Stallman's. I don't drive."

Max chuckled while grabbing her briefcase, and together they walked to the front door. Max inserted the key into the lock. "I know, but what if I told you that you own this house?"

"I'd say no money to pay for this house."

They walked inside. Max was impressed that Helen Barrett loved her employee this much that she would gift her something so expensive. An older home, it offered the typical floor plan with large rooms. A white-brick fireplace in the living room extended from the ceiling to the oak floors, present throughout, and the whole house was nicely furnished with traditional furniture. It appeared that Helen Barrett made sure Maddie had everything she would ever need. Maddie didn't say much, but the appreciative smile on her face was heartwarming. Making their way around from room to room, they stopped in the kitchen, and Maddie walked around the room admiring everything, stopping to slide her hand over the counters and cabinets. A long center island with a sink at one end and bar stools the length of the counter had Mandu and Fejoku taking turns trying out every stool. Old brick walls and white cabinets made the room spectacular. Off to the side of the kitchen was a breakfast booth built right into the wall with leather-covered benches. Maddie stopped to view the six-burner stove.

"And what if I told you that you'd never have to work another day in your life?" Max gestured toward the living room. Maddie's confusion intensified. All three family members sat down on the sofa. Max sat across from Maddie, pulling her chair close to the coffee table in front of the sofa. Unzipping her briefcase, she pulled out the documents. The boys were laughing and making noise until Maddie gave them a stern look. They calmed down, frequently releasing a low laugh, speaking in their native tongue.

"Do you remember going to an attorney's office, a John Paterno, with Mrs. Barrett?"

The woman thought for a moment. "Yes. I remember. I sign papers for Mrs. Barrett."

"Well, those papers you signed—it wasn't for Mrs. Barrett, it was for this house, and now you own it free and clear."

Concern crossed her face. "I don't understand."

"Maddie, Mrs. Barrett bought this home for you and your family."

"No. That's not possible."

Max gave a slow nod, and Maddie burst into tears. Max pulled out tissues from the pocket of her briefcase and handed them to the woman while the sons took off to check out each room, releasing frequent bursts of whooping sounds when they discovered something new.

"No. This too expensive of gift, Detective Max," she said in a wobbly voice.

"Mrs. Barrett did this because she loved you and your family, Maddie." Max unfolded the deed. "Do you know what this is?" Maddie shook her head negatively. "It's a deed for this home showing you as the owner." She pointed to Maddie's name.

"It's my name."

"It is. So that means that your Mrs. Helen bought this house for you and your family."

Maddie gasped, placing her hand against her chest. "I can't believe Mrs. Helen do this, but I can't keep it. I don't have enough money to pay for the bills people pay to keep their homes."

"Well," Max said, opening up the bank statement. She put it on Maddie's lap and pointed to the header. "See here? It has your husband's name on it. That means you own this house, it's all paid for, and she left you a lot of money to take care of everything. Now you can afford to pay for your family to come to the States."

"My Souley?" squeaked from her mouth.

"Right, the bank account is in his name."

"But if my Souley's name is on the account and he's in Jamaica, how I pay for him to come?"

"Don't worry, I will go to the bank with you to explain and get the money transferred to you." Max looped her arm through Maddie's. "C'mon, show me your beautiful new home." Maddie smiled, but Max wasn't sure she understood the magnitude of her good fortune. In the distance, the boys argued about which bedroom was going to be theirs, and by the time Max and Maddie made it downstairs to the game room, the boys were already playing pool.

"I think they're happy," Max said.

"Yes, Detective Max, I think so too. Thank you."

Max reached inside her briefcase and pulled out the letter from Helen addressed to Maddie and handed it to her. "Here's one more thing Mrs. Barrett left for you." Maddie immediately tore the envelope open. Her hands were shaking as she pulled out the letter and read, the tears flowing more freely now because she understood. When she was done, she looked skyward. "Thank you, Mrs. Helen. I love you."

CHAPTER
THIRTY-THREE

Later Sunday afternoon, Max dialed Cory's number. "Hey, want to meet us so we can discuss where we are with the case?"

"I'd like nothing better. Can you come over to my new office?"

Max's head jerked back in surprise. "I didn't know you were looking for a place to hang your shingle. Will it be for law offices or private investigator?"

"It could be either. I haven't totally decided yet, but I'm leaning more toward PI."

"Okay, give me the address."

"One-sixty-five Broadway, suite 504. My name isn't on the door yet, so text me when you arrive and I'll wait in the hallway."

Walking up the five flights of stairs to Cory's office, Riley stopped and bent over to catch his breath. He was panting.

"For chrissake, Riley, don't you ever exercise?" He wagged his head from side to side while taking in gulps of air. "You sound like you've been smoking two packs of cigarettes a day."

"I know. I have a physical coming up soon," he said between pants. "I guess I'd better hit the gym." He frowned at her. "Do you exercise?" he asked her.

"I have an elliptical machine in my apartment and use it whenever I'm free." Max gave him a quizzical look. "Don't you ever get outside and play football with the boys?" she said while texting Cory. It wasn't long before he appeared with a toothy grin.

"I guess I need to start," Riley breathed.

Max felt the stress leave her the moment she saw Cory's delicious body standing in the opening of the office doorway. He winked at her, and she knew he'd read her mind. Riley shook hands with him, and entered right behind Max, practically collapsing on the chair.

"Apparently, Riley hasn't climbed stairs in years."

Cory laughed. "I can see that. Anyway, welcome to my new home away from home. It's still a work in progress, but the conference room is set up. Shall we go in there?"

"Sure."

"Aha," Max said, forgetting Riley was standing right next to her, "so this is why you have an empty dining room," she teased until she realized what she'd just revealed. A sudden rush of heat colored her cheeks.

Riley laughed.

"Honestly, Max, did you think I didn't know? Seriously? The smile on your face all day yesterday when you didn't have anything to be happy about was a dead giveaway. I'm a trained detective too."

"Then let us hear the breakdown of your claim," she teased.

"Okay. You live alone, you don't have a dog, or a cat . . . so where else would you get that high school glow from if it hadn't been for a bite from the love bug?" He put his arm around her shoulders and squeezed her in a friendly hug. "If you both thought the way you ogle one another wasn't obvious, then you haven't been paying attention. Really, it's no big deal, so why hide it? Besides, I love seeing this side of you."

Max nervously cleared her throat. "Okay, how about we get back to work?"

"As you wish, my lady," Riley said in a British accent, sweeping his arm in a gallant bow.

Max rolled her eyes and sat down on one of the chairs. She pulled a file folder from her briefcase and set it down on the table. Now, it was Cory who couldn't stop smiling, amused by Max's reaction to Riley.

"I don't have a coffeemaker yet, but I have bottled water," he announced with pride, "Anyone?"

"No thanks." Seeing Cory's disappointment, Max reconsidered. "On second thought, maybe I will have one." Cory got up and practically waltzed to the small refrigerator sitting on the back counter, pulled out two bottles, and handed one to Riley even though he hadn't responded.

"So, you know some of our good news," she said. "Riley and I arrested the senator, the doctor, and Melanie Chambers."

"I'm happy about the first two, of course." His shoulders slouched. "Although I've never met Mrs. Chambers, knowing the horrific death her daughter suffered at the hands of a madman, I can't imagine how a parent deals with losing a child. So what went wrong?"

Max shook her head in disbelief. "What I can tell you is she seems like a sophisticated woman that no one would ever suspect. And I guess that was their whole point. No one would ever think that she would get involved in anything like this." She twisted the cap off her drink while she continued talking, "We only have fraud and conspiracy to commit fraud on Chambers right now, but . . ."

"Don't tell me it was that phony Barrett charm that convinced her to get involved?" Cory shook his head. "Is that why she agreed?"

"No, it was a lot more than that. Intimidation, loss of job, and money. This all happened before she'd lost her daughter. Dangling money in front of someone who has a dire need obviously trumped her common sense. We still haven't figured out how Valerie Morrison is involved, though."

Cory was nodding in agreement. "What about Jack?" he asked. "Surely with all these people charged, there's no need to keep him jailed." Max's facial expression showed she wasn't totally convinced.

"I did some more digging into Jack's life," Riley said, "and I haven't found anything other than the original circumstantial evidence and what is believed to be the threat to Helen. Maybe Cory's right, Max."

"Let's take it one step at a time. Given the circumstances, we haven't yet proved any of them actually conspired to kill Helen. I just need a little more time, Cory." He made a face. "I know you want to see Jack walk out of jail. I get that. We're very close; please be patient."

Cory leaned back in his chair and put his feet up on the conference table, much to Max's surprise.

"Will you look at this?"

He quickly pulled them down. "It's a bad habit."

"What about those other cases?" Riley asked, bypassing their conversation.

"I checked the status with Lucio and Howe this morning, and they still have not been solved. At one point, I thought it might have been a coincidence, but I'm not leaning that way anymore. They have to tie in somehow. Barrett and the senator swear they didn't have anything to do with Helen's death, and although I think it's hard to believe given the evidence, what if they didn't? That means we're back to square one again on the murder, and I'm not going to leave this case unsolved," Max said. "Even though the lieutenant hasn't pressured me about closing this case, I know it's coming, and I'm not about to rush to judgment just to have a closed case."

"I agree, Max," Riley said, "but he knows this is a complex case. I can't imagine him pressuring you to close it quickly."

"With a senator and a renowned heart surgeon at the center of this," Max said, "I think not, but we don't know what he's getting from the higher-ups. So, let's talk about these other unsolved cases. We know Lucio's victim was the Chambers girl, and Howe's victim was Morrison's niece, plus there's Helen's murder. Based on the missing file and the blank box, I think we need to talk to Chambers again and see if we can get her to spill her guts."

Max watched as Riley loosened the cap from his water bottle and drank. "We should get back to the precinct and talk to this woman. I'll catch up with you later?" she said to Cory.

"I'm not sure if I'm available," he said flatly.

"Oh," she said, the undertones of disappointment coming through loud and clear. "Okay, well, call me when you are."

"Just kidding, Max."

"I know."

Both men blurted out , "You did not," simultaneously, and broke into hysterical laughter.

"This is a very interesting side of you, boss," Riley said. "It's fun seeing her squirm just a little, isn't it, Cory?"

Cory knew better than to agree.

Max gave Riley a tap on his arm before slipping her arms into her coat. She headed for the door. "Thanks, Cory." She threw him a kiss. "Love the new office."

"Want to help me decorate it?"

She nodded her agreement with a wide grin.

Back at the precinct, Max called down to the guards and requested Melanie Chambers be brought upstairs.

"I'm sorry, Detective," the supervisor said, "but she's been given a sedative to calm her down. She wasn't in a good state of mind and the doctor thought it best to give her something pretty heavy. Maybe tomorrow."

"Okay," she said with disappointment.

"Chambers isn't taking this well. She's been given a heavy dose of sedatives."

"I'm sure," Riley said. "She's suddenly feeling the ramifications of her greed and the guilt is doing a number on her."

Max didn't respond. "Well, we have plenty of other things to do."

CHAPTER THIRTY-FOUR

"Hey, Max," Riley said, rushing up to her when she walked in on Monday morning. "I called to get Mrs. Chambers up here to have her ready for more questioning, but she's still in sick bay loaded up on sedatives."

"She's worse?"

"Apparently. The guard said she wasn't eating or drinking, she sobbed throughout the night, and became combative when they brought in food, so she was put on suicide watch in a padded cell and loaded up with sedatives. I asked if she was going to be available to talk to us tomorrow, but I was told to call in the morning." Riley's palm rose in the air.

"Damn," Max said and released a sigh. Rubbing her hand across her forehead, a thought crossed her mind, and her eyes opened wide. "That's it."

"What?" Riley said.

"Let's call Howe and tell him we want to talk to Valerie Morrison. I'm sure he'll want to tag along with us. We haven't ruled her out yet as to how she's connected, so I'd like to sit and ask questions to see how she responds."

"That might prove to be good, but up until now, she only related to the case indirectly," Riley said.

"That's probably true, Riley, but I'm out of ideas and thought maybe she could share the scuttlebutt in the hospital that might give us another avenue to take. So let's think positive about this, okay?"

"Yes, ma'am," Riley said. "Sorry. I'm just a little frustrated, and I wasn't being fair to you."

"No worries. Okay, I'll call Howe. You tell the boss where we're going."

A half hour later, the pair pulled out of the garage and drove in the direction of Mount Sinai where Howe was planning to meet them.

Howe was already sitting with Mrs. Morrison when they arrived. They greeted one another, and Mrs. Morrison herded them into her office and closed the door behind her.

Howe began. "I'm not sure you've met Detectives Turner and Riley?"

"Yes, we have."

"It's nice to see you again, Mrs. Morrison," Max said. "We're here today because we're hoping you can answer some of our questions."

"Have you found my niece's killer yet?" she asked Howe.

"No, and that's why we're here. We still have a lot of unanswered questions." Howe sighed. "We're still waiting on the lab results from our testing. The problem is, this killer, whoever he or she is, left very little evidence behind."

"There are a lot of rumors flying around this hospital about what Dr. Barrett and the senator did, but I'm having a hard time believing Melanie Chambers would ever be involved in something like that,"

Morrison said, the expression on her face was one of disbelief as she continued.

"I'd heard that Melanie's daughter was killed, too. I don't know if the things I'm hearing are true or not, but it certainly was brutal," Morrison said. "And if they're not related, then there's a killer who's still out there who could come back at any time."

"We're doing everything we can, Mrs. Morrison," Riley said.

"We also realize your primary concern is finding your niece's killer, but if these cases are in fact related, then it must have something to do with what went on here," Max said. "So we're hoping you might know something . . . maybe even something you think is insignificant, or maybe you don't think has anything to do with the heart transplant surgery, that you can share with us even though that aspect was handled by Mrs. Chambers. Give it some thought," Howe said, "and if there's anything at all that comes to mind, please give me a call." He handed her a business card.

"Boy, I really wish I did, but as I told that good-looking private investigator, my only function here is hospital administrator, and when patient cases get down to that level of detail, I'm just not privy to any of it."

"What other kinds of things are you hearing from the rumor mill?" Riley asked.

Morrison made a face. "Things like the senator and Dr. Barrett might have killed his wife because they wanted to be together. What a rat he is, and how stupid we were to have voted the senator into office. That's about it, but it sure has left us totally drained and not very trusting. Something like that just shocks the hell right out of your faith in the medical field. I really wish I had something to help you, but honestly, the only one who can help you is Melanie Chambers. She ran the whole show over there." She gestured in the direction of the transplant center as though it were down the hall and not several buildings away.

"Well, we knew this was a shot in the dark when we came over here," Howe said, "but we decided to give it a try anyway." He shook her hand while the others nodded a thank-you.

Walking outside to their vehicles, Howe continued to talk. "You've arrested that Chambers woman, haven't you?"

Max nodded.

"So why aren't you talking to her?" he asked. Riley shared what they'd done and finished with ". . . and rather than sit idle, we thought we'd try to find another avenue to fish out information."

Being the first to find his vehicle, Howe offered his hand. "Good to see you guys. Sorry this turned out to be a dead end."

"Yeah, us too. Thanks for meeting us here," Max said. "See you again."

On the ride back, Riley brought up Morrison's comment about Cory. "You'll have to tell that good-looking guy of yours what Morrison said."

Max released a low laugh. "Yeah, I'm sure he'll appreciate hearing that. Well, I'm really bummed, so I guess we'll just have to wait and hope tomorrow brings good news."

CHAPTER
THIRTY-FIVE

Max arrived at the usual time on Tuesday morning and waited for Riley to arrive. At nine-fifteen, Riley waltzed over to his desk.

"Sorry, Max. My wife is sick, my parents are away on vacation, and I was the designated carpool driver."

"No problem." She slid a cup of coffee over to him. "Here, I got this for you."

Riley dug in his pocket for change. Max rolled her eyes and shoved his hand away when he tried to give her money.

"All right. Let's call for Melanie and see what happens. Keep your fingers crossed," she said.

"Crossed," he said, hanging up his coat. He walked back and sat at his desk and listened to Max's phone call. Her expression changed to a smile, and when she gave him a thumbs-up, he knew Melanie was able to talk.

Disconnecting, Max blew out a breath. "Thank God for small favors."

It wasn't long before Melanie entered the interview room. "Mrs. Chambers, how are you feeling?"

"Numb."

"I'm sorry. Listen, we really need your help."

She did not acknowledge either one, nor did she look up until Max asked her again. Her brow arched. "I don't know anything."

"Look, in case you haven't heard, you're turning out to be the heavy in the Stansbury kid's transplant." Hearing that comment, Melanie straightened her shoulders and pushed back in her seat. "We have another theory we're trying to test, and you're the one in the best position to tell us who was deprived of the heart given to the Stansbury child. The prosecutors' office tends to go easier on those who cooperate. I'm sure after what has happened to you, the last thing you're going to do is let Dr. Barrett and the senator go free."

"What?"

"Trust me"—Max held up her hand—"that could happen if we don't have enough evidence. So will you help us?"

"What do you want to know?"

Max breathed a sigh of relief, certain she had her attention now. "Everything from the time Barrett implicated you. Help us understand how the process worked. We know the OPTN has very strict guidelines, and if someone was bypassed, then that's a break in protocol. It means Barrett will lose his license, not to mention the possibility of the hospital being hit with a civil suit."

"Yes, that's the way these things work," Chambers said.

"So did Dr. Barrett break that protocol when he asked you to fix the scheduling of the Stansbury child's transplant?"

She nodded affirmatively while her eyes focused on the floor.

"Mrs. Chambers, please say the words for the recording."

"I'm sorry." She cleared her throat. "Dr. Barrett told me there would be another heart forthcoming that afternoon for the primary candidate, a child I'd grown to love. With that in mind, I was to move her out of the way because I'd been told the senator's daughter's condition was a higher priority."

"But aren't you, as the coordinator, the first to hear about an available organ?" Riley asked.

"Yes, I am, and I questioned Dr. Barrett, but he told me he'd spoken to someone in the OTPN, and I would be hearing something soon."

"How did he know it was going to be a match for this child?"

"I asked him that, too, and he told me based on the information he'd been given there was nothing to worry about . . . so I believed him."

"And did that child receive the second heart?"

"No." She burst into tears. "I'm sick at heart because I'm just as responsible for that sweet little child's death as they are. Dr. Barrett lied. There never was another heart."

"Oh, no," Riley said. "How old was this child?"

"She was five years old." Max could see she was severely depressed.

"Have you ever had a patient prepped and waiting for surgery, then turned away after they'd been told their blood work was a perfect match because something was suddenly found to make it a mismatch?"

"That's unlikely, because every test imaginable is performed to make sure the candidate is a viable match. I suppose it's possible, but I haven't seen it when it's gotten that close to the countdown."

"What if both candidates are an even match? Who gets priority?"

"It's determined by the OPTN. The surgeon normally doesn't even have a say."

"That surgeon being Dr. Jeffrey Barrett?"

"Yes."

"So what you're saying is the OPTN is basically playing God."

"That's what I'm saying." Chambers sipped the container of water Max handed her.

"Had this child been prepped for surgery?" Melanie nodded in agreement. "A verbal, please."

"Yes, she was prepped for surgery."

"So the child had been brought into the hospital, had had her tests, and had been accepted as the likely candidate until Barrett decided to buck the system and dragged you into it?"

"Yes."

Max glanced over at Riley. Their exchange said they both understood what happened.

"The family must have been devastated."

"They were."

"Can you give me a name?"

"Yes, he's an orderly who works in the hospital."

"And his daughter was passed over for a VIP?"

She never responded because Riley shot out another question. "What is this orderly's name?" he asked.

"Charles Wiggins."

"Is he a full-time employee?"

"You'd have to contact the hospital. You'll want to speak to Roberta Harris, the director of nursing."

"I'll check the database," Riley said, heading to his desk. Max nodded agreement.

"Mrs. Chambers, how did you justify the death, the change in priority to the OPTN?" She didn't respond. "Please answer the question."

After a long span of staring into space, she spoke. "I fixed the records so that our department wouldn't get into trouble."

"When you say *fixed the records*, what exactly did you do?"

Tears sprung from her eyes like a geyser. She covered her face. "I'm so sorry. I'm so sorry. I can't believe what I've done. I deserve to die."

"Mrs. Chambers, please tell me what you did. Please. Let me help you."

She looked at Max with pleading eyes. "I was losing my home, Detective. The home my husband had struggled to afford all his life, and I was the one who was losing it. I couldn't handle the additional expenses. I thought I could handle it, but I couldn't. I wasn't making that much money, but my daughter was going through a divorce, she didn't have a job, and the father was fighting for custody of the child—a child he'd never wanted. They were all I had left in this world. I knew if he got my granddaughter, both our lives would have been destroyed, so I did an unspeakable thing. The pressure of helping her pay for her divorce, send my granddaughter to a preschool so she didn't have to deal with the stress, all that plus the expenses of food and electricity, and everything else that goes with maintaining a house and a family on one salary, I got behind in my mortgage payments. Dr. Barrett could see I was depressed, and he played on that when I was most vulnerable. I don't know how he heard about what was going on in my life, but he did and came to me and offered to help me . . . but he wanted something in return."

"Had he told you what it was that he wanted you to do at that time?"

"No. But just knowing I wasn't going to lose everything, I accepted his offer."

"When did you realize what he wanted in exchange for the money?"

"After Becky Wiggins died."

"And that was to fix the records to make it look like the Wiggins child was a legitimate rejection?"

"Yes, and now God has punished me. I've lost everything that mattered: my daughter, my granddaughter, and my home, all because I took a child away from her family in the name of money. Shame on me. I pray they put me to death, because that's what I deserve."

"Thank you for your help, Mrs. Chambers. One more question and I'll let you go with the guard. Did you collect your money through a fictitious company called M. C. Party Planning?" Although she never stopped staring at the floor, Chambers gave a slight nod of her head. "Did you receive two hundred thousand dollars?"

Her head jerked upright. "No, it was one hundred thousand. Why? Are they saying I collected twice?"

"No, there's two entries for the dollar amount." Max shook her head. "And how was the money paid to you?"

"Then they must have paid someone else too, but I have no idea who that would be."

"The money, Mrs. Chambers, how was it paid to you?"

"It was deposited into my daughter's checking account, but I never got a dime of it anyway. With it being under her name, her ex-husband became the recipient of the funds."

"And his name?"

"Jason."

"Had the divorce been finalized?"

"Yes."

"Then Jason Inghrams did not get one cent of the money. It automatically becomes part of your daughter's estate, and it will be awarded to your granddaughter. I don't know what the state will do about that money. It was Barrett's to begin with. She may just be able to keep that money for her future."

"I'd hate for her to know that her grandmother let a child die to collect that money."

"One more question, Mrs. Chambers. Did you hide the Wiggins child's file folder?"

She blinked her eyes shut. "Yes, I did." After a few minutes, she swallowed hard, then continued. "You'll find it hidden in the trunk of my car under the tire well."

"And did you also delete the Wiggins' child's name from the list, but forgot to delete the cell?"

"I did." More tears rolled down her cheeks. Max handed her tissues. "I was so upset that day, even seeing Becky's name in print sickened me. I hated myself, I hated God, but most of all, I hated Dr. Barrett."

"Thank you for being honest. I'm going to have the officer take you back to your cell." By the time the officer arrived, Melanie Chambers was sitting erect, no longer crying, and her face resembled a shield of stone as though she'd hidden the remorse away.

The minute she was gone, Max rushed out of the room and over to Riley. "What did you find out about Charles Wiggins?"

"He was recently released from the military, lives on Second Place, and he hasn't been to work for a few days."

"Then let's go pay him a visit."

The detectives stood on the front porch of a small bungalow that resembled a beach cottage; the exterior paint showed signs of wear, and children's toys were scattered over the porch in disarray. Max pushed on the doorbell.

An elderly short, portly woman wearing a blue-flowered bathrobe answered the door. "Mrs. Wiggins?"

"Yes," she said in a timid voice.

"I'm Detective Max Turner, and this is my partner, Neal Riley, from the Homicide Division of the NYPD." They returned their badges to their jacket pockets.

"What's wrong?"

"We'd like to speak to your son, Charles."

"Is he okay?"

"We need to talk to him."

"He ain't here. He's been gone since yesterday morning."

"May we come inside?"

"Yes." She pulled the door open and ambled back to the living room.

Inside, the house was tidy, with outdated furniture. The shades were drawn, covering the windows to prevent light from seeping in. She motioned for them to sit, just as a tabby cat jumped on her lap and purred.

"Does your son go off like this for days at a time very often?" Max asked.

"No, only since our Becky died."

"And how long ago did she die?"

"She's been gone since July. You see the dining room in there?" She pointed. "Becky set that up with the red plastic dishes and blue plastic forks for the picnic we were supposed to have on the Fourth of July." Max and Riley turned in the direction of the room and nodded. A deep sadness made Max shudder, seeing the deflated helium balloons still hanging from the ceiling. "We were going have a picnic to celebrate. It had to be inside, because she couldn't take the heat, but all the neighbors were coming over to celebrate, and then we got the call that day from the transplant center to come in, they had a heart. I know I should put that stuff away, but our Becky touched it, and I can't bear to shove it in the cupboards." Tears rolled down the older woman's cheeks. "I know she's not coming back, but I just keep thinking she's watching from heaven and smiling." She wiped her tears with her apron. "As a matter of fact, everything has been left exactly as it was the day she died."

"I'm sorry for your loss. I'm sure it was difficult to understand how someone so young could die."

"Well, she wouldn't have died if they'd given the heart to her like those bastards promised. And what's even worse is Charles works there, so you'd think he would have had some clout."

"How long has he worked at the hospital?"

"Probably about eighteen months. He tried and tried to find a job when he got out of the military but couldn't find anything. One day when he was at the hospital for an appointment with Becky, he heard there was an opening for an orderly, so he took it, figuring it might not be a bad idea because he could keep an eye on Becky when she had to go to the doctor. He also thought she'd get special treatment, but that didn't work out." The woman seemed to fade into a trance until she started to grin and explained why. "We used to joke about Becky's checkups, and he would tell her they were 'tune-ups' to make her laugh."

"Tell us about the day you received the call about the heart."

"It was early morning, and we were told to bring Becky to the hospital right away. Those hearts only last six hours from the time the donor dies, and then the doctor has to harvest it from the dead person to get it ready to install it into the patient."

Max smiled at her use of the word *install*, but she wasn't about to correct an elderly woman in such a fragile state.

"And did you know they use them big helicopters to fly organs all over the country? The heart that was promised to my granddaughter came here from South Dakota, so there's no dilly-dallying around when it comes to a transplant. We rushed like crazy, telling Becky this was gonna be her best day ever. No more tubes, no more oxygen, she was gonna be a normal kid so she could play outside with her friends instead of standing by the door watching them. The poor kid has never been able to keep a friendship going, except at the hospital with the other kids who are gonna need transplants, so she pretty much stayed here with me while Charles was serving his country. I raised her like a daughter."

"I'll bet. What happened to her mother?"

"She died from a heart attack at thirty-three."

Max swallowed hard. "Please continue about your experience at the hospital."

"So we rushed her to Mount Sinai in time for the surgery, which can take as much as twelve hours." Her eyes opened wide. "You know, those doctors actually stop the bad heart from beating, even cut most of it out before they can install the new one." She nodded her head up and down. "So whatever doctor you've chosen for such a delicate surgery better know his stuff, because he could lose a patient just like that." She snapped her fingers.

Max didn't need all the scientific data, but she wasn't about to cut off this grieving grandmother.

"Anyways, Becky got to the hospital, was all prepped and ready to go. Charles was walking back and forth like a crazy person, so nervous he could hardly stand it, but then I told him he might be scaring the poor child. So he stopped his pacing and sat with her, telling the child she shouldn't be afraid. Funny thing is she wasn't afraid, we were. But he still told her it was going to be all over before she knew it. They checked her test results again to confirm that she was in fact a good match, and she was, and when it was time, they wheeled her down the hall to the OR, and then some woman stopped us; Charles knows who she is. I guess she was the lady in charge, I think he called her Mel, but I can't remember for sure. You'd think I'd remember the name of someone I hate, and yeah, I know it's not godly to hate, but I can't help myself. I pray to God every day begging his help so I won't hate her." She made a face. "It's not easy. So, yeah, this Mel stopped us and said to take Becky back to the room, she wasn't gonna get the heart after all. I can still picture that woman holding her hand up to the orderly who was taking Becky to the OR, righteous, like she was one of God's disciples. Sooner or later, the Lord will punish her for her sins, but I'm never gonna forget that face. Never. She killed our Becky."

"Did she say why Becky wasn't getting the heart?" Riley asked.

"She gave us some cockamamie story about a test not coming back right, after they'd already told us minutes before that she was a perfect match."

Mrs. Wiggins' head wagged in disillusionment. "Charles couldn't believe that woman Mel. He tried to talk to her about it, but she brushed him off like he was a piece of garbage. Charles demanded a response from her, but she never gave us a good excuse. She just kept saying the blood work doesn't lie, but we knew *she* was lying. Becky, the poor little thing, was so weak she could barely hold our hands.

"Our little Becky was so brave, struggling to stay alive as long as she could—for us, I guess. And then she told us not to cry, she was gonna see her mama up in heaven, and she'd tell her that we all still loved and missed her." Mrs. Wiggins swiped at the tear rolling down her cheek. "Then she wanted to know what we were going to have to eat for the Fourth, so she could dream about the feast on her way up to heaven. Charles could hardly get the words out. Two hours later, Becky told her daddy she loved him, closed her eyes, and took her last breath . . . and then our little princess was gone forever. I guess the last-minute disappointment was too much for her poor little heart." Mrs. Wiggins took a deep breath before continuing.

"And you know, not one of those bastards from the team, or the doctor himself, ever came out to tell Charles how sorry they were." She sniffed. "And then the next day, there it was in the newspapers—the senator's daughter got Becky's heart. A couple days later at the hospital, Charles overheard that Dr. Barrett had been having an affair with the senator for many years and that's why she got priority treatment. He saved *that* child so they could live happily ever after, and put the light out on our little girl. Charles heard the nurses on staff were furious, but no one wanted to say anything for fear of losing their jobs. Charles went nuts when he heard that. He tried to get in to see Dr. Barrett, but he wouldn't see him.

"My poor son ain't been right since he came home from the military, and he's even worse since Becky died. He has a lot of anger inside that head of his. That's why I don't say nothing to him about being away overnight. I just hope he's found some woman and he's hanging out with her, or he's talking to Reverend Warren from our church. He needs someone, because, Lord knows, I ain't gonna be around forever.

So . . . maybe that's where he is. You know, these soldiers see some pretty bad things, especially when they're constantly blowing up all that stuff, killing them people during combat in Afghanistan—it's hard to forget."

"What did your son do in the military?" Max asked.

"He built them bombs and blew up the enemies."

Max and Riley looked at one another. "Was your son diagnosed with an illness?" she asked.

"Yeah, the VA hospital said he was suffering with something that starts with the letter *T*?"

"Do you mean PTSD?" Riley asked.

"Yeah, that's it." She pointed a deformed arthritic finger in Riley's direction. "I don't even know what that is. All's I know, he's pretty angry most of the time."

"Is he being treated for it?"

"He was, but he stopped taking his pills. He said they weren't helping him, and he didn't need them."

"We'd really like to talk to your son. Can you tell us where we can find him?"

"I don't know. I think he'll be just fine. It's Becky's birthday today, you know. He said he wanted to do something special in honor of her birthday so that our little angel could finally rest in peace. I don't know what that meant, and I suppose I should have asked, but he's always talking crazy, so I just let it be."

Riley and Max looked at one another, the panic filling Max's insides. "What do you suppose that meant?" Riley questioned Mrs. Wiggins.

"I don't know," she said.

"Where would she rest in peace? At the cemetery?"

"Yeah, he goes there quite a lot to talk to Becky and her mama. They're buried next to one another, you know."

"Do you have a picture of your son so we know we're talking to the right person?" Mrs. Wiggins pointed to the mantel. Riley snapped a picture of the photograph on the mantel with his phone.

"What's the name of the cemetery and plot number?"

"New York City Marble Cemetery." She got up from her chair, pushing the cat off her lap, and hobbled toward the kitchen. "I need to check the address."

"I don't like the sounds of this, Riley. Let's thank her and get the hell out of here before he hurts someone else."

Riley keyed the name into his phone. "I got the location of the cemetery, Max—72 East Second Street. I'll call to find out the plot number."

"Send a car over right away. I don't want to chance what he's about to do. Thank you, Mrs. Wiggins. We'll keep you posted," they said on their way out.

"All right then."

Riley rushed outside and keyed in Charles Wiggins's information in the DMV database and obtained the information he needed, then called dispatch. "This is Detective Riley, badge number 107, and this is an emergency," he told the operator. "I'm sending you a photo of our suspect. He's driving a dark blue sedan bearing license plate Alpha Boy Lima 9843. Send a few cars over to the vicinity of New York City Marble Cemetery and apprehend him. If they can't find him, tell them to drive up and down the rows of gravesites; he could be hiding."

"Riley," Max said, rushing outside toward the car, "this killer is going down the list of anyone dealing with the heart transplant. My best guess is the surgical staff on Barrett's team is next." She dialed the lieutenant's number. "Lieutenant, we need to send SWAT and the bomb squad over to Mount Sinai. We are on the hunt for Charles Wiggins, the father of the child who was denied the heart that went to the senator's daughter. We believe he is exacting revenge on the heart center at the hospital. He's trained in explosives, did four tours in Afghanistan, and he's suffering from PTSD. He told his mother that his daughter would rest in peace after today—it's the kid's birthday." Max continued to fill in the gaps.

"After my tours in Iraq, I witnessed this firsthand. After so many tours on the front lines, there's no way these guys come back unaffected. I can almost guarantee you that his mind may be bouncing in and out of combat, killing people he believes to be the enemy. We now believe he's Helen Barrett's killer, as well as Candace Morrison's and Sharlene Chambers-Inghram's killer. Riley and I have a team heading out to the cemetery where the child is buried to see if he's there, but we can't be sure he hasn't already taken some action. There are too many variables here, Lieutenant. We can't be sure what more this man will do to avenge his daughter's death."

"I'll put out an APB to find him and also send reinforcements to you right away. We'll contact the hospital and get the surgical employees' names and addresses. You focus on those who are at the hospital, and keep in touch," Wallace said.

"Yes, sir." They disconnected.

Gunning the engine, Max turned on the lights and whipped around corners on the back streets as she weaved in between cars on the main thoroughfare. Traffic was unusually light and they made good time.

"We need a miracle, Riley," Max said.

"I think we already have someone watching out for us, because the hospital is just ahead. Christ, my heart is pounding like a banshee chicken ready for slaughter."

Riley blew out a hefty breath. "We'll get him, Max. We'll get him."

Max and Riley pulled right up in front of the hospital, where uniforms blocked off the traffic on the main street. The bomb squad was already fast at work checking the hospital. Max hit the brakes, shoved the gearshift into park, and made a beeline for the person in charge.

"Nothing yet," the bomb squad leader said. "We're still looking. Uniforms are guiding workers who were wheeling panicked patients and their relatives outside."

"Take it easy, folks," the officer in charge was saying. "You're going to be okay. Just relax and we'll have you out of here in no time."

Mrs. Morrison, the administrator, saw Max and approached. "What's going on, Detective?"

"We believe Charles Wiggins, an orderly at this hospital, is going to kill someone on the transplant staff." She took a deep breath.

"Oh my God. I'm scared to death." She began pacing in her panicked state, hyperventilating. "Is he coming after me?"

"I don't know, but I'd like you to go with my officers for safekeeping until we figure this out."

She agreed and latched onto a uniform's arm. "You think he killed my niece, don't you?"

"We aren't sure yet, but we believe so." The painful look in her eyes made Max want to hold her tight, but catching the killer was more important.

"Why her?" Her voice cracked. "I never should have taken this job." Mrs. Morrison's hands trembled as she swiped at the tears streaming down her cheeks. "My brother and sister-in-law will never forgive me. I killed my niece." She screamed. "Why would he do this to me and my family?"

"Because you run this hospital. In his PTSD state, you're the enemy, and we believe he went on a killing spree after his daughter died. He learned that the senator's daughter received the heart intended for his daughter, and he's blaming anyone who he thinks is responsible."

"But I don't even know him," she said just before she passed out. Max called out for the medics, who rushed over and lifted the woman onto a gurney and tended to her needs.

Seeing the fury that Jeffrey Barrett created, Max prayed the man would rot in hell for what he'd done to so many innocent people. Her mind replayed the words: *Becky would rest in peace after today.* Suddenly realizing the magnitude of that statement, she repeated the words again and gasped. They were in the wrong place. Panicked, she keyed in the lieutenant's number.

"Oh my God, Lieutenant. Wiggins doesn't want to blow up the hospital, he's after Arianna Stansbury!"

"Take a deep breath, Max, we've got this," the lieutenant said. "Where is the Stansbury kid now?" he asked in a rush of words.

Max checked her watch. "I would imagine she's in school, but I don't know what school she attends."

"Hold on." She could hear the lieutenant's fingers hitting the keyboard. "Alexander Robertson School—Upper West Side. I'll contact the precinct and tell them to evacuate the school and detain Arianna Stansbury."

"I don't think that's a good idea. If he already has her, it might push him right over the edge. Remember, this is his last deed, and he no longer cares what's going to happen to him."

"Then hurry and get over there before school lets out. You'll make it," he encouraged.

"We're on our way. Will you call Detectives Lucio and Howe to let them know what's going on?" Max said and disconnected. Stepping on the gas, she warned Riley, "Hang on tight."

Charles Wiggins left his daughter's gravesite and slid behind the wheel of his car. He cranked up the engine and drove out of the cemetery, noticing several police vehicles heading for the entrance he'd just passed through.

He sped away and headed for the back roads he knew so well, parking his vehicle just long enough for him to change into a black suit, and then make his way over to the Alexander Robertson School, where he'd spent every afternoon for the last few weeks to determine Arianna Stansbury's routine.

"We got 'em, Becky," he whispered as he pulled up in front of the school and parked next to a limo in the space beside him, checking the plates to make sure he had the right car. When he was certain, he rushed inside the limo on the passenger's side, surprising the driver.

"Who the hell are you?" the driver asked in a thick German accent.

Charles said nothing, but with one swift motion, he placed his hand over the man's mouth to silence him and pointed the barrel of his gun directly at the man's heart. The driver's eyes bulged with surprise.

"I knew that would get your attention. Now, you listen very carefully, because I'm only going to say this once. You got that?" The driver nodded. "As soon as the school bell rings and the Stansbury child is released, you and I will get out of the car and wait for her. Once she's in the car, you will get in on the passenger's side, Edward." The driver's eyes opened wider, apparently surprised Charles knew his name. "Let me tell you how this is going to play out," he said, wielding his gun. "I'm a sharpshooter and have no qualms about using this gun to get what I want. And just in case you're trying to figure out how you're going to outfox me when we do get out of the car? Don't waste your time, because I know where you live on West Forty-Second Street and Tenth Avenue and that your two children, Alex and Mickey, are alone every afternoon until your wife comes home." Edward's eyes began blinking rapidly from nerves. "So trust me when I say, I won't feel an ounce of remorse about killing your entire family. Am I making myself clear?" Edward agreed with a nod.

Things were silent until the bell rang and sent Charles's heart booming inside his chest in anticipation of the outcome. The aftereffects of avenging his daughter's death would be even better, knowing he was fulfilling a promise he'd made to Becky as she lay dying. After today, she would finally rest in peace.

The students exited out of the front of the building in single file. "I'm going to remove my hand from your mouth now, Edward." The man released a noise as his head bobbed in agreement. "Good." Charles gestured toward the door. "Let's get out of the vehicle nice and easy."

The minute Charles spotted Arianna, the pretty little towhead, the fifth one back from the front line talking a mile a minute to the girl next to her, Edward was calling out to her.

"Hello, Edward," the headmistress said, "I see you have a companion today."

"I'm Charles," Wiggins said, extending his hand, "and I'll be filling in for Edward while he's on vacation the next few weeks." Edward didn't say much except to smile and nod, causing Charles's suspicions to kick in. "Tell her where you're going, Ed."

"Home to Germany to see family."

"Well, good for you," she said, and turned to Arianna. "Do you have everything, Ari?"

"Yes, ma'am."

"Good, then we'll see you tomorrow," she said and turned her attention to someone else.

Ari? Charles thought. Becky always talked about her friend, Ari.

"Good-bye, Mrs. Hastings," the child said, waving to her friend. She latched onto Charles's and Edward's hands then skipped along with them. The warmth of her small hand in his confused state had him thinking it was his daughter. He looked down to see her cherub face looking up at him and realized she wasn't Becky, she was the enemy and she had to be destroyed.

Edward opened the back door of the limo while Charles stood a few feet away from him waiting for the child to get inside. Once the door was shut, Charles opened the passenger door for Edward. The man did not resist, he simply slid across the seat and stared ahead. Charles glanced his way and noticed him shaking. He liked that. It meant Edward was listening.

"You look very pretty today, Ari," Wiggins said to the child.

"Thank you. My mommy bought this dress for me to wear for special occasions. She's away, so I wanted to wear it to remind me of how much I miss her."

Hearing the child tell him how much she missed her mother made his heart ache. He knew what that was like. It brought tears to his eyes and made him realize he could not kill this child. Charles looked skyward. "I'm so sorry, Becky. I can't."

"What did you say?" Arianna asked.

"I'm going to take you home now, sweetie."

"Thank you, Mr. Charles."

"I'm Mr. Wiggins."

"Wiggins? My best friend's name is Becky Wiggins." Arianna covered her eyes and he could tell she was crying. "My friend died." She wiped her tears with the back of her hand. "Mommy says I'll see her again someday and that she's in heaven dancing with the angels and watching over me. I still talk to her in my prayers. Do you think she can hear me?" Charles tried to respond, but the words caught in the back of his throat. "Are you Becky's daddy?"

He nodded his head, unable to find his voice. Tears rushed down his cheeks. What was he doing? Flashbacks of Becky talking about her best friend, Ari, made him realize this beautiful little girl was *that* friend, and maybe those messages he thought his daughter was sending from heaven had nothing to do with hurting anyone. He'd done that all on his own to avenge her death. Visualizing Becky dancing in heaven gave him comfort but had him wondering what she thought of him after so many deaths. He suspected she was plenty mad at him.

He pulled the gear into drive and stepped on the gas to drive away when a crossing guard signaled for him to stop and roll his window down.

He retracted his window. "Can I help you?" he asked the woman. "I have a book of Arianna's that one of the moms asked me to return to her," she said as she handed the book to him. He turned to look over his shoulder as he passed the book to Arianna, when he suddenly felt the cold hard steel of a service weapon against his head.

"You make one wrong move, Wiggins, and you die where you sit. Do you understand?" Max spoke quietly but emphatically to him. Wiggins nodded his understanding.

Within seconds the police surrounded the car, Edward was removed, and Riley whisked Arianna from the backseat into the school before she saw what was happening. The sudden rush caused her to cry.

Max relieved Wiggins of his weapon while he recited his name, rank, and serial number. "Charles Abraham Wiggins, E-7, 195-45-6398."

Seeing Charles' behavior, Max knew he thought he was on the front lines in Afghanistan and had been captured by the enemy.

"You are under arrest for the abduction of a minor, the abduction of Edward Schubert, and car theft." Wiggins stared into space and continued to recite his name, rank, and serial number.

Max slipped her left hand inside the opened window and released the door handle. She kept the gun pointed directly at his head as several officers stood by with their guns aimed at Charles. "Now get out of the car nice and easy, soldier, or I'll blow your brains out."

Charles kept his hands in the air and got out of the car, immediately getting down on his knees. Once he was cuffed and ready for transport, Max yanked him to his feet. Wiggins shouted, "Ma'am, yes, ma'am!" The smug expression on his face would normally have infuriated her, but she knew he was mentally incapacitated.

"Please deliver Mr. Wiggins to the 51st Precinct for questioning, gentlemen. Thank you," she said. "Good job, folks." She turned and headed inside the building to see the child.

◆ ◆ ◆

Max blew out a breath, thankful this case was over, and walked into the school searching for the child, who was sitting with an older woman. Max presented her badge to the woman and introduced herself.

She could barely respond with her own name. Holding her head in her hands, Mrs. Hastings was in a state of panic. "I can't believe I let Arianna go with that man, but Edward, her normal driver, was right there with him. I never suspected anything could be wrong." She was visibly upset. "I'll be fired for this one."

"I think what's more important here, Mrs. Hastings, is Arianna's well-being, not your job."

"Of course. I'm sorry. I'm just so nervous I'm not thinking clearly."

Arianna had been crying since Max entered the room. "I want my mommy."

Max could feel the lump in her throat as stabbing pains jabbed in her stomach. "Hi, Arianna," she said, squatting down next to her. "I'm Detective Max, and this nice policeman next to me is Officer Mike. He's going to stay with you until your grandmother comes to get you. Okay?"

Shaken, but no longer in a state of panic, Edward rushed over to Arianna. "Are you okay, Wiener Schnitzel?"

Her mouth cracked into a weak smile. "That man called me Becky, Edward."

"I know. He was a little confused."

Max felt a heaviness inside her chest, knowing what could have happened to Arianna if the words hadn't replayed in her mind. "I'm going to leave you now with Edward and Officer Mike. Okay?"

"Okay. When is my gram coming?"

"She's on her way, sweetie."

All the way back to the station house, Max couldn't stop the pain of knowing Arianna would never again live a normal life. When she entered the interview room, Max wanted to lash out at Charles Wiggins, but she knew it was the wrong thing to do.

"This is Detective Turner," Riley said. Charles stared blankly as though in the room by himself.

"Can I get you something, Mr. Wiggins?" she asked. He shook his head negatively.

Riley motioned for Max to join him away from the suspect. "He seems to be Charles Wiggins, the father, right now. He's talking about his daughter."

"Good to know. Okay," Max said, "let's get down to business then. Can you tell me what happened?"

"My daughter is dead."

"I'm sorry, Mr. Wiggins. How did she die?"

"They gave the heart my daughter was promised to her best friend." He began to cry. "I'm not even angry anymore. Ari was my daughter Becky's friend. I thought Becky was speaking to me from above telling me to kill, but she wasn't. If she's watching me, she's mad. I disappointed her."

"Why don't you tell me in your own words what happened to cause you such pain?"

Charles told them about the day his daughter died. "I wanted those people to suffer too, but it didn't make me feel better. I killed Mrs. Barrett. Did you know that?" Max listened while he poured his heart out. "I hadn't planned to kill her. I wanted to kill Dr. Barrett. He's the one who killed my Becky, but when a pretty woman came out and got into his fancy car, I figured she was his wife and decided killing her was better because then he was going to feel the pain and suffering I felt. Afterward, I'd heard Dr. Barrett was sleeping with the senator, so I knew he didn't feel any pain, and that I had actually done him a favor. So I went after the two women who were in command and killed their relatives. I was saving the senator's daughter for last so my Becky could rest in peace. It's her birthday today, and I thought killing Ari was my gift to her." He started to cry again. "I'm a bad person. My sweet little angel is mad at me."

"Mr. Wiggins, she might feel a little sad, but she'll always love you. Can I ask a special favor?"

"Yes."

"Will you please write down everything you've just told me and sign it?" Max asked, sliding the tablet over to him. He took the pencil in his hand and began writing, but then suddenly stopped, got off the chair, grabbed Riley's bottle of water and hid behind one of the steel chairs, holding the bottle like a gun as though ready to fire.

Sadly, Max recognized what he was doing and pretended to be his commander. "Soldier, hold your fire."

"No. The ambush commander gave the signal." Turning his head to and fro suspiciously, he raised his hand in the air and whispered, "Initiate ambush. I repeat, initiate ambush," and pointed forward. "Commence ahead."

Max watched Charles with tears in her eyes, knowing what he'd felt on the front lines. "At ease, soldier. You did a good job today, E-7, Wiggins. It's time for your battalion to rest now. It's been a long day."

Charles stood and saluted Max. "Ma'am, yes, ma'am." Moving his hands behind his back, he spread his legs apart and stared into space.

Max buzzed for the uniforms. "Please escort our soldier to the van and take him to Bellevue for observation. He suffers from PTSD." Max looked Charles directly in the eyes but knew she'd lost him to some faraway land.

Following behind, Riley sighed. "Sometimes this job sucks, you know? All these people suffering heartache because of what two friggin' selfish people did, greedy for the heart that killed four people. The good news is those two bastards will never have the kind of life they've left. But that poor child will have to learn to live without her mother. What a travesty."

"Yep. It sucks, all right. I'd like to give Howe and Lucio a heads-up about the results."

◆ ◆ ◆

Detective Howe was sitting at the table in the interview room when Max entered, a disconcerted scowl covering his face. Lucio was the first to greet her.

"Good job, Max. Everyone in my district is sleeping a little easier tonight."

"What I want to know, Detective," Howe barked, "is why didn't you call us during the takedown?"

"Surely you jest. Do you know how close I came to missing him? You know what it's like in a takedown. You expected me to stop what I was doing and call you?" What she didn't want to tell him was that she'd asked the lieutenant to call. At least she thought she had.

"I've spent a great deal of time trying to find the killer, and you just wiped out my efforts," he complained. "Giving me an 'assist' status isn't going to make me any more of a hero in my captain's eyes."

"Perhaps not. But it's likely to get you a sizeable raise or a promotion. It's a shame you aren't more cooperative with your peers. You might just find you have more friends than you ever thought."

"I don't need friends. I need to solve cases."

Max threw her hands in the air, realizing there was no convincing him. Howe stood and walked out of the room.

Lucio snorted. "Don't give it another thought, Max. He's just one of those disgruntled people who takes his insecurities out on everyone else. I thank you for doing an outstanding job."

CHAPTER
THIRTY-SIX

Max dialed Cory's number. "Well, hello there."

"Hi, yourself. What's happening?"

"The case has been solved, and the guilty party is on his way to Bellevue for observation. I'm exhausted, I'm sad, and I can really use a shoulder to cry on."

"Then that ought to work out well. I have two shoulders and a lot of hugs. Do you want to have dinner out or here at the house?"

"I don't really feel like celebrating at the close of this case, so why don't I pick up a pizza and bring it over?"

"Good idea, only I'll pick you up, and we can choose our food together," Cory said.

"By the way, Jack's papers are in the works," she said. "I thought it would be nice if we went over to the jail together to tell him. He should be free within the week."

"Thanks, Max. I'm sure he'll be relieved to know he's been cleared."

"I'll meet you downstairs in an hour after I type up the DD5."

"See you then."

Max disconnected and pulled the form from her file drawer, slowly turning toward one of the empty rooms to fill it out. Riley had already left for the day, and the night shift was just beginning to arrive. She waved to Gary Johnson, the detective who occupied her desk at night, and continued to walk. Gary was one of those overly sociable men who could talk to a stop sign. She was in no mood to entertain him or anyone else. Sitting down, she looked over the familiar form and took a moment to reflect on the events of the past few days.

She was thankful the case was solved, but it was a bittersweet conquest. Charles Wiggins, who suffered PTSD from his four tours in Afghanistan, had served his country proudly. He had come home to a daughter who was in desperate need of a heart transplant, which was denied because two individuals corrupted the system, sending him into a meltdown that brought out the worst in him. Having served two tours in Iraq herself, Max felt a kinship toward him because she knew what he'd gone through, and she hoped the courts would take some pity on him due to his mental state.

She knew that Charles would live the remainder of his life in a six-by-six-foot cell. What she didn't like was knowing the senator and Barrett would never feel the kind of pain Charles Wiggins felt.

Walking the finished form into the lieutenant's office, Max turned and headed for the elevator, taking it down to the sidewalk level where Cory waited. Seeing the opened door of his car, she slid inside.

"Hey, I see an awfully long face." Cory latched onto her chin. "I know this was a tough case for you, but think about the positives. The Stansbury child is alive, the bad guys are behind bars, and you're sitting next to a man who's falling madly in love with you."

Max smiled. "I'm sorry. I'm suffering the aftereffects. This job doesn't always have a pleasant ending, but it's the nature of the beast."

"Would you rather wait to see Jack?"

"No. I don't want him to have to wait another day to hear the news. Seeing him might help lift my spirits, although I'm sure he doesn't hold me in the highest regard."

"He might not, but he has to respect you for doing your job." Cory pulled her closer to him and held her hand.

The drive to Rikers Island was quiet, with only the background noise of the radio. As they pulled into the parking lot outside the facility, Max took a deep breath. They entered the prison, and she held up her badge for the guard. "Detective Max Turner of the 51st here to see Jack Hughes, with private investigator Cory Rossini."

"I'll call down and have Mr. Hughes brought to the visiting area. Please sign in."

"I haven't seen you before," Cory said to the guard. "Are you a new hire?"

"Yes, sir. Tonight is my first night, and the natives are restless."

Cory snickered. "Don't let them get to you. That's their initiation for new guards. Stay firm and show your confidence or they'll try to walk all over you."

"Thank you, Mr. Rossini. The warden told me the same thing." Pushing a button on the wall panel, the heavy steel door unlocked, and the pair walked through. "I assume you know where the visiting area is located?"

"We do. Thanks." The heavy door clunked to lock behind them. Max shuddered. "That noise gets me every time," she said. "It's so final."

"Yeah, I hear you. Thanks for doing this tonight, Max. You could have waited until the morning."

"I know. But if I were in Jack's shoes, I'd want to know right away too."

Walking inside the room, Jack looked surprised to see Max. "Did you come to give me more bad news, Detective?"

"Not unless you think putting the bad guys behind bars is bad news."

"Does that mean what I think it does?"

"Yes, Mr. Hughes. That's precisely what it means. You're getting out of here. The paperwork has been initiated through your attorney, Bill Cates, who is currently going through the process. It should take about a week and then you'll be a free man."

Jack blew out a breath. "Thank God."

Cory shook his hand. "I told you, buddy, didn't I?"

"Yes, you did. You said she was one of the good guys."

"But you didn't believe him," Max said.

"No, I'm afraid not." He stared at her for a few minutes. "It's going to take some time for me to warm up to you, Detective, but knowing how Cory feels about you gives me more of an incentive to get over my snit." Cory shot him a look of despair. "I know you were only doing your job and that you don't know me the way Cory does, so I have to say, I respect you for that. As soon as I'm out of here, we'll have plenty of time to get to know one another."

"I'm sorry I was mistaken about your guilt, but I'm sure, given the same set of circumstances, you might have come to the same conclusion."

"You're probably right."

"Okay," Max said and stood. "I'll let you two visit with one another."

"No. Please don't leave," Jack said, reaching for her hand. "Getting to know you starts right now. Can you tell me if Barrett is behind bars?"

"Yes, he and the senator are both behind bars."

"Hot damn. That's music to my ears. And he killed her, right?"

"No, he didn't, although he's still being charged for the murder of the child he denied the transplant. I can't give you specifics, but just know that the right person is behind bars."

"So he didn't kill her? That's a big surprise. Maybe he did love her after all." Jack shrugged.

"I think not."

"You look exhausted, Max," Cory said. "We're going to say good night, Jack. I'll come back tomorrow and spend some time with you."

"Should I start packing?"

"You don't have anything to pack, do you?"

"No. I was trying to be cute, but I can see it failed." He eyed Max. "Were you in the military, Max?"

"Yes, sir, two tours in Iraq."

"I could tell by your stature. You walk like military. So, I guess we have more in common than I thought. I'll look forward to sharing war stories."

On the ride back, Max seemed more upbeat. "It's nice to see you coming back to life again," Cory said, squeezing her hand.

"Yeah. I sulk for a while and get it out of my system. There's nothing much I can do about the poor choices other people make."

"I understand. I was like that when I practiced law. Some cases could tear your heart out." He leaned over and kissed the tip of her nose. "Hungry?"

"I am. How about we go to our favorite Italian restaurant?" she suggested. "That was where we had our very first date."

"It is, isn't it?" He reached for her hand. "Now that the case is over, we pull out all the stops, right?"

"We've already pulled out all the stops." She leaned in and kissed him.

"I just want to be sure." He gave her a loving smile. "You've just made me the happiest man on earth."

"How so?" she inquired, knowing full well she was baiting him.

"I've been waiting for the right time to tell you how I feel, and now I can say it." He looked in her direction. "I love you, Max Turner."

A wavy feeling fluttered in her stomach. She reached for his hand. "You do?"

"With every breath of my being."

She was taken back by his comment. She'd never had a man be that straightforward about his feelings. "That's the most beautiful thing anyone has ever said to me."

"Then I'm glad to be the first one to say it. You know, I'm going to tell you how much I love you whenever I feel it."

"Really?"

"Why hold back?" Cory said.

"I wasn't suggesting you hold back. I'm just surprised to hear a man express his love the way you do. But you know what? You're exactly the kind of man I want in my life. I need to know I'm not the only one working on the relationship. I've had enough of those one-sided relationships to last a lifetime."

"Yeah, but that's a thing in the past now. Erase all that trash from your mind, because this is the first day of the rest of our lives. So what do you think about our future?" he asked.

"I think it's looking mighty good." And she meant it.

AUTHOR'S NOTE

All too often, our military veterans come home after having served several tours in countries like Afghanistan, Iraq, and elsewhere fighting wars to keep us safe, only to return with a serious disability: PTSD. My own nephew did four tours in Afghanistan and struggled through this disorder himself.

Based on what I know and what I've seen portrayed in movies like *American Sniper*, to help make people aware of this horrible disorder, I will be donating a portion of my royalties to the Chris Kyle Frog Foundation. This nonprofit organization's mission is to help those men and women affected reenter society as well as their marriages.

I have a deep respect for our veterans and hope that by playing a small part in their recovery, I can do justice to their sacrifices. May God bless them, and may God bless America.

ACKNOWLEDGMENTS

As has been said many times, no book would be possible without the help from others who so willingly share their knowledge: A heartfelt thanks to my sister, former Detective third class L. Jessie Esposito, for her knowledge and thirty-six years of experience working undercover in the Port Authority of New York and New Jersey. She makes sure I'm always on the right track.

Additional thanks to retired NYPD Detective third class Donald Hamilton, who bestowed good fortune upon me when he moved into our neighborhood. He has willingly taken time from his golf to answer my unending questions.

On the home front, a warm thank you to my wonderful husband, Bob, who spends an inordinate amount of time brainstorming with me, researching, and continually showers me with his ongoing support and encouragement. I will be forever grateful he came into my life.

And lastly, to Montlake Romance, the best publisher on the planet, for consistently going out of their way to make sure recognition is given to their authors. I'm extremely proud to be a member of the family.

ABOUT THE AUTHOR

K. T. Roberts writes romantic suspense with sass and brass, and she is the alter ego of Carolyn Hughey, an author of humorous contemporary romance. In 2012, Carolyn decided to try her hand at self-publishing and wrote her first mysteries, the Kensington-Gerard Detective Series, using the pen name. *Blind Retribution* is her first romantic suspense for Montlake Romance.

Originally a Jersey girl, she lives with her real-life hero, Bob, in Arizona; they have four children. And as a former chef, on those rare occasions when she's not writing, she loves to whip up some gastronomic treats for family and friends. For more information about K. T.'s books, visit her website at www.ktrobertsmysteries.com.